Cast in Paradise

Howard Chadwick

'Front Cover : Primitive Chapel, Witton Park / Back Cover : Church Street looking down to the Iron Works. Little boy, seated, is the father of the author.'

Note for Librarians: a cataloguing record for this book that includes Dewey Decimal Classification and US Library of Congress numbers is available from the Library and Archives of Canada. The complete cataloguing record can be obtained from their online database at:
www.collectionscanada.ca/amicus/index-e.html
ISBN 1-4120-2640-7

TRAFFORD

This book was published *on-demand* in cooperation with Trafford Publishing. On-demand publishing is a unique process and service of making a book available for retail sale to the public taking advantage of on-demand manufacturing and Internet marketing. On-demand publishing includes promotions, retail sales, manufacturing, order fulfilment, accounting and collecting royalties on behalf of the author.

Offices in Canada, USA, UK, Ireland, and Spain
book sales for North America and international:
Trafford Publishing, 6E–2333 Government St.
Victoria, BC V8T 4P4 CANADA
phone 250 383 6864   toll-free 1 888 232 4444
fax 250 383 6804   email to orders@trafford.com
book sales in Europe:
Trafford Publishing (UK) Ltd., Enterprise House, Wistaston Road Business Centre
Crewe, Cheshire CW2 7RP UNITED KINGDOM
phone 01270 251 396   local rate 0845 230 9601
facsimile 01270 254 983   orders.uk@trafford.com
order online at:
www.trafford.com/robots/04-0468.html

10   9   8   7   6   5   4   3   2

Dedicated in memory of my parents,

both born and bred in Witton Park

also

to my grandson

ROBBIE

my father's namesake.

Author's Notes

Cast in Paradise is true to fact and historically correct, to the best of my research and I extend my gratitude to those who have helped make this book a reality.

The events are as seen through the eyes of the typical, but imaginary, Morris and Bryan families and the real bystanders around them, whose involvement in a new village shaped events to a larger or lesser degree. Throughout, I have used real events, and have taken from the 1841 – 1891 censeii the real names of people who lived out real lives in the latter part of the nineteenth century. Those persons created, in a place where previously nothing existed, a community in the fullest sense of the word. The time scale is correct except for a few minor events, which have been slotted in to help the reader understand the momentum of continuous developments. The history of Witton Park is clearly defined from the first phase, its inception in 1845, until the mass exodus of the population in 1884. A second influx of 'immigrants' filled the empty houses after then, and another story unfolds, but this book restricts itself to 'Phase One' of events in Witton Park.

This humble work is for the people who built and fought for the very life of this community. Today little remains of the original village yet despite attempts to kill it off it refuses to die.

My special thanks go out to the late Mr. Derek Hebden whose own publication, *Witton Park,* inspired and proved so valuable in my research; to my long-suffering wife Ann, who has laboured daily proof reading; and to Phil Atkinson—I cannot pay enough praise nor heap on him enough thanks for years of dragging me to the typewriter and editing the work. Their encouragement throughout has been unstinting, and I seize the opportunity to publicly say, "Thank you."

Howard Chadwick
September 10th, 2004

Chapter One — 1845

The Liverpool canal appeared to run into the harbour but it stopped just short. Docks at night took on a relative sleepy aspect after the hectic routine of daytime commerce. Harbour staff was minimal and only a few mariners and a handful of others were about. From the direction of the canal a party struggled with their cases towards the harbour office. Strangers, having travelled north to Liverpool on one of the canal boats, they sought directions. A lone customs officer came out of the office and approached.

"I won't keep you long," he said, studying them fleetingly as he passed. "I must speak to the captain first."

"Excuse me, sir," Patrick Bryan shouted as he led his family onto the quayside. "I wonder if you can help us?"

The customs officer's face was hardly visible behind the huge upturned collar of the full-length overcoat protecting him from the elements. Wedged firmly over his ears, his cap defied the blustery northeasterly and stayed put, the badge above the shiny peak glinted gold in the light from the storm lantern he carried.

"I'll be back in a minute," he said. "Wait with them if you like." He nodded to the group already on the dock then walked off.

"Wish I had a bloody coat like that," muttered Patrick. Pulling his own jacket tighter about him only succeeded in removing a button.

"Damn, bloody well damn," he said, cursing the other man's good fortune. Last to leave the brig returning from Boston, the captain walked down the gangplank. Ignoring the passengers he walked towards the customs man.

"Why, you old sea dog! How long has it been?"

"Too long, my friend. What have you brought us this trip then?"

"Spices, wheat ... and them," he said nodding in the direction of the other group. "Oh, and a drop of the finest Jamaican rum for you and I to sample tonight." He relaxed the firm handshake and laughed loudly.

As Patrick paced up and down, his eldest son Michael stood patiently on the dockside awaiting the official's return. Annie, his mother, tired from the canal journey leaned against their offloaded luggage.

"Here, Ma," said Michael, gesturing to the luggage. "Sit a while." Annie sank gratefully down onto one of their battered blue trunks. The stout cases, with shiny brass corner protectors and banded about with leather straps, represented all they owned in the world.

"Michael, let's go and ask yer man if he can help us," Patrick said.

"Da, the man said he'd come as soon as he had seen the captain."

"Well, he's seen him has he not? Does he not know that it's freezing?"

"He'll come soon, Da," Michael replied patiently.

"Aye, and so will bloody Christmas. And before he does, I'll bet! It's just my bloody luck to arrive in Liverpool at the same time as a wind from Siberia!"

"Patrick, stop your swearing," said Annie.

"No, I bloody well will not woman, it's just my bloody luck," he repeated. "Come on Michael, let's go."

"Gather round your Ma," Michael urged his younger sister Jane. "Philip, come away from the water's side and sit with Mamma, we'll be right back." The youngster, impervious to the freezing conditions, reluctantly returned.

"Here, get in here," Annie beckoned. Unbuttoning her herringbone coat she pulled her youngest close and gathered it around him, but all their effort to escape the icy wind met with little success. Outside the harbour office, a dark man who towered head and shoulders above them joined the captain and customs official.

"He's a big bugger isn't he, Michael?" Patrick said as he and Michael walked towards them.

"John ... this is Richard Blackman," the captain said. "He worked his passage here and let me tell you he has the makings of a fine seaman, but I can't convince him to sign on again." The harbour official held out his hand.

"If you ever change your mind Richard, come and see me and I'll get you a job with a proper captain!" he said smiling.

"Bloody officials!" Patrick shouted to Michael through the squall. Patrick glowered at the customs official as he strolled towards the shivering immigrants.

"Excuse me ..." said Patrick.

"I'll be with you as soon as I can," said the official, sternly enough to stop Patrick dead in his tracks. "My first priority is to these folks who've come all the way across the ocean, if you don't mind." Gripped tightly in his gloved hand he held their landing papers. Patrick growled and Michael smiled behind his back as they rejoined the family. The customs officer finally approached.

"How can I help you then?"

"We've just arrived from Cornwall, sir," said Michael. "And the boatman of our barge told us that you could help us find lodgings."

"Try at Mr. Campbell's store over the road," he said indifferently, pointing to the only lit premises, and, touching the peak of his hat he turned and headed back towards the waiting captain. As each of the family sought to gather a share of their luggage, Patrick made yet another inventory. Since arriving on the dockside he had counted and recounted the trunks numerous times.

"Are you sure it's all here, son? Them pirates would steal the pennies off a dead man's eyes, I'm sure they would," he said pointing to a group of sailors.

"It's all here, Da," Michael reassured his father. Like pack mules they started for Campbell's store.

"How many times is this we've moved?" Michael asked his mother.

"Why worry, son? You should be used to it by now!" she joked.

"How long has Da been promising that one day we'd be rich and go to Ireland and buy back his Granda's farm? Yet here we are heading up north this time."

"Ever since I met him, son. But we all need our dreams don't we?

"Has Da ever even been to Ireland, Ma?"

"No never, it was his grandfather's family that came to England"

"Why is he always on about going to Ireland then?"

"Cos somehow, son, it's in his blood and in his heart. Don't be too hard on him. We haven't done so bad as some now have we?"

"I suppose not, Ma."

"There you are then, what more do you want?"

"Yer right Ma, you alone are worth yer weight in gold," Annie smiled lovingly at her son. "But I liked Cornwall," he concluded.

"Aye, so did I."

"Will we ever settle down do you think, Ma?"

"I'm sure we will, maybe this will be the last move, hey?"

"I hope so Ma, I hope so."

Patrick Bryan was a miner. He had first gone down the mines at the age of eight to help his father. His one wish was to provide a better life for his family than he had received. To those who did not know him well, he seemed a hard man, rarely showing emotion, and indifferent towards family life. But those closer to him were aware of his ambitions that something good would become of his family. Patrick had always both worked and played hard. Gregarious by nature, the atmosphere of alehouses and bars was where he felt most comfortable. Patrick was aware of his personal shortcomings as husband and role model for his children and fought hard to control his excessive drinking. He abstained for long periods but then lapsed and drank continually for weeks.

In England there could be as many as thirty small mines in thirty square miles. Often working the same seam of coal simply in different areas, men tunnelling underground for different employers occasionally—and unexpectedly—met. Conditions in some of the pits Patrick had worked were horrendous, and he liked to brag that it took a

3

special kind of man to win coal in seams often as low as eighteen inches. Always wet, a miner—half on his side and half on his back—lay in pools of black water hacking at the rich fossil fuel.

Patrick drifted from small mine to small mine. From the midlands to the southern coast, he had mined tin or coal, he didn't care which. He never had to worry about being fired, which often he was. Almost every village had either a deep shaft or drift coal mine that fuelled industry. If he chose not to work, and go instead on a drinking spree or he did not like his boss, he would pack up his family and move to the next village. During his career he had almost exhausted potential employers in the south. Now he was moving his family to Newcastle. The first plan was that Michael would remain in Cornwall with one of his sisters. The others would go up north. Ireland, always Patrick's dream, without a grubstake had little to offer. Rumours were coming out that the potato crop was failing and the dissident Young Irelanders were set to take up arms against the British. Michael eventually changed his father's mind.

"Ma, I've thought things over and I want to go with you. After all who would look after you?" said Michael. Patrick knew this was a direct reference to his failings and he squirmed.

Michael turned and saw Annie and Jane labouring along the Liverpool dock.

"Can you manage?" he shouted. "Leave the cases there and I'll come back for them if you want."

"We're fine," Jane reassured her big brother and carried on chatting to her mother as they struggled. Jane was unusually quiet reflecting the events of the past five years.

"Are you missing Cornwall?" Annie asked her. A small smile, derived from happy memories of her childhood, fell from Jane's face and for a moment she was silent.

"Very much, Ma, and it's only been a little while, hasn't it?" she replied sadly.

"I know how you feel, pet. I feel just the same," Annie replied, her voice tailing off.

"Do you think I'll find work up there?" Jane asked.

"And why not? What's so different about Newcastle? Why within the month you'll be making dresses for the Duchess of Northumberland herself!"

Jane laughed loudly, before her tone saddened again.

"But I don't know anyone."

"You'll be fine, just fine. You wait and see," Annie reassured her.

"If yer talked and giggled less we'd be across the bloody road by now," Patrick mildly chastised as he relieved Jane of one of the larger cases. This made mother and daughter giggle more.

4

Patrick was also thinking of the past. Annie and Patrick had grown up in the same close-knit Cornish village. After drinking away the family farm, Patrick's Irish grandfather had brought his family to England where Patrick's father later married an English lass. Not long after, Patrick was born and as he grew he earned himself a reputation as something of a wild man. His mother thought he'd never marry but Annie stole his heart.

"Are you sure you know what you're letting yourself in for dear?" Annie's mother had asked. "You'll never tame him."

"I wouldn't want to Ma," she replied. "I love him the way he is." She listened through the ledge and brace kitchen door as her mother broke the news to her father.

"What!" he screamed, the blood vessels in his temple fit to burst. "Has she gone mad? If she marries that Bryan lad she'll never even have a pot to piss in! For God's sake she's still a child!"

"She's nothing like a child. She's twenty-one and old enough to make up her own mind and there's nothing we can do," her mother said to him.

"It'll never last the course!" Yet he had been wrong about that. In another two months they would be celebrating their silver wedding anniversary.

Liverpool waterfront even by night was a bustling place. Across the broad roadway, in front of Yorkshire stone buildings, evenly spaced gas lamps on tall cast iron poles fought against the dark.

"Careful as you cross. Watch out for them carts," Patrick shouted to his straggling group. Hackney cabs for ships' passengers, horses and carts for cargo and handcarts for seafood trundled back and forth. Even the prevailing high winds could not eliminate the smell of fish from the dock.

"And watch for the potholes!" he shouted as he twisted his ankle in a particularly big one. The road surface was reverting to a quagmire as wagons hauled ships' wares to various warehouses. Patrick stopped to let a huge cart pass. Spray flew as giant iron-banded wheels rolled into potholes that filled and refilled with water. The sheet of water did not reach him.

"Missed, you bugger!" he shouted at the driver who shook his head.

On top of the impressive civic building a flagpole, pennant removed, pointed skyward against a backdrop of taller ships' masts on vessels berthed opposite.

"What's that git building, Da?" Philip asked.

"It's where the English keep the food that Ireland needs, son."

"Is it full, Da?"

"Aye, probably son, they'll give nothing to the Irish that's for sure."
Beneath the flagpole, fronted by Gothic columns and protruding
beyond all the other buildings, the Corn Exchange dominated the
quayside. Next to it was Mr. Campbell's brightly lit double fronted
shop. Strange-shaped fruits and brightly coloured pots and basket ware
from around the world were displayed in neat rows inside and out.
Despite the weather that kept prospective customers indoors, the
owner had no thought of closing early. The broad-striped canvas
canopies, protecting goods on trestles outside, danced in the wind like
Viking-ship sails. Patrick Bryan ushered his family across the final few
yards of the broad waterfront road towards the store.

"Are we going in here, Da?" Philip asked.

"Aye, we are son."

"Do you know the man, Da?"

"Philip, haad yer tongue, lad."

"What's them, Da?" Philip said pointing to some unknown tropical
fruits.

"I don't know lad, but by the price on them they're fit for a king."

"Can I have some, Da, please? I'm hungry."

"You can have some when Nelson gets his eye back. How's that?"

"It doesn't matter, Da," a puzzled Philip conceded. Arm around his
youngest, Patrick entered the shop while Michael, Annie and Jane
waited outside with the baggage. Michael had not noticed the dark
figure that came up behind them.

"Hello." The voice made him jump and he turned quickly.

"Oh! Hello," Michael said puzzled "You nearly scared the life out of
me!"

"And us," said Annie.

"I'm sorry, really I am," the man said. "My name is Richard
Blackman. I think I saw you all on the docks."

"Was that you talking to the captain and that other man?"

"Yes, it was. The customs man told me that like myself you are
looking for lodgings. Any luck?"

"No, not yet," Michael said. "But me Da's in there now." Although
almost six feet himself, Michael felt dwarfed beside the crewman.
Against his dark olive skin, the crewman's eyes shone eggshell-bright
with pupils brown as horse chestnuts and Michael marvelled at the
whiteness and uniformity of the his teeth. Through the shop windows,
close to the rolls of silk, Michael could see his father and Philip
listening intently as Mr. Campbell gave directions. His hands moved
first left, then right, then ahead, then up and down, reminding Michael
of the sailors' ship-to-ship semaphore. Without a noise, Richard

entered the shop and received a nod of acknowledgement from the storekeeper.

Mr. Campbell was a fountain of information. He received a small commission for every customer he sent to local hotels and hostelries, and he furnished several addresses. Once again outside, Patrick shared the information with Annie and Michael. Jane paid little heed, more interested in silks for dressmaking. Philip was fascinated by the ships, and decided his future was at sea, fighting pirates.

One other person was listening intently and nodded occasionally as the family discussed where they would stay the night. Richard Blackman had come out of the shop with Patrick and Philip and stood beside Michael. Annie counselled on the side of thrift, although they were financially sound. Patrick's last few months' excessive drinking had depleted their resources a little but not sufficient to cause concern. She had got good prices for their chattels prior to leaving Cornwall and methodically, over the years, she had saved a little.

"We've never starved in a winter yet and we're not going to," she always said and often her prudence had saved the day after Patrick drank excessively. Jane's wealthy clients, disappointed that their talented dressmaker was leaving, had placed large orders. In the final days before departure, assisted by her mother, she worked tirelessly. Often by lamplight, she sewed into the early hours, fulfilling every order. Her labours brought her in what her mother called 'a tidy sum'.

The consensus of opinion was that they should seek lodgings at the house closest by, which, according to the shopkeeper, was reasonable in both price and comfort.

"If we don't like it we can move out in the morning," Michael reasoned.

"I agree," said Blackman involuntarily.

"Who invited you?" said Patrick, surprised.

"Are you coming along with us?" Michael quickly intervened.

"If you don't mind."

"I don't think we have any objections, what did you say your name was...?"

"My name is Richard Blackman and I'm from the East Indies, although I've just come back from America."

"Well, Patrick it'll be good for Michael to have someone nearer his own age to talk to, won't it?" said Annie. But Patrick, more uneasy than unhappy with their uninvited guest company, chose for the moment to say nothing, but positioned himself between Blackman and the females.

"C'mon then, we best be off or we'll miss supper," said Jane trying to break the ice.

For the second time that night, distribution of the family baggage restarted. Richard carried only a long cylindrical canvas bag, so favoured by mariners. Drawn closed by a cord, it was carried over one shoulder. As he took up the rough canvas bag the rubbing of coarse material against the stubble on his face sounded like a file on iron.

"Let me help you," he said flashing a smile at Jane that brought a look of disdain from Patrick. But he quickly moved onto Patrick's good side when he grasped the largest trunk by the handle. He swung it effortlessly onto his other shoulder as though empty, or full of feathers and strode away. Very soon he was almost fifty paces ahead.

"Quick you lot, we'd better catch him ... he could be off with our gear," Patrick said in amazement. The rest of the family gathered themselves, and quickly followed.

"Did yer see the size of his arms? They're bigger than my legs!" said Philip.

"I saw them, aye," replied Michael with a smile.

"Do you think that man is the strongest in the world, Michael?"

"Looks like he could be, doesn't it?"

"I bet he's not as strong as me Da. Can you remember when Da told us about lifting that horse above his head?"

"Aye, I remember," sighed Michael.

They followed Richard past the Corn Exchange into a cobbled street aptly named Green Ginger Lane, the hub of Liverpool's spice trade. The light from the dockside street lamps was disappearing fast as they approached a giant flat-topped building proportioned like a European castle. The tall double wooden doors tapered like the bows of a boat. To the left and the right of the doors, leaded windows gave the building even more of a fortress appearance. A constant rumbling, the whitewashed glass and intermittent squeals and thumps had Philip's furtive imagination convincing him that this really was a giant's castle. Chiselled out of the huge keystone above the doors were the words 'Liverpool Flour Mills'.

Richard looked up at a rusty street sign that indicated they had reached Beck's Yard. Around the courtyard were tall three-storey dwellings, each with tiny windows that had reflected the comings and goings of commerce for almost a century. Outside the largest of the buildings burnt a welcoming gaslight, and together they proceeded towards the illuminated entrance.

"My goodness," said Annie knocking on the low door. "They must be midgets!" They were laughing as the lodge keeper answered.

"Well, this is a merry gathering!" he said. Stepping out to inspect his visitors caused him no headroom problem, as he stood no more than five feet tall. Long strands of fiery red hair, arranged over the top of his very large head failed to conceal his baldness.

"Have you rooms?" asked Annie.

"Well," he replied, gazed fixed firmly on Richard who towered in comparison. "I'm almost full. But I can probably squeeze you in." Patrick and Annie looked at one another with relief.

"But," added the lodge keeper, panning around the group and resting his eyes on Richard, "I only have three double rooms to spare."

"I can look elsewhere," said Richard, picking up his holdall.

"No need," Michael said, quickly chasing the slight smile from his father's face. "This'll do us fine. Philip and father can have one room. Jane will share with Ma, You and I will share the third!"

There were a few moments of awkward silence, and then a demure smile crossed Annie's face as she turned to the perplexed proprietor.

"We'll take the rooms."

"I either charge a price per head or the price per room," he said, recovering. "Candles to be put out before going to sleep and no boots to be worn in bed. Oh and payment is in advance, of course." Patrick watched in disbelief as the others stooped to carry the bags indoors.

The proprietor had not lied; his establishment was indeed busy. When the meal bell rang there was a cavalry charge to the dining area. Seats at the table were at a premium despite most of the guests taking their meal to their rooms. The fare was plentiful but limited in choice. Fish soup for starters and fish pie for main course. Dessert was treacle pudding steamed many hours earlier.

"Thank God for that," said Annie in a whisper when it was served. "I was worried it was going to be haddock and custard!" Influenced by what he considered a very civilized custom of serving girls continually topping up emptied ale jugs, Patrick congratulated himself on having found such an oasis in a foreign land.

Seated at the oblong dining table, with legs almost as thick as the columns of the Corn Exchange, were fourteen people. To avoid his lank hair falling into the soup, the proprietor constantly needed to push it back. Like a wig on a windy day it just kept moving. The lodge keeper's wife was a plump-faced woman, whose silver hair was held back by an intricately carved whalebone comb. She and the two serving girls shovelled food onto the plates. From her pinafore pouch pocket protruded the neck of a corked bottle that she periodically produced, uncorked with her teeth, and took a sip.

"Medicinal purposes," she announced to no one in particular. After each 'treatment' the distinctive, pleasant aroma of sloe berries filled the room. The serving girls were too young to be the lodge keeper's children, and although not much over ten years old, seemed to carry the greater share of the work.

In addition to the Bryan family and Richard Blackman, there were more than a dozen other diners. A young couple, no more than eighteen years old, complicated eating their meal by holding onto one another's hand. Next to them, a gentleman of some years and his family ate in silence. As the room filled, he spoke quietly to his wife and she and their daughter gathered up dishes and took their supper to their room. As she passed, the daughter cast a quick glance at Michael, who returned it with a smile, which made her blush.

Occupying the end of the table nearest the fireplace, two noisy men with guttural sounding voices, laughed continuously.

"Russian whalers," said the matron, noticing Michael try in vain to identify their strange language. "Been here nearly a week while their ship's in for a refit."

Curiosity satisfied, he watched his mother still daintily picking her way through the main course. Whenever chastised for rushing his food, Philip always politely suggested that it was not he that ate quickly, but his mother who ate slowly. Fortunately, there were others who ate slowly, and Michael waited for an opportunity to speak to them. On finishing their meals, most of the women returned to their sleeping quarters while men gathered at the smaller tables around the fireplace with huge flagons of ale. Patrick was soon the hub of small talk and doing what he did best.

"Excuse me, sir," he said to the quiet gentleman who had sent his wife and daughter off to their room. "I could not help noticing your steadfast refusal when the ale jug goes around."

"Strong drink is not for my family, thank you," the man replied quietly.

"Well, then, that's all the more for me!" roared Patrick to his family's embarrassment. "I trust you don't mind if I have a drop? Your good health!" Michael stepped between the two.

"Don't mind my Da," he said. "He a good man sober and harmless drunk."

"I don't mind at all," said the man in the singsong accent of South Wales.

"Welsh are you?" Michael said, stating the obvious.

"Yes," he replied.

"My name is Michael Bryan, You've met my father ... " said Michael, pointing to Patrick who was attempting to teach the Russians to sing. "And this is an acquaintance of mine Mr. Richard Blackman, and this is my young brother Philip. That's my mother next to him, and that's my sister Jane."

"I'm William Morris," he replied, extending his hand across the table. "These are my sons Samuel and David, and young William on the end there. And that's Mr. Jones our companion who is travelling with us." He pointed to a slight man whose round spectacles sat on the end of his nose.

"All boys then?" Michael ventured, and got the answer he was looking for.

"Oh, not quite. My daughter Tamar is upstairs with her mother."

"Great," thought Michael.

Each of the Welshmen was dressed similarly in dark respectable suits.

"Are you Quakers?" Michael asked innocently. William Morris came as close to raising his voice as he ever came.

"Pardon? Quakers? I'll say not we are Methodist, through and through. Samuel here is considered the best lay preacher in Wales, and I'm not considered too bad myself."

"Sorry, Reverend," Michael said, embarrassed.

"We are lay preachers not ministers, young man," said William

"Oops I guess I got it wrong again, sorry."

"Not to worry. What denomination is your family?"

"Church of England — sort of," he replied, hoping to move off the subject. "So what brings you to Liverpool then?"

"Samuel has been given a job of great importance in the north east of England."

"Doing what?" Michael asked.

"He's to be one of the top men at a new ironworks, and we are all going with him."

"Tell me more" Michael asked as Richard leaned closer to hear.

Meanwhile, Patrick was becoming louder by the minute bragging to his drinking partners.

"I once worked in one a mine where the ceilings were less than two feet high. It was so low that one day the shovels arrived at the coalface upside down and we were unable to turn them over. Would you believe they had to be sent back to the surface to be righted? That they did." The audience laughed and scoffed.

"Oh, so you don't believe me?" Patrick said indignantly.

"No one could shovel coal in so small a space," one of the group remarked.

"Is that so now? I don't suppose you would like a little bet that not only could I fit under that form but I can crawl all the way from one end to the other?" Men scrambled to take up his wager.

"Mister lodge house man, how much height would you say there is between the floor and the bottom of that bench there?" Patrick asked pointing to the seats against the wall.

" I don't know, — maybe a foot or two? What the hell are you up to … don't you break anything, now!"

"That's near enough," Patrick said " And don't you worry, sir, just watch this." While the room fell silent he stripped to the waist.

"What's them marks down your back, Patrick"? One of the Russians asked in thick English.

"Marks, what marks?" he asked looking over his shoulder. "Oh, them you mean. Them's me medals."

"Medals?" Stripped to the waist, miners who had been in low seams were easily distinguishable from those that had only worked only in underground caverns. High roofs left no 'pitman's medals'. These were 'won' through hewing coal in seams so low, that—but for these men's exploits—have proved uneconomical. On each raised disc along the length of the spine was a round blue-black dot about the size of a small fingernail. Daily rubbing against the black roof of low seams scraped the skin off and let coal dust into the wound, leaving identical marks on each of the human moles. So even and consistent were the markings, that they became a tribal tattoo of the subterranean brotherhood.

Patrick lay on the floor on his back, sliding through the sawdust and debris as he wriggled under the bench. He mimed the skills of putting props and straps into position, filling imaginary coal into imaginary woven corf baskets. As a child dragging these to the surface had been his first underground job. "Somebody pass me that shovel from the fireplace!" Patrick called out from somewhere under the seat. The curious lodge keeper obliged.

"Not that way up you idiot!" Patrick yelled. "Did you not hear a word I said?" The man turned over the shovel and once more slid it under the form. Scratching and brushing could be heard from beneath. Suddenly the shovel—filled with years of muck - reappeared, followed by a filthy Patrick. The place was in uproar. Men applauded while others argued trying to renege on their bets. Patrick stood up and with a grin from ear to ear showed his astounded companions a shiny gold sovereign, rescued from under the bench. Scooping the wagers from the table into his cap he stood on a chair.

"Landlord!" he shouted "Fill every glass, the drinks are on Patrick Bryan!" A huge hooray filled the room just as Mrs. Morris and Tamar re-entered.

"William!" she howled. "What are you doing? Get our family upstairs, now." She then turned to Patrick who still stood on the chair in the silenced room.

"And you, sir, you should feel ashamed of yourself!" As she turned and led Tamar from the room, Michael hung his head in his hands. Ann and Jane helped Patrick down and led him back to where Philip sat with Richard. Before Patrick' antics had caused the Morris's hurried exit, Michael had gleaned a lot of information from William.

"Listen to this, Da" he began. "There's a new ironworks, with new houses for the workers, under construction right now in the middle of the County Durham coalfields. They need over three thousand men, skilled and unskilled, and..." He leaned in close and whispered, "Mr. Morris says these jobs pay double the national average! Four and five times that of farm labour!" The Bryans and Richard were astounded, and suddenly Patrick burst into inebriate tears. Annie put her arm around him.

"What on earth's the matter? This is such good news Paddy. We can start a new life there."

"All my dreams are coming true, my dear," he replied. "I am going at last to the Emerald Isle, it's nothing short of a miracle!"

"Good grief, Da," said Michael. "County Durham is in England!" But Patrick was not convinced. In his mind the only counties prefixed with the word 'County' were in Ireland.

"I've never heard of a County Sussex, or a County Lancashire. Have you?"

"No Da, but there's any number of things you've not heard of."

"It doesn't matter where it is, Da," added Jane. "County Durham sounds like a place we can settle and make a good life." This seemed to pacify him. Michael and Richard helped Patrick up the stairs, out of his clothes and into bed. As they laid him down, he opened one eye.

"County Durham's in England?"

"Aye, Da. Honest."

Back downstairs, Michael shared a late-night beer with Richard.

"Well," said Michael. "Our family decided to journey on to this new ironworks place."

"I've been thinking a lot about that, too," Richard said. "It sounds good to me."

"So you going as well?"

"I guess so ... any objections if I tag along with you lot?"

"No, none at all, welcome aboard as they say!"

"Will we leave first thing in the morning then?"

"Yes, why not?" said Michael, smiling at the prospect. "Next stop Witton Park."

Chapter Two

Standing on Liverpool's new railway station, the Morris family occupied themselves watching small steam engines shunting back and forth.

"When will ours come, Da?" young William asked his father and namesake.

"It won't be long now," he replied. "Watch for one that has the Liverpool and Manchester Company painted on the coaches."

"Are we going to Manchester, Da?"

"Yes, then York, then Darlington then just another short ride and we'll be there."

"Phew, will it take a long time?"

"Quite a while son, but I thought you liked trains anyway?"

"Oh, I do," young William said as he looked longingly down the single track, urging their train to arrive. The boy had shown a fascination with the railway and had often watched in delight as the great steam engines thundered past the lower end of his village. At every opportunity, he had stood on the second rail of the wooden fence by the railway line and waved furiously at the passing drivers, who sometimes waved back and made his day. But today was this was to be the first time he would actually ride on a train.

"Isn't that the family who were in our lodgings?" Tamar asked her brother David.

"Where?" he asked

"There," she said, nodding in the direction of the Bryan family as they approached along the platform. Mrs. Morris rolled her eyes.

"Oh no! Keep your heads down. Pretend you don't see them and they might pass."

"But why, Mammy? They seem a nice enough family."

"Nice?" Margot stammered. "Did you not see the drunken behaviour of the father?"

Margot held a fiery hatred of drunkenness and strong drink. At nine, she had joined the Temperance League at an initial meeting of The Band of Hope. The same day, she approached a local drunkard and demanded he sign the pledge. At ten she won a prize for one of the shortest essays ever written on drunkenness.

"The cause is drink, and the cure is abstinence!" she wrote.

By the time she was twelve she had become prominent enough in temperance circles to successfully oppose the election of a cleric to the Band of Hope committee, claiming she had seen a barrel of ale delivered to his back door. In addition to her fanaticism against drink,

Margot carried a Protestant work ethic and was fastidious around her house. She hated the clutter of ornaments or crocheted doilies on every chair arm and back. And although she loved her children deeply, she never kissed them.

Yet Margot never turned beggars away from their door although her husband never earned more than two pounds per week in his whole life. Her family recognised she was no ordinary human being; she never forgot that she had known want and hunger and was a queen of compassion. When there was a death she was as good as a doctor, nurse and vicar all rolled into one. Her honeymoon consisted of a half day trip to Tredegar to hear a brass band play in the park, then back to work again the next morning. Margot had always made a special effort for William returning from work and each day she would put on a clean and ironed apron. Among the many studded boots that turned into their street, she swore she could recognise those of her husband.

The Bryan family stopped once they reached the Morris's.
"How nice to meet you all again," Patrick said as Margot shuffled her feet.
There followed a good deal of uncomfortable head nodding and handshaking.
"We're off to County Durham," Patrick continued. "There's work waiting for all of us my son says. Where are you all off to then?"
"Da," Michael interrupted "It was Mr. Morris who told us about Witton Park!"
"Oh, of course it was, how daft of me, forgot about that." Patrick said undaunted.
"No wonder," Margot muttered under her breath.
"Pardon?" Patrick asked
"Nothing," she replied curtly.
"Perhaps we should travel there together," Michael said. This brought a demure smile from Tamar and a scowl from her mother. Margot felt her knees buckle slightly.
"Perhaps," William Morris said in a non-committal tone. Philip Bryan sidled over to the young William. Both boys were about the same age.
"What's your name then?"
"William, but most people call me Squeak. What's yours?"
"Philip. Where do you come from?" he asked
"Wales. Where do you come from?"
"We're from Cornwall, but my Da's Da was from Ireland."
"Oh," Philip said slightly perplexed.
"We came from Wales by coach and guess what?"

"What?" Squeak asked.

"I sat up on top with the driver and he let me hold the reins."

"He didn't"

"He did you know. How did you come from Cornwall?"

"Well, we walked a lot, then we got a ride on the barge."

"What's a barge?" the other lad asked.

"It's a sort of flat boat that like only goes on rivers."

"I saw big ships in the harbour? Did you?"

"Yes, and when I grow up I'm going to be a sea captain."

"I'm going to be a stage coach driver." Squeak replied. "Mr. Blackman has been on one of them big ships", he continued.

"Who's that?"

"My brother's friend Richard Blackman. That's him there. The great big bloke talking to your uncle."

"That's not my uncle. That's Mr. Jones. He's a friend of me Mam and Dad's."

"Anyway he's been on a ship, he's a proper sailor you know."

"Do you think he has been to America?"

"I suppose so," Philip said uncertainly.

"When's our train coming? Do you know?"

"Not really, but my Da says it will be about another half hour yet.

Next to Richard Mr. Jones looked like a midget and had to strain his neck to have a face-to- face conversation.

"You a long-time friend of the Bryan's?" Mr. Jones asked.

"Oh, no. In fact we just recently met, sort of thrown together you could say. I'm from the East Indies originally. My father was a Dutch trader and my mother English. I was apprenticed as a locksmith but it wasn't for me.

As I grew older my wanderlust got the better of me."

"Oh, it sounds interesting, tell me more," said Mr. Jones.

" My first trip away from home was to America," said Richard.

"That must have been fascinating!" Mr. Jones interjected.

"More of a disaster really. The food was bland, and the winter weather had my teeth chattering in my head!" Richard answered.

"Like a snow goose, I decided to head south towards the warmth of the sun. That decision nearly cost me my life." He paused and Mr. Jones shifted from one foot to the other.

"Do go on," he implored.

"Ever heard of the Mason Dixon Line?" Richard asked.

"Never," Mr. Jones replied." What is it? A railway line?"

Richard laughed.

16

"Well, it's a very special line my friend — a line that separates the free state of Pennsylvania and the slave states of Maryland and Virginia. I'd crossed it and a day later I was accused of being a runaway slave."

"Oh, my goodness!" Mr. Jones whispered, looking around suspiciously.

"Exactly what I thought!" said Richard. "Ever heard of a Mulatto?"

"No, I've never heard of one of them either," Mr. Jones said, this time not venturing a guess.

"Well it's what I am. I am not a black man, and I was never a slave. But they chose not to believe me. Two men took me to a nearby town, where I was literally dragged before a local judge and I did not have any papers to prove who I was he ordered that I be put in jail until someone came forward to claim me!"

"How did you escape?"

"The jail was a way out of town and two men put me in the back of a wagon and we set off. At the first opportunity I banged their heads together and while they were senseless I ran off and I did not stop until that awful land was a long, long way back. Then I went to a town called Boston and shipped aboard a brig bound for England. It's still too cold here, but people are much kinder."

Mr. Jones was slack-jawed.

"I only heard tales like that in books," he said.

Richard laughed again.

"And that's when I first met Michael Bryan and his family, standing outside a shop on Liverpool water-front. Anyway enough about me. How come you are leaving Wales for Witton Park?" Mr. Jones paused as though he was unable to answer.

"Nothing left for me there," There was another pensive pause. "My wife died," he said quietly.

"Oh, I am sorry Richard said I did not mean to intrude on your grief"

"No apology necessary" said Mr. Jones.

"Have you and the Morris's been friends a long time?" Richard asked, eager to move away from the subject of Mr. Jones' grief.

"All my life," he said, "William and I went to the same school, and I played at their wedding."

"You play the piano?" Richard asked.

"And the organ. It was I who taught Tamar. Now she is the master."

Michael was standing next to Tamar and had overheard the comment. He was quick to pick up the thread.

"Can I hear you play sometime?" he asked.

"You'll have to come to chapel," she said with a smile.

"I will," Michael said with conviction.

""Well there may be some hope for the boy, "Margot said in Welsh to her husband. "But the father?"

"Pardon?" Patrick said baffled by the language

"Oh, nothing" she said. "I was just saying what a nice boy Michael seems."

"Takes after his father," Patrick said proudly.

Quietly reverting to her native tongue she said, "I pray not."

"Pardon?" Patrick said again, and again got no translation.

"Who is your favourite composer?" Michael asked Tamar, eager to keep the conversation flowing.

"Apart from hymns I think I like Chopin best."

"But isn't he that man that they say has hands like shovels?"

"He has true pianist's hands, if that's what you mean." Tamar said.

"Not many people can play Chopin's music," Mr. Jones joined in. "Because of the size of his hand he can cover and play a chord of ten keys. Tamar can do that, too."

"Never, not with such beautiful hands," Michael exclaimed. He reached out for her hand but she instinctively withdrew it.

"I'm sorry," he said. "May I look at them?"

Tamar glanced quickly at her mother who was preoccupied in keeping an eye on Patrick. She held out her hands. They were almost as long as a man's but so slender that Michael felt as though they would slip from his grip.

Shaking her head slightly and blinking as though waking from a dream she pulled back as a rush of blood brought a colour to her high cheekbones.

"That's enough of that," she said in a whisper.

Michael backed away, happy that he had accomplished not just a touch of Tamar's hand, but certain that he had made a favourable impression. He turned to David Morris, still smiling.

"Are you sad to be leaving Wales?" he asked.

"In one way, yes," David replied. "Like, sad at leaving friends and family and those you know. Did you not want to leave Cornwall?"

"Oh I wasn't that bothered really. We have been on the move most of our lives. Almost gypsies," Michael joked.

"I'll miss the countryside and the valleys most, I think," said David "Not so much Nantyglo itself."

"You didn't like it then?" Michael asked.

"Oh, it wasn't that," David said, almost apologetically. "I was brought up there and I suppose I loved the place. But when I came up from underground I longed for open spaces and fresh air. We lived in a drab uninteresting terraced street. When we were little the kerbstones outside our house was our playground. Not a tree, a flower or blade of grass grew in the immediate area. The only colour — the only break from the monotonous grey uniformity — was the window display of the little shop next door to our house. No birds other than dull brown sparrows. No singing of blackbird or thrush, only the constant whirr of the wheel above the coal shafts, or the blowing of hooters broke the silence. Luckily the countryside was within easy walking distance. When I got older I had my allotment garden. I'll miss that, but maybe I'll get another one day."

"Hopefully," said Michael. "But in them surroundings communities existed and people had a sense of belonging didn't they? They walked a common path"

"Yes, they did that," David said in a melancholic whisper.

"Who knows," Michael added cheerily. "Perhaps this Witton Park will be all that and more."

"I hope so," said David.

"Is this our train, Da?" Squeak suddenly shouted.

"Possibly son, what does it say on the side?"

The young boy started to build up the words, "Liv ... Liver..."

"Yes! That's the one son. The Liverpool and Manchester Railway Company."

"Hooray!" both lads screamed as they ran about the platform.

"Philip, put your cap on straight and come away from the edge of the platform," Margot called. The noisy engine drew its carriages to a halt and exhaled a giant plume of hissing steam.

"Well let's hope we all meet again," Patrick said. His sentiment was echoed by all but two of the company: Margot avoided eye contact with Patrick, and Tamar avoided the smile from Michael by lowering her head.

The Morris family began to board the third carriage from the front as the Bryan's walked towards the back of the train. As the Morris's seated themselves on the church pew type wooden seats, but even before they had settled in, a commotion could be heard outside.

"Bloody toffs!" Patrick shouted. Squeak had his head out of the glass-less window.

"What ever is that?" Margot asked.

"It's them Bryan's ... they are coming back. I think they're going to get into our carriage," he said.

"Oh no..." Margot said in Welsh.

"Bloody toffs," Patrick was cursing as he boarded. "Kept the best seats at the back for the rich. They won't get covered in soot and shit from the engine will they? But it's all right for us bloody peasants, eh?"

"Patrick, please stop your swearing," Annie pleaded as they bundled their belongings into the Morris's carriage. Patrick looked around the coach occupants.

"Small world eh?" he said, with a huge smile which brought a lump to Margot's

"It certainly is!" said Michael also smiling, and looking directly at Tamar.

A booming voice outside their carriage was a precursor to the start of the journey.

"Last call for passengers for Manchester!" With a shudder the little engine moved forward hauling its line of coaches and passengers northwards.

Chapter Three

Aboard the train, the travellers dozed or became lost in thought. With each puff of black smoke this wonder of the industrial revolution took them further away from their roots. Was this relative modern marvel, a blessing or a curse? Was it transporting them away from, or propelling them towards health, wealth and happiness? Each of the adults harboured their own hopes and fears.

"Look at that!" Philip said every few minutes to Mr. Jones who, although seated next to him, appeared not to hear. "And look at that," Squeak marvelled as new sights rolled by. Only the novelty of the journey was keeping him awake. Mr. Jones tired from the journey was also beginning to flag.

"Squeak, c'mon up on my knee, Son," Margot bade him. "Leave Mister Jones rest awhile, now."

Despite a slight embarrassment he cuddled into his mother and the steady rocking of the carriage put him to sleep almost immediately. Amazed at his surroundings Philip could not sleep.

The least expensive coaches were unlined, oblong wooden structures with unglazed windows cut along either side. The spokes of the four wheels were artistically shaped as a letter S and almost reached shoulder height. Entrance and exit was by a centralised door in the rear, and even the contour of the slightly arched roof failed to negate the impression of a box on wheels.

From the onset of the journey, Patrick grumbled and complained about the primitive conditions of the coach.

"There's no bounce in this coach at all. My arse is in agony!" Annie cast him a disapproving glance. "If I could afford it I would transfer to one of them posh coaches at the back of the train. That I would ... to be sure. I'd give anything."

Everyone ignored him, especially Annie who controlled the purse strings.

Similar thoughts never entered the heads of fellow passengers, the Morris family, forever content with their lot in life. Having seldom travelled far, and this for the first time by train, they had marvelled at every aspect of rail travel. Although it would mean being exposed to the elements, Philip would not have minded sitting outside, especially on the footplate with the driver. He had always shown an interest in the railways. Now, having ridden the train, he was besotted. Discarding earlier aspirations of becoming a cavalry or ship's officer, Philip decided he would become a famous engine driver and break the current record of nine hours from London to Gateshead — set the previous year.

Pocket watch in hand Samuel passed the time attempting to calculate the speeds at which they were to travel to achieve their estimated time of arrival at Darlington, over forty four miles farther north. He looked over towards his brother, who was engrossed in a novelette.

"What's that you're reading now?" Samuel asked David."

"Sorry, what were you saying?" David apologised. "I was miles away."

"I asked what the book was called you're reading,"

"Oh, it's called ' The Birth of Public Railways."

"Oh? Interesting is it then?"

"More appropriate than interesting I would say," he said lowering his left hand and book to rest on his lap.

"Appropriate? In what way?"

"When I chose to bring this book along with me I honestly had no idea that a whole chapter was devoted to it"

"Devoted to what?" enquired Samuel half wishing he had not started the thread of conversation.

"Witton Park and the railways. They started at Witton Park you know."

Margot leaned towards Annie and whispered. "Our David's book daft you know, he's forever reading."

"Not a bad thing that at all," Annie replied, nodding her approval.

"I thought the railways started in a place called Shildon?" said Samuel.

"No, the track definitely started at Witton Park colliery," David said with conviction. "The first public railway was built by a man called George Stephenson and started at Witton Park. It says so right here," he said with an air of authority, once again waving his book in the air. "It was for the coal."

"What was?" Richard Blackman asked becoming interested in David's story.

"The railway," David replied. "They were going to build a canal, but someone, — a Sir William Chaytor, who owns a castle there — wanted a railway.

"Why did they need a railway or a canal at all?" asked William Morris.

"To get the coal to the coast I suppose," said Michael keen to enter the debate and impress Tamar.

Patrick laughed.

"How do you think they got it out of Cornwall before canals or railroads lad?"

"Or out of our Welsh valleys" William interjected.

"I know, they used pack mules and carts, but the railway is progress," a slightly ruffled Michael concluded.

"Progress? What's wrong with mule trains or carts?"

"It doesn't cost as much to send coal by rail to the ports," David said to his father.

"I can't believe that," said Patrick. "Why I've seen a mule carry up to three hundredweight of coal up to fifty miles, and many a horse and cart with a ton of coal do the same journey."

"According to this book," said David, "The cost of carrying coal to the ports is a grain of that of mule or carts and takes a fraction of the time."

"Does your book say why this Sir William, or whatever he's called, wanted a railway rather than a canal?" a now interested William Morris enquired of his son.

"It says a railway was cheaper to build and could get nearer to the pit which made it cheaper again."

"I knew it would have something to do with money, it always has," Patrick sighed.

"Aye, them that has it don't like spending it do they?"

"I bet this Chaytor bloke come out of this railroad business smelling of roses."

"Aye. I'll wager the same. Money goes to money as they say," said Patrick.

Little they knew how close they were to the truth. The Chaytor family had bought Witton Castle and Witton Park Colliery for £78,000 in 1815, then they soon resold it for £100,000. Investing half of the profits into the embryonic Stockton and Darlington Railway Company, Chaytor became its first chairman. An important co-investor was Joseph Pease of Darlington. Many would later refer to him as the father of the railways. His association was to be directly instrumental in the development and fortunes of Witton Park and its inhabitants. The man who had bought the castle from Chaytor, Mr. McLean, MP, some years later filed personal bankruptcy. William Chaytor shrewdly rushed to secure repossession. It was never disclosed what he paid to get it back. With a vested interest in both coal and the railways, Chaytor continued to expound his belief in a railroad and produced sound financial statistics to back up his argument. With support for a canal diminished, the Stockton and Darlington Railway engaged George Stephenson to begin building the world's first public railway, commencing at Witton

Park colliery. In September of eighteen hundred and twenty five the miners of Witton Park wrote themselves into the history books as their coal left Jane Pit Witton Park bound for Stockton aboard the worlds first public railway.

"Is there a castle at Witton Park?" Philip asked his father.

"So you heard the man say," Patrick replied

"And are we going to live in it, Da?"

"No, not that one son, but one day, I'll build us one of our own."

"Will you really Da," an impressed son asked his father

"Aye I will that, I will that."

"Patrick stop filling the lad's head with all your nonsense," Annie interjected.

Patrick smiled and winked at his youngest.

Philip, puzzled, looked to David for an explanation.

"David please tell me if my Da's kidding. Is there really a castle in Witton Park?"

David smiled at the boy.

"Not exactly Philip. On the map it looks more like Witton Park is in the castle grounds, that's how it gets its name you see."

Endowed with coal and other minerals below ground and beauty above, the area was idyllic but the landscape of the old park of Witton Castle was undergoing radical changes. For centuries prior to 1845, there had stood only scattered farmhouses and the castle. For hundreds of years, large convoys of mules and horses-and-carts had carried coal from the deep Brockwell seam but there was also coal near the surface. Like giant molehills, pit-slag littered the meadows and pastures of Witton Castle, pockmarks from centuries of surface excavations. Anyone with a broken down pony, or even a handbarrow and a pick and shovel, could earn a living open casting. The miners who were journeying towards Witton Park – men like Patrick Bryan and William Morris – were not open-casters but deep-shaft miners who would descend deep into the earth. Down through the Harvey seam to the Five Quarters, down even further to the Brockwell, then deeper again to the Victoria and Marshal Green.

Soon in this ancient setting, there would stand a metropolis of nineteenth century industry and commerce. A great flood in 1771 had altered the course of the nearby river Wear and brought it waters closer to fields known locally as Paradise fields. In 1844, this beautiful spot, bordered north and northeasterly by a huge dogleg in the river and to the south by woodland, was chosen as the place to construct the new ironworks.

Philip looked up at David. "Does it tell you about the castle in your book?" he asked.

"It certainly does, Philip. What do you want to know?"

"Everything it says please," he said eagerly.

"Aye go on David, amuse the lad," Patrick said, curious to hear what was written.

"Well, it doesn't say much. Let's see. It was there when King Henry II was on the throne, he is supposed to have hunted there."

"When was that?" Philip enquired.

"Oh, hundreds of years ago. Then a warrior family called the Eures bought it. They had to build a wall around to defend it against the Scots with whom they were constantly fighting. That was about five hundred years ago. It was later surrounded and captured by Sir Arthur Hazlerigg for Oliver Cromwell."

Philip looked at his father and said "I know about Cromwell, Da. Miss Cornish told us at school."

David scrolled his eyes over the page before starting again.

"In 1689, it was dismantled and the materials were sold by auction, only to be rebuilt just over one hundred years later."

David now had every ones attention including Squeak who had woken and was rubbing the sleep from his eyes.

"Just over fifty years ago it burned down. All the inside was destroyed and only the outer walls were left standing.

"So it's gone now?" Squeak asked, disappointed.

"No, it was built up again and is there now," David said.

"I wonder if there are any knights there?" Squeak said, brightening.

"I suppose so," replied Philip.

"Good," Squeak says, "I think when I get there and grow up I'll be a knight, ride a big white charger, kill a dragon and save the princess."

The adults laughed and Samuel patted his little brother on the head.

"David are you sure the railway started at Witton Park colliery?" Samuel once again questioned his brother.

"Positive," David assured him. "The tracks of the Stockton and Darlington railway started at Witton Park Colliery." David turned back a page and scanned it. "It says so right here. And the first train was called Locomotive Number One. Ah, here, let me read you this it may explain the confusion," said David.

"Initially railway wagons, laden with coal, were pulled along the railway tracks by horses, then hitched to a long tow rope which ran down from the summit of Etherley incline. Sited on top, the stationary engine built by Stephenson, drew in the rope, hauling the laden trucks up with comparative ease. To lower them down the other side the exercise was repeated. Up and over the second steep hill to where they were hitched to Stephenson's Locomotive Number One railway engine, waiting near Shildon..." Everyone looked on intently as David turned the page.

" ... The little engine, whose chimney-stack rose like an elephant's trunk was serrated at the top, like the blade of a bow saw, or more appropriately, as that of a crown. Befitting, for that day when, Locomotive Number One was elevated to the status of King of Transportation, and booked its place in history."

"So the train *did* start from Shildon ... and your brother's right?" Patrick contributed to the debate.

David felt uncomfortable and squirmed, wishing he had never opened his mouth.

"Not exactly, the railway lines and some of the train started out from Witton Park, but Locomotive Number One started from Shildon. Listen: ' ... Pulling its tender, five wagons of coal, one of flour, and twenty-one other wagons of assorted workmen and guests, plus the companies long coach containing directors and their families, the historic thirty-five mile rail journey from Witton Park to Stockton continued."

"Does it really matter where it started?" Annie asked Margot.

Margot shrugged her shoulders and offered a questioning, wry smile in reply.

"Why did the loco not start at the beginning then?" Mr. Jones enquired.

"I just read that, it couldn't get over the big hills and stuff," David said recovering his confidence a little. "Anyway, that was all more than twenty years ago, it says here that a little later on they built a tunnel so the train can go right through."

"What does it say about that?" asked Patrick, who had specialised in the construction of new tunnels into parallel coal seams back in Cornwall.

David cleared his throat.

"... Advancement of the Stockton and Darlington Railway was rapid. In less than seventeen years from its conception, the hill that prevented Locomotive Number One initially getting nearer to Witton Park colliery was overcome. After almost three years digging, the hill was no longer an obstruction. The line ran almost to Bishop Auckland, bringing the train and colliery ever closer. The final obstacle — the river Gaunless — was bridged just one year later, and, as predicted, Locomotive Number One, still in service, halted only yards from Jane Pit, Witton Park."

"No specifications on the construction of the tunnel, then?" asked Patrick, slightly disappointed but none the less impressed.

"Not in this book, sorry," David replied.

"Never mind lad, all the same, Witton Park seems an interesting sort of a place to be going to does it not?

"Time for a smoke I think," William Morris interjected, patting the pockets of his jacket to locate his beloved pipe.

"What a good idea," said Patrick "I think I'll join you."

"Don't you think there's enough smoke coming in here?" Margot questioned.

"We'll sit at the back dear," William replied. Rising from the uncomfortable wooden bench seat he stepped into the central aisle.

At the rear door Patrick who took from his coat pocket a rigid pipe case, bound in well-worn leather, joined him. A small brass lever allowed it to open like a violin case, and inlaid into the red velvet lining was a golden shield and crown. Secure in the hand-tooled relief of the case lay a prestigious Meerschaum pipe. The bowl was ochre yellow turning to hazelnut brown at the bottom. An ornate hall marked silver band separated it from a well-chewed stem.

"What a beautiful pipe, where did you get such a thing?" asked William.

Patrick looked lovingly at his pipe.

"It was me Da's. I think it was the only thing of value he ever possessed," he said softly.

When Patrick inherited the pipe, he was aware of the importance of the hard case in which it snuggled. The marshmallow consistency of a new clay bowl needed protection, like a baby. When smoking from it, cupped hands were used to support it, and only numerous years of use rendered it less delicate, but it always remained fragile. Producing a length of twist tobacco from a pouch, he cut pieces off with a penknife stained by constant use and offered a slice to William.

"Like to try this baccy?" he asked.

"Why thank you, don't mind if I do." William's pipe was fashioned from briarwood. Covering the basin was a bell-shaped silver dome, and the stem was bent downwards so that the bowl rested on his chin. Both men addressed themselves to lighting their pipes. Patrick stared at the cover on his companion's pipe.

"That's a nice bit of silver work on your pipe, William. It reminds me something."

"It always reminds me of the hinged bell flanges on top of the blast furnaces back home, that swung open for loading."

"Well, I've never seen a blast furnace."

"I suppose we will be seeing a lot of them where were going eh?"

"Yes, I suppose we will."

"Then you'll be looking for work in the ironworks with your Samuel, will you?" Patrick enquired.

27

"No, not if I can help it. It's back down the pits for me I hope. Why, anything else would be the death of me I fear. What about you?"

"I'm the same as that. A miner first and foremost. Like yourself, I'm hoping to go back underground. Who knows? We might end up working together."

"As you say. Who knows? If it's written so it will be," William philosophised

"I guess so," said Patrick sceptically.

The two men sat in silence, each savouring the flavour of the tobacco. Smoke from their exertions was sucked to the open windows, then, mixed with smoke and steam from the engine, was drawn back into the carriage. Patrick removed his pipe to exhale and pointed the stem towards William's family.

"And what of the rest of them then?" he asked.

"Well, as you know, Samuel is the reason for us all being here. He'll take up his position at the ironworks, although one day he hopes to enter the ministry and be a preacher. David will probably go back down the pit with me, and of course Philip is still at school. Tamar wants to be a schoolteacher as well as teach music, but we will have to wait and see. Mr. Jones is a clerk so he should have no problem finding work."

"Sounds good," said Patrick. "Well, as I said, I'll be going back down the pit, but it's not for my lads. I'm hoping Michael will get the start at the ironworks. His friend Richard Blackman seems an adaptable man, and with his strength should hold down a job in either coal or iron. Jane is a first-class dressmaker so she'll be all right. Anyway, I expect it won't be too long before she'll find herself a husband and be off."

William detected a little sadness in his voice.

"There's time yet for Philip, he's only ten years but he's becoming an impatient boy," Patrick continued. "He sees some of his mates working and at times gets himself annoyed."

"I know what you mean," William agreed, nodding towards Squeak. They settled back to their smoking and watched the countryside roll by in silence.

At Manchester, a second change of train at Manchester was uneventful except for an hour delay. The children occupied themselves watching the various activities on the railway station while the adults stretched their legs along the platform. At last, a distant train approached from the south. A breathless Squeak saw it first.

"Is this our train coming in now?"

"Could be," Samuel said. "Stay close."

"Will you come away from the platforms edge, lad?" Annie shouted to Philip. "How many times do I have to tell you?" Oblivious to her calls, Philip waved his cap frantically to the driver as the train pulled in.

"I'll get him, Ma," Michael said, and he dragged his protesting brother by the jacket collar back to his mother and safety.

Within the confines of the shared wooden rolling stock the journey from Manchester to York was consumed with conversation, intertwining the two parties together. Soon their lives were almost open books.

"Did I hear Samuel tell our Michael that you already have accommodation in the village?" Annie asked Margot.

"Yes, you probably did. Fortunately along with his job goes a furnished house. What about you? What will you do when we get there?"

"Oh, we'll be all right. A guard at Liverpool station looked up the area on his map for us. We have decided to stay overnight at Bishop Auckland. It's a market town only three miles or so away from Witton Park and sure to have hostelries."

"You will have to come and see us as soon as you are settled," Margot said.

"Does that include me Mrs. Morris?" Patrick said sarcastically. Margot did not immediately answer.

"Of course it does Patrick," William said, "It includes all of you." Patrick smirked at Margot.

"Mrs. Morris, it will give me great pleasure to call on you and yours tomorrow when my son and I visit Witton Park. Please have the kettle on," he mocked.

"I'm sure you will be made welcome Mr. Bryan," she said mimicking his tone, then sternly and seriously said, "As long as neither your pocket nor your belly contains strong drink." Although all laughed at her witticism, most knew she meant it.

In this convivial atmosphere, time passed quickly and soon York appeared on the horizon. The now familiar change of trains ensued, except here, unlike Manchester, there was barely time to visit the toilets before shouts from the stationmaster urged them to board the third train.

"Passengers for Darlington! Passengers for Darlington! All aboard," he called between loud peals from the great hand bell he carried.

They soon arrived at Darlington station.

"How many more trains are we getting on Da?" Philip enquired, his enthusiasm beginning to falter.

"This will be the last."

"Then we'll be there?"

"Yes."

"Squeak, did you hear that? We're nearly there!" he shouted

Both lads danced and skipped about on the platform. Enquiring of a porter they learned that their train would leave in fifteen minutes, from a different platform.

"C'mon stop that now, give a hand with the luggage," Margot called to the boys.

William Morris stared at the steam engine that would pull their coaches on the next leg of their journey, and he tapped his son David on the shoulder.

"Have you noticed that the name of our engine is the Witton Castle? Do you think it a coincidence or a good sign?"

David looked first at the polished brass nameplate riveted on the train's boiler then smiled at his father.

"It's a good omen Dad, definitely a good omen."

The two younger boys were peeking through cracks in the side of a closed wagon hitched behind theirs. Suddenly, the sound of frightened animals made them jump.

"There's horses in there," Philip said excitedly, looking back through the cracks.

"Can you see a white one?" Squeak asked

"Why?"

"I thought they were maybe going to the castle, and I could look after it," he said hopefully.

"No, can't see a white one."

" Ah, they must be just pit ponies then. Let's go and get on the train," a slightly disappointed Squeak urged his friend.

"Why, this little station is busier than any of the major ones through which we have travelled," observed William.

"To be sure you're right. Do you think all these people are going to try and get on our train?" said Patrick.

"Looks like it," said Michael. "We'd better hurry and get a seat."

Minutes after they boarded other travellers who jostled and pushed for space joined them. In the same decade as the Californian gold rush, families flocked to Witton Park and its days of prosperity were to last ten times longer. In search of riches, the émigrés came to an area rich in black gold with an abundance of employment in the new ironworks. They came in droves from all points of the compass to a place not yet even on most maps. Depending on their means, migrants often travelled on foot, sometimes walking for weeks, while others pulled handcarts up hill and down dale, they came by horse-and-cart, or simply carried their worldly goods upon their backs. For some sleeping rough was common, while in contrast, others travelled in the relative comfort of the expanding railway system.

The short journey to Bishop Auckland was uneventful until the train entered Shildon tunnel. Unlit and almost three-quarters of a mile long, it caught the passengers by surprise. The high arched tunnel roof was designed, yet failed, to dissipate the engines smoke and it filled the coaches. The echoing noises were deafening and as the alarmed passengers reached the mid-point, women and children screamed as others fought for breath. Like a million fireflies, sparks flew past the unglazed square holes in the side of the carriage that acted as windows. Fascinated, Squeak stuck his head out to discover their source. The only thing he could see through the smoke was the illuminated wire net contrivance on the engines funnel designed to trap the escaping hot ash. Suddenly he felt something brush his hair. A cold shiver ran down his spine as he realised how close he had come to his having his head smash against the wall of the narrow tunnel. Shocked and drawn, he slid back onto his seat.

With near euphoria they emerged into the bright daylight, the intensity heightened after the blackness of the tunnel.

"Thank God were out of that," Annie sighed with relief.

"Amen," Margot replied, equally relieved. Nervous chatter and excitement filled the coach as the occupants related their personal reactions to the tunnel experience. Squeak sat silent.

The train slowed as it approached Bishop Auckland station, which was no more than a wooden hut by the side of the lines. This was where Patrick and his party disembarked. During good-byes and reassurances that they would meet the following day, their attention was drawn to a quarrel that was ensuing only yards away. On the platform was a broad shouldered man and a woman, her crying baby wrapped in a shabby shawl.

"If I want to take a shortcut down the lines, Mr. Crawford, I will do so."

He appeared about thirty years old, and at five feet nine he stood some four inched taller than the stationmaster. His swarthy face was thin and his dull-black eyes matched the colour of his long rough hair, which curled about his ears. A recently healed scar was clearly visible under his left eye and another on the right jaw gave him an altogether menacing appearance. On his right hand, the first joint of his thumb and first two fingers were missing. He wore a coarse slouched hat, a black silk neck cloth, and a fine blue waistcoat that looked out of place with his dark blue overcoat and dirty brown trousers.

"I'll report you," said the newly appointed stationmaster.

The man laughed as he picked up the shafts of the large handcart and set off along the platform towards the tracks.

"Damn you and damn your railway company! Tell your English masters that Seamus Hickey will bow to none of the bastards."

Crawford ran ahead and stepped in front of the cart with outstretched arms, but the look in Hickeys eyes suggested he'd enjoy running someone under the iron rimmed wheels. At the last moment Crawford stepped aside. Hickey spat on him as he passed and the mess clung to the shiny brass buttons before running down onto Crawford's tunic.

"Sadie!" he growled. "Move. And shut that howling brat up or you'll both be sorry, I promise you."

His dejected companion appeared to be about 35 years old and was unkempt. She had light hair, and a fair complexion, and her once pretty face was marred by a squint in her right eye. A black silk bonnet was tied about her head with a handkerchief, and a short red cloak covered flowered skirts had seen better days. On hearing Hickey shout she seemed to freeze and wither a little, then clutching the baby close to her bosom, she scurried after the burly Irishman.

"I hope I never have a run in with that one," said Patrick aloud.

To the sound of clanking chains and the hiss of steam the train moved off. Standing at the rear door of the coach, Margot and Samuel waived their farewells to their new friends. Squeak, since the Shildon tunnel and the close proximity of head and wall, had ceased offering himself for decapitation and waved his good-byes from the inner sanctum of the carriage. After a steady increase in forward thrust, the train—whistle blowing—began to slow. Heads and hands of curious passengers appeared at the windows, as though in the stocks. The cautious driver edged slowly past Seamus Hickey and his family. Hickey stopped and watched the carriages slowly pass, directing a look of resentment towards the engine driver and passengers. Safely past the travellers beside the track, the driver gradually increased speed and within five minutes the train arrived at Etherley Station, Witton Park.

Margot slipped her hand into Patrick's and squeezed.

"Were here at last," she said.

Chapter Four

"All off for Witton Park," boomed a voice from the platform.

"We're here at last," Margot said to her daughter.

"I thought we were never going to get here," agreed a tired Tamar. Slowly, the compartment emptied as the Morris family and Mr. Jones gathered their belongings and stepped into their chosen future.

"Are we at the right place Da?" Squeak asked his father. "The station board says Etherley."

"Yes, this is it son."

"Hooray, hooray," shouted the boy.

Although since 1774 engravings by the famous Dixon family of nearby Cockfield had promoted the sale of Witton Park coals the new community was to suffer an identity crisis for many years. Referrals to the area years after its development would be as diverse as Witton Park Ironworks, Carville, Old Park - even as Escomb, although the latter was some miles away. It would struggle for recognition until granted full parish status almost twenty-five years after its inception.

William's shadow now fell on almost the exact spot where less than a year previously ironmaster John Vaughan had stood, also for the first time. Upon that first visit, the entrepreneur had admired the undeveloped, unblemished countryside, and spawned plans for its development. Here Vaughan had discussed with local mine owners the coal needs of Bolckow & Vaughan for their ironworks in Middlesbrough.

Born in Worcester to Welsh parents, John Vaughan had worked in the iron mills of Dowlais, then the Black Country before moving to Newcastle. On Tyneside he was manager at the Josh Wilson ironworks, then later at Bell's ironworks at Walker, where he met his partner, Ferdinand Bolckow. They had courted two sisters, whom they eventually married. Bolckow, three years Vaughan's junior, originated from an upper class northern Germany family who had immigrated to Newcastle and amassed a fortune dealing on the Corn Exchange.

Some years into the successful partnership, they purchased land at Middlesbrough from Joseph Pease, a prominent Quaker businessman from Darlington. There, near the north east coast of England, they built their first ironworks. Vaughan had gone to Witton Park to test the quality of the local coal, hewn from the Witton Park and surrounding collieries. He found the coal bountiful and worthy of its high reputation. The main colliery owners of the area were the Stobbart family who had grouped together the product of their different mines and marketed it under the prestigious brand name 'Etherley'.

Stobbart's influence even extended to having Witton Park railway station named Etherley.

At the time, there existed a geological belief that where there was coal, there was ironstone. It was no more than a rule of thumb. Vaughan's thought turned to a second ironworks near to the rich coal seams. He knew that in the unlikely event that ironstone could not be found in the area an abundant supply was available around their Cleveland plant, just 20 miles away. Grosmont or Whitby stone would transport at little cost in the railway wagons that left Stockton empty to fetch Etherley coals back to the coast. Back in Middlesbrough he sold the idea to his partner and without any more ado or geological surveying he instigated plans to build an ironworks at Witton Park.

That warm autumn afternoon, William stood with his arm around Squeak's shoulders and looked over the land to which he had led his family. Quietly he bowed his head and whispered.

"Thanks be to God the Almighty for our safe journey and for bringing us to this land of milk and honey."

"Amen," said Squeak. "What's that over there Da?" The boy was pointing to a giant whirring wheel on top of ramshackle buildings.

"It's the pit son. Just like the one back home." William's voice saddened a little.

"Are you and David going to work there?"

"Don't know yet. Have to wait and see, won't we now?"

Two hundred yards behind them stood the historic Jane Pit, starting point of the world's first public railway. High against the skyline, out on a beam, like the boom of a crane, rotated a pair of grooved iron wheels. Strong ropes blackened by coal and friction lowered and raised men and coal from below ground. The ascending and descending ropes disappeared through a patchwork roof of thick pieces of overlapping rough sawn wood. Exposure to countless days of sun and alternating rain had warped the roof in every conceivable direction and the ageing bark curled and reached skywards. Trees with only the branches lopped supported the whole structure; where inside the ramshackle building lay the concealed mine shaft.

"What's them lads doing up there?" Squeak asked. William diverted his gaze from the opposite banks of the valley and looked again towards the mine.

High up, near the rafters, two boys sat. They looked more like chimney sweep boys than chimney sweep boys did. With faces as black as soot their eyes, from rubbing, and their lips, from licking, even from a distance, stood out as though painted white.

"They're working."

"But what are they doing up in the roof?" an unsatisfied Squeak asked again.

"Wait and you'll see. When the wheel starts to turn, watch and you'll see."

Squeak now occupied himself watching the boys; William turned back to view the valley. He suddenly felt homesick.

To the sound of a hum the giant wheels began to turn. Slowly at first they spun, then faster and faster then slowed and stopped again .The taut ropes hauled to the surface tubs containing coal or waste. The boys laboriously tipped the tubs of coals down a corrugated slope, where it thundered into in rough-hewn wooden trucks standing on iron rails. The second tub contained stone. Squeak watched the boys turn it and tip the contents down a second, less-steep chute. The rocks and stones clattered against the sides of the iron causeway that carried the waste material away from the main building. Then, as the dust clouds rose, they lay silent on an expanding slagheap close by.

Beneath the boys, accustomed to the rumblings and banging, men watched the coal as it travelled to the railway wagons below.

"What are those men doing?" asked the ever-inquisitive Squeak.

"They're banksmen," said William.

"What's banksmen?"

"Men who work on the bank. It's what they call surface workers"

"So they're not real pitmen then?"

"No, not really, son."

Taking a break between ascending loads, the stone pickers and other banksmen sat around eating their meagre fare that they washed down with tepid water. An old horse waiting to be hitched to coal-filled trucks filled was contentedly grinding hay in his nosebag as his co-workers, in turn, stuffed their faces with bread and jam. Behind and to the right of them, black smoke billowed from the tall chimney of the brick powerhouse where a steam engine - needing no break - drove the winding cables and pumps that fought underground water.

"So what's them then?" Squeak asked, pointing over the tracks.

To his left, over the spider web of rail track, lay the coke works. Completed ahead of time, back to back, six brick constructions formed two regimented rows. Clearly visible on the side of each oven was a large metal door through which coal entered and exited as coke. Each circular, domed fabrication, ten or eleven feet high and seven or eight feet in diameter closely resembled a brick igloo. From the top a round chimney allowed flammable gasses to escape. All around the ovens the cratered area, covered by the red ash of coke manufacture, looked like the surface of Mars.

"That's where they make the coke for the blast furnaces."

"Oh," said Squeak, pointing along the railway lines. "So what's them for then?"

Towards the viaduct over the river, there stood the brick works. Situated on the south sides of the tracks, the square buildings with their peculiar shaped chimneys were easily distinguishable from those of the coke ovens. Pig iron production started there, and the kilns supplied an almost unquenchable demand for firebricks.

"That's where they make the bricks to line the blast furnace."

"Oh," said Squeak, no wiser, but with his youthful curiosity temporarily satisfied.

A little farther off, William could see the Witton Park colliery and six miner's cottages, but directly opposite the most imposing architectural monuments were rising. Against the contour of a massive artificial hill nestled the blast furnaces. The circular base or bosh rose straight for approximately ten feet before the main body tapered slightly to the fifty-foot summit. There on the top, just like the silver cover of William's pipe, sat the bell-shaped hinged flanges where the raw materials were tipped in. Protruding from the base were large wooden buildings that would be the first mills to receive the molten contents. Somehow they reminded William of riding boots standing against a wall. The tops of the furnaces were level to the top of the great man-made hill. They were attached one to another by stout beams, giving rigidity and providing gangways between for the workers. From the top of the escarpment to the throat, supported on the strongest of vertical iron girders, ran a single-line overhead railway track that would transport the charge of iron ore to the bell-shaped flange then down into the belly of the molten mass.

"I know what them are, Da, them's blast furnaces aren't they?"

"That's what they are lad, all four of them."

Down in the basin of the alluvial plain, a former farmhouse was put to new use. Paradise Cottage was a square, two-storey building with numerous outbuildings. The many windows and chimneypots revealed the large number of rooms. From there, surrounded by small puddling furnaces and ancillary mills, Bolckow & Vaughan's manager and clerks controlled the works complex.

Finally, William looked down into the picturesque valley where the river Wear flowed through an area as yet undeveloped.

"It reminds me somehow of home, the valley and all," said David, who had quietly approached from behind.

"Yes, it does to me too," William's heart skipped a beat and the nausea of homesickness returned. "The only thing missing is the mountain," he added sadly.

"I hope we don't spoilt it," said David. "It would be such a shame, wouldn't it now?"

Thus preoccupied, the party failed to be aware of Samuel's approach accompanied by the recently appointed station and postmaster.

"Da, this is Mr. John Hogg. He is the station master and today our reception committee."

"Pleased to meet you, Sir. These are my other two boys, Samuel and Squeak."

Each of the lads nodded as their names was mentioned.

"As I have just explained to your son Samuel, Mr. Raine, the works manager, intended to be here to greet your son personally. In the event, he has had to travel to their head office in Middlesbrough. He has conveyed his regrets at not being here and asked me to deputise for him."

"But surely you work for the railway don't you?" William asked innocently.

"Around here, Mr. Morris, you will find that Bolckow & Vaughan call the tune. I'm to take you to your accommodation and see everything is to your satisfaction. You're to get one of the new houses ... there's only a few built so far. It's yonder," he said, pointing to the row of houses along the track. "That side of the track is called 'Paradise,' although around here most folks just call it 'the works' you know." He turned slightly and swept his arm to the west. And that is Weardale," he added in a matter-of-fact tone.

"Right then, which is your luggage? I'll have a porter bring it along."

As the zealous Mr. Hogg turned, Samuel shrugged his shoulders and smiled at his father.

"Ready?"

"Err, yes, I suppose so. Leave the luggage you say?" Samuel asked.

"Yes, here's the lads to fetch it now. They'll follow us along."

"I think we had better collect your mother, sister and Mr. Jones though, don't you, Samuel?" David said light-heartedly.

In the distance they could see their destination. Nestling among the railway sidings, Stable Row was a huddle of eight houses, the only ones ever built on the north, works-side of the tracks. As close to the works as possible, the purpose-built terrace had five stables attached to one end. These smaller houses were in use as transient accommodation for key workers, although the stables had housed the equine animal workforce for some months. From the temporary railway station no uncomplicated route was available to Stable Row. It involved, either crossing the lines and clambering down the opposite embankment, or walking along the south side past the housing construction site. A third alternative was to walk back along the tracks then double back. Since he felt he had the necessary authority, a most important consideration to a man of his disposition, Mr. Hogg elected for the route along the tracks and led the group off.

Squeak enjoyed himself trying to step on each railway sleeper, but on occasion needed to lengthen or shorten a stride. The rest of the party walked along the flattened black loco boiler ash that formed the dusty surface, well away from the track and the sharp rocks that filled the gaps between the sleepers. They walked towards an iron bridge, a viaduct that allowed works traffic to pass beneath, and trains above. Elevated on the embankment, the group were roof high to Railway Row, the latest housing project. In the bedrooms, workers could be seen adding finishing touches. Outside, on the pavement, a mangy dog scratched at its bald patches and waited for workmen's scraps of food.

"Won't get much of a view from their parlour window down there, will they, Mam?" said Jane.

The only thing visible from the downstairs windows was a high stone wall retaining the earth of the embankment.

"No they won't pet, and I think the rooms would be dark. Look over there, they look better."

Behind Railway Row, running parallel, the construction of Middle Row, a terrace of twelve similar dwellings was well under way. Beyond, labouring with picks and shovels, men with backs bent excavated foundations upon which masons would raise Old Row.

Close by, built higgledy-piggledy around a large wooden hut, were upwards of fifty white ridge tents. Squeak caught up with Mr. Hogg.

"Who lives in them tents, Mr. Hogg ... soldiers?" he asked.

"No lad. Them's mostly the construction workers families and some are them what have arrived and ain't yet got an 'ouse."

"Which is our tent, Mr. Hogg?"

"Your tent lad? There's an 'ouse waiting for you. Your brother now he's an important man, he is."

"Oh," a slightly disappointed Squeak thanked him.

In the distance, as far as the eye could see, Weardale remained rustic countryside.

"That's pretty over there," Margot said to her husband who walked beside her. "But it seems so out of character with the works and all."

"David and I have just been talking about that," William replied. "It's men that builds towns but God that built the country."

"Yes, and its people that make slums, not houses. Let's hope these folk respect what they are getting here," Margot responded, looking down at the new housing. At the end of Railway Row there was a small gap. Then, towering twenty feet above the end house, was a detached, square building. Recently whitewashed, it was impressive even when approached from the rear. Next to the large double gates lay the hoop of a barrel, waiting for some child to come along with a stick and bool it away.

"What's that big place, I wonder?" Margot asked.

"Don't know, maybe a chapel," William replied with the first thing that came to mind.

Around the front, a sign writer was balanced precariously up a ladder. The huge sign he was completing left no doubt that this was the Vulcan Hotel. Margot paused, taking in the implication of the hotel's designation. Vulcan, god of fire and iron making.

"A public house. I should have known. I wonder how many lost souls will come to worship the mythical fire god in this den of iniquity."

Her face was full of anger, but William made no reply. As they crossed the iron railway bridge they could hear the echoing noise of horse and cart passing directly beneath them in the tunnel. Although having passed their destination by some hundred yards, the embankments were too high for Margot and Tamar to descend. Mr. Jones shared their trepidation at being unable to descend. At the end of the embankment, they traversed the level ground to the road that would lead them back past the mouth of the underground passage to Stable Row.

"Watch out for trains now ladies," Mr. Hogg shouted as he led the party across the interwoven tracks of the railway sidings and reached the fifth house in the row. Far enough away from the odorous stables.

Plainly built, they differed only in room size from the larger houses of other streets that would follow. They were a simple design of two rooms up, two rooms down, with a pantry extension.

"Here we are then," Mr. Hogg enthused. Producing a key, he unlocked the door then stepped aside to let the ladies enter first.

"That's the parlour," Hogg said, throwing open the first door on his right. Directly in front was another door which, to Margot's slight embarrassment, led only to an under stair's cupboard. To the right of this was the door that led into the kitchen.

"And this is the kitchen," Hogg said with authority.

Dominating the room was a huge black cast iron fire range, almost floor to ceiling and occupying two thirds of the far wall. Ornamenting the oven door was a pattern of flowers, above the embossed maker's name. A long brass rail was suspended from under the mantle piece while on the floor was a brass fender with leather covered small box seats at either end. To one side of the fireplace was the entrance to the primitive pantry.

"And this is the pantry," Hogg explained. He stepped to the back of the kitchen to make room.

Above an earthenware sink was a cold-water tap. Concrete shelves were built into the walls and could support weights far greater than expected in a larder. From the rafters protruded large meat hooks held an array of pots and pans pots and pans.

"If it's all right with you, sir," Hogg said to Samuel. "I'll leave you to look around the rest for yourselves. I must get back to my other duties now. I'm sure Mr. Raine will look in on yers as soon as he is back from Middlesbrough."

"Of course Mr. Hogg. You get along; we'll be fine now. Thank you very much for your help, you've been most kind," Samuel said.

"Thanks, Mr. Hogg," Margot called from within the little pantry as she filled a pan from the tap that reluctantly provided running water.

"All part of me job, Mrs. Morris, no need to thank me. All part of the job," he said proudly and left.

"Well what do you think Ma?" Jane asked.

"If upstairs is as nice as this pet, I'll be over the moon. Everything is so new, it's beautiful!"

"Let's have a look in the yard," Squeak urged David.

"Yes, take him from under our feet," Tamar said.

The staircase door and the door leading into the back yard were adjacent. There, on the right, a protruding pantry extension further reduced the size of the small concrete area. Separated from the pantry by a small gap, the earth closet filled another corner. The closet was both toilet and dustbin. Ashes from the coal fires capped the previous day's waste. Facing the back of the house was a gate that led only onto more railway lines. To the left of this, further reducing the size of the enclosure was the coalhouse, with its low sloping grey tiled roof. Between theirs and their neighbours yard was a dividing wall. High enough for some privacy but low enough to lean on and chat.

"There's the poss tub!" Squeak observed.

To the left of the back door, in the only corner void of any sort of outbuilding, stood the familiar household item. An opened wooden barrel, in which, when filled with water, clothes and other household items were pounded manually with a heavy wooden stick, until clean. On one side of the rim, an idea adopted from iron manufacture, was the mangle or squeezer. Squeak skipped over to it and turned the handle.

"Mind you don't get your fingers in there'" Samuel cautioned.

"I won't," Squeak assured him. As he turned the huge cast iron wheel, a pair of, large, wooden nip rollers rotated. Adjustment of a worm screw allowed varying thickness of wet clothing to pass between.

"And there's the bath," Squeak said.

Hanging above the poss tub and mangle, from a six-inch spike hammered into the wall of the house, was a long tin bath with handles at each end. "Yes, and I think it's time you were in it," Samuel said, looking at Squeak's face and hands.

"I like getting bathed in the poss tub best," he said.

"As long as you get bathed somewhere, I don't care. Why lad, you're as black as coal!"

"As black as Richard?" Squeak said innocently.

"Oi! Don't be cheeky! Anyway, Richard's not black, he's brown."

"I heard people say he's a blackie, Samuel. But I think everybody's brown," said Squeak. "Just some's dark brown and some's light brown."

"God bless him, did you hear that?" said William aside to Margot. "The things that come out of that boy's mouth."

Samuel's new employers seemed to have anticipated every need. The house seemed self sufficient in every aspect. Coal for the fireplaces, fitted in all the rooms, was bursting from its store, and in each bedroom in addition to a double bed was a spare mattress and bedding. Throughout the orientation, Mr. Jones had stayed in the background until a suitable chance to speak occurred.

"I've been wondering," he said to Margot. "Do you think I should seek lodgings at the Vulcan or should I have gotten off the train at Bishop Auckland with the Bryan family and Mr. Blackman?"

"What? The Vulcan did you say?" Margot shrieked.

David heard Margot's raised voice and hurried inside to investigate.

"Oh, David I've just been asking your Mam advice about lodgings."

Now Margot was speaking with her husband to one side of the small room.

"Mr. Jones," William said firmly, "We will not hear of your leaving. There's room enough here."

"But..." Mr. Jones began.

"Mr. Jones," Margot reiterated, "The matter is closed."

"Thank you."

"Ma, here's our baggage arriving," Samuel shouted from the front door.

"Ah, good. We'll be able to get out of these dirty clothes a last," Tamar said.

Margot, as effective as any quartermaster, rolled up her sleeves and set about organising the household.

"You men light all the fires, it'll help air the rooms. All this new plaster on the walls will have to be dried out or we'll catch our deaths, we will."

"Is there anything I can do to help?" Mr. Jones enquired.

"You can make us all a nice cup of tea, if you'd be so kind Mr. Jones."

"Delighted to, Mrs. Morris where do you keep it?" From her bag, Margot produced a silver tea caddie.

"Don't be overdoing those leaves now, Mr. Jones, the price of the stuff as it is. Tamar you come help me with the beds." The front bedroom was larger of the two by the width of the staircase.

"This is the biggest room so the men can sleep in here," Margot concluded. She called downstairs for David.

"Yes, Ma?"

"While Tamar and I make up mine and your Da's bed in the back bedroom, I want you to take that little bed to bits and put it up in the parlour. That will be Tamar's room. The rest of you will have to make do with one big bed and two mattresses for now."

"Right, Ma," David said. "Squeak, come up here and give me a hand!"

Within minutes the dismantled bed was transferred the parlour.

"Mind them new walls," Margot shouted as she heard the beds irons knock against the staircase wall.

"Sorry Ma," Squeak replied.

"Well, that's the best we do for now," Margot said to Tamar. "Things will get better when our own stuff arrives."

"When will that be?" Tamar asked.

"Not too long, about another week, your Da said."

"What do you want us to do now?" William asked.

"When you've done with the fires somebody will have to go and seek some food," she said.

"We'll all go, it'll give you more room to get put right."

"Yes, take them all with you, William."

"I'm ready now," Squeak said excitedly.

"In a minute lad, let's finish my cup of tea will you?" William replied.

As she neared full term of her pregnancy, Margot enjoyed a well-earned rest in the company of her daughter once the men had gone. She put up her feet and enjoyed the surrounding of her new house with its fresh smell of pine from the wood used in the construction. Happy to be outdoors, heeding Mr. Hogg's earlier advice, the four males stepped cautiously among the railway tracks. At the end of the terrace was the iron bridge that earlier they had walked across. The tunnel beneath, built before the works came, restricted the width of carts collecting and delivering through it. Despite regular levelling, the transit of overloaded wagon and carts' wheels left two deep ruts near the walls. The depressions filled with water, and mixed with the clay and ash, used as infill, had become two muddy swamps. Down the centre was apiece of high ground here no wheels had been.

"We'll never get through there," Mr. Jones said emphatically.

"Of course we will," said Squeak. "Look there's a dry bit right along the middle."

"It's too narrow, we'll have to go back and over the main line."

"That's a long way. Back to the house, then up and over the embankments. C'mon Mr. Jones, where's your spirit of adventure?" David said. "Look I'll go first."

"No I will," shouted Squeak and sped under the bridge. With the recklessness of youth, he literally took it in his stride. Arms outstretched, like the wings of a bird, he placed one foot in front of the other and quickly exited from the other end without incident.

"C'mon, it's easy," he shouted back. Like airborne geese, David and Samuel ventured along the ribbon of protruding road. A cautious William, putting down one boot in front of the other as though pacing the tunnel's length followed them. Midway, hearing no following footsteps, William halted and carefully looked over his shoulder. As he turned he rocked a little but quickly regained his balance. By this time David and Samuel had joined Squeak at the other end.

As though frozen to the spot, Mr. Jones would make no attempt to negotiate the narrow strip protruding slightly above water level.

"C'mon Mr. Jones. It's quite easy once you get going"

Upon hearing William call, David and Samuel joined in the solicitations. Their voices amplifying and echoing, spurred Mr. Jones into action.

"That's it, you can do it Mr. Jones," the brothers shouted. "You can do it!"

Arms rigidly outstretched, palms down, one foot placed directly in front of the other, he set off, toe to heel.

William finally cleared the tunnel safely wearing a smug smile. Mr. Jones was still not halfway. The collective shouts of support gave him the courage to take his eyes from his feet, and he raised his head for the first time. He gave a nervous smile to his waiting friends then hiccupped loudly.

With only ten more yards to go fate intervened. A horse and cart entered the tunnel behind Mr. Jones. Panic gripped him. His arms began to flap, firstly in a co-ordinated effort to restore his balance, then erratically. He appeared to be trying to fly. As the cart drew closer, throwing caution to the wind he closed his eyes and lengthened his stride. Ten paces from safety he slipped slightly. Stretching for the wall, which, alas for him, was out of his reach, and he fell, tumbled into the cart rut.

"Oh no," Samuel uttered.

The grimy water, at its deepest, was only about twelve inches but the splash sent it upwards, until gravity pulled it back down - onto Mr.

Jones! Motionless he stood with filthy water half way up his trouser leg whilst sludge rained onto his head. Down his face it travelled, behind his spectacles and into his eyes as he coughed and spluttered. Arriving at his neck the slurry met the oversize stiff collar, which acting as a drainpipe, allowed the sludge to flow down into his 'Long Johns'. He stood motionless as William re-entered the tunnel

"C'mon man it's no use just standing there," William urged him.

Slowly he walked the remaining distance to join the others, wiping his muddied spectacles on his handkerchief. His companions were too shocked to laugh.

"I think I should go back," Mr. Jones whimpered.

"I think you should," said William "Do you want us to come with you?"

"No, that won't be necessary thank you."

The others stood and watched a wet and dejected Mr. Jones walk back under the bridge, back through the mud with no regard for his water filled shoes.

When Mr. Jones was out of sight, the rest of the party allowed themselves a smile before going on. Not far from the tunnel entrance, a short row of four dwellings was well under construction.

"It looks like someone has big, big plans for this place doesn't it Da," David said.

"It certainly does. Look at the size of the window on that end building. Must be going to be a shop, eh?"

"Must be, Da," David replied. They crossed the few yards to the large front window though which they could see a large counter being fitted.

"I don't think so," said Samuel. "Look again."

The man they had earlier seen up the ladder outside the Vulcan was busy again. Using chalk he was outlining on the window the sign he was to paint.

"What you going to write, Mister," Squeak asked.

"Oh, hello lad. Write?" He pulled a piece of paper from his pocket. "This one ... this is to be the Ironworks Inn. Busy times, eh?"

"Another tavern?" William exclaimed. He paused. "Better not tell Ma just yet about this anyone or she'll wonder where I have brought her." They said good-bye to the puzzled workman and left. In the field behind stood a large wooden building, surrounded by the mass of ex-British army tents. Rain had ruined the lists of products and prices painted on the outside walls of the store in whitewash.

"I guess that's the store," Samuel said to David.

"Looks like it to me, brother," he replied, and they headed towards it. Access was by way of double doors on the gable end. Inside was like Aladdin's cave. Having a monopoly the proprietor was 'all things unto all men' being butcher, baker candlestick maker, and more. About two-thirds down its length a long wooden counter ran the full width, separating the customers from the proprietor and his neatly stocked shelves. Behind the shelves could be seen the living quarters. A woollen army blanket suspended from a hemp rope afforded little privacy to a mother breast-feeding her child.

The customer's side of the store was like an obstacle course. Piled high - often to the ceiling - were large boxes, tea chests and butter barrels. All items as yet unpacked or too large to make theft easy littered the room. Tents by the dozen occupied the whole corner next to the double doors. The emporium's owner sought to sell almost everything, except the tents, which he rented on a weekly basis. With so much merchandise to wade through, the Morris's took their time and walked around the premises perusing, pricing and selecting items. The point of service was a central smoothed area of the otherwise rough counter. With his wife busy feeding the child; the owner scampered back and forth to a waiting couple that he was serving. The

Morris family was patiently waiting their turn when the doors burst open and in strutted Seamus Hickey.

"It's that bad tempered man from the railway station," said Squeak quietly.

"Never mind him," said William. "Pay attention over here."

Circling the store, walking stick in hand, Hickey quickly scrutinised its contents then strode towards the end of the counter. The floorboards groaned under his deliberate stride the steel segments hammered into the soles and heels of his boots resounded off the wood. The storekeeper was interrupted as he was about to turn his attention to William and his family.

"How much do I owe you for these?" Hickey growled, throwing onto the counter several small items.

The shopkeeper ignored him.

"You. Shopkeeper. I said how much do I owe you for these? Do you want bloody paying or not?" He banged on the counter with the handle of his stick.

"These gentlemen are before you, you must be patient."

"An Irishman waits for no bloody Englishman!"

"Welsh, we are," David said, stoically.

Unaccustomed to having his authority challenged, Hickey looked coldly towards David who, unabashed, met his stare.

"It could have been worse ... they might have been Hibernian Orangemen."

William grabbed David by the arm.

"Go ahead and serve him, we are in no hurry," he said.

Without hesitation the grocer checked the items and spoke with a tremor in his voice.

"That comes to one shilling and three pence, sir."

Raking through his coins, Hickey counted out the money and slammed it on the counter. Before anyone had time to say good riddance Hickey spoke again.

"And how much does a thieving English bastard want off an Irishman for one of them, then?" he said pointing to the stack of tents.

"They're five shillings a week, in advance?"

"Five shillings? I could get a damned house for five shillings a week."

"Not around here you couldn't," the storekeeper said, and immediately wished he had not.

"What did you say you little bit of shite?" The storekeeper was almost quaking by then.

"Nothing sir. I simply meant there are no houses ready to let here, at the moment that is, sir."

"I'll pay you after I get a wage packet, and you think yourself lucky at that." Hickey strode across to the great heap of tents next to where his spouse and child waited, he paused for a moment, then selecting quickly, threw it over his shoulder and left. William at last relaxed his grip on David's arm.

"I'm sorry about that gentlemen, we get all sorts in here I'm afraid," said the storekeeper.

The Morris family collected and paid for their supplies, then left for home without mentioning that they had met Hickey once before.

Chapter Five

Goods' trains passing at all hours of the night, within yards of Stable Row had failed to disturb any of the occupants of the Morris household. Although in strange surroundings, the long journey of the previous day ensured sleep.

"Sleep well, son?" Margot, already up and cooking breakfast, asked her youngest as he came down the stairs into the kitchen.

Squeak still rubbing his eyes nodded several times.

"Rub your face under the tap, it'll help wake you up. And comb your hair son."

"First I wanna go to the lavvy," he said through thick lips.

"You'll have to wait your Da's in there."

"And I'm next," David said from the comfort of the fireside chair.

"Aww," Squeak complained.

"David give your Da a shout, he's been in their ages."

Father and son passed each other in the yard under an 'Indian Summer' sky.

In the nearby town of Bishop Auckland the Bryan family and Richard Blackman were also about early. Over a cooked breakfast they discussed the days plans.

"What's the best way to Witton Park, landlord?" Michael asked their host as he served the meagre breakfast. Fat covered the majority of the surface of the plate. An egg only eclipsed the size of the lone small sausage. So small it must have come from a pigeon thought Michael. The bacon he could not face and slid it along the plate in its own fat and hid under a rough-cut wedge of stale fried granary bread.

"You'll not find any signs pointing the way, that's for sure. You can either walk along the riverbanks, upstream through Escomb, or catch the train. They run all the time. Seems all of a sudden everyone wants to go there," the hotelier said grumpily. Anybody will point you the way. Some walks along the railway tracks but if Mister Crawford, sees you near them tracks he'll report you, that's for sure.

"I believe so," Michael concluded.

"He didn't stop the Irishman did he Da," Philip whispered.

"Ssh lad, said his father.

How long will it take to walk there along by the river?" Michael enquired.

The landlord looked at the party,

"Even with the two women and the bairn you'll be there in less than an hour," he said.

"Then I vote we take a morning stroll," said Annie

"Me too," said Patrick. The cheeks of me arse is still sore from them trains"

Patrick "Do you always have to swear?" Annie criticised.

"Sorry," he said before falling silent.

Jane sent a small sympathetic smile to the father she adored.

"It's beautiful, isn't it?" Jane said to her mother as they walked along the river valley.

"It certainly is," Annie replied.

"What's its name I wonder," Jane asked

"I believe, although written it looks like the word wear as in clothes, the local pronunciation is River Wear as in a tear from your eye," Michael informed her.

"Wear, as in tear. How pretty Jane murmured to herself

"Can we go in for a swim Da?" Philip asked.

"When?"

"Now," said Philip.

"Don't be daft lad."

"I'll take you swimming. Once we're settled in," Michael offered.

"Smashing, but I can't swim properly yet. Will you teach me?"

"I will Philip," said Richard. As I lad I swam regularly in the warm sea back at home.

"Great," an excited Philip said before running ahead knocking down tall green plants that looked like rhubarb, their tops as wide as an umbrella. Ahead of them, beside the river in Paradise fields, the works began to reveal itself.

"We're nearly there son," Patrick said to Philip who did not answer. He looked around, but Philip was nowhere in sight. Looking to the river, his heart skipped a beat.

"Philip! Philip!" he called out anxiously. Everyone stopped and looked around them.

"Up here Da," Philip shouted from up in a tree.

"Philip, get yourself down here now before I kill you. You little sod you frightened the life out of me," Philip began to climb down. "And if you fall and break both of your legs, don't come running to me."

Annie and Jane burst out into giggles.

"There's nowt funny about it," he said angrily. Both Michael and Richard stifled their laughter.

Before long they were knocking on the door in Stable Row.

"Have you got the kettle on Margot?" Patrick shouted as he entered the house. She smiled a welcome.

"Did you have to bring him with you?" she said frivolously to Annie.

"Afraid so."

48

"Shame, but I suppose we all have our crosses to bear don't we?"

The gathering filled both the tiny kitchen and parlour.

"Fancy going for a walk?" Tamar asked Kate.

"Good idea", Margot said. "Take the two lads with you. There's not enough room to swing a cat in here with all these men."

"Oh, Ma, must we?" Tamar groaned.

Sitting on a gate, the girls were happy to relax in the morning sun.

"I saw loads of lads pass by here this morning Jane said excitedly. "On their way to the works I suppose."

"Yes, I suppose so," a disinterested Tamar replied.

"Let's run up to the top of that hill we'll be able to see the men and horses working from there," Squeak said.

"Yeah, let's go. Race yer," Philip said and took off up the hill with his friend in pursuit.

"How old is your Michael?" Tamar probed, trying hard not to make her interest obvious.

"One year older than me," Jane replied. "Why? What do you want to know that for?"

"Just curious. So he's the same age as me then?"

"I suppose. You don't fancy him do you?"

"No, I don't," Tamar said unconvincingly. "And don't you be telling him any other." Jumping down from the gate Jane shouted teasingly:

"I will, I'll tell him that you fancy him." Frock hems flying as they ran, Tamar raced after her friend, shouting.

"You dare, just you dare." Panting they arrived back at the house. Inside the reunited groups gossiped.

"What's Bishop Auckland like," William enquired of Patrick.

"It seems like a quiet market town."

"Yes, it must be quiet, why there's grass growing through the cobbles in the market place," Michael added. "A bloke was telling me that years ago one of the Bishops who lived in Auckland Castle was almost as powerful as the King of England himself."

"Never," exclaimed William.

"Aye, they could raise their own taxes, armies. Why they ran County Durham. That's why it's still called The Land of the Prince Bishops."

"Never," William repeated himself.

"Oh, it's right enough, but like I said it's a quiet place now."

"Not like this place," Annie said to Margot.

"No?" I hope you haven't been too busy, overdoing it the baby near due and all."

"Oh, I'm all right, there wasn't that much to do."

"That's good," Annie said.

"Smoke time do you think Patrick?" William said inviting him to step out into the yard.

"Certainly is." Besides the two smokers all the other men followed into the warming sunshine. David started to tell Michael about poor Mr. Jones' misadventure.

"Ssh, you'll embarrass the man".

"It's all right William," a blushing Mr. Jones said.

"What happened?" asked Patrick and Richard.

David related Mr. Jones unfortunate experience.

"Poor Mr. Jones," Richard said smothering his laughter. Patrick let out the greatest of belly laughs. Tears rolled down his face. Only a bout of coughing, brought about by his uncontrollable laughter, saved Mr. Jones further embarrassment. Clutching his stomach and retching, Patrick rushed up the three steps into the lavvy and slammed the door behind him. Silence fell over the yard. Returning, calmed, he stood with his back to the unfortunate man; for to look at the little Welshman made him chuckle. Diplomatically William changed the subject.

"There's not much else we can tell you since we didn't arrive until late. The agent is called Mr. Raine and I understand he is coming to see our Samuel. Perhaps then we will find out more."

Samuel nodded in agreement.

"Oh and we bumped into that horrible Irishman again, the one that was arguing on the station platform" said David.

"Wasn't Hickey his name?" Patrick asked.

"I'm not sure," David answered. "But one thing I know. I wouldn't like to meet him on a dark night."

"Me neither," Patrick said.

"Speak of the devil, they say, and he will appear," Margot said leaning out of the kitchen door. "He's at the front."

"Hickey at the front door?" blurted out Mr. Jones. "What can he want of us? It'll be trouble I bet."

"Calm down, Mr. Jones. It's not Hickey it's the other 'devil'–Mr. Raine." Relieved, Mr. Jones exhaled loudly then gulped in a great intake of air.

Standing in the front doorway, Mr. Raine, a kind and handsome man, no way resembled the devil either in appearance or nature. Samuel strode along the passage to introduce himself. Entering the kitchen a scene similar to musical chairs unfolded, the comfortable fire side chairs being offered to the guest.

"The rest of my family and friends are in the yard. They are all anxious to meet you."

"Let's not keep them waiting then." The works agent said excusing himself to the ladies. Mr. Raine introduced himself to the group.

"It seems the journey has brought together some previous strangers eh? Good to see different people from different cultures getting on so well in this time and age. What with the Irish 'troubles' and all if you understand what I mean? No offence meant to any Irishman, mind you."

"And non taken," Patrick interjected for which Annie dug him in the ribs.

"Time for introductions all round I think," Mr. Raine continued. "And what of you all? Are you all seeking work in the iron trade?" Samuel, his position as stock taker assured, stood by the side of his new boss.

"Not us, sir." William said, arm around Squeak. "We're pitmen, though I believe my other son, David, would like to work for you."

"Not me either. I'm going with them ... back to what I do best. It's back down the pit for me, so it is," Patrick said firmly. "But my son Michael he's in the same mind as David, so he'll be looking for the start." Without intending it, they divided into two groups.

"That leaves who else then?" Mr. Raine asked Samuel.

"Mr. Jones and Richard Blackman, sir," he said to his superior as he introduced the two men. "Also my brother David ... and Michael Bryan standing next to him."

"And what type of work do you do Mr. Jones?" The agent listened intently to Mr. Jones as he delivered his curriculum vitae in a nursery rhyme, musical manner. Mr. Raine nodded occasionally but occasionally was also lost!

"Good," he said when Mr. Jones finally finished his monologue. "We need a weighbridge clerk cum timekeeper. Would that suit you?"

"It certainly would sir, thank you, sir."

"Good," he said. "Now what about you Mr. Blackman?"

"I'm a locksmith and blacksmith by trade sir, but I can turn my hand to anything. I'm not afraid of hard work."

"You're certainly big enough to eat hard work," he remarked. "Iron working needs strong men with brains."

"This is my brother sir, he worked in the Nantyglo ironworks," Samuel said, steering him towards David.

"Did you now? And what did you do there?"

"I'm was a leading hand roller, sir."

"Excellent. We're short of good men for the rolling mill. I hope you soon work your way back up to that position in our mill. And last but not least, Michael isn't it? Now what do you do?"

"Anything sir, I can do anything."

"Ah, the confidence of youth, wonderful," Mr. Raine commented. "Right, all three of you accompany Samuel to meet the works manager in the morning and we'll have you all placed. Idle hands and all that, you know." They all nodded in agreement.

"What about me?" Philip interrupted.

All around him boys as young as seven worked in both the coal and iron industries. Patrick shot a look of anger at his son.

"Philip ... apologise this minute. How many times have I told you little boys should be seen and not heard?"

"I'm sorry," an uncomfortable Philip said.

"There's job's for fire boys if he's looking for work," a compassionate Mr. Raine said, smiling at the lad.

"No, thank you, sir. He needs more schooling yet."

"But Da, I don't want to go to school. I want to go to work."

"When you're older son, there's plenty of time."

"Michael Fannon helps his Da in the pit and he's not as big as me. And Squeak works," Philip argued.

"Enough," Patrick said firmly. "Enough I tell you." Philip knew by his father's tone that he had over stepped the mark and fell silent.

"There will be plenty of days left for you to work," Mr. Jones said to the disappointed boy. You'll have a lifetime of toil; don't be in such a rush. Get your schooling in first lad, like Michael did." Philip ran into the house in tears.

Before leaving, Mr. Raine thanked Margot for the courtesy extended him and informed her that he expected that they would be in the larger house of Railway Row within the week. Life was full of expectations, and everyone was in high spirits.

"Well, William, I guess it's down to us and the lad to find work now. Are you ready to start looking?" Patrick said.

"There's no time like the present, in my book. Ready when you are. David give Squeak a shout for us and we'll be off. We'll try Jane Pit first, it's nearest."

"Hang on a minute while I get my jacket and I'll walk a while with you'se." Richard said.

"Me too," said a recovered Philip.

"C'mon then," said Squeak to his pal.

The two family heads and Squeak stepped out onto the tracks first. Emerging from the tunnel without incident, they began to walk along one of the developing streets. The new flagstones in adjacent Vulcan Terrace were laid in place on Friday and by noon Saturday the little girls had filled in the patterns on the pavement with numbers and were playing hopscotch and itchy-dabbers. For both games the children weighted an empty shoe polish tin with dirt. The tin was thrown onto squares one to nine for hopscotch. For itchy-dabbers it was thrown onto square one, then kicked onto succeeding squares by girls on one leg. In both cases landing the 'dabber' on a crack meant the end of the turn.

"Well that's Irish," said Patrick.

"What is?" a curious William asked.

"Calling a street Old Row and it isn't even finished yet."

"You'll feel at home do you then Patrick? With all that Irish blood in you?" Richard mocked.

Although only eleven in the morning, a group of men, whose priorities did not seem to include securing work, gathered at the rear of the Vulcan. Where the large rear gates stood open, lined up on the wall of the yard, stood numerous ale jugs. As they approached, they saw hoops of iron, weighing over three pounds, flung through the air towards an iron spike hammered into the ground. Fashioned by blacksmiths the large iron links of chains had been almost flattened. The outer edges thinner than the main body the thin leading edge allowed these heavy objects to cut through the air when thrown.

"You play that don't you, Da?" Philip asked his father.

"Yes, I don't mind a game of quoits now and then," he replied.

"I thought you played," Philip said. "Bet you could beat them, couldn't you, Da?" William smiled at his son and fondly ruffled his hair.

Walking a little further up the slight incline, they gave way to a mechanical giant; a steamroller worked ahead of them. They stopped and watched the driver spinning the small steering wheel a hundred times for small changes of direction. Giving the machine a wide berth, they sank up to the ankles of their boots into the unrolled mix of ash, riverbed silicate, pebbles and broken masonry. Later, when compressed, it would form the finished surface of the street.

The loud clank of iron on iron of the quoits was still audible halfway up the street, as Jane Pit, at the top of the incline, became visible.

"If this is Jane Pit what's that other one over there then?" William asked David.

"I'm not sure, Da. There's so many round here. We'd have to ask."

"It makes no matter does it?" Patrick said. " One's as good as another isn't it?"

"I guess so," said William. "I was just curious."

"Now we are here let's try this one first."

"Fine," said William.

Less than five hundred yards separated the Jane and Witton Park collieries. The old white fat horse, seen earlier, slowly turned its head towards them as they approached. Hoping for at least a crust of bread, it turned away in disgust when it got nothing from the strangers. Squeak stroked its ancient head. Suddenly, its black and yellow teeth grabbed and began to chew a button on his woollen jacket. Startled, he jumped back, to howls of laughter from Philip who had been more cautious.

"That wasn't funny," Squeak complained.

"I thought it was," Philip said sniggering.

"Let's ask that bloke if there's any work here," Michael suggested.

Using a long rake, the man pulled at coal reluctant to tumble down the chute into the coal wagons. Patrick approached him as he completed his task.

"Is the gaffer about do you know?" he asked. The man pulled down a scarf, which was covering his nose, mouth and chin. Secured around his neck, when dropped his face appeared a distinct two-tone.

"He's underground at the minute, won't be up for about an hour I reckon. What's it you're after? Work?"

"Yes, for all three of us."

"I know for sure he's looking for two, at least. Men are leaving on piece and going to yon ironworks. Do you want to wait?" Patrick looked to William for guidance.

"Look, we'll take a walk over to that other pit while we're waiting. If we don't get fixed up there we'll call back."

"Right, I'll tell him you've been." To the sound of more cascading coal he re-covered his nose and mouth and went back to work. Thanking the man, they headed for Witton Park Colliery. They followed a well-marked path, the stud marks of the early morning shift workers boots clearly visible in the flattened soil. Before rolling countryside started again, the pit was the last eastward scar on the landscape. It was a mirror image of Jane Pit but for a row of cottages, old coke ovens and bigger slagheap. Even the fat old horse dragged away from the chutes a string of filled coal wagons looked the same. Pulled to the railway sidings and unhitched from the colliery nag they joined more wagons from the 'Old Witton Park' and 'Phoenix' collieries. Coupled to a railway engine the coal tubs set off on their journey to the Cleveland ports.

"We won't be long," Patrick said as the three job hunters left Philip and Richard sat in a lush pasture over looking the river. They watched the two men and Squeak walk the final fifty yards to the mouth of the colliery.

"Why does me Da and them want to go underground and leave all this?" Philip asked Richard.

"It's a way of life son. They love it," Richard said unconvincingly.

The three job seekers were in better luck at the second pit. Richard could see much talk being exchanged between his friends and a man who appeared from a ramshackle building.

"There's jobs for you all," the manager said. " But there's only one problem."

"What's that?" Patrick asked.

"I've only one pit house empty." He pointed in the direction of the six pit cottages with communal privy.

"That's not a problem," William explained. My family doesn't need one. My son has taken up the important position of stock-taker and accompanying benefits as befits that status! Including a *new* house."

The manager smiled, but inwardly winced at the mention of the ironworks, since prior to its inception they had always sold their total production, without labour problems. After much nodding of heads they all shook hands started back to where Richard and Philip lay outstretched.

"Look, they must have got jobs. They're shaking hands and coming back," Richard said to Philip.

"I can't believe the wages they're paying," Patrick said to Richard, upon their return. The effect on the supply and demand of labour when the ironworks opened had local mine owners worried. Anticipating a possible exodus they had systematically raised their rates to the iron industries average unskilled worker pay.

" I could hardly believe me ears," said William.

"Because of the ironworks they're having to pay good money. They can't get enough men," said Patrick. Philip looked longingly at his father.

"Son, will you please get this work idea out of your head once and for all. Anyway, while I'm going down the pits again, I'll tell you this for the last time. Since my grandfather drunk away the Bryan farm and your grandfather was forced to come to England and work in the pits, I made mesel' a promise. I vowed I'd be the last of this Bryan family ever to crawl underground."

" But, Da ..." Michael began to say. Patrick cut him off.

"There'll be no buts and there'll be no pits for you. That's final lad," he said firmly.

"But I thought you liked pit work," William asked, slightly surprised at Patrick's answer.

"I do that," Patrick said. "But I'd sooner be sitting with me feet up on me own farm in County Cork."

"Point taken," William said.

"Let's go and break the good news to the women folk, eh?" William said.

"Good idea," said Patrick. "But I want to call and get some baccy at that store on the way back."

"Could do with some myself I think," said William trawling the bowl of his pipe along the bottom of his pouch. On reaching the store Patrick and William went inside. Waiting outside the others watched the men they had passed earlier playing quoits. The man Hickey had joined the game. He looked over to the innocent spectators.

"Look lads, there's a bloody monkey watching us," he said loudly. The others laughed. Squeak looked at Richard with anticipation, but he appeared passive. William and Patrick came from inside and looked to Richard who seemed transfixed.

"Good game?" Patrick asked. Richard did not answer.

"Where'd yer get your monkey at, Taffy?" Hickey called to William. Richard edged forward.

"Forget it. Ignore him; he's not worth the bother. He's scum," Patrick said, reaching out to restrain Richard by the forearm.

"Patrick, remember that promise you made yourself? Well I also made one. After the carry on in America I vowed I would never stand for such things again. I've got to nip this in the bud, here and right now. If I don't, my life around Paradise will be nothing but hell. Let go of my arm please." He tensed his forearm muscles and Patrick's hand was stretched open. William's pleas for restraint were wasted as Richard strode towards Hickey. As he was about to launch one of the iron rings, Hickey stopped in his tracks.

"Were you talking about me?" asked the advancing Richard.

"Aye, I don't see any other blacks here. Do you lads?" he asked looking over his shoulder and smiling at his associates. "That is unless you don't know I hate the black slaves of the English more than the English themselves. You surrendered your liberty to the colonial bastards without so much as a fight. You Africans are nothing but cowards and the lackeys of your English masters."

"Me? Are you talking about me, you ignorant, thick Irishman? First, I'm not from Africa, or anywhere near it," Richard, said firmly. "And secondly I was never a slave."

Now that Richard was close to him Hickey could see Richard was not black. But he was not prepared to back down.

"Did you hear that lads? He says he's not a black. What do you think lads?" Hickey shouted. "Light brown or black ... they's all the same to me." Sensing trouble brewing the others fell silent.

"I'll give you one chance to apologise," Richard said quietly but firmly. Undaunted by Richard's bravado, Hickey sneered.

"Apologise? What me?" he said, laughing loudly, exposing decaying teeth and yellow furry tongue. Expecting an assault, Richard watched Hickey's biceps exposed beneath his rolled shirtsleeves for any movement. The muscles twitched. But before the hand holding the quoit that was to crown him moved, Richard struck. If Hickey's teeth had been together the clenched fist that buried itself into his mouth may have done less damage. Propelled back against the wall, with one front tooth missing and others slackened, Hickey lay slumped, stunned. His companions took a step forwards. Richard, with the pink palm of his hand held out towards them, indicated they should halt.

"Who's next?" he said to them. Suddenly they backed away, excusing themselves, after all they hardly knew the man, one could be heard to say. Richard walked towards his opponent who sat sprawled against the wall. Two yards away he stopped and adopted a crouching position. Sitting on his haunches, he watched him steadfastly.

"Here. You. Help me up, and pass me my stick yonder," Hickey ordered one of the men, nodding in the direction of his walking stick. Leaning against the wall was a cherry walking stick with an iron band near the handgrip, which was as big as a cricket ball. Hickey appeared unsteady on his feet and incapable of moving without assistance. Anticipating his intentions Richard reached the stick first and threw it as far away as he could. The feigning Hickey seized the moment and ran fowards. Richard lifted his leg until it touched his chest; his knee on his chin, then straightened it, as a penknife opens. Like a piston, it shot out straight in front of him. The sole of the giant limb crashed into the oncoming torso of Hickey. Ribs groaned before breaking under the impact. Catapulted backwards, the aggressor, for the second time, collapsed against the wall. Richard walked forward and resumed a studious crouching position close to his opponent.

Recovering once more, Hickey dragged himself to his feet. There he found Richard in a classic pugilist-boxing stance waiting for him. Puzzled, he fleetingly copied, before abandoning the idea and attempted to deliver a roundhouse kick. Catching and trapping the foot under his armpit, Richard made Hickey hop comically on the spot. His own leg then became the battering ram that ran him backwards until his back thudded into the masonry of the wall. Hickey for the third time crumpled to the floor in an untidy pile of humanity, while Richard went back down onto his haunches and waited.

Each time the duration of his opponents' recovery lengthened and while he sensed victory, he waited patiently.

"Have you had enough yet?" he asked Hickey. There came no answer. Eventually, helped to his feet, a thoroughly beaten Hickey made no attempt to continue the fight. Assisted, he headed for the sanctuary of the Vulcan. Helped through the gates, spitting blood from his busted mouth he cussed Richard, but made no reference to his colour. Unnoticed, standing in the shade cast by the giant building,

Hickey's woman stood quietly. Rubbing the side of her bruised face she muttered to herself.

"Yes, you bastard, it hurts doesn't it?"

Life settled into a daily routine. The cart containing the goods of William and Margot arrived at the same time as they received the keys to the new house in Railway Row. With Richard as lodger, the Bryan family settled into their less well-appointed miners cottage but were content. As the first snow of winter fell, Christmas approached rapidly. Christmas that year was to be a double cause for celebration as Margot went into labour early on December 25th.

"I think you better go fetch Mrs. Bryan," she told her husband. Tell her the baby's coming."

Large canine paw marks in the light snow preceded William along the street. Outside the Bryans front door a patch of yellow snow defined where the animal had relieved itself before wandering off. The whole Bryan family arrived. By teatime the contractions were one after the other and Annie, assisted by Jane and Tamar, performed the duties of midwife admirably. Hour upon hour Margot strained, bearing down with each contraction, then after a momentous struggle, the baby's head appeared, allowing a brief respite from her labours. Downstairs, the house was filled with people and anticipation, the holiday festival almost forgotten.

"Da, I'm hungry," Squeak said.

"Not now, son, not now," William said puffing continuously on his pipe. "Why don't you and Philip go out and play in the snow?"

"It's freezing, and I'm hungry."

The two lads occupied the little boxes on each end of the fender, closest to the roaring fire. Impervious to the heat, the smell of scorching caused Patrick to look to his son.

"Philip," Patrick shouted to Philip. "You're bloody well burning. Get up you silly little bugger. Can't you smell that? Right that's enough. Outside you both go, there's little enough room in here without youse." Feeling dejected, the boys left the room as Tamar came from upstairs for more hot water.

"Phew," she said, waving her arms, causing the thick pipe smoke to swirl like mare's tails. "Someone open that back door before you all choke." Michael obliged. Patrick looked to William.

"You nervous?"

"A little."

"There's nutten to it," Patrick said. " Why I've had three meself you know. After the first one, Michael that was you know, it got easier. Take my word for it there's nutten to be nervous about. Anyway I think I'll stretch my legs."

"Afraid it's snowing again," William said watching the large fine snowflakes fall like white feathers onto the poss tub in the yard.

"Ah well, maybe I won't be going outside then." With a taper lit from the fire he stoked up his charged pipe before stepping into the passage leading to the front door. Despite his bravado Patrick had been reduced to a drunken wreck on each of the occasions Annie had delivered. Births or deaths were a bad time for him. In the semi darkness, Patrick paced up and down the corridor. From constant drawing the contents of his pipe glowed red in the dim light. Draughts from the ill-fitting front door blew his smoke into the kitchen adding to William's pollution. Like ghostly flying apparitions the trails of smoke were pulled to where William stood at the open back door, before vanishing into the yard.

"Well, I was saving this for wetting the bairns head, but needs must," Patrick said to himself. From his hip pocket he produced a flask of Irish whiskey.

"It's Margot's fault anyway. If she hadn't taken so long then I wouldn't have drunk it, now would I?" he asked himself. I've been more than patient have I not? With that he savoured the distinctive taste of the Irish favourite as it warmed his inside.

"Ah, that's better now."

Upstairs, on the next contraction, Annie eased out the shoulders, allowing the whole baby to emerge.

"It's a healthy boy," Annie said. The exhausted mother relaxed her grip on the bed head for the first time in hours.

"Is he all right?"

"He's perfect, mother," Tamar reassured her.

"Praise the Lord," Margot whispered.

"Aye praise the Lord," Annie echoed. "Someone pass me the scissors please." Jane retrieved the scissors from the pan of boiling water kept hot on the bedroom's petite fireplace and handed them to her mother. Annie deftly cut and tied the umbilical cord as the two young women watched and learned. Holding the silky child upside down by the ankles with consummate care, one slap on the tiny rump caused a sharp intake of air and the infant to wail. Using one of the many white cloths in the room Annie gently cleaned the baby's face, then wrapping him in a clean white sheet placed him onto his mothers waiting breast. Margot gazed at the child with the expression of tenderness and love that artists have attempted for centuries to capture on canvas. He was complete in every detail. Even the bruising and swelling, to the face, could not take away the beauty of a newborn child.

The gathering downstairs heard the child cry and waited with bated breath for Ann's footsteps to descend the stairs. Discreetly Patrick emptied the contents of his flask in one great gulp.

"You're the father of a healthy son Mr. Morris," Annie announced.

"Are they both well?"

"Both are doing just fine," Annie reassured him.

"And the baby? Is he all right? You know what I mean don't you?

"Mr. Morris, for your information I have delivered upwards of twenty children in my time. I tell you the child is fine."

"Thank the Lord," William said instinctively.

"I'll drink to that," a slightly inebriated Patrick. " Well I would if I had something to drink." A look of disdain from his wife silenced him, but he simply smiled back at her.

William gazed lovingly at his wife and new son for almost half an hour. The nurseling seemed so perfect.

"Can we come up William, the boys and me that is," Patrick shouted up the stairs.

"Yes, c'mon, Tamar and Jane are on their way down now." David, Samuel, and Squeak anxious to see their new brother climbed the stairs. Patrick was close behind. They stood without speaking, gazing on the nativity scene. They stood like that for a good five minutes before Patrick broke the silence.

"Look at them hands," he gasped. Why they're as big as pan shovels."

"Aye, he's a Morris so he is," his proud father said.

"It's rest you'll be needing now Mrs. Morris so it is," Patrick whispered. "I know after we had Philip how it took it out of us. Yes, you have my sympathy so you do." Annie shook her head in disbelief. By the time the New Year's celebrations were over the bruising and swelling on the baby's face had diminished. The features were that of a handsome child.

At the end of January a prominent Independent minister was to preach at Railway Row, in the room that acted as the place of worship to the Welsh speaking community. Margot and William made preparations in order to capitalise on the big occasion. They would bring their child for baptism.

"You'll also have to register the bairn, Da," David said.

"Yes, I suppose so but I think this new law about registering births deaths and marriages is a farce. It won't last you watch."

"A lot of folk are still not bothering, or forgetting."

"Can't say I blame them, who'll give me time off work to go to Bishop Auckland?"

"You have ten month to do it,"

"I'll have to do it at Easter then, remind me will you son?

"Have you and Mam decided what you are going to call the boy?"

"Your mam wishes to give recognition and thanks to Mrs. Bryan for her help."

"How?"

"Well, we can't call him Margot can we?" Both men chuckled.

"No we are going to christen him Will Patrick Morris." A surprised David looked to his father.

"And mam agreed to that?"

"Well, she preferred Michael or Philip. I explained to her that the initials of Will Patrick would be a constant reminder to him of his birthplace. WP for Witton Park, you get it?"

"I do Da, but I'm hanged if I know how you got away with that." William smiled smugly

"Despite all this new fangled registration business, we'll still have a traditional christening," William continued.

"Who'll walk in front with the child ... Mrs. Bryan?"

"Of course, she was midwife wasn't she?" his father said. "It's customary."

On a dry, crisp, Sunday morning in January Annie proudly carried the new child out of the Morris household. She took with her a large slice of the christening cake and a corresponding piece of cheese, wrapped in a clean piece of paper. She was to give this to the first person of the opposite sex to the infant that she met. The procession behind her consisted of firstly, the godparents, Mr. Jones and Jane, followed by Richard and Michael. Then came the parents and the rest of the family. Only one person was missing—Annie was becoming concerned about Patrick. He had left two hours earlier, 'to honour the bairn in his fashion,' He had promised to return within the hour. That was over two hours ago. A strange relief overcame her anger as she saw him appear from the alleyway behind the Vulcan. With his disarming smile, cheerfully he joined the cavalcade, at the rear. As the procession walked along the street towards the chapel it approached two urchins. Brother and sister, children of the tent dwellers they watched with childish curiosity. Halting, Annie handed the little package to the mystified girl.

"Here, take this," she said. "Eat it, you'll enjoy it." She smiled at the waif before leading the procession on. The girl, watched intently by her brother, opened the gift and, revealed the contents. To the excited children this provided a rare godsend. Running as fast as they could, they overtook the cortege. With their benevolence of innocence then raced home to their mother to share their good fortune.

Immigrants arriving daily, the little room filled with the growing Welsh-speaking congregation. Samuel read the lesson before William delivered the sermon and announced the first hymn. Standing and gazing at the pages, illiterate Patrick bluffed his way through. Occasionally he would add a discordant note or two, at the top of his baritone voice.

"Doesn't Tamar play well, Da?" Michael whispered to his father. Patrick was doing his best to accompany her. The tune seemed familiar, but he could not recall the words at all.

"Don't know this one," he whispered to Michael. His son smiled then quickly reverted his gaze to Tamar. During the baptism the minister handed over ritual gifts to the parents: an egg, representing the germ of life; reading a verse from the book of Levictus he added bread and a lump of salt, used for centuries in religious rights.

"What's he saying?" a perplexed Patrick asked Michael quietly. He was ignored. Nudging his son in the ribs he said loudly, "I asked what the hell is he saying?" His voice echoed around the little chapel. Heads turned towards him and the service halted.

"Sorry," he said sheepishly.

"The service concluded with a final hymn, once again Patrick seemed to know the tune, but not the words. Outside, Annie, relieved of her responsibilities walked slowly over to her husband.

"Patrick Bryan, one day I'll swing for you so I will."

"I'm sorry, pet, but that service was no more understandable than the Latin them Catholics use."

"It was in Welsh you stupid, drunken, idiot, what did you think it was?"

"Oh," he replied. Annie shook her head and walked away.

Chapter Six 1846 – 1848

As Samuel and David walked the short distance to the works Richard and Mr. Jones greeted them.

"Happy New Year to you both," said Mr. Jones.

"And the same to you," said David.

"How are your mother and the baby?"

"Both fine thank you, Mr. Jones."

"Good, give your mother my regards will you?"

"And mine," interjected Richard.

"Of course we will," Samuel replied.

"Well do you think we will be ready in time for the grand opening then?" Richard asked. "It's less than five weeks away now you know."

"Can't say for you lazy lot in the puddling mills or them as works in the offices, but us in the rolling mills will be ready," David teased. After the holidays, men and machines were tested to the limits of endurance, in readiness for the big opening day. Inexperienced men and boys discovered to their cost the price of their lucrative employment. One man was killed less than one week after arriving with his wife and two children when his head was trapped between cogwheels while greasing a blooming engine. Three construction workers crashed to the bottom of a furnace when a crane failed, and a moulder suffered fatal burns. Children were especially vulnerable, and while many had lucky escapes others were not as fortunate. In a short space of time two twelve year olds perished, one crushed in a scrap iron rolling machine, the other beneath a horse-drawn cart weighed down with rails. Inquests on these and numerous other unfortunates held in the local pubs were often scenes of chaos.

The five hundred people initially employed in the Witton Park ironworks enjoyed a lifestyle unknown to millions of their countrymen. In the middle of 'the hungry forties' much of the population of the United Kingdom lived in poor sanitary and housing conditions. Families unable to support themselves faced either the workhouse or death by starvation. In Ireland, the potato blight had led to half a million dying in even worse conditions than their English counterparts. Almost two million Irish fled to the United States or various parts of Britain. In pockets of England they found sporadic places of employment, usually where the new railway systems were flourishing, or in the coal or iron industries.

Saturday 14th February 1846 was an historic day in the life of the expanding community and the opening of the works had a carnival atmosphere. Six hundred workers brought in from the Middlesbrough plant swelled Numbers. Even people unconnected with the works came from miles around—agricultural workers jostling with miners for the best viewpoints. The sound of the two brass bands aboard another train heralded the arrival of performers and entertainers. A large marquee, erected for the dignitaries, stood on a small area of Paradise where the last grass struggled for survival. Some distance away two of the larger sheds had been tidied and fitted with tables, benches and bunting for the migrant workers.

"Who's that with Mr. Raine?" David asked Michael as they patiently waited for the start of the festivities.

"It's one of the bosses' daughters I think. Miss Vaughan perhaps? Ask Samuel he'll know, working in the offices and all. Why? Do you fancy her?"

"Can't say I wouldn't mind marrying the boss's daughter. Wouldn't you?"

"I suppose," Michael said half-heartedly. "By the way, is your sister coming today?"

"That's it isn't it? I wondered why you were being so friendly to me!" he chided. "Tamar! Is that all you think about? I don't know what you see in her."

"Well you wouldn't, you being her brother. Anyway I don't know what you mean."

"Don't know what I mean. Why man I've seen the way you look at her." Michael suddenly realised how obvious he had made himself.

"C'mon lets go and watch, it looks like they've started," said Michael, eager to change the conversation. Let's try and get a seat."

To the roll of drums the opening ceremony began. An encircled Miss Harriet Vaughan cut a ribbon that held back a cleverly built devise releasing a hammer ten yards away. With a loud crack, a clay plug was knocked from the side of one of the blast furnaces, allowing molten metal to run into the odd shaped moulds. The resulting heat caused Miss Vaughan and the others to retreat quickly to a safe distance. Cheers and smoke went up as a number of moulds were filled, and the first 'litter of pigs' was cast in Paradise!

"We're in luck. See, right down the front there's our Samuel and Tamar," said David. "Look, there's space enough beside them. Wonder who's the bloke in the fancy suit Tamar's talking to?"

"Search me," said Michael. "Let's go find out, eh?"

In front of a sturdy platform stood two rows of benches, reserved for staff and families of overseer status and above. Behind, hundreds of other people stood waiting for the speakers and guests to take their places. Sitting beside Tamar was Joseph Vaughan junior, nephew of one of the owners, and brother of Harriet.

"I am sorry I must leave right now and join the others, up there," he said to Tamar nodding towards the podium. I hope I bump into you later."

"I hope so too," she replied with sincerity.

"Who was that? David asked.

"And what did he want?" Michael interjected.

"That, my brother, is Mr. Joseph Vaughan junior, son of your big boss. Mister Raine introduced us." She turned to Michael. "As to what he wanted? That is for me to know, and you to find out."

"But why did you say you would see him later?"

"Michael Bryan! I'm not sure who I speak to is of any concern of yours, thank you very much!"

"I'm sorry Tamar. I didn't mean to be rude. It's just that I thought we might have spent the day together," Michael said hopefully but despondently.

"That's your problem Michael, you always just think, you never do! You never ask or tell me anything. How am I supposed to know what you are thinking? I'm not a mind reader."

"I'm sorry Tamar, I meant to ask you, honest. I just couldn't figure out how to!"

"And stop saying sorry, It doesn't suit you," she said, her voice softening. Michael bit his tongue, as that word was about to form on his lips again.

"C'mon Samuel I think it's time we had a walk round. And left these two lovebirds alone. "Bye," David mocked. Tamar blushed and Michael squirmed.

"I hate our David at times," she said as the two brothers left.

"Now we are here, shall we sit together a while or do you wish to walk?" Michael suggested.

"There! At last! It wasn't so hard to ask me something, was it?"

"Not at all, no not at all," a relieved and ecstatic Michael replied. All the notable persons and their special guests climbed onto the podium. Seated behind a long table that was covered in a white linen cloth, they waited their turn to deliver speeches. Railway owners, and others, lauded Bolckow and Vaughan for their business sense, and thanked them for the imminent prosperity expected from employing upwards of two thousand people in the area. John Vaughan, in reply for the owners, rose to his feet.

"Who would have thought that it was less than a year ago when I first arrived here?" he boomed in his unmistakable Welsh accent. "Yes, here in Paradise there was but meadows and a cottage. Now as we look at the completed works we can see the industrial might of Great Britain. This picturesque site was an unusual choice for an ironworks some may say. This valley has often been spoken of for its beauties; but when I see the smoke emanating from those tall chimneys I cannot but exclaim that those beauties are much enhanced."

Tamar and many of those sitting and standing in the attentive audience winced at the statement, but applauded enthusiastically anyway. The ironmasters, Bolckow and Vaughan, toasted by the dignitaries as visionaries, were well aware of the treasures of the Wear Valley. Limestone and coal, well adopted for coking, was in abundance. Firestone and fire clay used in the building of the furnaces was at hand. However, one major component was proving frustrating. The quantity of ironstone around Witton Park was minimal. Frustratingly, less than fifteen miles away, in the Derwent valley, all these minerals were in abundance, but owned by a competitor.

On the podium, from behind a white-gloved hand, Miss Vaughan seated next to Mr. Raine asked him, "Who is that handsome young man in the front row?" He looked down into the crowd.

"There," she said. "On the end, next to that girl in the tasteless brown frock."

"Oh, you mean Michael Bryan; he's one of our new workers. Seems a bright lad."

"Is that his sister with him?" she asked. Mister Raine looked down again.

"No, I don't think so," he answered coolly, anxious to get back to the speeches. "It's the daughter of another of our workers. I've met so many new faces these past days—it's hard for me to remember them all."

"Then he is not married?"

"No ... well, I don't think so," he replied uncertainly, but with finality in his tone.

At last the speeches ended and the people migrated to the food areas. Inside the wooden huts, workers and their families sat down to a feast of bread, beef and ale of magnificent proportions. Close by, inside the marquee, the sixty special guests washed down their oysters with the finest of wines. During the meal Miss Harriet Vaughan let her thoughts wander to Michael Bryan. After a while, the men in the marquee retired to a respectable distance and lit their cigars. Inside the long sheds men and women were lighting clay pipes. Bored by the ladies' small talk, Harriet Vaughan stepped outside.

In number two shed Michael and Tamar had finished eating.

"Would you like to go to the fair now?" Michael asked.

"Oh yes please. There's so much I want to see and do ... with you." Michael blushed. Scattered over Paradise were various attractions, whose acts had changed little since medieval times. Mr. Jones joined a small, spontaneously assembled male-voice choir. Unrehearsed, it left a little to be desired, but the crowd was not critical. Accompanied by one of the brass bands, their renditions brought great applause and the finale of 'Men of Harlech' brought shouts and cheers from the Welsh contingent.

A man had brought a dancing bear. Michael, intending to stop and watch, was dragged away by the arm.

"What's the matter?" he asked Tamar.

"It's cruel. Poor bear, chained through the nose like that. It's degrading. Please lets move." With a slightly puzzled look Michael nodded, and turned his back on the spectacle. The day seemed as though it could get no better for him. For the first time since they met, they touched. Tamar had linked her arm through his to pull him away from the bear act. She felt comfortable with it there, and made no attempt to withdraw it. So on they walked, arm in arm. Miss Vaughan spotted them at a hoop-la stall and approached. Tamar saw her first as her fine regalia made her stand out from the crowd. Suddenly, despite all her efforts to look pretty, Tamar suddenly felt dowdy. As Harriet came level with Michael, her lace handkerchief slipped from her hand and floated to his feet. He instinctively bent, and retrieving it handed it back to Miss Vaughan.

"Excuse me, Miss, I believe you dropped this."

"Well, thank you most kindly. It's good to know that there are still some gentlemen around," She tucked the kerchief into a sleeve and, without acknowledging Tamar, rose to her tiptoes, exposing her ankle in the process, and frantically surveyed the crowd. "It does not seem to be my day, today."

"Why? What's wrong? Can I help in any way?" Michael asked.

"Well, I seem to have lost my brother. He was to have been my escort. You will understand that it is not the done thing to be abroad alone on such occasions."

"No ... er ... I suppose it isn't," Michael stammered.

"Perhaps you know him ... Mister Joseph Vaughan junior? He is your employer I believe."

"Sort of."

"You must help me find him," she said linking her arm through that of a bewildered Michael and led him away. As they left, she looked at Tamar for the first time. Her gaze held an unmistakable air of contempt and triumph. Tamar felt foolish as Miss Vaughan's intentions became perfectly clear to her. She watched Michael walk away, constantly looking back over his shoulder, carried along by the whirlwind that was Miss Harriet Vaughan. A minute later Joseph junior stood next to her. He had watched his sister's performance from the luminary tent.

"A penny for your thoughts?" he asked, startling Tamar.

"I'm sorry, Mr. Vaughan. I was miles away."

"Please call me Joseph. May I call you Tamar? It is such a beautiful name."

"If you wish," she replied, slightly flustered. "Your sister was here a moment ago. She appeared anxious at having lost you. She took my friend off with her in her search."

"Oh?" Joseph said but thought it prudent not to enlighten her that he had seen it all before.

"Yes, she must be anxious by now. Shall we go look for them?"

"In a moment," said Joseph. "Please give us the opportunity to become better aquatinted. After all you sort of promised didn't you?"

"Sort of, I suppose," said Tamar as she continued to scan the crowd for Michael and Harriet. Joseph was about two years here senior, and slightly taller, and she found she liked his company. He had a quick wit and was highly educated but did not parade it ostentatiously. They stood awhile discussing the day's events. He asked many questions about her family and personal tastes, but still Tamar scanned the crowds, hoping to catch a glimpse of Michael. After a while Joseph stepped right in front of her and looked straight into her face.

"Have you heard a single word I have said to you?" he said, sadly.

"Oh yes, it's just I'm concerned for my friend."

"There's no need my dear. After all my sister is not a man eater," Joseph smiled.

"I'm not so sure about that," Tamar muttered under her breath. Joseph reversed the situation when he noticed the anxiety in Tamar's voice.

"Right, will you help me find my sister then?" Tamar smiled.

"Of course I will," she said.

He held out his arm, which she linked without any ado and they set off into the crowd. Joseph was in no hurry to be reunited with his sister. He insisted upon stopping at every stall and amusement. Suddenly Tamar shouted excitedly.

"There they are, over there. I can see them." She could see Miss Vaughan and Michael watching the dancing bear. Disappointed, at having found them so quickly Joseph steered through the throng towards the other couple. The look of astonishment and disbelief on Miss Vaughan's face was worth a king's ransom to Tamar.

"I've found your brother for you," she said to Miss Vaughan. "Here he is, safe and sound. Sorry we can't stay a little longer but Michael and I have a long day planned together. So I hope you will excuse us. Good bye and thank you, Joseph." The couples separated. Tamar looked triumphant and Miss Vaughn was stunned.

Since the official opening, cast iron production at the ironworks had steadily increased, but the market was sluggish. Sufficient iron ore had still not been found locally, so Whitby stone, shipped to the port of Middlesbrough then transported to Witton Park by rail, was proving expensive. Bolckow and Vaughan attempted to renegotiate transport costs with the railway owners. Trucks that came from the coast to transport local coal to the docks came to Etherley station empty. Bolckow and Vaughan suggested that the Whitby ironstone could be carried in them free of charge, for an initial period. The railway owners insisted on payment Lengthy and often-adjourned meetings with the Railway Company followed. Eventually a compromise was reached. Half the normal rate would be charged for the otherwise empty trucks to bring ironstone from Middlesbrough.

Building work proceeded unabated on the housing for the ever-expanding workforce. Four more parallel twin rows were completed. Each street, built on a slight incline, consisted of seventy-five houses, with commercial premises at each end. Overcrowding was widespread. Into houses of the familiar design of 'two up, two down' squeezed families of ten, plus upwards of four lodgers. Very early in the development of the village, although not planned, a form of segregation grew. In Albion Street there lived, as a lodger, a solitary Irishman, while in Thompson Street where one of the two public houses was appropriately named 'The Shamrock,' the population was almost totally Irish.

The business premises soon filled with prospering traders, tailors, boot makers and yet more public houses with local farmers taking up shops as butchers. The gap between Railway Row and the Vulcan Hotel had narrowed. The Welsh Independents having raised the money by subscription built the first multi-purpose place of worship. On Sundays, the pedal organ and solemn hymns competed with their neighbour's honky-tonk piano and bawdy songs. The large room at the front, open only for religious services, was the chapel. In the upstairs backroom the Welsh established the Cambrian Co-operative Society. This proved very popular, the goods store and mutual help fraternity were much in demand. The large ground floor kitchen doubling a storeroom had an improvised lift to hoist heavy items. In the first floor front room a library of almost four hundred books flourished. It was also used as a reading room. The running of the library fell to David Morris, a volunteer, who considered it a labour of love. Jane Bryan was a willing helper.

"Who's your favourite author?" Jane asked.

"Dunno' really. Probably Dickens," replied David unconvincingly. The author had once occupied pride of place in the library. "I like to read about the Chartist's also." David's recently acquired interest in politics absorbed his reading time almost exclusively. He had become involved with the Chartist movement and its six-point plan for social justice at an early stage. Resulting from disappointment in the Parliamentary Reform Act and indignation at the harsh Reform Act of 1838, the Chartists pressed for change.

"Well, the Chartists are a group of people who want social justice for everyone. Not just a favoured few," he tried to explain briefly. "Nearly two thousand people signed a petition called the 'Peoples Charter'. Parliament has twice refused to implement it, so we are going to try again. 'Third time lucky' we hope."

"Too deep for me, I'm afraid," Jane said and let the subject drop.

The reading area with its large drop leaf oval table and an assortment of chairs provided a pleasant place to study. The chairs had varying degrees of comfort. An abundance of candles illuminated the room and on winter nights, when the crackle of the cheerful fire was the loudest noise heard, the reading room filled to capacity. Every Tuesday the table was folded away and long wooden benches, carried from the chapel below, were arranged in rows to fill the room. Inspired by David, on a rota basis, members of the community would read novelettes to all and sundry, of all religious persuasions. Whenever 'penny readings' were held every seat was occupied, except the 'hot seat'. The end of one bench was directly next to the heat of the fire. These evenings proved so popular, that occasionally, rather than be turned away, someone would endure 'the hot seat' ... but usually only ever once. The sole exception was Patrick Bryan, whose enthusiasm for the readings far exceeded the discomfort of the hot seat.

"Good morning, Margot!" Annie hailed to her friend who was down on her hands and knees scrubbing the concrete doorstep. "I see you are getting new neighbours again."

"And good morning to you, Annie. Yes, new neighbours again. They seem to move in and out every day, so it seems."

"It should be our turn soon, shouldn't it?

"I hope so."

Building work had continued apace since their arrival. The occupation of newly constructed houses emptied others. New people continued to appear. As some of the first arrivals were moving into the new streets, others were being evicted. House moving became almost a way of life as people climbed up the housing ladder. Most moves meant, at the most, five hundred yards, into adjoining streets. So bonds of friendship remained, and the community knitted closer and closer together. There were also other building programmes. Parts of the community tried to keep the balance in favour of temperance. Erection of the Wesleyan, Primitive Methodist and Zoar Baptist chapels kept pace with the growth of public houses and inns. It was an ongoing struggle for the tee-totalers.

Annie sidestepped the removal men as they struggled with a huge set of drawers so she could continue to chat with Margot.

"How long will it be before the new street will be ready, do you think?"

"Why it shouldn't be long now. Well let's hope not, I can't wait. Sometimes I can't believe we are moving into a brand new house."

"Me neither," said Margot. "I've been happy here in this little house, but can't wait to move. What will I do with all of that extra space?"

"Stretch out and enjoy it all" said Annie with a smile that bordered on a giggle. Patrick and Annie eventually got their move, as did William and Margot. Moving into the same street as their firm friends made life seem even better. Their vacated little pit cottages, small and ancient, were soon re-let. Richard Blackman and Mr. Jones ceased being lodgers and each became a tenant of one of the cottages—small and compact they made ideal bachelor habitats. And so they became neighbours.

Another year passed. Samuel walked up to the railway station. A General Post office had yet to be built. Mr. Parr was both stationmaster and postmaster. Samuel stooped to look through the low, arched window with its half-moon opening at the bottom. The brass plate over which tickets and letters were passed was worn by the constant rubbing. He could see Mr. Parr, sitting in a captain's chair, shuffling papers at a huge mahogany table.

"Good morning, Mr. Parr," Samuel greeted the most likable overweight man, "Have you any mail for us today, please?"

"Good morning, Samuel. It's always good to see you. His tone implied it had been some time since they'd met, but it was only the day before that Samuel had had to prise himself away from the affable, talkative Mr. Parr. "Excellent, yes excellent sermon you gave yesterday. I hope all of us can live up to the moral of the parable." Mr. Parr was a devout Methodist and rarely missed chapel.

"Thank you, sir, I hope so too," said Samuel. "And the mail?"

"Oh, yes. Sorry! Got carried away for a moment there, didn't I? Yes. Now let me see. I do believe I saw a letter with your name on it. It came on the last train. You expecting a letter are you then?" The walk to the station to check the mail had almost become a habit. To find that there was a letter came as a small but pleasant surprise.

"No, not exactly," said Samuel.

Mr. Parry went methodically through the pigeonholes that almost covered the back wall of the office. "There we are, I knew I had seen one," he said sliding it under the glass screen, and over the brass plate. The beautiful scroll handwriting seemed to frame his name on the manila envelope. Portrayed on the penny brown stamp, a youthful Queen Victoria—complete with tiara and ponytail—seemed to stare at his name. Outside he looked at the envelope again.

"To Samuel Morris Esquire," he read aloud with a strange sort of pride. Curiosity overcame him—he could not wait to get home to read the contents so in the middle of the station yard his manicured thumbnail gently prised open the envelope. He read the single sheet of paper, and then re-read it. Very slowly he digested the substance.

"Oh no! Not again ..." he exclaimed. He felt the colour drain from his face as the implication of the letter sunk in.

"Something wrong, Samuel?" asked a porter, going about his work in the yard.

"Wrong? No, no, there's nothing wrong, thank you." Slightly stunned he walked away from the mildly concerned railway employee. Samuel found himself in a quandary yet again. Through the ministry he was invited to attend a theological college in America. After two years residency he could gain a doctorate and become a Methodist minister. It was something he had always wanted.

"I can't go. I won't go," he said aloud. "I will not." On his return home his father, William, was standing at the front door.

"No mail for us, son?

"No, not today, Father." William noticed the crumpled letter in his son's clasped fist.

"Well, what's that then? Who's that for?" He pointed at Samuel's hand and his words were delivered in a cloud of smoke from his beloved pipe. Samuel's mother, Margot, appeared behind her husband and looked into her son's pale face.

"Sorry," he said. "This letter is for me. I think we had better step inside. There is something I need to tell you."

"Are you all right son? You look as though you have seen a ghost." Squeak was just finishing up his lunch when they all came into the room.

"Run out and play, now, Son," said Margot. "Hurry now for we have things to talk about."

"Let him stay, Mother. What I have to say affects us all. David's not home yet, no?"

"He'll not be home for some time yet. He is working over," said William.

"That's all right. I can tell David myself, later," said Samuel.

"What's wrong, Son?" his mother pleaded. Taking in a deep breath, Samuel read out aloud the letter.

"Before anyone says anything I would like to say something first, if I may ..." Samuel looked at the faces of his parents for their consent. Squeak nodded. With finality in his voice, he told them that he had no intentions of going. "It was I who brought you all here. If I left I would feel that I was abandoning you." He fell silent. William drew long and hard on his pipe and the burning tobacco crackled. He held the smoke in his lungs for what seemed an eternity. Tilting his head back he released the inhaled smoke, slowly and deliberately.

"Son, you did not bring us out of Wales. God did," William said resolutely. "As sure as he led the Israelites out of Egypt. If God wants you to go on and do his work in America, then you must go." All afternoon they discussed his going or staying. After two hours David came home and joined in the discussion. He agreed with his father. Margot, although devastated at the thought of her first son leaving the family home, knew she must urge him to go.

"You said it won't be permanent, didn't you?" she asked. "You'll be back in no time. We'll all pray for your swift return, son," she said wiping the tears from her eyes. Until then Squeak had remained silent.

"This time you really are leaving me," he said sorrowfully.

"I haven't changed my mind yet," Samuel said half-heartedly, although inwardly he felt he was weakening and deep down he felt destined to go.

"If, I go—if," said Samuel. "It won't be forever. Not for long at all, my little brother. Anyway, you're a young man now, doing a man's job. Soon it will be your turn to fly the nest."

"Never," Squeak said firmly and rose to go to his room. Samuel smiled at him.

The day arrived when Samuel left, and when they were alone his mother kissed him on the cheek. They both blushed slightly. In all his twenty-five years, Samuel had never known her kiss anyone. When the very moment to leave arrived she cried quietly, which upset him, for he had never seen her weep either.

"I'll write often, Mother, I promise," he said as he touched her tear-soaked face. "Please be happy for me." Margot put on a brave face, but her heart ached.

The following two years, despite frequent letters, were a silent anguish for Margot and she longed to see her eldest again. Michael and Tamar initially drawn together by family ties, now by choice, spent more time in each other's company. Michael also became a regular visitor to Carwood House, the home of the Vaughan family. Sometimes it was in a professional capacity but usually at the invitation of Joseph junior. Joseph's father had died suddenly and now he was joint owner and manager of the iron-works. At the age of only twenty-three, he found the responsibility demanding. He often sought the advice and company of someone his own age.

"You going up Carwood House again tonight?" Tamar asked Michael petulantly.

"Yes, Joseph's invited me again. I can't really refuse him. He did get me the job as foreman, didn't he? Anyway you want to me get on in the firm don't you? Besides all that, I enjoy his company."

"Obviously, more than mine," she tetchily responded.

"Now, now," Michael rebuked her lightly.

"Are you sure it's his company you enjoy when you're up there?" Tamar continued unabated. "There's no other reason you go up so regular is there Michael?"

"C'mon, Tamar if you are referring to Harriet, you're barking up the wrong tree. You know there is nothing between me and his sister."

"It's not for the want of her trying, I know. And how would you like it if I went visiting Miss Vaughan and Joseph was always there? The thought distressed Michael.

"Oh, please, give it a rest will you, Tamar? Don't you trust me?"

"Michael you know I have every faith in you. It's that conniving woman I don't trust." When first invited to Carwood House, Michael also had been apprehensive. Wondering if Harriet had somehow encouraging the visit he laid down two simple ground rules for himself. First, he would avoid ever being left alone with Joseph's effervescent sister. Harriet had made it obvious from the onset she wanted him, and everyone knew that what Harriet wanted, Harriet usually got. Michael had no intentions of being hung out to dry because of her brother's friendship. Second, he would not encourage chat with Joseph regarding Tamar. He was not above a little guarded jealousy himself. Michael still considered Joseph a potential adversary in love.

The village continued to grow. Law and order became a problem. A police station, manned by two constables, was built. Leaning over the adjoining fence of their new homes, Annie Bryan called to Margot.

"Guess who was the first customer in the new police cells?"

"Let me guess, now ..." responded Annie pausing from her washtub toil. "Was it Seamus Hickey by any chance?"

"How did you know that? Or was it a lucky guess?" Annie laughed.

"Call it a well-read guess, if you like. I've just seen Hickey's woman, with the child, on her way to Bishop Auckland workhouse."

"So, he been beating her up again, has he?"

"Looks like. She's black and blue and she's limping this time."

"Poor soul, why doesn't she leave him?"

"Better still, bury a knife in his ribs. That's what I'd do if he were mine." Anger raged in Margot usually passive voice." No one would miss him, that's for sure. It seems to be every week now doesn't it? God forgive me for what I have just said, but I'm sorry, I mean it." She looked up apprehensively to the heavens.

"Yes, but have you noticed anything extraordinary?" Annie asked her confidant.

"Like what?"

"Next time, you take notice. One day she's all black and blue then the next day there's not a mark on her."

"She must have good healing skin," Margot said.

"Nobody has that much of a healing skin. It's almost miraculous. You mark my words and take notice next time," Annie concluded sadly, knowing that there would definitely be a next time for the poor woman. Hickey's notoriety had increased over the previous two years. Sadie, his battered partner, often sported black eyes, bruises and cuts. Beyond comprehension, time and time again, she returned to Hickey, and despite horrific injuries, she steadfastly refused to prosecute. Hickey never forgot the incident with Richard Blackman. He almost growled when he saw Richard, though he had never accosted him again, and he left his friends alone. It seemed he preferred to beat up on people like his wife, and the weak and vulnerable.

Many merchants came to live in the village. Next to the Queen's Head hotel, in Commercial Street, more affectionately known as the 'bottoms,' the widowed Mr. Lodge established a hardware store. He brought with him his spinster daughter. Miss Lodge was as plain as a pikestaff, and when agitated her left eye drooped into the corner of the socket. This gave her a peculiar appearance. Naturally shy, and acutely aware of her affliction, she averted her gaze downwards, rarely raising her head. With her naturally quiet demeanour, in all her thirty years she had not made a single friend of either sex. The first Witton Park customer she served was Patrick Bryan.

"Our first customer, eh?" Her father asked appearing at the sound of the ornate cash register opening and closing. "Who was it?"

"A very funny man."

"Funny?" her father asked, quizzically.

"Funny ha-ha. Very humorous," Miss Lodge explained. After that Patrick called in at the shop fairly frequently. He had found a new captive audience who would listen to his fanciful tales. He would tell her the wildest stories. They all had the same theme. One day he would return to Ireland, rich! Miss Lodge, between serving customers, was a good listener and Patrick always brightened up her mundane day. Before leaving he never failed to flatter her but she took it all with a large pinch of salt.

"I think you have definitely kissed the Blarney stone, Mr. Bryan," she would say to Patrick. Summoned by the tinkle of the shop doorbell Mr. Lodge arrived in time to see it close.

"I bet that was Patrick Bryan again, was it?

"Yes it was, Father. Calling on his way to work."

"It would be better if he called to spend some money," Mr. Lodge retorted. "Instead of wasting people's time."

"Last time he was in I asked him to speak to his daughter. It seems she is quite an accomplished dressmaker. He called to say that she will be stopping by to see me, later."

"Oh," her father said grumpily, going back to his weekly stock check.

Jane Bryan was an immediate success with Miss Lodge. She found her a breath of fresh air and much admired her seamstress work. Miss Lodge became Jane's first important dressmaking patron. The hardware shop was among the most important in the community. Excluding groceries, Mr. Lodge stocked almost every household item. The Bryan family were regular visitors. Much to her embarrassment, Michael also made a fuss of Miss Lodge.

"Like father like son," she said to him. Having become a regular visitor to the Bryan home, it seemed she could not escape Michael. Not always for a clothes fitting, but in the parlour, after the shop had closed, she and Jane chitchatted for hours.

"Is Tamar round tonight? Jane asked Michael.

"No, not tonight. Why?"

"Because Miss Lodge is coming round. It means that the parlour will be free." When Michael had first met Miss Lodge he felt sympathy towards her.

"Enigmatic, that one."

"What does that mean?"

"It doesn't matter," he replied to a slightly puzzled Jane. What had grown out of sympathy for Miss Lodge was developing into a family friendship. He ribbed her like he would a sister. That night, before he left to see Joseph, Miss Lodge arrived.

"I saw you last night," Michael lied to her.

"Saw me? Afraid not Michael I was never over the doorstep all night."

"Exactly. That's where I saw you, on the doorstep with that young man."

"Will you stop teasing Miss Lodge please Michael? Jane begged him.

"I tell you I saw her," Michael insisted.

"Michael Bryan, you should tell the truth and shame the devil."

"All right" he conceded. "Ah it's all in good fun, now isn't it Miss Lodge?" Michael, smiling, winked at her. Miss Lodge avoided his gaze.

"I'm sure it is brother, but can you please leave us alone now. Have you no better things to do?"

"Bye, Miss Lodge, be careful now. You never know whose watching, do you now?"

"Get out," his sister said pushing a laughing Michael out of the parlour door. From the inside passage he could hear the women giggling. He smiled as he turned towards the front door.

"What time you in, Michael?" his mother shouted from the kitchen.

"When I land," Michael answered. He always felt embarrassed when his mother asked him that question. Sitting in the kitchen, Annie resumed her knitting and sighed.

"That boy," she murmured. "He's twenty five years of age and still I worry about him. Have you a minute, before you go son?" Michael looked at the pocket watch that his father had given him. It was habit. Time was unimportant when it came to his mother. He adored her. The quiet click of Annie's needles did not miss a beat as she spoke.

"Michael, what is going on at the works? Why your father's pay packets seem to be getting smaller by the week."

"I know Ma, but don't worry ... things will get back to normal soon. I promise you. These past two years has seen a drop in the use of pig iron." Pig iron took its name from the peculiar shaped moulds into which it was collected from the blast furnaces. This was the mainstay of the works until the national depression of 1847. Trade had been erratic during the first two years and the fledgling works struggled. Wages related to the selling price of pig iron seesawed as demand rose and fell. There was also a demand for a more refined iron. In his earliest trials, the railway engineer George Stephenson established that a softer iron, rather than cast or pig iron, was preferable for the manufacture of railway track. The railway entrepreneur, Joseph Pease, turned to his old acquaintances Bolckow and Vaughan. His large orders for 'puddled' malleable iron rails saved the day.

New smaller furnaces were being built apace. Within a month, looking like rows of bakers' ovens without shelves, the puddling furnaces, with individual tall chimneys, were suddenly working at full capacity. They were divided into two sections by a low wall over which the heat of the firebox section flowed and reflected against the low arched ceiling and onto the hearth. Using an iron raddle—a long oar shaped tool like those favoured by Egyptian and Viking ships—the under-puddler plastered the surfaces of the furnace section with a red iron oxide paste. The pig iron still had many impurities that the blast had failed to remove, and the little puddling furnaces would refine it further into the desirable malleable iron.

Weighing about six hundred pounds, 'pigs' of cast from the blast furnaces were loaded onto the sloping hearth of the puddling furnace. There began their refinement. The sloping hearth allowed slag to run away. The tiled door was closed and the process of puddling began. Steadily the temperature increased with the addition of more fuel, until, after about half an hour, the pigs became molten. Men, stripped to the waist, their trousers held up by large belts with buckles befitting pirates, poked a raddle through a hole in the furnace door into the molten mass. As some impurities burnt away, others ran off, and the puddler continued to re-oxygenate the red-hot lump of liquefied iron. Relying solely on experience, the puddler methodically moved certain portions away from the bulk. He would roll a little onto the end of his raddle, like toffee, allowing more to weld to it, and then release the ball at a point away from the fire bridge wall. Two and one half-hours later the whole puddling was complete.

The balls of hot metal, weighing about sixty to seventy pounds were lifted out by the use of giant tongs, then their journey continued to the steam hammer or squeezer, for further refining. Down the continuous production line the red hot metal continued its journey, through the blooming and into the finishing mills. A series of diminishing roller gaps, not unlike the washing mangle, shaped the elongated bars. Side rollers finished the forming before shears cut the lines to length. The ends were cut to an angle. Stephenson specified that the ends be cut at forty-five degrees, in an attempt to lessen the impact on the transgressing joint. Finally, hammered to flatten the cropped ends, the finished rails were inspected, loaded onto carts, and left the mills. 'Rail end boys' returned the croppings to the blast furnace for recycling to complete the circle.

A period of prosperity followed for the whole village. Despite a regional infant mortality of over twenty per cent, Will Patrick survived and thrived through his second year. His namesake Patrick fared well also, and had become a regular at the 'penny readings'.

"Are you not going tonight?" one of his compatriots asked as he saw Patrick rush along the street towards his house.

"Of course I am, I'm just a little late. I've followed this one from chapter one. Try and keep me a seat will you?"

"You'll be lucky. It's the final chapters tonight isn't it?"

"Aye, and I don't want to miss it, which I will if you keep me talking much longer. Try and keep me a seat if you can."

"I'll get my tea later," he shouted into the house without entering. "I'm late for the penny reading."

"You'll be late for your own funeral one of these days," Annie shouted back from the kitchen, but Patrick was halfway along the street by then. By the time he arrived, the room was packed. The only available seat was the dreaded 'hot seat'. Without a choice Patrick sat down to listen to the end of 'Joan of Ark'.

"Who's doing the reading tonight," he asked the man sat next to him.

"David, I think," he replied.

"Ah, good he's definitely the best." David Morris knew where to insert a pregnant pause—how to emphasise certain words and phrases and tonight he was at his finest. Totally engrossed, Patrick was transported back through the centuries. He was there giving Joan, tied to the stake, a drink of water as the flames licked about her. He heard the noises of great confusion, and the cries of pity surrounded him. Even the smell of smoke seemed real. It was then that he realised the pocket of his coat was on fire.

Chapter Seven 1848

It was the year of the French Revolution and the Young Irelander's doomed uprising resulted in the majority of the leaders of the Irish party being arrested or fleeing into exile. Many whispered that Hickey had been involved and only barely managed to escape with his life, but no one knew for certain!

During the summer months the local health board water cart weekly sprayed the streets, much to the entertainment of the children, including Philip who, stripped naked, followed the showering water around the village. The road surface had settled and taken on an uneven and hazardous nature. Exposed by the elements, large rocks protruded through the street surface of clay and ash like the tips of icebergs. Miniature lagoons formed between the small rocks. Iron hoops protecting the wooden wheels of the carts clanked up against and slithered back down them, as they rolled through the village.

"Have you seen the notices?" William asked his wife.

"Yes, it seems so far we have been lucky. Cholera is everywhere again."

"That will spoil the bairns' fun."

"What do you mean?" Margot asked.

"The water cart that sprayed the streets now and then. Well it is coming every day now but the water has a disinfectant added."

"The place stinks," Margot said with disdain, her mouth pulled down at the corners, as though sucking a lemon.

"Mind, it wouldn't hurt some of the bairns to continue taking a shower when the cart comes," William said, only half jokingly.

"Someone said they are going to start emptying the lavvies, as well, every day."

"Are they? It must be serious," Margot exclaimed.

"It is," William confirmed. "I've also heard that every house is to receive a supply of free disinfectant."

"I didn't know it was that bad but if they are giving away free stuff it must be. Are we safe?"

"As safe as we can be I suppose. Just follow the precautions, my dear. But at the end of the day we are all in God's hands aren't we?" Margot nodded her agreement.

It was the second outbreak of cholera in eighteen years. The first outbreak, having originated in Hamburg, claimed over fifty thousand lives. It arrived from Europe courtesy of ship's crews. The victims were usually the poorest of society that lived in the unsanitary conditions of industrial towns. It was contracted by swallowing some item of food or drink, usually water, contaminated with the faeces of a cholera patient or carrier. Two or three days later, a teeming painless diarrhoea occurred. Many precautions, enforced by the national authorities, had changed little since the bubonic plague. The quarantining of large areas and even whole cities proved impractical and unpopular. Yet, as the epidemic raged around the country, southwest County Durham fared well. Only isolated cases were reported and Witton Park appeared to have escaped totally.

Although not on the agenda for the night, the second annual meeting of the Cambrian Co-operative society debated the national cholera crisis before moving onto the main business of the evening.

"I am pleased to report that the year's trading of our society has proved very profitable for our members," the treasurer told a packed meeting room audience. Loud applause thundered around the small room.

"Can you tell us how much dividend are we getting?" a man called from the back of the room.

"Everyone is different, you all know that. It depends on how much you have spent with us over the year." said one of the men on the improvised stage.

"Is it better than last year then?" the man pursued the treasurer.

"All I'm prepared to say is that everyone will be pleasantly surprised on Monday. The total payout will exceed over five hundred pounds." Gasps of astonishment proceeded yet another round of applause. The chairman interjected.

"And there will still be enough for the purpose built store we promised."

A lady stood up and proposed a vote of thanks to all who had made the Society such a success. The committee and workers received a thunderous standing ovation. Having being actively engaged in the day to day running of the store since the onset; Margot and Annie felt proud of their association. When the room went quiet and everyone was seated, the treasurer continued.

"Next Monday is a Bank Holiday. The vast majority will be off work. This is when you can collect your money." Facing the audience, the committee members were looking on rows of smiling faces. Prior to the meeting, those involved and associated with the society met to iron out any problems. In the area there still roamed a felonious element. Transporting such a large amount of money safely from the Bishop Auckland bank could be perilous for an individual. Michael told his mother that it was unfortunate that the chosen date of the pay out did not coincide with the fortnightly armed-guard payroll for the works.

"I'll ask Mr. Raine to loan us the payroll dogcart. I'm sure he will. Once the money is locked in the strongbox with Dad and me bringing it back, it should be no problem." After some discussion, it was agreed that the dogcart might attract too much attention. They felt that a money belt, hidden about the person, might prove inconspicuous. When Michael told his Dad he had been volunteered to go with him it seemed fortuitous.

"Good," he said to his son. "Will I have time for me to go to the dentists first?"

"Of course you will," Michael replied. Patrick's tongue played with a slack tooth. "Good," he repeated. "I should have gone months ago. I'm owed three or four days leave from work. I'll put in for one for the Friday. It'll make a nice long weekend."

"You better get in quick," Michael warned him. "A lot of people may be thinking the same way. I'm sure it will be first come, first served. Hot iron does not have days off."

On Friday morning, as Patrick and Michael were almost ready to leave for Bishop Auckland, a messenger boy arrived at their house. It was one of the young boys from the works.

"Excuse me, Mr. Michael, sir," said the well-trained boy. "Mr. Vaughan sends you this. He says I am to wait for a reply." Michael took the sealed note from the boy and read it.

"What is it, Michael? Patrick asked his son as he joined him on the doorstep.

" Mr. Vaughan wants me to come to the works immediately. It seems the blast furnace men are threatening to walk out."

"It doesn't take a genius to work out why lad, now does it? They just want to extend the Bank Holiday weekend. Why money's not a problem at the moment, them getting the divvie and all." Patrick halted midstream then exclaimed, " Aye the divvie! Who will collect that if you have to go into work?" Michael turned to the patient messenger boy.

"Tell Mr. Vaughan I'm on my way."

"Yes, sir," the youth said. Then he turned and fled through the tunnel that led to the works.

"Give me half an hour, Da. I'll go and see what's to do. I'll come back and let you know what is going on as soon as I can," Michael said, hastily slipping on his best tweed jacket. Still adjusting the turned-in collar, he hurried along the street in pursuit of the errand boy. Jonathan had summoned all members of staff to his office.

"I have some good and bad news for you all I'm afraid," he started. "Since sending for you many men had decided to stay at work. Sadly others, more determined, have downed tools."

"Why?" asked one of the overmen.

"Supposedly over shift rotas," Jonathan explained. "But I believe that is just a ruse."

"So do I," interjected Michael. Jonathan smiled at his friend, thankful for his support. "However, that does not alter the fact that there is a full blast of iron that needs finishing. It cannot be allowed to cool. There is only one way to save it, I'm afraid. Management will have to fill the labour gaps." Loud groans came from all parts of the room. Michael placed in the undesirable position of being torn between two loyalties returned home to explain the situation.

"You get to work," His mother urged him. "There's plenty of others who will go with your Da to Bishop Auckland. Work puts the bread on the table all year round, the divvie but once. Go on, get changed and be on your way. Joseph needs good men like you. Hurry yersel along now."

"Are you sure Ma?" Michael asked.

"Michael," said Patrick firmly lending support to Annie. "Do as your Ma tells you and get going." Quickly changing into his work-clothes, Michael was soon on his way back to the works.

"Who *shall* we ask then?" Patrick asked his wife. They each suggested names for consideration. They had not realised that the majority of men were still at work, and the actions of the few hothead strikers eliminated them. It seemed they were reduced to either old men or boys from whom to choose.

"I'll go with you," Annie declared. "No one will suspect a man and wife as being money couriers. Is that not a good idea now?" Patrick was flabbergasted.

"That's the worst idea since my grandfather said 'Let's go to England!' And what would I do if we were attacked? Why I would be so busy looking out for you I would not be able to see to myself. I might be able to see off six or seven men on my own," he blatantly boasted. "But not if I have to look after you."

"Patrick, can't you take this serious—a lot of poor people are relying on us."

"Sorry, Annie. Well maybe only three or four men at a time?" Ann cast him a cold glance.

"I'm coming."

"You're not—if you insist on coming, I will not go at all," he said with a determination that surprised his wife. "And if I do not go today then there will be no money to be had until after the Monday bank holiday."

"Patrick Bryan, that is blackmail," Annie declared.

"Call it what you like," Patrick said. "But that's the score. Take it or leave it." From the minute he walked out of the front door Annie had a feeling of foreboding. She would not settle until he returned.

Patrick arrived in Bishop Auckland and made his way to the dentist's. His tongue now played constantly with the large molar that rocked back and forth.

"I'm sorry, sir, but Friday is the day Mr. Holmes visits the rural areas," the dentist's wife informed Patrick.

"What time will he be back then? Do you know?" Patrick asked.

"Well not really. All I can suggest is that you call back later. Come anytime really, he never closes for emergencies."

"Thank you," said Patrick, bidding the woman goodbye. "I'll do just that. I'm in no rush; I've got the full day of work so I have. As long as it is done sometime today, that'll be fine." He closed the garden gate and stepped into the street leading to the market place.

"Leave the matter of the money till last," he said to himself. "That makes sense. That way you'll not be carrying it around for so long. Well thought out my lad. In the meantime why don't you have a couple of ales while you wait of the man? And another good idea Patrick!" The nearest inn was but yards away from the dentist's house. On the edge of the bar lay a push-halfpenny board, the retiring players having taken their coins with them. After an hour he reluctantly left the inn, but within minutes he was back.

"Why, you're soon back," the landlord welcomed him. Patrick explained about the dentist, but made no mention of the bank.

"So, what can I get you? Whiskey and water wasn't it? Irish whiskey *of course.*"

"No, forget the water this time. Just make it a large whiskey this time, if you please." And so he sat, and waited, and drank. Hourly he made enquires, at the surgery, of the dentist's return. Three visits and hours drinking later, the landlord had to arouse him from a drunken slumber.

"C'mon my lad. Lets be having you. I think it's time you went home," the landlord said compassionately but firmly. Patrick tottered out of the door and headed, once more, towards the dentists. Still the dentist had not returned.

"I can't understand it," said the dentist's wife. "He is usually home for lunch. He has missed his two-thirty appointment with the Bishop, and that's not like him. Perhaps you would be better calling tomorrow. I'm sure he would see you."

In his stupor, Patrick decided to forget the whole dentist idea and to conclude his business at the bank then walk home. He staggered from the railway station down the long straight road leading to the market place and the bank.

It was dark when Patrick awoke. He lay beside the path that ran the course of the river from Bishop Auckland to the village, via the

Ironworks. He could vaguely remember stopping to relieve himself, then nothing else. His waistcoat had ridden up above his beer belly exposing the money belt still around his portly waist. He dragged himself slowly to his feet. On the back of his left hand there was blood and his mouth felt caked. Spitting to clear his throat produced more blood on the ground. He patted the money belt for reassurance as he pulled down his waistcoat. It felt conspicuously flat. He checked every little pouch, expecting to find the folded large white five-pound notes, but every one was empty.

"My God," he cried. "I have been robbed."

His flattened stovepipe hat with the broad green ribbon lay on the ground. Picking it up he stretched it open it from its concertina shape. He placed it firmly on his head and began to retrace his steps. After half of an hour he gave up and turned slowly homewards. When he poked his tongue around his mouth he discovered his bad molar was gone.

The whistle that signalled the end of the shift brought Michael home to find his distraught mother weeping. Jayne was just as bad.

"What in heaven's name has happened?" said Michael, fearing the worst.

"Your Da's not back. He should have been back hours ago. Have you seen him Michael? Annie said, fighting back tears.

"Is that all?" Michael exclaimed, relieved. "Why that's not the end of the world. He has been late a thousand times before."

"This time there is something wrong. I can feel it, here in my heart," Annie said placing the palm of her hand to her bosom.

"Ma, please settle down. We'll go find him. Squeak run along and ask Mr. Jones and Richard if they will help us search for him. We will start with the fourteen public houses, here, in the village, and then widen our search.

"He has got the divvi money with him, you know?" Annie said.

"Aye, I know he has, and when we find him he'll still have. If my Da's nothing else he is a honest as the day is long."

Annie felt insulted. "Do you not think I know that Michael? It's them rogues that would rob a blind man I'm worried about. Why, if they have touched a hair of his head, I'll' — *I'll*," her voice tailed away into sobbing.

"Ma, here's Mr. Jones and Richard now. Please try and pull yourself together." Michael conveyed quickly what little he knew. "If we pair off we should be able to get round all the pubs and ale houses pretty quickly. Agreed?"

Mr. Jones broke the habit of a lifetime and to puzzled looks and often jeers, entered licensed premises for the first time ever. They could not find Patrick.

"Richard, Richard," someone was calling from down Low Thompson Street. Richard peered into the semi darkness to see Squeak approaching them.

"He's home. Me Da's home. Michael said for to tell you to come back."

Mr. Jones said a little thank you for Patrick's deliverance, and his own that saved him from further embarrassment. The two search parties arrived back at Michael's home at the same time. Anxiously Michael asked, "Where is he?" His mother put her finger vertical to her lips.

"Ssh, talk quietly, he's gone upstairs."

"Where' he been?" asked Michael.

"What happened?" asked Richard.

"Ssh. One at a time." She answered as she tried to regain her composure. "In a nutshell, he has lost the money."

"What?" an exasperated Michael uttered. "What, all of it?"

"Aye all of it," said a saddened Annie. The others stood and listened in astonishment.

"How?" Michael asked.

"He doesn't know. He came in here his face and mouth covered in blood. All he can think is that he was robbed on the way home. Says he can't remember a thing after heading for the bank. The next thing he remembers was waking up, bloody, halfway home. The money belt was empty. Michael went to speak to his father but, in shame, Patrick feigned sleep.

"How's about we all go to William's house? It will be easier to talk there, and after all it concerns Margot," suggested Mr. Jones. Leaving dejected, guilt-ridden Patrick, they walked the short distance to the home of William and Margot. Inside the small kitchen, suggestion followed suggestion.

"One thing is for sure—this matter must not go beyond these four walls," William said firmly. They all agreed.

"What can we do we have but two days to try and raise five hundred pounds. It seems impossible." Michael said despondently.

"Well lets see," said David producing pencil and paper. "I presume we all want to help?" David estimated that, from all sources, there would be a shortfall of about two hundred and fifty pounds. This assumed that none of the gathering collected their dividend on Monday.

"There's little more we can do tonight, "Michael said. "Lets all go to our homes and we will talk again in the morning, eh?"

"That sounds like a good idea," David Morris concurred.

On Saturday morning Patrick did not come down stairs. Returning home after morning a stroll Michael asked cautiously, "Where's Da?"

"He's still in bed and says he's staying there. Doesn't want any food or to talk to anyone. Not even me," Annie replied sadly.

"Taking it bad is he? Have you told him what we are going to do?"

"Yes, I told him."

"And what did he say?" Michael asked.

"Nothing. He doesn't want to talk, I tell you."

"Well that won't help anything, will it?" Michael said.

"Look son, if that's what your Da wants, let's leave him alone, eh?" Annie said. Defensively. Michael, Jane and their mother sat in silence in the little kitchen. The rock of the pendulum and tick of the little wall case clock seemed hypnotic trance. On the stroke of mid-day the movement whirred and the little repeater began to strike. Before the twelve chimes had finished, a knock came to the front door. Michael answered it.

"Jane. It's Miss Lodge for you," he called. Miss Lodge noticed an obvious change in Michael's usual full-of-life demeanour.

"Oh my," Jane said to her mother. "With all the bother, I forgot about Miss Lodge coming."

"Show her into the sitting room will you, Michael please? I'll be but two minutes." Jane looked into the old mirror and rearranged her hair before leaving the kitchen.

"I'm sorry, I almost forgot about your fitting. It's been that sort of day. Please forgive me," Jane apologised as she entered the parlour.

"Is there something wrong? Have I called at a bad time? Shall I call another time?"

"No, no," Jane said contritely. "Not at all." She handed Miss Lodge the object of her visit. "I think with today's fitting you will definitely be wearing your new dress for the Bank Holiday."

"But there seems so much to be done," said Miss Lodge, looking at the half finished garment.

"It will be ready for Monday," Jane said firmly. "Or my name is not Jane Bryan." Miss Lodge smiled.

"Right. While you try on the dress I'll pop into the kitchen. There are a couple of things I must tell Michael before he leaves. I'll draw these curtains for your privacy. Would you like the gas lamp lighting?"

"No thank you, Jane. That will be fine," she concluded. Back in the kitchen concern over Patrick and the lost money continued for the five minutes Jane left Miss Lodge.

"You all right in there? About ready for me are you?" Jane called.

"Yes. Just about," Miss Lodge called back. Through the half-closed parlour door, the conversation between Michael, Jane and his mother was clearly audible. Re-entering the sitting room, Jane closed the door firmly behind her. If Miss Lodge had overheard what they had been saying in the next room she discreetly concealed it well.

The weather that Sunday morning was dark and gloomy. Inside the homes of those privy to the financial crisis, the atmosphere was similar. Everyone knew that time was running out. No one wanted to dwell on the outcome. Since Miss Lodge's visit, Jane had worked furiously on her new dress. She was so agitated that she dropped more stitches than she sewed. She seemed to be sticking pins into herself all day. Yet she made progress and it kept her distracted.

The Morris household was similarly affected. They welcomed the noon Sunday service at their little chapel. As they walked through the damp fret that left miniscule droplets on their clothes, Mr. Morris quoted from the scriptures.

"Where so ever they shall gather under one roof, in my name, so their voices shall be heard."

"Amen," the Morris family chimed. Tamar could not seem to string together a dozen notes correctly on the chapel organ and her tutor, Mr. Jones, understood why. Sunday evening arrived. Michael had not changed out of his Sunday best clothes after chapel.

"Are you still going to Carwood House tonight, Michael?" she asked him. "I thought maybe under the circumstances ..."

"Yes, I'm still going. I may as well. I am going to tell Joseph of our dilemma."

"You're not!" an astonished Tamar exclaimed. "I thought it was to be a secret?"

"It was, but time is running out and I can't think of any other way. I won't ask for help mind, I still have some pride. But if he offers, I'll take his hand off! I'll pay him back somehow. Swear to me though you will say nothing to anyone while I'm up there. No one," he emphasised. "There's no point in building up hopes. Promise me, Tamar, please."

"I promise," she replied with lover's conviction. Arranged for some weeks, the musical soiree at Carwood House was in full swing when he arrived. Harriet who led him through to the large music room greeted him. There were upwards of forty people there, but he could not see Joseph.

"Where's your brother Harriet? Where's Joseph then?"

"Oh, he left his apologies but he has suddenly had to go to Middlesbrough. Something important came up and he has to meet the board first thing Monday morning. He left this afternoon. This being a Bank Holiday as well. It's not fair on him at all is it?"

"No, not fair at all," Michael mumbled. A thousand blades seemed to cut at his body and he became oblivious to his surroundings. Michael felt gutted. He breathed faster and he was overcome with a feeling of panic.

"Are you unwell, Michael? You have gone such a strange colour." Harriet's voice seemed muffled to Michael as he fought to clear his head.

"I'll be fine in a moment," Michael reassured her. "It must have been the heat on entering here."

"Would you like to step outside into the orchard perhaps?" Harriet said hopefully. Michael declined gracefully.

"No thank you, as I said, I'm feeling a little better already." Fine music, wine and song could not raise his spirits. During a break in the renditions he feigned illness.

"It seems, Harriet, I am not as well as I believed. Would you forgive me if I left?"

"What next, I ask? My two favourite men deserting me in one day? What ever shall I do?" she asked dramatically. Michael's put-on illness was not one hundred per cent contrived. The burden of his problem was weighing on him heavier by the minute. He needed to talk to someone, anyone, not directly involved. If only Joseph had been there he would have had a shoulder to lean on. As it was, he did not feel in control.

"Will you see me to the door, Harriet?"

"Reluctantly, yes I will. Are you sure you won't stay a little while longer?"

"No, I'm sorry but I really can't."

At the door she asked him, "Michael, is there something wrong?" Michael looked at her momentarily then, almost involuntarily, confided in her. It was like an out-gushing of emotion as he related the events of Friday and his family's quandary.

"Harriet, I do not know why I told you that. Please forgive me. I have no right or desire to burden you with my troubles. Please pardon me," he implored. "No one must know of this, I don't know what came over me."

"Sometimes it helps to talk to someone not close to a problem, don't you think?" Harriet said sympathetically. He had to agree that the outward eruption of his pent up emotions seemed to have helped. Harriet was quick to seize the opportunity to put Michael in her debt.

"Can I help? Financially I mean. Call it a loan if you like. Would you like me to?"

"Harriet," Michael said firmly. "I must thank you, but that is the last thing I would do even if it were my own problem. I know me Da, he wouldn't hear of such a thing. He'd sooner face the village than think I went begging on his behalf."

"Don't tell him then! This will be a loan between you and me. What you do with the money is up to you. Is my money tainted or something? If it was my brother offering, would you not take up his offer?" Michael felt defensive and inwardly cursed himself that he could have been so foolish as to confide in Harriet.

"I can't, I'm sorry," he said, and turned and walked away.

The Bryan home was quieter than usual, even for a Sunday evening. Squeak read intently from a book borrowed from David Morris and ignored Michael's homecoming. His mother sat in the kitchen staring into the flames of the coal fire. She acknowledged her son with a tiny smile before returning to her own personal flicker show. Jane sat working on the finery of lace that would add the finishing touches to Miss Lodge's new dress.

"You're back early," she said to her brother.

"Aye. Joseph had to rush off to Middlesbrough so I felt a bit left out. Anyway, all that singing and piano playing was a little much."

"It's called a musical soiree, " Jane said with confidence.

"I know it is," Michael said, then changed the subject. "How's Da? Has he been downstairs yet?"

"Not yet," his mother replied without lifting her head.

"What about food? Has he eaten anything?"

"Not yet," his mother repeated, thrusting the poker hard into the fire. The atmosphere of the little room was gloomy.

"Was that a knock at the front door?" Michael asked as a tiny rap on wood startled him.

"If it is they'll knock again. It might be about the money and tomorrow will come soon enough," Annie said sadly. Michael looked anxiously to his mother.

"Do outsiders know about the money then?"

"Not that I know of, Michael," his mother reassured him. "But you know how these things leak out. Bad news always travels faster than good, it seems, Anyway I know you're almost at your wit's ends, like the rest of us, but you will have to try and calm down. For your own sake. We're all in the same boat but we will have to try and grin and bear it. For your Da's sake, if for nothing else. Maybe you're hearing things? I heard nothing."

"I'm sure I heard a knock," said Michael, reluctantly rising from his kitchen chair. In the dark of the passage he instinctively reached for the cast iron door handle of the heavy, ledged and braced front door and pulled. It swung open easily. There was no one there. He stuck his head out into the drizzling rain and first looked along the street to the left but there was not a soul in sight.

"No wonder on a night like this," he thought. Then looked right towards the Vulcan. He was just in time to see a figure, wearing a long dress, vanish into the small gap between the hotel and the Cambrian building. A heavy raindrop fell from the top of the doorframe and made the sound of a pea on a drum as it landed. Michael looked down and saw the parcel on the doorstep. About the size of a shoebox, it was neatly wrapped in brown Manila paper and tied with string. He bent down and picked it up cautiously.

"Who was it?" Jayne asked, keeping her tired eyes on the intricate lace work.

"There was no one there," Michael said.

"Told you so," his mother said smugly, still staring into the fires flames. Squeak was snuggled into his book.

"But someone left this," said Michael. Suddenly he had everyone's attention.

"What is it?" Squeak asked.

"Haven't a clue," Michael shook his head.

"Open it then, Michael. Let's see what's in it." Squeak pleaded. Michael laid the mystery parcel on the table.

"Who left it then?" his mother asked. Everyone stood around the kitchen table and stared down at the package.

"I haven't a clue, Ma," Michael answered his mother. "All I could see in the street was a woman going between the Vulcan and the store. It was too dark and miserable to see who it was."

"Is there anything written on it?" Jane asked.

"No, nothing," Michael said, turning the parcel over and over.

"Then how do we know who it is for?" Squeak asked. "Maybe it's for me eh?"

"Do you want to open it, Ma?" offered Michael.

"No, thank you. The way my luck is running it will be full of dirty washing. No, you do it Michael."

"Aww," a disappointed Squeak moaned. "I wanted to do that." The neat bow when tugged allowed the twine to fall away from the outer wrapper. Carefully, he folded back the wrapping paper to expose a cardboard box.

"There's nothing written on the box either," Michael said. "I expect there will be a note inside. Let's see, shall we?" He lifted the lid. The box was stuffed with bank notes.

"Are they real?" an astonished Squeak gasped as he gazed at the white, five-pound notes. With shaking hands Michael lifted the banknotes out onto the tablecloth, handling them as though they were of the finest silk.

"How much do you think is there?" Jane asked.

"Soon tell you," Michael answered in a quivering voice. "Let's see shall we?" He began to count. "Ninety eight, ninety nine, one hundred. There are exactly one hundred five pound notes."

"Who can have been so generous?" Jayne asked.

"Who cares right at this moment!" a mightily relieved Annie exclaimed. "Jane, you best pop next door and let the Morris's know. Michael, take Squeak and go tell Richard and Mr. Jones of our good fortune. I have someone to tell in person." As her children left carrying the good news Annie fell silent. Hand clenched she looked up, closed her eyes, and whispered, "Thank you, Lord." She then went to the bottom of the stairs and called.

"Patrick Bryan! Come down these stairs this minute. If you do not I will never speak to you again. Come down right now I say. There is something very important I must tell you." Momentarily she heard the sound of her husband's feet on the bedroom floor, then on the bare stair treads. Ten minutes later the kitchen was crammed with family and friends looking in astonishment at the neatly stacked piles of bank notes.

"Has no one any idea who our benefactor can be?" William Morris asked, but no one did.

"Why, nobody outside this room knew of our troubles did they?" Mr. Jones enquired. Only Michael had a suspicion who it might have been. While relieved beyond belief, he was also saddened. Now he was indebted to someone he could never love. He knew the price that must be paid.

"While we are all gathered here. I have something important to say, to you all like," Patrick announced. Everyone listened intently.

"Firstly, let me say how deeply sorry I am at letting you all down. I am deeply ashamed that I let the drink get the better of me. As a sign of penance, next Sunday I intend to sign the temperance pledge and join the 'Band of Hope'."

"And the band played 'Believe it if you Like', " Annie murmured.

"What was that?" Patrick asked his wife.

"Nothing Patrick," she replied, "Nothing at all. I was just thinking aloud!"

On the holiday Monday, as the village celebrated unaware of the near calamity, Michael reluctantly but steadfastly walked to Carwood House. Harriet opened the door to him.

"Why, good morning, Michael. You must be feeling better—you certainly look it! Joseph is not yet back though, I am afraid."

"It is you I have come to see, " Michael replied, uncomfortably.

"In that case, Michael, don't just stand there on the door step. Come on through to the parlour." Michael felt as though he were stepping into a lion's den as he followed Harriet through the house. When they were both seated on the sofa, Michael began.

"I've come to thank you for the help."

"And what help would that be, Michael?" Harriet asked.

"Why the money you left on our doorstep last night."

"I know nothing about any money on doorsteps I'm afraid. That was not me," Harriet replied flatly. Michael found the denial unconvincing, accompanied as it was by a coy smile.

"I know it was you, Harriet. It all makes sense. Firstly, earlier in the evening, I refused your generous offer of help. Secondly—but more importantly—only you and you alone outside of our circle was told of our predicament. I promise you, even if it takes a hundred years, my family will pay you back every penny."

"Michael, there is no need, for it was not I," she reassured him. "Will you stay for lunch?"

"I should be getting back. I promised to spend the holiday with the family."

"With that girl don't you mean? Tamar is her name isn't it?" Michael squirmed but did not reply.

"I'll make a deal with you," Michael said. "I'll stay to lunch if you promise to let me pay back the money and for the rest of the morning we speak no more of it."

"And will you promise to call more regularly? To see me, that is?" Harriet bargained. Michael reluctantly agreed.

"I guess that's the first repayment met, " he thought, nervously nibbling his bottom lip.

Joseph arrived home just after lunch and delayed Michael's departure even further. Michael watched the hands on the marble cased clock on the mantelpiece above the fire rotate, hour after hour. Several times he rose to leave but was discouraged. Finally, he knew he must make his excuses and go.

"Joseph, you must excuse me. The day is almost over and I have hardly seen my family. I really must go. Thank you for a wonderful day."

"I'll see Michael to the door Joseph," Harriet insisted.

"Somehow, I thought you might," an astute Joseph sneered.

"There's one final thought for you to take with you," Harriet, framed in the doorway, said to Michael as he was leaving.

"What's that, then? He innocently asked.

"Let's say ... hypothetically of course, that a woman loaned her husband some money. Now she wouldn't ask for restitution would she I don't suppose? They being man and wife, that is."

Swallowing deeply, he looked at Harriet and said, "No, I don't suppose she would."

"What a mess," Michael thought as he trudged back home. Silhouetted against the open door of her parents' home was Tamar. She had waited for him since dusk. He stopped but could not find words to say to her and for a long time, as though ashamed, he looked down at his dusty shoes.

"You've been a long time," she said.

"I'm really sorry Tamar, but it's along story. I'll maybe explain to you in the morning. I'm ready for my bed now; it's work in the morning. Goodnight."

"And maybe I don't need an explanation," she snapped. "It's obvious why you spend so much time at Carwood." She stepped into her house and slammed the door. As Michael locked the front door behind him he felt as though he was also locking Tamar out of his life.

Tuesday morning found Margot and Ann busy in the Cambrian store. A growing Will Patrick played happily among the goods. It was like an Aladdin's Cave to a child.

"What time train is that?" Margot asked Annie as she watched the little engine pass the window way up on the embankment.

"It'll be the five past eleven from Bishop Auckland. It seems to be on time for a change. Are we expecting anything?

"No I don't think so. Are we? I was just curious, that's all." Both women continued with the stock check. Five minutes later a dapper little man entered the store.

"Can I help you?" Margot asked from behind the long wooden counter.

"I would like to speak to someone in charge, please," he said looking around the room. "Is there anyone about?"

"Well you can speak to either of us," Annie said straightening her hair and joining Margot.

"I'm sorry, no disrespect but I was instructed by my employer to speak to the manager."

"Well I guess that's us," Margot said smugly. "Did you see the sign when you came in? It says the Cambrian Cooperative Society, that means it belong to it's members. It has neither an owner nor a manager, just us. Will we do?"

The bank courier looked slightly baffled. "I'm sorry," he apologised, "It's just I was expecting a man. Like I said no disrespect meant."

"None taken, and like I said, can I help you?"

A slightly embarrassed Mr. Dewhurst, senior clerk of Messrs, Backhouse bank shuffled his feet.

"It's the matter of the five hundred pounds we readied for your collection, Friday last."

"What about it?" a puzzled Margot asked.

"Mr. Clarkson, our manager, requires instructions as how you wish to proceed."

"Proceed. What on earth are you on about?" Annie asked.

"Simply, do you wish to make new arrangements for the collection?" The two women looked at each other in amazement. Annie, bewildered, looked the courier hard in the face.

"Do you mean that my husband did not collect it on Friday?"

"He certainly did not, and do you think Mr. Clarkson would send me on such a fool's errand, had he so done?" Margot tried to take in the implications of this stupendous news.

"No, no, I'm sure he wouldn't. Tell him someone will call this week. Thank you for coming Mr. Mewhurst," she said, ushering the messenger to the door.

"It's Dewhurst, madam," he corrected her as he found himself out on the pavement. Inside, a joyous pair of women flung their arms around each other and did a few steps of the polka. Young Will Patrick ignored them and continued to eat, what remained, of an opened tin of biscuits.

"He never got to the bank, he never collected the money!" Annie cried.

"And so he couldn't have lost it!" Margot shouted.

"I'm going to Jane Pit," Annie said.

"Why?" Margot asked. "You know they won't bring Patrick up just for that."

"I suppose you're right. But I feel I need to tell someone."

"Michael will be home for lunch in half an hour won't he? You can tell him. In the meantime can you mind the store? I think this news is worthy of waking William," Margot said as she pulled her shawl around her shoulders.

"Of course I will," Annie said. " And I'll look after the bairn."

"Eeh - the bairn. I totally forgot about him!" She looked over to where Will Patrick happily sat munching the remnants of the biscuits. "You stay with your Aunt Annie now. And be good. I won't be long," she said as she left.

The atmosphere in the kitchen was entirely different to the night of Friday past. Family and friends gathered to listen to Margot and Annie relate the day's events,

"There's something I should tell you." Michael said bringing the gathering to silence. He relayed the conversation of the previous day with Miss Vaughan to them.

"Can you be sure it was her?" someone asked.

"As sure as I can be." Michael said.

"She did try to say it wasn't her though didn't you say?" David Morris asked.

"Well yes, sort of, in an unconvincing way," Michael responded.

"That's settled then," William recommended. This week we can ask to have it sent with the works payroll, and Michael can take it personally to Carwood.

"If you don't mind, I'd rather David did that."

"William looked slightly puzzled. "I'm sure David will take the money, and all our gratitude, to Miss Vaughan, if that's what you'd prefer Michael."

"I don't mind," said David.

"Thanks," Michael cast a glance at a smiling Tamar and remembered what his father once told him regarding Daniel and the lion's den: *Once out, he did not go back in!*

That evening, bang on the stroke of eight, Miss Lodge called on Jane.

"You seem happy tonight Jane," she said as they settled in to the comfort of the sitting room.

"I am," she said. "Very happy and even more happy that at last I can tell you everything." In the privacy of the parlour, Jane entrusted to her friend the details of the last few day's events. As the drama unfurled Miss Lodge listened closely in disbelief. At ten, Jane greeted her older brother at the door of their home and guided him into the parlour.

"Have you seen Harriet tonight? Since you got the news I mean?"

"No, I've been with Tamar. And why are we whispering?" he asked his sister

"I have something of great importance to tell you Michael, I think you had better be seated."

"Not more bad news I hope?"

"No, not at all." Michael listened intently as he heard how it was Miss Lodge and not Harriet who had placed the box on the doorstep.

"I should have known," he said quietly. "What a fool I am! The manila wrapping paper, precise at each fold and the neatly trimmed ends of the string should have been a giveaway. In the hardware store I've have admired Miss Lodge's handiwork a hundred times. Why did she not say it was her?"

"She didn't want us to know that she had overheard our plight. It's only now when I told her that we intended to repay Harriet that she confessed that it was her who bailed us out."

"And Harriet was prepared to let me believe it was her. The witch!" a vexed Michael blurted out.

"Michael, watch your language, please," Jayne rebuked her brother.

"Sorry, Jayne. I am just so angry."

"I can imagine brother, but you may want to consider pity as an alternative. Someone should tell Miss Vaughan that you can't buy friends – only rent them. What do you intend to do now?

"Do? First thing in the morning, before I go to work, I intend to ask Tamar to marry me."

"What are you doing straight back from work—did you forget something?" Annie asked as Patrick rushed through the house.

"I haven't got there yet," he said. She watched him tearing off his clothes, throwing his jacket and waistcoat to the kitchen floor.

"Is there paper in the lavvy?" he asked anxiously as he sprinted across the concrete back yard.

"There was this morning," Annie called after him. By the time he climbed the steps and closed the door his braces were around his waist and he carried his unbuckled belt. Annie waited anxiously until he came back into the house.

"What's wrong?" she asked. "You got the runs?" During the night he had developed painless diarrhoea that he attributed to the preceding days of anxiety, stress and excitement.

"Aye, the runs all right. I'm run off my feet. Didn't think I was going to make it home without shitting mesel," Patrick declared. It's just like milk coming out of me arse so it is." Before she could scold him for his choice of language he rushed back into the yard and vomited down the drain.

"I think we'll have the doctor," Annie said to him as he sat on a kitchen chair feeling very sorry for himself. He didn't put up an argument.

The doctor, a youthful medical graduate of Edinburgh, arrived promptly after receiving Annie's message.

"What have you had to eat or drink recently?" Doctor McKechnie asked Patrick as he began his examination.

"Nothing yet today, sir," a weak and subdued Patrick answered.

"And yesterday?"

"Nothing really. In fact I haven't really eaten since I went to Bishop Auckland on Friday."

"What did you have there?" the doctor asked. Patrick could not answer until the practitioner removed a giant wooden spatula from his throat.

"Cold beef" he gargled, clearing his passageway.

"And to drink? Any water?" Patrick was about to laugh at the suggestion when he remembered…. He had added water to his first few whiskies.

"Yes, I drank some water. Is that important?"

"It could be, we will have to wait and see. Have we any boiled water that is now cool?" he asked.

"It's not exactly cold, Doctor," Annie said emptying the contents of the kettle into a mug.

"That will be fine," he said as he added medicine from a large bottle that he produced from his bag.

"Here drink this," he said. "Then I think we will have you off to bed."

"I'll leave you this for now," the physician said to Annie as he placed the bottle on the table. "He is to have the same dose every half hour. I will arrange for more to be made available for your collection."

"Thank you Doctor," said Annie gratefully. With his back to Patrick the doctor discreetly nodded towards the door and Annie followed him out.

"It's not cholera is it?" Annie asked.

"I cannot be sure," Doctor McKechnie answered. "He's a lucky man having such an astute wife. Time is of the essence in these circumstances. That is, of course, if indeed it is cholera. Even if it is I'm sure he has gotten life saving liquids in time. The greatest danger to cholera patients is in the first hours."

"Then he will be all right?"

"I cannot make any promises at this stage. As I said, I am not yet sure that it is cholera although I suspect the worst."

"Is there anything we can do?"

"Yes, there quite a lot you can do. First, I must ask that you conform to the health authorities guidelines." From his bag he produced a roll of printed sheets and gave one to Annie. "It's all there, what you need to do. The medicine is a mixture of salt, sodium carbonate and a little glucose. It's a new idea I learned at college. Given every half hour— although unable to stop the muscle cramps and severe physical weakness that will develop—it's said to be one hundred per cent successful if administered regularly. I've seen many people slip into a coma and die within a couple of hours without fluids. Once the sickness and diarrhoea has started that is. Odd ones lasted up to two days, but never longer without liquids."

"You can be sure he will get it. Every half hour, on the dot," Annie declared. The young doctor shifted from foot to foot and looked down at the floor.

"I need to report the case to the local medical officer, Mrs. Bryan," he said softly. "And I'm afraid I'm required to post a notice on your front door." Annie was alarmed.

"But they'll think my house is filthy! And I scrub every day!" The doctor held up a hand.

98

"If it's cholera—*if* it's cholera," the doctor deliberated. "It's most likely he picked it up in Bishop Auckland. There are no cases here in Witton Park. It's also unlikely that any of the family will contract it, unless he's a carrier, but that's unlikely either."

"Thank God," said Annie, although she instinctively knew that some of the neighbours would not be so understanding as the doctor and was certain they'd be blamed for the outbreak if it spread.

"In the meantime," continued the doctor, "Although you are not legally required to do so, I suggest that the rest of your family stay within the confines of your own home. Just for the time being. I will call again in the morning, unless you need me before then of course." Closing his bag, he donned his hat, smiled reassuringly, and left.

After putting her husband to bed, Annie brought out a can of disinfectant from under the kitchen sink. With the sterilizer in one hand and a bucket of ashes from the fire in the other, she crossed the yard. The wooden toilet seat was scrubbed and disinfected and half the bottle of sanitizer poured into the midden. The ashes were then sprinkled into the hole, capping its contents.

"Squeak. Find Jane then run to the works. Tell Michael he must come home straight away. Just tell him your Da's poorly." As fast as pans boiled, Annie and Jane disinfected every item and surface in the house. Michael arrived home half an hour later and, upon learning the news, slumped into the fireside chair.

"What next?" he said.

Upstairs, Patrick retched into a bucket, while downstairs the family received instructions from their mother. Within an hour of the precautionary notice being posted on their front door, Annie's fears were realized and panic swept through the village. People crossed the street when passing or avoided it all together. Back in number ten, as predicted, Patrick suffered painful cramps. Annie mopped her husband's furrowed brow and gazed lovingly onto his contorted face.

"Do they hurt that much my poor dear? Never mind the doctor said they would soon pass." Patrick was a good patient and suffered in relative silence. "There," she said as she stroked his hair, "Try and get some sleep now will you?"

Patrick nodded his head gently and closed his eyes. Annie allowed no one else to nurse him. Throughout the night she boiled then cooled water and every half house gave Patrick the prescription.

The following morning Doctor McKechnie called.

"And how is your husband this morning?" he asked.

"I'm a little bit worried doctor," a very tired Annie replied. " I'm sure that over night his face and the soft bits of his body have shrunk a little." The doctor smiled.

"That's quite normal, it's due to the dehydration. Come take me upstairs lets have a look at him, eh?" She led the way.

"How have you and the family been coping confined to the house?"

"Not bad," Annie said wearily. "Everyone has been good, considering." To relieve the boredom, the prisoners of their own home assisted in twice daily disinfecting the house. Dressmaking for Jane, and dominoes and cards for Michael and Philip also helped reduce the monotony.

"And the neighbours and friends have been wonderful," she added.

"The neighbours?" the doctor asked, surprised.

"Don't worry," she reassured him. "We have stuck to the rules. Maybe it's the fairies that have been leaving all sorts of things for us on the back wall. For we have not seen a soul these past twenty-four hours." Dr. McKechnie smiled and fastened up the buttons of Patrick's pyjama jacket as he slid his stethoscope into his bag.

"Well, if he gets no worse I think he will soon be up and about again," was his welcome prognosis. Patrick managed a smile and Annie breathed a huge sigh of relief.

"I'll call again in the morning then, unless I'm needed before then. After that I feel Saturday will be soon enough. That will be three days since the symptoms first showed. No more problems in the family before then and the house will have a clean bill of health."

"Roll on Saturday," Annie prayed.

"In the meantime you should get some sleep, Mrs. Bryan."

"I will," Annie reassured the doctor as he left. He gave her a parting quizzical look.

"That's an order mind you," he said finally. She smiled at him sweetly.

On Saturday morning, when the three-day incubation period had passed, the Bryans received the all clear. The official from the board of health made a grand show of tearing up the cholera notice so all the eyes that peered from behind lace curtains could see. Not another case of cholera appeared in Witton Park. This in the main was thanks to Annie's alertness, a new simple treatment brought by an intern, and the unselfish behaviour of the Bryan family. Emerging into the freedom of the little street, friends and neighbours greeted and applauded them, although a few still kept their distance.

During the days of Patrick's convalescence, the lay preacher William visited often.

"God moves in mysterious ways, His miracles to perform," he said. "Had the money crisis not developed, Patrick would not have taken to his bed. It was this that averted the possibility of spreading the disease." Patrick agreed.

"I feel I have suffered God's personal retribution," he observed. "I will not presume to punish myself further by signing the pledge after all."

It was just three weeks until Michael's wedding day.

Chapter Eight

"I'd better be going. Can't be late on my first morning Tamar said.

"Are you nervous, daughter?" Margot asked.

"A little, but I won't be on my own in that, I think. I bet the other two pupil teachers are feeling pretty much the same. Then there's Mr. Richards. He must be apprehensive. After all, being head of a new school is a large responsibility."

"I'm proud of you lass," said Margot as she watched Tamar fashion her long brown hair into a bun at the back of her head.

"We all are," added her father.

"Thanks, Father," Tamar said lovingly.

"You haven't far to go to work," Squeak piped up. "Just the end of the street, eh?"

"Yes—nice and handy if it's raining. Anyway, I must go."

"Can I come with you, Tamar?" little Will Patrick pleaded.

"Next year, Will. When you're five I'll take you," she said as she stooped and kissed the top of his head in farewell.

The first 'National' school opened twenty years before compulsory education came about in England. A stout stone construction was available to all religious persuasions and after two extensions was capable of holding two hundred and fifty pupils. Village pessimists were betting the attendance would never exceed fifty. Sitting in the reading room of the Cambrian building, Richard Blackman turned to the librarian, David Morris.

"It's packed in here tonight isn't it, quite a few new faces as well?"

"It's been like this since the school started adult night classes, three nights a week. Seems they go there then come here and practice what they have learned. And it's winter, even the kids pack in at this time of year," David concluded, nodding in the direction of Squeak, Philip and friends.

"I don't blame them," said Richard. "I think it might snow tonight."

"Tamar tells me that they are averaging one hundred and fifty pupils a day for the juniors."

"I bet that doesn't please the pit owners," Richard said.

"Who cares about the greedy coal barons? Bairns, seven and eight years old ... working underground? Why, it's a sin."

"You'll never stop it," said Richard.

"We'll see," David declared passionately.

"What's that you're reading?" asked Richard, changing the subject.

"This? Oh, it's a new book, just arrived all about the Chartist movement. Stirring stuff," David said happily. "And you?"

"Well, I thought it was time I brushed up on a bit of local history. I think a man should know where he is, so to speak. Don't you agree?"

"I suppose so," David answered, slightly baffled.

"You'll never believe what I've just found out," said Richard, distracting David once more from his studying. "See these pictures?" David looked down at the open, illustrated volume of the historical account of County Durham.

"What about them?" he asked.

"Well they were done by two fellas from Cockfield. That's just up the road from here isn't it?"

"Yes, about six or seven miles, but what has that got to do with anything?"

"Well, you remember me telling you about my narrow escape in America? These pictures are by the Dixon family. Him there, Jeremiah Dixon, was the one who drew the Mason – Dixon line, the one what separates the slave states from the rest." Richard stabbed the point of his index finger into the picture. "He would have been better drawing it on the ground. What use is it on a map? I've a good mind to walk up to Cockfield and tell him exactly what I think of his line."

"He's dead," David said trying to calm Richard.

"Who's dead?" Richard fumed.

"Jeremiah Dixon's dead. Look it says here, he died shortly after completing his survey." David pointed to the words beneath a study of the man. Feeling cheated, Richard reacted angrily.

"Dead? Never mind, I suppose it is the best place for him."

"Come now, Richard, you know we should only speak good of the dead," said David. Pushing back his chair, Richard rose, looked straight into David's face and spat each syllable.

"Is that so? Well how's this? Jeremiah Dixon is dead. *Good.*" He then left abruptly and David returned the book that had caused Richard so much upset to its place on the neatly indexed shelves. He studied the faces of the people who were crammed into the reading room and felt proud that a pitman could volunteer to contribute so much to so many. His gaze fell on Squeak and his friend Thomas Whitton Davies who was reading a book on Jewish history.

"A strange subject for the son of a Welsh Methodist to be reading," thought David. He watched the as boy read intently, elbow on desk, head supported by his hand, oblivious to his surroundings and to David's curiosity. No one could have guessed that this young Welsh boy would one day be honoured by Durham University and become one of the greatest Hebrew scholars of all time.

"Can't we read something different for a change?" Philip asked Squeak. "Some of the words are too big for me."

"Don't worry, I'll help you. Would it be better if I read it to you?"

"Yes, that would be better." Squeak began to read out aloud from 'Folklore and local Customs Lost'.

"Ssh," resounded around the room as though a hundred snakes had been released. Innocently, the boys looked up to meet David's disapproving stare.

"If you're going to read to Philip you will have to do it quietly. Whisper like this, understand?" Both boys nodded their heads in submissive agreement.

"Maybe it will be better if I read it again then tell you about it after," Squeak suggested. Philip agreed and, as his friend continued reading, he let his attention wander aimlessly around the room. Later, squashed into the little lean-to shed that was their gang hut, Squeak tried to explain what he had read and what he wanted them to do.

"It's like this," he started firmly. "A long time a go villages had customs."

"What's a custom?" one of the band asked.

"Well, it's sort of things that people always used to do."

"Oh."

"One custom was, like, if a man—who was married like—went with another woman he would be punished. Or if he beat up his wife he would get it done to him as well."

"Get what done to him?" someone asked.

"Get the piss taken out of him."

'Ugh, with a knife or something?" the youngest member of the band asked.

"It doesn't mean that," Squeak said firmly.

"What does it mean then?"

"It means shown up in public, where everyone can laugh at him, like."

"Oh, whose gonna get shown up then?" With a little help from his friends, Squeak was about to resurrect a custom, long neglected, for the wife beater Seamus Hickey.

"*Hickey*?" one boy gasped, almost blowing out the lowly candle.

"Yes, Hickey. We're gonna make him 'Ride the Stang,' just like they used to in the book."

The custom of punishment by riding of the stang began with the mounting of a volunteer on a plank of wood or short ladder. Four other people then carried on their shoulders both plank and rider around the village. A crude rhyme was usually shouted or chanted by the rider, which set out the name of the villain and the type of crime they'd committed. At the end of the speech, the mob that always accompanied the procession finished with a round of hurrahs and howls. This was repeated on the second night; then on the third and final night, an effigy of the guilty party was burned either in the market place or in front of the house in which the scoundrel lived.

Having listened to every word in amazement, Philip was the first to speak.

"What's an effigy?"

"It's like a scarecrow," Squeak explained.

"Oh, that's all right. Then it's not Hickey we burn?"

"No, stupid. Have you not been listening?" There came the sound of Squeak's name being called over the terraced roofs.

"That's me Ma calling! I'll have to go in now. I'll tell you more at school tomorrow ..." The gang dispersed to their homes, supper and bed.

Over the next few days they got hold of a ladder, some old clothes that they stuffed with straw, and they practiced carrying Squeak aloft. By the fourth night they were ready, and Squeak, legs dangling through the rungs of the ladder, was carried to Hickey's house in Old Row.

Outside the front door the pageant and accompanying din emanating from borrowed musical instruments, halted. All fell silent as Squeak, from his elevated position, read from a piece of crumpled paper.

"Hey Derry! Hey Derry! Hey Derry Dan!"
It's neither for your cause, nor my cause that I Ride the Stang.
But it is for t' hammer man Hickey for hitting his deary,
If you'll stay a few minutes, I'll tell you more clearly.
One night he came home with a very red face-
I suppose he was drunk, as is often the case,
Be that as it may; but — when he got in,
He knocked down his wife with a blow to her chin.
She jumped up again and, and knocked off his hat,
And he up with his hand, and laid her quite flat.
She ran out to the yard and shouted for life,
And he swore he would kill her with a great gully knife.
So all you good people that lives in this row,
I'd have you take warning, for this is our law;
And if any of you husbands, your wives you do bang,
If they come to us, we'll Ride the Stang!

A great cheer went up from the gang who thought Squeak's verse the best they had ever heard. Front doors opened along the street. Some occupants, with heads shaking, went back inside while others complained about the noise. Hickey's door remained firmly closed as the group carried Squeak away triumphantly.

"Maybe he wasn't in, Philip," someone said as they gathered back at their den.

"We'll see tomorrow night. Maybe he was frightened of us."

"Oh, yeah, I bet," Philip said sarcastically.

On the second night their numbers grew. Once again they marched round the village repeating the scene of the previous. The neighbours were less curious and more hostile.

"You lot again? Get yersels away into your own streets," a man shouted from his front door.

"Aye, bugger off home you noisy buggers, there's bairns in bed here," an irate woman called from another house as the sound of a child crying could suddenly be heard from the upstairs front room. The troupe stood its ground but still Hickey's door stayed shut.

When the important third night arrived, youths with all sorts of instruments gathered behind the cavalcade and marched noisily towards Hickey's house. They lowered Squeak to the floor as he read out the rhyme and another lad lit the effigy. Suddenly the door flew open and an enraged, drunken Hickey leapt out.

"Come 'ere, you little bastards! I'll show you what us Irishmen do to British brats!" The boys bolted and scattered in every direction. Squeak tripped over the ladder and fell, and was grabbed by the collar before he could recover. Hickey's face was so close that the smell of rotting teeth and stale alcohol made Squeak want to vomit.

"Well, what have we got here? If its not one of them Morris's, eh? One of them Welsh sheep shaggers, is it not? Where's your friend Blackman now? Not here to save you, to be sure. If I ever catch you again, taking the pish, I'll cut off your head and stick it up your arse," he barked, shaking Squeak like a rag doll. Hickey held onto the petrified boy by his jacket while he rained down more threats and insults. He swiped Squeak full force across the face with the back of a hand before throwing him semi-conscious to the floor. Then he kicked the burning mannequin and went back inside the house. Sparks flew up into the darkness of the night silhouetting Squeaks still form.

Philip, Thomas and some of the other boys watched in horror from a safe distance. Others had run all the way home.

"Do you think Hickey has killed him?" asked Philip, almost in tears.

"Dunno, let's find out." The boys cautiously went to the aid of their friend. Squeak lay so still.

"Is he dead then?"

"Dunno. Never seen a dead person before, except me Granda."

"What shall we do? Get his Ma?"

"Maybe we should get the polis."

"Let's pick him up and carry him to Dr. McKechnie."

"We'll pick him up and carry him home, that's what we'll do," an authoritative Philip decided. "His Ma and Da can do what they want then. Right?" But as they jostled to get hold of a piece of Squeak, he suddenly groaned and wriggled.

"Put me down," he said, putting his hands to his aching head. The startled boys gladly obliged. Blood from his nose and bottom lip dripped of his chin.

"What do you want us to do?" Philip asked. "Do you want us to get the police? Or maybe the doctor?"

"No, I'll be all right in a minute, but let's get outta this street."

Squeak's injuries, though extremely painful, were not crippling and he rose to his feet. Handkerchiefs, both dirty and clean, were offered to stem the flow of blood, but eventually it stopped of its own accord. Squeak's tongue identified the cut to the inside of his lip and licked it clean.

"How bad do I look?" he asked.

"Pretty bad."

"Maybe, if I can get all the blood washed off, me mother and father might not notice?"

"I doubt that, but let's try, eh?" The cut to his lip was not outwardly visible and the bleeding from his nose had stopped, so he was determined to try and conceal the injuries from his family.

"You must all swear, on the gang's honour, that you won't tell anyone about this."

"If that's what you want, we swear," they declared.

Philip and Squeak walked the back streets until they found an unlocked water butt. In the back yard a caged ferret was restless. Hanging upside down on the nearby wall, blood dripped from the nose of a recently caught rabbit.

Squeak washed away his own blood but he could not wash away the pain, yet considering his ordeal, he felt reasonably well. Entering the kitchen where his mother and father sat reading, he kept his back towards them. The candles, drawn close to his parents, darkened the back of the room.

"Hello son, you're in early," his mother said to the back of his head. "Would you like some supper?"

"No thanks, I'm tired and off to bed. Goodnight." He yawned loudly through thickening lips and climbed the stairs to his bed. Margot thought it strange that he should refuse the offer of supper but shrugging her shoulders, she returned to her book. Hiding his blood stained shirt under the mattress, Squeak lowered his sore face onto the pillow. He spent a restless night, but in his prayers was thankful that he had not also incurred the wrath of his family and hoped that by the next day it would all seem just like a bad dream.

The following morning, Squeak struggled out of bed on his mothers' call.

"Time for work Squeak, come and get your porridge!" His father and David, already at breakfast, looked up to say good morning. David's spoon froze half way between bowl and mouth. His father seemed transfixed. Margot turned from the huge pan bubbling on the fire and gasped.

"My God!" she said. Squeak could not understand why his entrance had caused such an impact.

"What's the matter?"

"What's the matter?" his shocked mother asked. "What in heaven's name happened to you? Just Look at yerself." The octagonal kitchen mirror, framed only by its bevel edged glass, reflected a pitiful sight. His nose was twice its usual size and his eyes had blackened. The bottom lip had swollen and rolled outwards, exposing the deep cut.

"You been fighting lad? What have I told you?" Squeak did not answer his father.

"Whisht, William, can't you see the boy's hurt? Come here son, let me take a look at you." Breakfast forgotten about, Margot replaced the ladle of porridge into the pan.

"Do you want to stay off work today? One day off won't hurt, I'm sure,"

"No, I wanna go to work."

"You sure?"

"Positive."

"C'mon then lad, lets be off," his father encouraged. Squeak and his father set off in one direction, for the pit, while David walked in the opposite way towards the ironworks. Upon arrival at the weighbridge office, Mr. Jones greeted him.

"Good morning, David," he said presenting the time book for signature. "Will you be at choir practice tonight?" The reply was non-committal.

"I'll try." Mr. Jones countersigned and entered the time of arrival. As he walked away, the man next in line tapped him on the shoulder.

"Sorry to hear about Squeak. Is he all right?"

"He's not bad, but how do you know?"

"Why, them lads of mine were there. But they got away."

"Got away? Got away from who?" The man relayed what they had told him about the previous night.

"I hope the lad's all right and that bastard Hickey gets his comeuppance."

"You can bet on that," David assured him. "And it won't be long from now." Mr. Jones steadfastly followed every word uttered.

"One day, that evil man will burn in hell. That's for sure."

"And today might just be that day," David said as he walked away.

Hickey was already at his workplace when David entered the mill. The twenty-five ton hammer, banging seventy-six thunderous beats to the minute was deafening. Although David almost shouted into Hickey's ear, the worker along side heard not a word. He only saw him grin at David. Nevertheless, by time the six o'clock whistle blew, over five hundred men had gathered in the station yard. Word spread like wildfire of the coming fight and most spectators hoped to see David beat the living daylights out of Hickey. Inside the circle of onlookers both men stripped to the waist. Richard walked over to his friend.

"Are you sure you know what you are doing?"

"I'm sure," a determined David replied.

"But you're no fighting man."

"Richard, stop worrying. You have only see one side of me. I can take care of myself. Then there are these, the Morris family trait." He held out his enormous hands and clenched them. "I wasn't given these for nothing." Both men smiled. The Irishman looked over.

"Mind you Blackman, this is none of your affair."

"He'll take no part in this," David said firmly.

Inside the ring the pugilists circled each other. Hickey lunged at David who wrestled him to the ground. As they rolled in the black boiler ash, it stuck to their sweating bodies and gave them a sinister appearance. Neither gaining an advantage they released and stood up. Time and again they locked, fell to the floor then got up. David, attempting to land a right hook, missed his opponent's jaw with his fist but connected with the point of his elbow. Hickey went down as though shot and David stood over him panting heavily.

"Finish him off," Richard roared. "Get stuck in, now." As the dazed Hickey rose to his feet David waded in with both fists. The crowd roared encouragement, a minority for Hickey. Blood flowed from the Irishman's nose. Time and time again he fell, but time and time again he staggered back to his feet. His mouth bled and cuts above both eyes obscured his vision and it appeared just a matter of time till he had to submit. Suddenly, as Hickey was down on one knee wiping away the blinding blood, someone in the crowd threw his walking stick. He reached out grabbed it and used it to help himself to his feet. As David rushed forward to take it, Hickey twisted the handle one-way and his body the other. From within the hollowed cane a blade glinted.

"Watch out," Richard yelled, but too late. The blade penetrated David's chest, stopping him in his tracks. With a look of total surprise, he sank slowly to his knees. Smirking, Hickey stood over his opponent like a matador. Withdrawing the blade he callously wiped the blood from it on his bare forearm. Hickey took advantage of the crowd's stunned silence and vanished amongst them. Richard rushed to his stricken friend as the crowd stood motionless.

"Someone fetch the doctor ... hurry now, anyone!"

"Put him on here, it'll be quicker," said one of the foundry workers. "Put him on this cart and we'll take him there."

With his immense power Richard scooped David from the floor and gently laid him on the wooden boards of the flat cart. He covered him with his jacket and made a pillow of his waistcoat.

"Doctor, I think you had better come quickly," the nurse called into the house as she watched Richard carrying David's limp body through the garden.

"Bring him in here, lay him down there," she urged, pointing to a cotton covered table in the surgery. Once he's laid David on the doctors' couch in the surgery, Richard was asked to retire to the waiting room. Soon, other members of the Morris and English families arrived, followed by PC Hart. A small crowd began to gather outside the walled garden and inside the doctor began his examination of the stab wound.

"I don't think there are any serious internal injuries, but a urine sample will confirm that. I'll clean up the wound and stop the bleeding. This is going to sting quite a bit, David," he said without looking up from the wound. The doctor doused a piece of wadding with iodine and applied it with pressure to the injury. "Hold that down firm please, Miss Moore, then we'll bandage him tight. How are you feeling David?"

"I'm thirsty, awful thirsty," David whispered as he fell into a faint.

"Quick, Miss Moore, I think he is going into shock. Leave the dressing for now, place pillows under his feet and fetch more blankets. Hurry now. David, can you hear me? Come now, you must stay awake!" David opened his eyes momentarily. His face and skin were pale and wet from profuse sweating, while his lips and ears were ashen.

Doctor McKechnie found David's faint pulse rapid and his breathing irregular and shallow. Despite the sweating his temperature was subnormal.

"Is there anything else I can do, doctor?" nurse Moore asked after covering David with heavy wool blankets.

"Yes. Ask cook to fill all watertight jugs with hot water and bring them to me. We must get his temperature up. Oh, and make up some saline water for drinking will you please?"

"Yes, doctor," the compliant nurse replied, as she hurried out of the surgery.

"David, speak to me. You must not go to sleep just yet," David's eyes fluttered then opened. Weakly he again asked for a drink. "In a moment, it's on its way. Just stay awake and talk to me till it arrives."

As Miss Moore arrived back with the saline drink, frantic knocking came to he front door. The doctor took the jug from Miss Moore.

"See who that is—if it is the family tell them that he is alive, stable but not out of the woods yet. We're keeping him here and they should come back in the morning. I fear we will have a long night ahead of us, Miss Moore."

"Yes, doctor."

Early the next morning, as the wane light filtered through the lace curtains of the surgery, Dr. McKechnie checked the patient and yawned heavily.

"Well, it looks like he is going to make it," he confidently predicted as he watched the night clouds begin to roll back. "He has had a good night. He's out of shock and if he remains stable I think we should transfer him to the work's infirmary. He will need considerable bed rest and nursing. After that, Miss Moore, I prescribe a little sleep for both of us. What do you think?"

"Yes, doctor."

The fugitive Hickey was easily found. The few Irishmen drinking in The Shamrock alehouse fell silent when Constable Hart entered.

"You'll have to come with me, Hickey."

"What the hell for?"

"You know what for. Now will you come peaceably or not?" Constable Hart's grip tightened on his truncheon.

"It was a fair fight. Anyway, he started all the carry on. How the hell can it be myself you're after?"

"That's for sure it was a fair fight, I saw it mesel, with me own eyes, I did," said Hickey's drinking companion Patrick Keanan. "I heard him offer him out, after work like. And I'll swear that on me blessed mother's bible so I will."

"You'll all get your chance to tell the magistrate what you know, Keanan," said the policeman. "He'll be given a fair trial." Hickey's eyes filled with fire.

"A fair trial? When did an Irishman ever get a fair trial offa a fiken English magistrate? Can you be tellin' me that then?" He slammed his pewter mug hard down onto the table, sending ale flying in all directions.

"Now Hickey, I'll ask you just once more. You are under arrest, will you come quietly or not?" Hickey looked at the landlord.

"Don't close early tonight, Pat ... I'll be back in a crack, so I will," he mocked.

At the village police office he was formally charged with attempted murder before being escorted to a cell in Bishop Auckland. He did not get back to the Shamrock that night, but next day he was the talk of the place.

"Is Seamus not out yet then?" Keanan asked the barkeep Murphy.

"No, but it'll not be long now," said Murphy. "Did you not hear? Why there's a top man going to defend him. Coming all the way down from Newcastle so he is."

"How the hell is Seamus going to pay the man? I don't think he has got anything put by, has he?"

"It's all paid for, so it is."

"How the hell did he manage that then? I mean who, around here, in Jesus' name has that sorta money?" Murphy tapped the left side of his nose with his finger and winked with his right eye.

"Saints preserve us," said Keanan. "I shoulda known dat.... Enough said."

The next morning, Hickey appeared in front of the local magistrate, Sir Arnold Clark- Henderson. The court was relatively empty except for friends of the accused. The counsellor was quick to his feet.

"Your worship, my name is Roland Steen of Steen and Fortescue whose chambers are in the Quayside, Newcastle, in the County of Northumberland. We are partners to Messrs. Fletcher and Tempest who have chambers in Lincoln's Inn. I believe your son is studying for the bar there?" Hickey smiled from the dock and PC Hart raised an eyebrow.

"I am here to day to represent Mr. Seamus Hickey," continued the brief. "My client wishes it be known that he is prepared to plead guilty to the lesser charge of actual bodily harm. The court consequently would drop the charge of grievous bodily harm. We will, of course, be calling witnesses as to the mitigating circumstances surrounding this case."

James Parry, the prosecuting counsel, stood up.

"May I remind the court that the defendant is fortunate not to be charged with murder or at the least manslaughter? Why the victim is as we speak barely clinging to life."

"As I understand it sir," countered Steen. "Mr. Morris was deemed well enough to be released from the local doctor's care an hour ago. If the Crown is unable to indulge our request, then I must inform you we intend to ask this court to send my client to the next assizes, to be held in Durham. There he will plead not guilty in front of a jury of his peers. Perhaps it is not for me to remind your worship that only last month the Lord Chancellor instructed magistrates to deal with such trivial matters themselves. I do believe the assize calendar is bursting at the seams."

Sir Arnold nodded in agreement. "Quite. Let it be known that in the matter of the Crown versus Hickey I am prepared to listen to a plea of guilty to the charge of actual bodily harm. Are you ready to proceed, Mr. Steen, or would you prefer an adjournment?"

"We are ready your worship," said Steen. "But perhaps a short adjournment would be of benefit to the court. I wish you to summon the doctor who attended Mr. Morris. Can that be so arranged?"

"Very well. Clerk, instruct the bailiff to fetch Dr. McKechnie. This court is adjourned until two o'clock this afternoon. Take the prisoner back to the cells." Steen looked to Hickey and smiled discreetly.

Court reconvened on the stroke of two. The doctor informed the bench that the blade of the swordstick, having struck the breastbone had only entered the plaintiff's chest cavity about one and one half inches, causing no damage to vital organs. The onset of shock, as a result of the injury had caused concern but was overcome. He said his patient hopefully needed no more than bed rest and nursing.

"You say 'hopefully.' Can you qualify that for the court doctor please? Are you saying that in fact there is still danger to his life?" asked Sir Arnold.

"There are always dangers associated with such injuries. Septicaemia being an ever present threat."

Mr. Steen rose to his feet and chose his words carefully.

"Doctor, do you feel that Mr. Morris is any imminent danger at this precise moment?"

"I would have to say no, not at this precise moment."

"Thank you, doctor," He turned to the bench. "I would like the doctor's assessment entering into the court records. What we are interested in, here, today is whether Mr. Morris is alive or dead. Well, according to his physician he is much alive. As to the future ... the law provides for such events. It is a fact of law that the Crown, should Mr. Morris die within one year and one day, has recourse to bring the ultimate charge against my client. We understand and accept that. Sir, with your approval I would like to move on and call, in mitigation, my first witness. I would like to call Seamus Hickey to the stand." Hickey took the stand and the clerk approached him with a bible.

"Can you read?"

"No, I can't."

"Then hold the bible and repeat after me." Hickey hesitated and glanced at his barrister who nodded encouragement. Reluctantly he complied and took the oath.

"Your name is Seamus Hickey? Is that correct?" his barrister asked.

"Yes, sir."

"And you are gainfully employed at the Witton Park ironworks?"

"I am sir."

"Could you tell the court what transpired yesterday while you were at your place of work?"

"I'm sorry, I don't know what you mean."

"I mean, did anything happen at your place of work between yourself and one Mr. Morris? For example, did he come up to you and make threats?"

"That's for sure he did all of that," Hickey replied. "And he said that after work he was going to give me a good hiding."

"Did he say why he intended to fight you?"

"It was 'cos I'd clipped the ear of his cheeky young brother. I've had a rake of trouble with that one. A bad lot he is."

"A *rake* of trouble? Can you explain that for the court please?

"It means 'a lot,'" said Hickey, who then went on to describe the scenes that had occurred outside his house when Squeak had revived the act of Riding the Stang. Neither magistrate nor councillor was familiar with the tradition and both looked on with distain as Hickey placed himself as the victim in the episode.

"So not only did you not you provoke David Morris, but you were yourself the focus of mistreatment?"

"Yes, sir. I clipped the lad's ear, but I told David Morris I wanted no further chew."

"Chew?

"Trouble. I told him I wanted no trouble."

"But he insisted in this fist fight after work?"

"He did that sir, and while I'd sooner walk away as fight I will not be put on."

"I'm sure that any man would feel the same, Mr. Hickey. Tell me, then what happened?"

Hickey told the court that neither man had stuck a serious blow and for fifteen minutes or more, the contest was more like Cumberland wrestling. Then unexpectedly, he believed he saw the plaintiff produce a blade, and he feared for his life.

"You believed Mr. Morris produced a blade and you feared for your life. Is that what you are telling this court?"

"Yes, sir." Somebody threw me my swordstick, but I only intended to use it to defend mesel. Make things fair like, the same for both of us."

"When you got hold of the sword stick did you have specific intention of stabbing Mr. Morris?"

"No sir, it was an accident. He rushed at me and got himself stabbed."

114

"So, you feared for your life?"

"Yes, sir. "I was only flashing the blade to keep him away from me."

"What did you do after the fight? Did you run away?"

"No sir, I did not."

"What did you do?"

"I went to the Shamrock ale house."

"And that's where Constable Hart found you?"

"Yes, sir."

"Did you resist arrest?"

"No, sir."

"Thank you Mr. Hickey. I think that will be all from me. Please wait there, Sir Arnold may wish to ask you a few questions. Sir?"

"No, I think you have covered things pretty well. Do you intend to call more witnesses?

"With the courts indulgence I will call just one more."

"Proceed, Mr. Steen."

"Thank you, sir. I call Patrick Keanen."

"You are a roller in the same ironworks as Mr. Hickey? In fact you work on the same press I believe?"

"That's right, sir."

"Please tell the court in your own words everything you can remember about what happened yesterday, with regards to Mr. Hickey."

"Well sir, I was working alongside Seamus when a Welshman called Morris came storming up to him. Red in the face he was and screaming and shouting at him. I heard him, Morris that is, say to Seamus 'I'm going to knock seven sort of shit out of you'– begging your pardon, sir—then he challenged Seamus to a fight in the station yard at five o'clock that night. Seamus said he didn't want to fight. After work I watched the fight, and it wasn't up to much at all. I think Seamus could have taken him anytime, if he'd wanted, that is. Then I saw a flash of light and thought Morris had produced a knife from somewhere."

"You definitely saw the glint of a knife blade?"

"Yes, sir."

"Did others see this metal reflecting in the evening sun?

"I would say so, sir."

"So Mr. Hickey could have seen it also?"

"Like I said, lots of us saw it, so I guess Seamus would have seen it too."

"What did you do when you thought your unarmed friend was in danger of his life?"

"At first I shouted 'watch out he's got a knife' but I don't think he heard me."

"Then what did you do?"

"I threw him his sword stick."

"Finally, are you sure it was a knife you saw?"

"Well I was then. We all were. Since then folks are saying that it might have just been a reflection of the Welshman's trouser buckle. I'm not so sure now."

"But at the time you though it a blade of a knife?"

"Definitely, sir."

"Thank you, Mr. Keanan. Would you remain there just a moment please? The magistrate may have a question for you."

"I have no questions, thank you. You may step down Mr. Keanan. Are you ready for your summation now, Mr. Steen?

"Yes sir, I am, thank you."

"Sir, may I remind the court that my client has not shirked his responsibilities in any way. He has pleaded guilty to assault. He is aware that it is not in the public interests that people should try to cause or should cause each other actual bodily harm for no good reason. The court has heard today that the defendant tried to avoid this. He was not the protagonist. He wishes the court to know he is full of remorse for the injury to Mr. Morris and wishes him a speedy recovery. My client had no malice aforethought but at the worst was reckless. Therefore I ask the court to show leniency to Mr. Hickey who was quite clearly forced into this fight by Mr. Morris following sustained provocation by other him and members of his family. Given such circumstances, it is understandable that Mr. Hickey feared for his life when he saw the flash of a knife blade and only then moved to protect himself. I now rest my case, sir."

The magistrate returned from his deliberations after only ten minutes and fined Hickey five shillings and sixpence plus one shilling costs to Dr. McKechnie. The weapon was confiscated, and he was bound over to keep the peace for three months.

The town head area of Bishop Auckland was the one favoured by Irish immigrants. It was here that jubilant Hickey spent the rest of the day. By nightfall—hardly having had to put his hand in his pocket to pay for a drink—he was near collapse. Undaunted by his previous run-in with the stationmaster he set off to walk the tracks to Witton Park. As he stumbled and fell along the railroad he cursed Mr. Crawford and anyone else connected with the English railway company.

"Oh my God, not again! There's someone on the line," the driver of the 'Elephant' screamed to his assistant.

"Did we hit him?" the fireman asked.

"Dunno, but this time I ain't gonna stop to find out. I need this job."

Only two weeks earlier, on the same stretch of line the locomotive 'Elephant' had accidentally run over and killed two similar trespassers.

"Someone told me Hickey got hit by a train last night."

"Did he say if he was dead?" Michael asked his father.

"No, he never said."

"I heard the same. Dunno whether it's true or not, though. I've heard different stories. One said he was cut to ribbons. Another said his head was cut clean off."

"Wishful thinking, I fear me lad," said Patrick.

"Wonder who paid for his fancy lawyer?"

"Haven't a clue. Maybe they will pay for his funeral as well?"

"*If* he's dead," said Michael

"That's right son, it's doubtful. They say only the good die young." Patrick concluded.

Chapter Nine

By springtime, David had made a full recovery but he was to face a bitter disappointment. For the third time the Chartist's petition, containing nearly two million signatures was rejected by Parliament on dubious claims that there were fewer names than claimed and some were fictitious.

"Michael, I cannot be more pleased for you," Joseph said upon learning that his friend and Tamar planned their wedding for mid-summer. "At the same time though I cannot help but feel a little envious—you know I'm only kidding! I knew from the start that Tamar only had eyes for you. Wait till Harriet hears of it. I wonder what she will have to say?" Michael did not wish to even guess.

"Have you set a date yet?" asked Joseph.

"Not exactly, but I'll let you know as soon as we do. Joseph, do you think, when the time comes, we might get a company house?"

"I can assure you of that my friend. You leave it me. I'll give you Carwood House if needs must."

"Thanks Joseph, you are a true friend."

Three days after Michael broke the news to Joseph, the engagement of Harriet was announced in all the local newspapers. In the summer she would marry one Lieutenant C. Allbury of Leeds.

"I see they are going to build on the Black Road," said William to Patrick as they walked to work. Black Road ran from Jane pit to the abandoned engine house used by the famous engineer George Stephenson at the top of Etherley incline. Years of coal spillage provided its ebony surface.

"Who is?"

"Bolckow and Vaughan of course, who else?"

"More houses for the Paddies they keep bringing in?" Newspapers reported the growing numbers of new Irish arrivals in places like Manchester and Liverpool. At the same time more arrived at Witton Park. Although the Welsh outnumbered the Irish by over ten to one, the Irish were always more evident.

"Suppose so. Seems they can't get enough men for the ironworks these days."

"Went for a walk up there the other day," Patrick said. "Got talking to this bloke who said there was going to be over ninety houses up there plus three public houses and an ale house." William shook his head in disbelief. Building of licensed premises was almost at fever pitch; even the local farmers were getting in on the act. One changed his farmhouse to the 'New Inn'. It was not just tradesmen who jumped on the bandwagon—locals who could afford to buy a single barrel of beer opened alehouses and sold it from their front rooms. John Street sprang up north east of the original streets. Although it was a small street of only twenty-seven houses, it had three pubs. Closest to the ironworks, all day, boys could be seen scampering back and forth to quench the furnacemen's thirst.

"And they are building along Woodside aren't they?" Patrick asked.

"So they tell me, why we'll soon be living in a city so we will. And how many more pubs will they build I wonder?"

Running out of the village towards the Saxon village of Escomb was a long, straggling, roller coaster of a road at a wood side. Either side of the road was being developed for housing and there also would be one hotel, two public houses and two beer houses. The houses, separated from the heart of Witton Park almost became a divorced community and were much sought after.

"It seems as though all the Paddies are moving out of Thompson Street to up there," said William.

"Aye, I saw you-know-who pushing a cart up there followed by that poor woman of his." Hickey, it turned out, was not dead but neither had he returned to the ironworks. He never seemed to work but often disappeared from the village for varying lengths of time.

"On about building. Has David said owt about them building on the garden allotments?"

"Yes, he reckons they want to build another four streets there."

"Why ye bugger, it's right then," exclaimed Patrick. "Where's it gonna stop?"

The plan for the new rows of houses was simply a mirror image of the existing terraces. But for a gap at the end they would have been but extensions of the existing streets. The incline of the land increased towards the elevated Black Road placing the new streets above the older ones. So the existing streets became known as Low King Street, Low Albion Street, Low Thompson Street and so on, and the new extensions were High King Street, High Albion Street, etc. There was a gap between the old and new high terraced streets that became formally named Cross Street, but villagers, used to calling it 'the tops' continued to do so, perplexing generations for the next hundred years with the quandary that 'the tops' was in the middle. The building of the new high streets and the development of Black Road and Woodside added another three hundred houses but overcrowding still existed.

Between the 'top's of the original streets and the developing Black Road, lay the allotment gardens—pieces of land that were rented out to villagers to grow their own food. Plot holders were enraged that, after clearing and cultivating the meadowland their landlords made them move. The little piece of land was becoming locked in a horseshoe grip of development. Bordered on three sides by housing, the land was ripe for further development.

"And after all the work the likes of David have put in. What's he say about it?" Patrick asked William.

"He says there's nothing to be done, but move." Angry meetings had been held, but without any real choice, the gardeners agreed to leapfrog east over Black Road, and start again. As compensation, the owners agreed to pay for a well to be dug on the new site.

"My Da had an allotment all his life," said Patrick. "I spent many happy hours helping him. I'm thinking I might put in for one of the new 'uns, ... in fact I think I will, now you don't have to fetch and carry water from the river anymore." Domestic water still had to be brought into the village and was stored in locked household water butts.

"I've never had an allotment," said William.

"No? Why, after a shift down the pit there's no place like it, honest. Getting away from the dust and the suffocating stench of that place makes you feel ten years younger. Just to breath the clean fresh air is a godsend. William, do you not think that there is something marvellous about a tiny little seed that can grow to a thousand times its own size? Every year when I used to sow me Da's cabbage I'd think about that, so I would. And when I watch your David's pigeons flying, wings fully outstretched, it makes me forget how we work, all day, hemmed in down that bloody pit."

David had always had a fascination about pigeons. He was captivated by their mysterious ability to find their way home over hundreds of miles of foreign terrain. In his readings he learned how man had utilised this to his advantage. As the family sat quietly at home, David looked to his father who was relaxing beside the fire.

"Father. Have you heard of the Rothschild family?"

"They are the richest people in the world aren't they?"

"Yes, that's them, but I bet you don't know how they made their money?"

"Well, no, not really. How?" David had got his interest now.

"Pigeons!" David affirmed.

"Pigeons? How in Heaven's name did they manage that?"

"Shall I read it to you, from the book?"

"Certainly son, I'd love to know how someone made millions out of pigeons. Maybe there's hope for the Morris family yet."

David began to read: "Nathan Senior was the first prominent member of the Rothchild family. He was a familiar, but relatively insignificant player of the London Stock Market who had two sons. One lived in Paris, and one who was to witness the important Battle of

Trafalgar. Had England lost the decisive battle the stock market would have collapsed. When the result became clear, Nathan Rothchild Junior, at the battle scene, released a homing pigeon to his brother in Paris. From Paris, another feathered Eros carried his valuable note to his father in London. Upon receipt of the historic news Nathan Rothchild Senior began selling British Loan Stock and War Bonds. The market, aware that Rothchild had sons in France presumed he knew something that they did not, and a panic rush to sell followed. Secretly, Nathan Senior began buying back more and more of what to others seemed worthless bonds. The message of Nelson's victory was carried by relays of horse and riders across France. Crossing the channel and galloping to London, the messenger brought news that brought forth jubilation, except in the financial institutions. Nathan Rothchild, courtesy of homing pigeons, became an overnight millionaire and household name."

"Incredible," Patrick said.

Having moved to the new allotment site, men raced against time to ready the land for spring planting. Beyond, where a borrowed goat grazed down an overgrown plot, endless rows of potatoes would be planted. These were the allotments of the Irish.

"Are you going up the allotment after work, Patrick?" his wife asked.

"Aye. I will be after a bath and me tea that is."

"What time will you be back?"

"How the hell should I know woman? When I'm done I suppose."

"Don't you be calling at that public house. You come straight home you hear? We've a wedding coming up and we'll have to careful with the pennies from now on."

"I hear you Mrs. Bryan. I hear you," Patrick sighed. An hour or so later, Patrick took a break from digging and leant on his spade.

"Not much more now. Its back's broken," he said to himself as he looked at his plot. As he walked over to put more weeds on his smouldering bonfire William Morris appeared.

"I thought I would find you up here. Been up long?"

"Oh, about an hour. Just finishing up. That's enough for one day."

"It's looking good, Patrick. It's marvellous what man and God can achieve, isn't it?"

"Man and God? Well I'm not at all sure about that now. You should have seen the state of the place when he had it on his own!"

The summer months were sunny and hot. Sundays invariably included an after-church walk down to the river. In the late summer, the families of coalminers took their father's tea can and filled it with blackberries from the abundant hedgerows. Pride in pie making was fierce in Witton Park and women swore by recipes they had brought with them from other places: Scotland, Ireland, Wales and other parts of England.

During the school holidays, evenings and weekends the village children spent the majority of their time on the banks and in the waters of the river Wear. The banks were sandy and made ideal family picnic areas. Varying in different stretches, the water ran fast or slow, from ankle deep up to the 'twenty-oners' a pool reckoned to be at least twenty-one feet deep. Some locals even claimed it was bottomless. Beneath the high railway viaduct, children frolicked in the water, while high up above atop the arches, trains and people passed above them.

Sitting on top of Red Rock—a man-made mountain of bonded waste from the brick factory and the puddling furnaces—Michael and Tamar gazed on the beauty of the valley way beneath them. In the distance a late cuckoo could be heard calling.

"I feel a bit like Moses."

"Michael, come away from the edge. Come sit beside me, we have so much to talk about." Michael threw a small stone over the edge and watched until hundreds of feet below it vanished out of sight. He lowered himself down beside her.

"Michael, why can we not get married in our chapel?" she asked.

"I dunno really. It's some stupid law."

It would be another forty years before non-conformists could marry in their own places of worship. Marriages conducted outside of the Church of England or Roman Catholic church were illegal and not recognised. Many chose the new civil ceremony at a registry office, while fervent non-conformists ignored all three and underwent weddings by their ministers.

"I thought we'd decided to go to Bishop Auckland and get married in the registry office then have a ceremony in the chapel after."

"No, that's what you decided," said Tamar haughtily.

"Isn't that what you want?"

"Sort of. I'd always hoped that my father would be the minister at my wedding."

"He will be. It'll be no different, you'll see," he reassured her.

"I've written to Samuel in America and asked him if he will give me away."

"Good, and Jane and Miss Lodge are going to be your bridesmaids, is that right?"

"Yes. Have you decided on who is to be your best man?"

"No, it's a real problem for me."

"How?"

"Well, Richard should be my first choice, but would that offend David and Mr. Jones? I've heard some say that you should ask your boss. What do you think?"

"I think it should be Joseph."

Michael walked up to Carwood House to see his friend. He was relieved to find that Harriet was not at home.

"Joseph, now that we have set the date for our wedding, I've come to ask if you will be my best man. I ask you as a friend not as a boss as some might do."

"Nothing would give me more pleasure. I am honoured. Do you know I have never been a best man before? I suppose one could say 'the best man' lost," He laughed heartily. "Now let me write that date down somewhere."

Three days after Michael visited Carwood House the time and date of Miss Vaughan's wedding appeared in the newspapers. It was to be on the same Saturday as theirs.

"I don't believe in coincidences," Michael thought on being told. Joseph called Michael into his office the next day.

"Ah Michael, good come right in. Have a seat if you please."

"Better I stand I think," Michael answered, suddenly aware of his grimy work clothes.

"Michael, I really don't know how to begin. You will no doubt have heard of the impending marriage of Harriet to Lieutenant Allbury?"

"Yes, I have. Seems it's to be the same day as ours, isn't it?"

"That is the problem my friend. You see I find myself in a no-win situation. Harriet has asked me to give her away. Yet I have already said yes to you. What am I to do?"

"You know what you must do," Michael said. "Family comes first."

"Really? Is that what you really believe? I mean, are you sure?"

"Positive." Joseph knew that his friend had let him off the hook.

"Will you ever be able to forgive me? We will not part friendship over this will we? I pray not."

"I wouldn't do that. Never, especially over something that wasn't your fault."

"Michael, you are the gentleman in this room. One day I will make this up to you. I promise." Tamar was not surprised to hear of the reversal.

"Now what are you going to do?" she asked.

"You haven't told anyone of our plans have you?"

"Never. It's our wedding and ours alone."

"Good. That means I can ask Richard without making him feel second best."

"He was always in the starting line anyway wasn't he?"

"He certainly was. In one way it's worked out for the best. Neither of my best friends can feel let down can they?"

"No they can't, and like my mother says 'Out of all evil comes some good'."

"Are you saying Harriet is evil?"

"Your words, not mine," Tamar teased.

The weeks rushed by and during the early summer they saw little of each other, except on Saturdays. Michael worked every available hour and Tamar, in addition to her position in the National School, became a private music teacher.

"Are we going into town tomorrow?" Tamar asked during one of the rare moments they spent together as they worked and saved.

"I suppose so. Is it Saturday tomorrow? These days, one day seems the same as the rest. Yes, I'll be finished for twelve. We'll walk in?"

"Of course. If it doesn't rain, that is."

"What's wrong with a little rain ... you're sweet but you're not sugar are you? You'll not melt will you? Anyway down by the river path there's them big, wild rhubarb leaves. I'll pull you one and you can use it as a parasol. You'll look quite the lady."

"Like Harriet?"

"Tamar, that's not funny. You know I didn't mean that."

"I know you didn't that was my little joke."

"What are we after this week?" Michael asked. "We must have bought the whole of Bishop Auckland by now. Our bottom drawer must be bursting at the joints."

"We still need blankets and sheets and lots of other things. You haven't much idea have you, Michael?"

"Not when it comes to shopping. Have we got enough put by?"

"Well, after we pay something off the big stuff we have put away, there should be some left over."

"See what do I need to know? I've got the best banker and quartermaster in the world," He kissed her tenderly on the cheek. "Got to go now, don't want me losing my job do you?"

The Bryan's parlour was a hive of industry. Jane worked on two outfits for Tamar plus her own and one for Miss Lodge. Samuel had written back in despondency. Due to a chest infection he could not travel and he was devastated. He promised to visit home as soon as he was well enough. In the meantime he sent her a wedding present: the bridal gown was to be made from a roll of finest white silk that arrived from America shortly after his letter. All the while she worked painstakingly on the wedding dress Michael was banned from the sitting room.

124

For three weeks it rained continuously, but, just two days before the wedding, the dark rain clouds rolled back and the sun shone. The inhabitants of the village, in their new spring clothes, emerged in droves as though from hibernation. Friday was even warmer than Thursday.

"Will you take me to Red Rock tonight?" Tamar asked.

"Why?"

"Tonight is the last night before we get married and I just want to sit there with you, alone."

"If that's what you want. Let's waste no more time. Lets go." The river was in flood and they watched the swollen waters crash against the large rocks and boulders below. Whirls of white spray were sent cascading high into the air. Over the shallow section, around the bend, the river flowed ever faster, threatening to flood Paradise. Then, calmed, it reached the 'twenty oners' before rushing downstream.

At eight o'clock on Saturday morning, Patrick and the entire neighbourhood were suddenly awoken.

"What the hell were them bloody bangs?"

"I hope it's not the works," Annie said, rushing to dress.

"My God, it's not one of the furnaces blown up, I hope. Not today of all days." He rushed out of the front door where neighbours were running towards the ironworks. Michael hurried out of the house after him.

"What's happened?" Michael shouted to any one who would listen.

"No idea," a workmate shouted back. "Thought it must be the works but I can't see any smoke. Can you?"

"No, I can't."

"What about the pit?" Patrick asked, "Could it have had an explosion?"

"Don't think so, Da. It sounded too close for that didn't it? Tell you what, I'll check the works and you check the pit? Right?"

"Right ... see you back here." The mystery was solved quickly and Patrick headed home in an angry mood.

"Of all the bloody almighty stupid things I have ever heard of. Who in the bloody world would set off a canon at eight o'clock in the morning? A canon blast to announce Harriet Vaughan's wedding ... who the hell does she think she is? Bloody Queen Victoria?"

"Patrick please stop your swearing. Remember it's your son's wedding today. Let's not allow some idiot to spoil it."

"Stop me swearing you say? I could say a whole, bloody, lot stronger things so I could."

"Patrick. Please?"

The previous night, Annie laid out everything that her husband would need for the wedding. In front of a marble-topped dressing table, upon which stood a hand basin and water jug, Patrick put on his shirt collar. The starching was so heavy that it felt as though it were made of balsa wood and would snap when he tried to fold it around his neck. He secured the back stud through both collar and shirt holes and was working out his next move when Michael, extremely nervous, walked into the bedroom.

"Well, this really is it, Da. It won't belong now till I'm a married man."

"Aye, by tomorrow you'll have found that your tu'penny pie will be costing you fourpence."

"Don't be daft Da. With two jobs Tamar's bringing in almost as much as me."

"Aye, I suppose you're right lad." He hugged his father tight then slapped him on the back before leaving. Patrick gulped then gagged. He had swallowed the front collar stud that he'd held in his mouth. He reached for the water pitcher and drank heavily.

"Thanks son," he said to an empty room. "And I haven't got another one of them damned things either. Now what will I do? What a bloody start to the day."

"What are you wanting, Patrick?" Annie wife asked as Patrick searched the drawers downstairs. "Now's not the time to bothering folk. If you want something you'll have to see to yourself for once. Go on, get back upstairs out of the road." Holding down the errant shirt collar, he climbed the treads and stood in front of the bedroom mirror. Carefully he bent the collar to the shape of his neck but without a stud it sprung back, flat. It would not stay round his neck.

"I've got it," he exclaimed. "I'll string the bloody thing round me neck with me tie. I'll not be beaten, not Michael Bryan, so I won't." Holding his necktie on top of the collar, he slowly drew it closed, then secured it with a knot that almost choked him. With a smile like a cat that got the cream he set off downstairs again. His smugness did not last long. Any movement and the wayward piece of starched cotton took on a life of its own. By the time he reached the bottom of the stairs he had tucked one side or the other back behind the necktie.

"Damned thing," he muttered as he came down into the kitchen.

"Patrick, what have I asked you already about your language?"

Michael, in his new suit, and shoes polished to brilliance, paced the floor as he counted the minutes until he was to leave. His party was to go on an earlier train than the bride.

"What time is it now?" he asked Richard. "Should we not be leaving yet?"

"Michael, how many times are you going to ask me the time? We have loads of time, the train isn't due to leave for another twenty minutes."

"What if it's early?"

"Stop panicking man. Since when did ever a train go early? I fear the worst if you're like this now. What you going to be like while we wait for the bride to arrive?"

"I'll be all right when we are on our way. Can't we go now?"

"You mean you'd rather pace the station platform than here? Is that it?"

"Yes, I don't think I'd feel so fenced in. These walls are driving me crazy."

"Right then. If that's what you want so it shall be. Everyone ready?"

Patrick was still fighting with his shirt collar when they reached the registry. Tamar, and her cortege, boarded the very next train. The skilfully made, trim, two-piece suit enhanced her hourglass figure. At the same time Miss Vaughan, resplendent in a white antique-silk dress was boarding the first of six carriages that would carry her and her guests to the parish church of St John's at Escomb. The path into the church had been carpeted for her arrival. The houses and shops of Commercial Row were decked with bunting, creating a carnival atmosphere as a brass band accompanied the procession. The civil ceremony was in itself simple. From the welcome to pronouncing them man and wife took a little over ten minutes. The register was signed and they left the office to showers of rice, thrown by family and friends.

"That didn't take long did it?" Patrick said to William.

"No it didn't. Been to one before. Can't say I care for them. Wonder if they will catch on in a big way?"

"Do you know, I think if we hurry we shall catch the same train on its return to Witton Park."

"Did you hear that, you lot?" Patrick shouted to the newlyweds. "C'mon, shake a leg."

"Your Da sounds thirsty, Michael," said Richard. "We'd better go."

"He wouldn't dare. Not yet anyway. Me Ma would kill him." As Patrick led the group back to the railway station he passed the tavern that had caused him so much grief. He started to cross the road to be away from it and spat in its direction. From behind him, Annie said, "Patrick, I saw that."

"I don't really care," he replied as he fidgeted more with his collar, which by then looked little more than a piece of soiled rag.

Back in Witton Park Tamar ran to change from her town suit.

"Where are you going now?" Michael asked his new bride. "Can I come with you?"

"Of course you can't now go to *our* house and wait. I'll see you in chapel." It was the proudest moment of William's life to be officiating at the wedding of his daughter. In her pure-white, Chinese-silk wedding dress, carrying a small bunch of lilies-of-the-valley, she looked both beautiful and radiant. Behind her, Jane and Miss Lodge followed dressed in green embroidered crepe de chine. In total, they set a scene of regalia and beauty rarely witnessed in the village. Beneath the Methodist pulpit, the groom and best man turned to look at the bride as the organ began to play the wedding march.

"My, oh my!" Richard exclaimed. Michael seemed stunned, and he felt his knees buckle. Richard's hand reached for his friend's elbow and steadied him.

"You all right?"

"I think so."

The wedding ceremony of Miss Vaughan and Lieutenant Allbury seemed to drag on and on. The choir sang the same hymns chosen earlier that year by the Prince of Wales and Princess Alexandra at their wedding. Arriving back with her new groom at Carwood House, Harriet was greeted by a brass band. The tops of tall poplar trees had been drawn together and lashed to form an evergreen arch for the couple to pass beneath. The six coaches ferried guests the two miles back to Carwood from Escomb parish church. Dozens more, having brought their own transport, blocked the main street. But the new Mrs. Allbury somehow did not have the same glow as the new Mrs. Bryan who, once the ceremony was over, walked with her new husband to their little terraced house in Middle Row.

"It's time to celebrate!" a jubilant Patrick shouted as he left the chapel. Wedding celebrations were under way at two houses—guests spilling out onto the lush green lawns of Carwood and onto the brown chipped flagstones in Middle Row.

"Are you enjoying yourself?" Margot asked Annie as she handed around food.

"I certainly am. One thing though, I'd like to ask Patrick how he is the only man at the wedding not wearing a collar."

"Does it matter now? Patrick is Patrick, everyone knows that."

"I know. I just wish though, he'd take his tie off as well. He looks daft." In his son's little terrace house, Patrick took it upon himself to be the drinks host.

"What about you Margot? Would you not like to try a glass of this fortified wine?"

"No, thank you Patrick, I'd sooner choke."

"Only kidding Margot, only kidding. What about you then William ... can I tempt you?"

"You know you can't. As the good book says 'Get thee behind me, Satan'."

"More for 'em as does then, and like the good book says 'Waste not, want not', why I might have to drink it all mesel!"

As the celebrations continued, the children, faces stuffed with pie and cakes, became bored and began to wander away to play. Standing outside with his father, who was still avoiding Annie, Michael was the first to see the cart turn into their street.

"Isn't that Joseph alongside that cart?" Michael asked.

"It looks like him, but what brings him here? Shouldn't he be at his sister's wedding do?"

Walking alongside Joseph Vaughan was a cart man trying his best to negotiate the potholes in the unmade street. They stopped directly in front of Michael, who extended his hand.

"Congratulations, dear friend. Then it's done, is it?"

"Yes, it's done and thanks." Tamar stepped out of the house and the sight of her caused Joseph to gasp.

"Tamar, today you look especially beautiful." With perfect decorum he took her hand and kissed it gently. "For you and your husband I wish that there is a lifetime of happiness. I've brought you a little something to mark the occasion. Cart man, climb up then and loosen your load." The carter climbed up the tall cargo and loosened the ropes that held protective woollen blankets, which, like the unveiling of a statue, fell to the wooden floor. There stood the most beautiful carved rosewood tall clock. Gilded roman numerals were surrounded by gold leaf decoration that matched columns supporting the face.

"Do you like it?" Joseph asked.

"Like it? Michael said. "What is there not to like?"

"Joseph, it's beautiful," said Tamar. "But it must of cost you a fortune. You shouldn't have. Really."

"If I cannot spoil my two best friends on their wedding day, when can I, I ask? Here Michael, you take these," From the cart he produced and handed over the dismantled brass weights and pendulum. "And you take good care of this." To Tamar he handed from his waistcoat pocket the clock's brass key.

"I'll get it down from the cart," said Patrick.

"No you won't, Da. You've had far too much to drink."

"That's a lie. Not yet anyway."

"Either way. I'm not having you rolling off that cart with the clock. Can someone shout for Richard?"

Just then, an out-of-breath boy rushed past the startled partygoers.

"Hey lad, hold your horse! What's all the rush about?" Patrick shouted after him. Gasping for breath, bent over, hands on knees, the boy blurted out.

"Two, maybe three, lads have been drowned, down the river. They've took them to the work's hospital."

"Do you know who they are?"

"No, I don't." Annie and Margot looked first at each other then up and down the street. Only young William-Patrick could be seen, playing in the dirt.

"Where's Squeak and Philip?" Annie asked anxiously.

Chapter Ten

Outside the works infirmary, police constables Hart and Anthony fought to control the growing crowd that clamoured for any scrap of information. Dr McKechnie and his assistant appeared at the door and the gathering fell silent.

"Let me through," Joseph said firmly to the throng.

"Make way for Mr. Vaughan now. Come along make way," P.C. Hart ordered as he pushed the crowd aside.

"Come inside Joseph," the doctor beckoned. "It's not good I'm afraid." Joseph reappeared and scanned the anxious village folk. He turned to the other policeman who guarded the door and said, "Find Michael Bryan and fetch him to me will you please?"

"Yes, sir."

"Michael ... Michael Bryan!" the policeman shouted, and the crowd watched and waited as Joseph and Michael stood talking at the infirmary door.

"Can you hear what they are saying?" a woman asked another in front of her.

"Not a thing. They're sorta whispering."

After a short conversation Michael pushed his way towards his new bride.

"Tamar, where's your Ma and Da? I think you'd better get them." The colour drained from her face.

"Why, what's wrong?" she said. All the people strained to hear the reply.

"I'll tell you when we are inside. Do you know where your parents are?"

"I saw them!" a bystander said. "They're at the back, I think." Michael stood up on his tiptoes and craned his neck.

"Mr. Morris! Can you come please ... and you Mrs. Morris." he shouted to his in-laws. The crowd parted and allowed the fearful couple to come forward.

"What is it Michael?" William asked.

"Dr. McKechnie has asked for your and my family and one more to come see him. I'll let him explain why when we go in. The policemen are bringing my parents right now. They should be here any minute."

"It's not Philip is it? I mean he *is* all right isn't he?"

"Be patient a moment longer, Mrs. Morris. When we are inside the doctor will tell us everything." P.C. Hart helped Annie and Patrick to the front. Annie's legs buckled and she leaned heavily on Patrick's arm.

"Michael ... your brother's not one of them is he? Philip's not gone has he?"

"Ma, I don't know what to say. Let's just wait and see, eh?" Constable Anthony brought the third party, the Thomas family, and led them all through the little gate and up the path to the small hospital.

"They're all here, sir. All as 'em you asked for," he informed the doctor.

"Good. Bring them into the waiting room will you please?"

"One at a time, sir?"

"No, altogether thank you."

"Yes, sir," he said, turning to the families. "Can you all follow me, please?" He looked at Margot clutching young Will-Patrick.

"Why don't you leave the boy with P.C. Anthony, Mrs. Bryan? He'll look after him, won't you Mr. Anthony?"

"Yes, sir," P.C. Hart gently prised the boy from Margot's clasp and handed him to his colleague.

"Right, this way then."

In the waiting room they were silent as fear struck at their hearts. Men supported wives and brothers supported sisters. Doctor McKechnie addressed them.

"As you know, there has been a tragedy. Two boys have drown today. Another had a lucky escape. I must ask you all to prepare yourselves for a shock. Inside here are two bodies, each which must be formally identified. This will be a most difficult task. If any among you would prefer not to enter you may wait here. No? Then follow me please." Large double doors swung back and the three families entered the small ward. On two of the four beds, beneath clean white sheets that totally covered them, the outlines of two bodies were clearly visible. The sight brought a gasp from Margot and sobbing from Mrs. Thomas. Approaching in dread, the party stopped at the first bed. Dr. McKechnie reverently pulled back the sheet. There lay the lifeless form of young Evan Thomas, a fire lad at the works, and a wail erupted from his mother. His father, shaking his head and wringing his hands said repeatedly, "Why Lord? Why?"

The Morris and Bryan families turned to the second bed. While the Thomas family grieved only three feet away, the doctor drew back the sheet and revealed the lifeless, angelic face of Philip Bryan. Annie rushed forward and stroked her son's wet hair, crying uncontrollably. Patrick and Michael stood motionless.

"Where's Squeak?" Margot asked anxiously, turning to her husband, but before he could answer, the doctor spoke.

"Mr. and Mrs. Morris, will you follow me please?" Leaving two families to lament the death of their children, he led them into the second of the two wards. Tamar slipped her hand out of her husband's and followed her parents. The second small room was laid out in the same fashion as the first but only one bed was occupied. In it, with only an ashen face visible, was Squeak. Margot hurried to the head of the bed and gently pushed back a length of sodden hair from his sallow face.

"Squeak? Are you alive?" Squeak opened his eyes.

"Mother?" His thin smile was as welcome as the flowers in May to them.

"Gather round," William said to his family. "Lord, we thank you for the deliverance of our son this day. We also ask Lord, that you comfort those that were not so fortunate. Please give them strength at this time and help them through their mourning. Amen." As the nurse entered to administer hot water from a spoon, Tamar left to offer comfort to her husband of less than eight hours.

"David will you take some of this soup up to Squeak, please?" his mother asked. David took the soup and climbed the stairs to where his younger brother rested. "Now then young fella, here's your dinner and I'm stopping here till you eat it all. Got to get you up and about again. Why the pit will shut down if you are off work much longer." Squeak smiled as he sat up in bed and took the warm bowl. "Now might be a good time for you to tell me what exactly happened yesterday."

"It wasn't my fault, honest, David. It wasn't," he said defensively.

"Nobody's saying it was. I'd just like to know, for mesel like."

"Well ... me and Philip got bored while you lot were all at the wedding. We met Evan Thomas and went down Paradise ..."

Families not at either wedding were enjoying the fine weather, walking and playing beside the swollen river. No one was swimming. The rushing waters were dangerous and the temperature, after only a couple of warm summer days, was still close to freezing. Skipping stones across the river, playing in the sand and climbing trees occupied the young ones, while adults relaxed under the summer sun. Philip and Evan Thomas had been sitting on a bough that protruded over the water, washing the sand from between the toes of their bare feet when the branch snapped. Above the noise of the river Squeak heard the splash as the boys hit the water, then cries for help. Instinctively, he kicked off his boots, threw off his shirt, and ran into the swirling torrent. Ahead of him, he saw a hand reach skyward then disappear. Washed into the relative calm of the pool, he found himself struggling. Though his tired legs and arms fought to keep him afloat, he bobbed under the water. Thrashing out with hands and feet he resurfaced for a fleeting moment then sank a second time.

As he was swept downstream the water quickened again, carrying everything before it. Ahead, twin rocks about twelve feet apart rose horizontally out of the water. Trapped between them was the broken bough. It was against this that his rescuers found him and his two ensnared friends.

The Bryan family was in mourning. Patrick, unable to come to terms with the death of his youngest child, lost his humour and became dark and brooding.

"Your Da's taking it badly, isn't he Michael?" Tamar asked.

"Aye, but I suppose it's to be expected. It doesn't help me Ma though. She has enough on her plate." Patrick held himself personally responsible, thinking if only he had done this, or if he had only said that, Philip might still be alive, and guilt weighed heavily upon him.

"He's drinking a lot I hear."

"Too much."

"I think he was drunk at the inquest."

"He was. I spoke to him this morning and he can remember nothing of it."

"Do you think he will be all right for the funeral?"

"I don't know."

A mixture of strong drink and grief was overwhelming on the day of the funeral. Patrick would not remember the drunkard that lay across the path of his son's funeral cortege. Incapable of movement he had to be moved by disgusted mourners in order for the hearse to pass. There was little he could remember of the two-mile walk to the church, the service or the internment.

"How's your father?" William asked Michael three days later.

"Well, he still hasn't gone back to work. It's not like him is it?"

"No, it's not ... but we all know why don't we?"

"Aye, we do. It's just that he seems to be blaming himself."

"That's not unusual. Lots of folk feel like that. It's all part of the grieving."

"The good news is that he is not drinking as much, me Ma says."

"That's good. That's a start anyway. So he's not spending his days in the public houses?"

"No, he spends most of his time sitting alone on the top of Red Rock. Looking down at the river, I guess."

"Sometimes solitude can help. If you see him before I do, tell him I'm asking after him. Oh, and tell him not to worry about work, it's all looked after."

"I will, and thanks Mr. Morris. See ya."

Patrick spent hours gazing down at the river from the top of Red Rock, the huge, rust-coloured monolith that towered over the water. A mild breeze blew through his curly hair, cooling the heat of the summer sun. Three more days passed and still he kept his vigil. Suddenly, he began to cry. Deep, uncontrollable sobs wracked his body and a torrent of tears flowed. They ran down his face, salted his lips, ran through the cleft in his chin and dampened his waistcoat. He cried until he was incapable of any more tears, then, having taken the first step in handling his grief, he set off for home feeling a little better than he had in days.

Walking along, oblivious to his surroundings, he heard the sound of hooves and wheels approaching from behind. Instinctively he stepped off the crude roadway and looked over his shoulder. Drawing near was a gypsy wagon pulled by a large black-and-white horse. The green tarpaulin cover was stretched tight over many-hooped bows secured by light rope, as neat as any needlework. The body of the wagon and the shafts, decorated with gold leaf and scrolled lines of all colours, was a work of art in itself. The spokes of the four large wheels were painted bright red and the rims were a contrasting black. He watched as the man driving handed the reins to a full-busted woman and stepped into the covered section. The woman wore her dress off the shoulder and low cut, which showed off her healthy tanned complexion. At the waist of her layered black skirt she wore a broad silk sash, tied at the side in a huge knot. Large hoop earrings hung from both ears and every finger sported a gold ring. The clay pipe she puffed remained clenched tight in her mouth and it seemed a natural part of her. Alongside sat a pitifully sobbing girl that she totally ignored. Beside the caravan walked a boy about Philip's age.

"Gid up," the lad urged a smaller horse tied to the side of the wagon. Obligingly, the little horse helped pull the cart up the incline. Laceless boots exposed the lad's lack of stockings and the open neck of a grey woollen coat showed that he wore it next to his skin. As the colourful spectacle passed, Patrick doffed his hat.

"Good morning to you all," he said, to which he received no reply. Tied to the rear of the wagon was a bay mare followed by an endearing foal.

"Oh, don't Da. Please don't!" a young girl shouted from inside the caravan. Without warning, a dog dropped right in front of Patrick. Thrown from the wagon, it landed on its feet, rolled over and, picking itself up, shook its body as though it had been in water.

"What the hell?" Patrick shouted after the gipsies. "Did you fall off?" The dog looked at Patrick then at the disappearing travellers. About half the height of a large greyhound, its brindle coat was rough and wiry as an Irish wolfhound's. Its head and neck were pure white but for the ears that looked like two hares in corn stubble, and the white feet and tip of its tail were similarly prominent. It looked briefly at Patrick then set off in pursuit of the wagon as it rounded a bend and came broadside to him. With one giant leap the dog jumped up onto the smiling girl's lap, but a second later it was thrown back onto the road.

"Hadaway!" said the boy beside the wagon, but the dog still followed.

"Hadaway! Hadaway! Hadaway!" shouted the gypsy, lashing out with a foot. Then the dog skipped away and sat forlornly by the road.

Patrick was unaware that 'had a way' was slang for 'be gone, or 'go away', but he could see the dog was not wanted. He walked back to the dog and stood before it as they studied one another.

"Hello lad, have they gone and left you? Come 'ere lad ... let's have a good look at you. I wont hurt you," the amiable Irishman implored. "C'mon ..." The dog stood up and backed off a short distance before sitting down again. Patrick clicked his tongue and made a low whistle but the dog stayed put, so he turned and began to walk away. As the tunnel under the little railway bridge came into sight, Patrick cast a glance over his shoulder and saw the dog following a few paces behind.

"We'll call you Hadaway, shall we?" smiled Patrick. "Good lad. C'mon lets both of us go home." When he got there, Annie cast a sidelong glance at the dishevelled dog.

"What on earth is that?" she said.

"It's my new dog," he answered in a determined voice. "You can see he's best part Irish wolfhound. What do you think?" Annie didn't care; she was just too pleased to see the spring in Patrick's step and the glint back in his eyes. Man and dog became inseparable. Each day afterwards, Hadaway waited at the pithead for Patrick to surface.

Eight years later, the Cambrian Co-operative was flourishing in new, larger, premises at High Thompson Street. The older building was turned over to the Mechanics and continued in its popularity by expanding the library facilities. The increased capacity of the upstairs room proved popular and was much in demand. From church groups to debating societies, meetings of every sort were conducted there.

"Did you hear about the fighting on Saturday night?" William asked Patrick.

"What's new?"

"This wasn't in the pubs—it was in the Cambrian hall."

"Never? Who was fighting?"

"Our David says it was the Irish who had booked the room. They wanted to discuss the old chestnut of home rule for Ireland. Anyway, part way through some Orangemen burst in and started hurling abuse. The place is in a mess, he reckons."

"Anybody locked up?"

"Two of the Orangemen. They are up in front of the beak this morning."

"Who were they?"

"Patrick Carlen and John Nolan—do you know them?"

"Can't say I do," said Patrick. The arrested pair were bound over to keep the peace in the sum of five shillings. For weeks after the fight, some men—fearing for their lives—sought protection to and from work from the company's two private policemen.

In all the years after young Philip drown, not a day passed when Patrick did not think of him. His daughter-in-law, Tamar, suffered three miscarriages in the first three years of her marriage, and Patrick wondered if he was being punished somehow. In the following four years, the balance redressed itself, however, and she carried four full-term healthy children: three boys and a girl. Jane had recently married the son of a Welsh immigrant and in addition to dress making, she worked for Miss Lodge. Mr. Lodge had died suddenly around the same time of Philip's untimely death. Samuel had graduated from theological college and began a probationary period as minister in the New York circuit, but he wrote and kept his promise to visit. Squeak had become engaged to marry, and ten-year-old William-Patrick, insisting on being called 'Will', was a studious boy at the National School.

"Guess what mother? Bridie asked me to be her boyfriend today."

A half interested Margot asked, "Oh yes? Bridie who?"

"Bridie Hickey." That got his mother's attention.

"Oh my God," she exclaimed.

Just then, the front door was flung open and David rushed into the kitchen. "There's been a roof fall at the pit. It got father's leg pinned beneath it. They've got him out, they tell me he's all right, but he can't walk."

"Where is he now?" Margot asked as she took off her apron and looked for her coat.

"They've stretchered him to the doctor's. Get your bonnet and I'll come with you."

"Can I come?" Will asked.

"No, you stay here and mind that pan of stew on the fire. Keep stirring it and mind it doesn't set on now."

"I think you've damaged the leaders and tendons behind the kneecap," summarized Dr. John Beddingfield, the new assistant to Dr. McKechnie.

"Is it bad?" William asked the young doctor.

"Well, I'll have to relocate the kneecap, lets hope none of the blood vessels were torn. Nurse, will you hold down Mr. Morris's shoulders and arms please. He pushed a bone spatula between William's teeth. "Bite hard on that please ... or would you rather I gave you laudanum?" William shook his head, before the excruciating pain made him feel feint. With great skill the displaced joint was put back into place.

"You can let him go now nurse and help me position the splints please."

"Yes, doctor. Do you think he'll be all right? Will he be able to walk again?"

"Probably, but it will be with some difficulty. There's a lot of other bone damage. It's unlikely he will be able to bend that leg much. But at the end of the day he was lucky. Not many men live to tell the tale when the pit roof comes down." William lay listening to them talking about him as though he wasn't there.

"Doctor. Mr. Morris's wife and son are in the waiting room. Will you see them?"

"Certainly."

"How is he doctor?" Margot asked. The physician explained what he had found and what he had done.

"Now he will need nursing. In about a month, when the splints come off, he must try and bend that knee. He must not let that joint stiffen."

"Will he walk again?" David asked.

"Probably, but it will be with some difficulty. It's doubtful if ever he will be one hundred per cent mobile."

"Let's be grateful for small mercies," Margot said.

"Said a similar thing myself, just a few minutes ago. Now, would you like to go in and see him?"

"Yes, please doctor, and thank you—thank you for looking after him.

"What you going to do about the pit?" Patrick asked William on one of his regular visits. "I mean that young lad they've put marrers with me is all right but he'll never be as good as you. We were a good pair weren't we?"

"Yes, we were Patrick but I don't doubt that's over. It's now two months since the accident and I still can't walk properly. Mr. Stobbart's man came to see me yesterday and offered me a job as a banksman but I've no fancy working on the surface. Your Michael says Joseph can find work for me, but it sound a bit like sympathy. What do you think?"

"Me? I'd go to the ironworks. Why man, the pay's twice what banksmen get!" William took his friend's advice. He became one of the few miners to leave the pit to work in the ironworks, adapt and stick at it.

"I bet nobody else but Richard Blackman could have stopped that machine," Squeak said to his brother.

"Do you think he's the strongest man in the world?" young Will asked. "Were you there? Did you see what happened?" In the workshop, machinists toiled, turning down the rollers worn by the squeezing of the billets. Four turners and two apprentices were kept busy as giant lathes driven by huge belts revolved the rollers against the turner's chisel. Twelve-year-old John Raine, a clerk and son of the under-manager, had stopped to talk to one of the apprentices when his coat became snagged on the belt. The mechanism was pulling him in, as an angler pulls in a large fish, until Richard heard his screams. Grabbing the canvas drive-belt with one arm he somehow managed to slow down the flywheel around which it endlessly revolved. With his other arm, he reached an iron bar and threw off the cinch to halt the machine.

"He would have been mincemeat if Richard hadn't saved him."

"Ugh, that's awful," said young Will. "Who was the other lad he saved?"

"You know him, it was the policeman's lad."

The son of police constable Anthony was ticketing railway flat wagons upon which lay finished lengths of line. Given a small push, the laden wagon gained momentum and rallied down the incline, hooking on to its predecessor. The screams brought Richard from the weighbridge. The boy's trouser leg had wrapped itself around the brake pin and he was hanging on, attempting to prevent his puny legs from being severed between wheels and track. Unable to reach the shielded brake, Richard grabbed the side of the moving wagon and dug his heels into the rocky surface. He held firm as the wagon slowed then finally stopped. Behind him, his feet had dug a rut almost fifty yards long and six inches deep into the ground alongside the railway track.

"He must be the strongest man in the world," Will concluded.

The ironworks trade fluctuated but generally prospered.

"Have you heard what the Auckland Herald is saying about Witton Park?" Tamar asked Michael.

"No, what?"

"They're saying some people here have too much money for their own good."

"They could be right," Michael replied as he poked the kitchen fire. Earnings from the ironworks and local mines were astronomical compared to other industries, but were nevertheless often squandered and resulted in destitution for some. Not used to such sudden wealth, some men drank or gambled away their wages and their families suffered.

"Do you think these 'Tommy Tickets' are working? They sound a good idea."

"No, but I think Joseph's new plan might help." In an attempt to protect the vulnerable wives and children, the company had introduced 'Tommy Tickets'. As part of the wage packet, the tokens could be exchanged for provisions. Although a well-intended idea, it was open to abuse and some men sold the tickets in public houses for half their face value, which just increased the misery for their families. The new scheme—a variation on the old—worked better. Wives or mothers of company workers could receive provisions and the money was deducted from the wage packet. Despite the benevolent paternalism of Joseph Vaughan, resentment existed among many who felt that they should be able to spend their money at any store, and not just those owned by the company. But while some chose to throw away every penny, a few saved for a rainy day and the more prudent and sober families prospered with help from mutual help societies.

"What else does the paper say?" Michael asked.

"Listen to this," she said.

"In Bishop Auckland, gangs of men—some carrying revolvers—are now a common sight as the Fenian Brotherhood spreads. Meetings throughout the neighbourhood are taking place in members' houses. The movement also is spreading into the public houses of the town. The Town Head area, at the top of Newton Cap bank, is the Fenian's stronghold. Residents and travellers have complained that they dare not use the riverside path to Escomb and beyond. Fights involving the Irish community are commonplace. One victim of a gang assault told this newspaper that he had to swim and re-swim the river three times in order to escape men with coshes and a knife."

"Bet Hickey is in among it all."

"I bet!" Tamar said as she handed the paper to Michael.

"Will your lads be ready for the bank holiday show?" Richard asked his neighbour as they crossed the yard.

"They'll be fine. They'll sing like nightingales, you mark my words," he replied as both men vanished into their privies. Mr. Jones was very proud of his exiled 'men from the mountains'. Rehearsals were well under way for the first village flower show and gala. The grounds of Witton Castle were to be opened to the public for the day. Over the years, he had groomed his Welsh singers, vowing secretly that one day he would take them to Wales where they could compete in a truly Welsh eisteddfod. Both men emerged at the same time and stopped to chat over the low wall that divided the small concrete back yards.

"You're conducting the brass band as well as your male voice choir aren't you?"

"I certainly am. I'm pleased ... you know what they say don't you?"

"No, what?"

"Idle hands are the instruments of the devil."

"Do they now? Well yours won't get much chance to be idle will they? Waving that baton about all day."

"No, they won't. I'm looking forward to it and I think the village is too."

"Yes, everybody's on about it. Just hope there's no trouble."

"I hope so as well. Right. See you later. Gotta go to work."

The event was to be staged over two days, the Saturday and the holiday Monday, keeping the Sabbath intact. Day one would be the horticultural show and classes of small livestock as well as the much-awaited first homing pigeon race. David and three other pigeon fanciers had entrusted Squeak and his girlfriend to travel to York, liberate six birds from each loft and return.

"Now, Squeak you make sure you get the Gladstone train there and back won't you?" David instructed.

"What's the Gladstone train, David?" Will asked his elder brother.

"Back in forty-four our prime minister, Mr. Gladstone, brought in a railway act. This said that each company has to run one passenger train a day along the length of their line, at the cheap rate of one penny a mile."

"Is that how we got here? On the Gladstone train?"

"That's right, but not you. You were born here, weren't you?"

"Oh, aye"

Each pigeon carried in its leg band a number signed by Colonel Chaytor, and the owner of the first bird home and presented at the gala was to receive a pewter tankard. The committee, anticipating a drop in attendance on the Monday, engaged a circus, the highlight of which was that Miss Simmonette, daughter of the licensee of the Queens Head and favourite local artiste, would entertain. Boldly, she would enter the lion's cage and sing 'Break the news to Mother'. Witton Castle was only half a mile from the top of Black Road in the village. Estate staff occupied the two lodges at the entrance and exit to a circular drive that was only just wide enough for one carriage and formed a one-way system in and out of the grounds. Local people never used the road behind the first lodge as it was reputedly haunted. Woven throughout the ages, a tapestry of secrets, legends and myths became part of the fabric of Witton Castle, including that of the headless coach driver. No one who had heard the ghostly tale walked down the first lodge route. According to local superstition, each Halloween, a team of horses pulling a coach and driven by a headless driver appeared. Numerous accounts existed of it halting, as though to collect unsuspecting passengers. The folklore was so strong that—on Halloween especially—even estate workers would walk the extra half-mile to the second lodge to enter.

In the twelfth century, Henry II granted the Witton lands to the Prince Bishop, Henry de Pudsey. From the protection of the castle walls, knights had ridden out to fight at Agincourt. The same walls, besieged by Cromwell's men, had witnessed the master fall down the stairs and break his neck. Over the years the castle had burned to the ground and been rebuilt. At one time it fell into so much decay that the stone was bought and carted away. Rebuilt once more it survived the centuries.

At weekends and on holidays, Patrick Bryan threw himself into the role of doting grandfather.

"You'll keep your promise this weekend won't you Patrick? No drink at all?"

"I've said I would, haven't I?"

"Aye and you've said it all before. But this time you spoil the bank holiday weekend and I swear I'll swing for you, so I will."

"Stop your worrying woman. The weekend hasn't started yet and you're at it."

"Just you remember."

"How could I forget?" Patrick said with finality.

"I think the whole village is here," Annie said to Margot as they stepped onto the castle lawns. On the way from Black Road, Patrick had eyed the New Inn guardedly, thinking that maybe later he could sneak away for half an hour or so.

"Look at that bird—what is it? Why I've never seen anything as beautiful."

"It's a peacock, look there's another one over there." The bird nearest stood motionless with its tail fanned. Little Jacob in Tamar's arms pointed.

"Mammy look at the bird, it's got lots of eyes painted on its tail. Can you see?"

"Yes, I can see. Look over there. Who's that? It's your Grandpa Patrick."

"Grandpa," the little lad shouted as he wriggled down from his mother's arms and ran to him. "Will you take me to see the lions, Grandpa?"

"C'mon then, but I don't know if they're here yet." There was so much happening thoughts of the New Inn quickly faded as the morning flew over.

"I hear there's a pigeon back?" Patrick said to William.

"Already?" He took the pocket watch out of his waistcoat and opened the front. "Eeh, is that the time already. I had no idea did you?"

"No, I didn't. Like a man said 'doesn't time fly when you're enjoying yourself'?"

"Did you hear whose bird won? It wasn't our David was it?"

"No, they reckon he was second. Bill Atkinson is said to have come first."

"Never mind, second's not bad, eh?"

"Not at all," said Patrick.

"Did you win anything on the side stalls, Da?" Michael asked his father.

"Came close on a couple."

"So you never won nothing?"

"Well, er, no ... if you put it that way. Is it time to go yet?"

"Yes, I think so. I'll round up the tribe and we'll be off, shall we?"

"Aye, maybe I'll have better luck on Monday."

On the Monday, people arrived at the castle in droves. The circus and field sports were a big attraction. Tickets for the show in the big tent sold fast. Many arrived early to make sure they got to see the lions. Others hoped to see the lions eat Miss Simmonette. On the Saturday, Patrick had enviously scrutinised people winning dolls, commemorative earthenware mugs, and other trivia but he had not even won a booby prize.

"Today is going to be different," he thought. "Today I'm determined to win that prize of five pounds." Patrick intended to be the first person ever to climb the 'greasy pole'. A straight pine tree about two feet in diameter had been felled and stripped of bark and branches. The whole trunk was plastered in yellowish axle grease. Nailed to the end that was raised to the sky was a new, white, five-pound note. Hoisted upright, the pole was dropped into a hole that was then filled to support the naked tree trunk in a vertical position.

"What in heaven's name are you doing, Patrick?" said his wife as she watched in amazement as Patrick began to strip off his clothes.

"I'm going to get you that five pound note."

"You're mad," she exclaimed.

"That is as may be, but I'm going to climb that pole I tell you. You just watch me."

Patiently he waited as barefoot contestants struggled to get to grips with the tree. One after another he watched them fail. When his turn arrived, Patrick stripped to the waist and looked up the long smooth greased column where he could see the white bank note, fluttering in the breeze at the top.

"This is how it's done," he declared as he launched himself at the pole. He ran, jumped and hung onto the grease-smeared wood and remained there as though stuck. Without unlocking his arms he slid them up the pole gripping tight, then pulling his legs up behind him, he locked all his muscles, but he felt himself slide a little. His first move had advanced him one foot but he had slid back by six inches. Including his leap, still his feet were only a yard from the ground and his arms and shoulders over twenty feet from the prize.

All of Patrick's family and friends were amazed and speechless, except Michael.

"C'mon Da, you can do it," he shouted. Nudging Tamar gently in the ribs he said, "Shout Tamar, shout for him." Soon, the whole crowd was shouting encouragement. The older grandchildren sought out the rest of the family and urged them to come and watch their grandfather.

"Never mind, Da, you did well to stay up so long," Michael said as his father slithered back to earth.

"I'm not done yet son. It'll not beat me. That was just round one." As Patrick mounted his next assault on the face of the pole, Annie stood, aghast.

"Now I *know* he's mad," she said to daughter Jane.

His toe found the tiny remnant of a sawn off branch, but to Patrick, virtually hanging on by his toenails, it felt like the rung of a ladder. Advancing and sliding he laboured for over quarter of an hour and he was tiring. As he reached halfway point more people started to gather. The crowd seemed equally divided as to success or failure. Aching muscles needed re-oxygenating and he paused before making his next move. He slipped back slightly to a small gasp from some of the crowd while others urged him on. Exhausted, he eventually slid to the ground to loud applause and commiseration from the crowd. As Annie looked at the greying hair of his chest flattened and his navel filled with grease, her expression said it all.

"You'd better go and get some of that grease off. Wash up in that little stream we saw as we came in."

"I'm not finished yet. That was only round two. You watch if anyone can climb that bloody thing it'll be me. No one else but *me*."

"Go get washed, Da. No one's stayed up as long as you I think they should give you the fiver."

"Give? No way. I'll win that fiver fair and square, you watch me I tell you."

"All right, Patrick, but in the meantime will you please get a wash and put some clothes on?" Annie asked. Walking dejectedly, he set off for the stream scattering the displaying peacocks.

"Excuse me," he said to a group of house servants who had watched his exertions.

"We thought you did well there, mister. Thought for a moment you were going to make it, didn't we?" Her colleagues nodded in agreement.

"Thanks very much. So near yet so far eh? You wouldn't have a bar of soap I could borrow would you?"

"Certainly, mister. I'll get you one out of the kitchen. Just let me empty my scuttle."

"Right, thanks. Do you want me to carry that for you, it looks heavy?"

"No, thank you, it's not that heavy and the heap where I tip it is just yonder."

"What is it?" Patrick asked.

"Ash from the fires."

"*Ash*? And you say there's a pile of it?" He followed the girl behind the east wing of the castle. The startled girl could not believe her eyes or ears.

"Exactly what I need," he said then laid down in the ash pile and rolled over and over. "Now I'll get a grip on that bloody greasy pole." With a swig from his hip flask he left the girl who stood with her mouth wide open. One more drink from his hip flask and he emerged from behind the castle, looking like a coral reef. As he strode back towards the dwindling crowd, Jacob ran to Michael.

"Daddy, Daddy there's a monster coming—look!" Michael looked over at the approaching figure but could not make it out.

"Don't be scared, it's just a clown *or something*. It won't hurt you." Just the same, Jacob asked to be taken into his father's arms. Amidst giggles, laughter and shouts of encouragement, Patrick confidentially advanced. The closer he came to Annie the greater the look of shock registered on her face.

"Is that your father?" Annie asked exasperated. Michael looked again.

"You know what. I think it is. Has he fell down the midden or something?" Michael and David broke out in hysterical laughter and

Margot stifled her mirth. Tamar now had children hanging onto her dress as she tried to calm them.

"It's only your Grandpa Bryan, don't be frightened."

"What's happened to Grandpa?" Tabitha asked.

"I don't know yet, but we'll find out shortly," she said as Patrick got within earshot.

"In Heaven's name Patrick. What have you gone and done now?"

"It's all part of the plan dear. You just trust your old Patrick. You'll see."

"I'll tell you what I see," she said furiously. "I see a stupid man covered in ash."

"Annie, I worked it out. To get up that pole I need grip and this is what I'll get off the ash."

"Patrick Bryan everyone in Cornwall said I was marrying a mad man. I think it must have been me who was mad."

"Be patient, I'll show you who is mad—and it ain't me." Patrick stepped up to the pole once again. He slowly retreated five paces, looked up and then ran and sprang at the pole. Though winded, he locked tight and held his position with head and shoulders ten feet above the ground. The ash coating was working as cautiously he drew up his body and legs like a caterpillar. Each move saw him two foot higher than the last, and at each advancement the crowd roared him on.

"Do you know what? I think he is going to make it!" David said.

"I hope so," said Michael. "Just for his sake, for I don't think Ma's too happy." When Patrick got within six feet of the top, anxious looks appeared on the faces of the organisers who never dreamt anyone could actually win the money. With three feet left Patrick was tiring visibly, and he had to decide quickly whether to continue with caution and risk his strength ebbing, or to make one last thrust and risk slithering back to earth.

"Go for it Patrick, lad," he said to himself. "Go for it!"

Summoning all of his remaining strength, he hurled himself skywards. The feel of non-greasy wood under his fingers told him he had made it, and he picked off the five-pound note and held it aloft as the crowd below sent up a cheer that was heard for miles around. Patrick controlled his descent, waiving his prize for all to admire. As he landing back on the ground people surged forward to congratulate him but stopped short of actual contact. The coat of grease, red and black cinder ash and shiny tallow made him look a frightful sight. He picked his way towards an embarrassed Annie.

"I told you I'd do it. Do you forgive me now? After all I did it all for you." He presented her with the fair's major prize, one white bank note, greasy, but still worth over one week's wages. She smiled sweetly at her husband.

"C'mon Mr. Bryan. Let's be getting you home and in the bath tub shall we?" she said as he gathered up his clothes and boots.

By evening, news was reaching the village that a Fenian riot that had taken place in Bishop Auckland. According to available information twelve Irishmen, two armed with revolvers, were involved in a serious disturbance that resulted in the shooting of a police constable. The man who brought the news believed that Seamus Hickey was among those arrested.

Chapter Eleven

"How come you got involved in the cause then, Seamus? I mean, you with English royal blood in your veins?" Hickey looked angrily at his cellmate who stood on tiptoe to gaze out over Durham City. Through the barred window he could see people free to come and go.

"What of it? What if I have? Are you wanting to make something of it?" Hickey replied furiously. Submissively the man looked to Hickey but avoided eye contact.

"Seamus, I meant nothing by it. I'm your mate am I not? It's just what I heard ... it doesn't mean notten. You're as good an Irishman as ever I've known." From over in the corner a young man spoke.

"Lads, lets not be fighting among oursels. We're all true Fenians and we're all together in this mess. Lets get out of this pig hole and get back to fighting the fiken Brits and not each other." Hickey calmed a little.

Seamus Hickey's mother was a servant girl. She had been in service at the Irish household of a titled English landowner since she was thirteen.

"Katie," the master said to her as she fetched his breakfast. "Make sure Master Edward's room is aired and ready for Wednesday will you? He should have arrived by then according to this letter. I do hope he has learned something while at Eton. And please tell cook to do something special for dinner will you? That will be all."

"Yes, sir."

"One more thing, Katie."

"Yes, sir?"

"How long have you been with us now?"

"Over five years sir. Will that be all, sir?"

"Yes, that will be all. I just wondered." Katie left the bedroom and returned to the downstairs servants area.

"The master has asked me to tell you that Master Edward is coming home for the holidays. He wants something special for Wednesday's dinner."

"Fine," the cook said. "Well, maybe not for goosey, goosey gander I suppose."

Edward, the only son of the family, was a dashing, handsome young man, good-looking but youthfully promiscuous. He spent as little time as possible on the family estate. Time at home during the term breaks was always minimal. The rural Irish way of life bored him and he yearned for London's social life. The cost of keeping up such a lifestyle, for a student, was impossible and fell upon his widowed father and benefactor. So when his father wrote that he was overdue a visit he quickly complied. While walking the estate aimlessly one day, he rounded a corner and bumped into Katie Hickey.

"I am dreadfully sorry, Katie, I was miles away. Please let me help you up."

"It's no bother, sir. I am sure it was my fault, not looking where I was going."

"Neither of us can see around corners, can we? Are you all right?" Katie, regaining her composure, pulled back her mane of fiery red hair and tied it loosely at the nape of her neck. Edward looked at her with interest. How could he have not noticed this beautiful Irish girl previously? Her eyes were the brightest green, no emeralds held such beauty.

"Will I see you again?" he asked.

"Probably, sir, depending on how long you intend staying this time."

"Until you agree to take a walk with me."

"And what would your father have to say about that?" she mocked.

"We need not tell him. I can keep a secret if you can."

"No thank you, sir. I'm sure that there are plenty of ladies in the area who would be too pleased to take you up on your offer though."

"It's not them I wish to walk with. Please may I see you tomorrow."

"I'll be working all day. I'm off to collect blackberries for cook."

"Then I'll come with you," Edward said with an air of confidence.

"There's no law to stop you I suppose."

"Even if there was, it couldn't. Tomorrow you and I shall pick blackberries. I shall ask cook to put up a picnic basket for us."

"You'll have tongues wagging sir. You mark my words."

"Let them wag, I don't care."

"But I do, sir. I don't know what you think of me but I assure you I am not that kind of girl.

"Katie, please forgive me. There is no way I meant to insult you. Look may be I am being forward but I see no harm in two young people picking blackberries. Do you?"

No sir, there's no harm in that. But I'm sure you know what I mean."

"I get the message loud and clear and I promise to be on my best behaviour."

Edward, after his initial lustful interest became totally absorbed with Katie. By the autumn, the eighteen-year-old girl was pregnant. Edward seemed unperturbed and innocently assured her that, 'everything would be all right'. But every thing was not to be all right. He went to his father and asked for permission to marry Katie. His father's reaction was totally unexpected. He had reckoned on chastisement, or threats of disinheritance. Even the threat of being sent off to some obscure war seemed inevitable but his father would relent. After all he was an only son and he had never been refused him – *until now*. Lord Lowery swung between anger and mirth. At first he laughed at the suggestion but as Edward pressed him for permission it turned to anger. Even the thought of his son and heir wished to marry some peasant servant girl infuriated him. He could not believe that he was expected to give his blessing to such an outrageous union. Within the week, Edward was back at college and Katie was dismissed from service.

In disgrace, and broken hearted, she returned to her parents' small tenant farm. She was given no shoulder to cry on from her father. A dried up and bitter person with sandy hair and ginger whiskers, he had the coarse red complexion of those given to excessive drinking.

"Pregnant, so she is, eh? And to who? No less than an Englishman. I'll have no Brit bastard in this house. So I won't," he roared. "To be pregnant is bad enough, but to bring the child of an Englishman into my home? *Never.*" From then on he would rarely acknowledged his only daughter.

"Pay him no heed, he'll get over it," Katie's mother consoled her. Her mother was a kindly soul who attempted to comfort her daughter. Although unhappy with the situation she prayed that her daughter would be forgiven. The midwife who attended Katie's home birth was a wise old woman. She had seen and overcome almost every problem associated with childbirth. Following a fairly normal delivery, Katie began to haemorrhage. This was not uncommon, and the midwife administered hot water vaginal douches. At the same time she applied cold compresses onto Katie's stomach … but still the flow did not stem.

"That should slow down the bleeding," she said confidently as she washed her hands in the same basin as the compresses. "If by late tonight the bleeding hasn't stopped then mix this with some water and make plugs of absorbent cotton." She handed Katie's mother a half-filled bottle of perchloride of iron. "Take care now, you don't need a lot of it and it's not cheap. I'll collect what's left when I call in the morning." Katie lapsed in and out of consciousness which alarmed her mother, but not the old nurse.

"Don't panic," the midwife reassured her, "It's no bad thing so it's not. When she's like dat the heart doesn't beat so strong and it helps the bleeding." Opening her eyes, Katie handed her child to her mother.

"Please call him Seamus will you?" Before her mother could answer, Katie died. The midwife did what was necessary while trying to comfort Katie's mother.

"Strange, that's never happened before. I can't for the life of me work out what's gone wrong. Sure the bleeding was stopping, was it not? It's as though the girl had no will to live."

From the day he was born, Seamus was a surly child. Whether he followed trouble or trouble followed him was debatable but always he was in among it. Beatings from his grandfather were to no avail. Blinded by hate towards the English, the old man could not reconcile having an illegitimate grandson of a hated English landowner beneath his roof.

"Don't be so hard on the boy," his doting grandmother pleaded. "And remember that a tanned hide lasts for life so it does."

Edward, upon his father's death, returned to his Irish countryseat with his English bride. He married within his own class and moved into banking circles. Ireland held nothing but bad memories for him and he wanted rid of his holdings there. So he returned to set up the sale of his inheritance. While out riding he came across Katie's mother with a boy of five or six.

"Is that Katie's boy? Seamus isn't it?" he asked.

"Yes, sir, that's him."

"And a fine boy he is too. How is his mother?"

"She's dead sir. Died having him she did. We've been without her over five years now." Stunned and embarrassed, he reached in to his waistcoat pocket and withdrew a guinea, handing it to the matron. "Here. Take this for the boy. I am so sorry." With that he dug in the spurs and galloped away. Young Seamus Hickey urged his grandmother to throw away the coin that the English stranger had given her.

"Seamus, now you listen carefully to me. You must never speak of this to your grandfather, do you understand – *never*.

"Why, grandmother?

"It's for the best. Now remember not one word about the English man or the money. Swear on your mother's grave now."

"I do, grandmother. I'll never say nothing to him. Honest." He loved his grandmother and he would keep the promise. Until the day Edward returned to England, he sought out Katie's mother, and each time gave her money.

"For the boy," is all he would say before galloping away. Her secret safe from her spouse, she salted away the money for the boy's future. For Edward, it did nothing to appease his conscience.

Seamus Hickey grew into a man but not a gentleman. Locally, he was known as a bastard by birth and a bastard by nature. Few men dared cross him. A drunkard and a bully, he spent most of his youth in alehouses, working only now and then. It was during this time that he fell in with a character simply known as O'Donnell. Although he was some years older than Hickey, they were birds of a feather. When not involved in gambling, debauchery, or drinking they planned the fall of the British government. The first time Hickey was invited to supper, he met O'Donnell's two sons. Face up on the kitchen tables lay four hands of cards, left where someone had abandoned them. The sons were duplicates of their father, both in looks and mannerism. Also there was his downtrodden daughter Sadie, their mother had been driven to an early grave by beatings and neglect. The lack of a wife and mother for his two sons meant the burden fell upon the unfortunate girl. She became no more than a servant in her own home.

While gambling one night, Hickey cheated O'Donnell into owing him one hundred pounds. He knew the man had no chance of repaying such a fortune.

"You'll give me a chance to win it back though won't you?"

"Not this time. I can't." He demanded that O'Donnell pay the money immediately, or face the magistrate and debtor's prison.

"But I thought you were my friend?" an astounded O'Donnell asked.

"I am, but I'm tired of you always owing me money. Sometimes I no sooner get it back then you owe me it again. Why to be sure some times I don't know who the hell the money belongs to. You or me. This time you must square up. Look ... you know I'm a fair man, have you nothing you could barter?" The O'Donnell family looked round the hovel that they called home. The father shrugged his shoulders.

"Right," said Hickey. "For some time now I've been thinking of taking me a woman. Here's the deal: I take that daughter of yours with me and you and me are square."

"*What?*" the O'Donnell's said collectively.

"You heard. Sadie comes to look after me and the debt is square." Her father and brothers were outraged.

"And tell me this will you? While Sadie's looking after you, who's to look after us then?"

"Listen, I don't care about that. Here's my final offer." Producing a purse containing fifty guineas, he spilled the contents onto the kitchen table. While doing this with one hand, he kept the other on the butt of the revolver, concealed under his coat. Then he carefully replaced the shining coins, one by one, back into the leather purse.

"I'll write off the debt and give you them fifty guinea coins for the girl."

"I dunno," said the father, "I'll have to think about it. Lets have another drink while I'm thinking." Three bottles of whisky later, all the men were in agreement. Fifty guineas plus the gambling debt was a fair price, though no one bothered to consult Sadie.

Sadie's initial reaction was one of joy, as for years she had looked for a way out of her misery. Her elation was to be short lived. She soon discovered she had simply exchanged one life of hell for another; for life with Hickey was hell. He took her back to where he and his ageing grandmother shared a tiny home. There she had the tasks of the household heaped upon her, just as her father had done. For the first time she witnessed the demonic side to Hickey's nature. The black moods that overtook him and sent him into violent rages frightened her. Upon delivering him a girl child, Sadie hoped things might improve but if anything, they worsened and the beatings became more regular.

Ireland, in the grip of famine, was a population on the move, and Hickey decided to join the exodus. Upon being bluntly informed that her grandson was to leave for England, she waited until he went out.

"Sadie, I'm going to show you something. You must never tell Seamus what I am about to tell you." Using the strong blade of a meat cleaver she prised open a short floorboard.

"This money was given to me by his father. It was for him but I suppose he thought over the years I'd spent it. I never told him I had saved every penny. Here. Look." From inside the rusty tin she produced her cache of money. Sadie had never imagined that there was so much money in the whole world.

"Many's a time I was going to give it to Seamus but he would have just gambled it. Until now there never has been a right time. I want you to take it for you and the baby. Remember, just as I have done for years, you must guard the money and not let it be squandered. Use it carefully. Keep it for the bad times only and you'll not starve. You must know there will be lean times ahead of you, this will help."

"But what about you ... what will become of you? You may need it more than us."

"I'll be all right. I'm off to live with my sister once you have gone. I'll take no harm."

"I'll take the money, on one condition."

"What condition?"

"That you let me share with you."

"I don't want it, I tell you. I'll not need it."

"You can't be sure, things are so hard in Ireland now. And they can only get worse. Why if the price of potatoes go up again everyone will starve." Looking at the coins, Sadie divided them roughly with the edge of her hand and pushed one half to Hickey's grandmother and the grateful widow accepted the means to live out her few remaining years in her native Ireland.

"Will you come back one day?" Hickey's grandmother asked him as he was about to leave.

"Back? I'll be back that's for sure. And when I come it'll be with a gun on my back."

During his three years stay in Witton Park Hickey had worked feverishly supporting the Young Irelander party, awaiting the call to arms. In 1848, Seamus Hickey kept his word, upon receiving the command, he temporally returned to Ireland, 'gun on back'. Saint Columkill had prophesised the English would be driven out of Erin, and Seamus Hickey could not wait. His determination to be involved on that glorious day was unstinting.

Independence for the Irish was a fervour kept alive by seven hundred years of perceived wrongs and oppression. Independence was more of a passion than a desire and was an ever-burning flame in the hearts of some of the Irish. Care was taken from time to time to feed that flame with the appropriate fuel of public disorder. There was no secret plotting, there was no need for it; all the plotting was already done. It remained only to organise the various factions. Success was achieved by the establishment of 'clubs' that spread over the country with lightning speed. These clubs acted as fronts for clandestine plotting. Fifteen such clubs were formed in the space of one week. One of these, in Cork, registered two thousand members in seven days. Ireland was almost ready.

The leaders of the rebellion of 1848 had chosen Smith O'Brien as their chief. It was to prove a most unfortunate choice for his faults outweighed his assets. O'Brien was said to be in many respects wrong headed and apart from his physique he was without one commanding quality. His lieutenants, bold energetic, pushed for an immediate offensive. The peasantry and farmers did not wish to fight while crops were still in the ground as it would lead to financial ruin to many struggling to recover from the potato famine. They wanted to put off the rising from the spring until the autumn. But some leaders urged O'Brien to immediate action. Knowing that the probability of success was small a few still went along with it. In the end, the outbreak took place at least three months too late and, as expected, it proved an utter failure. Among those that rallied to the call, and fought at Ballingarry before fleeing back to England, was Seamus Hickey.

The British Government acted quickly. By the close of the year none of the leaders of 'forty-eight' committees remained in Ireland. Some were in self-exile while others were transported. One of the leaders, and Hickey's commandant, had been James Stephens who had covertly reformed the older Ribbons together with the Young Irelander Party, into the Fenian Brotherhood, taking its name from the ancient Irish warrior band of the Fianna. Everything that could be done to throw obscurity over Stephens was done. Five years after Stephens formed the Fenian secret society in Ireland, he carried the Brotherhood to

America and rumour was that it was there he fled after the uprising. Hickey, meanwhile, was lifted from a pub in Bishop Auckland and thrown into Durham jail with several others.

"Do you think they'll round up any more of the lads, Seamus?" one of them asked.

"Na. The chief saw to that didn't he? The way he has us set up now the Brit informers will never find notten out about the Brotherhood."

"Do you mean Stephens?"

"Never mention him by name! Even in here. Walls have ears you know," Hickey rebuked the man."

"Sorry, Seamus. What I was saying was it's clever the way the chief done it. I mean none of us know more than a couple of others do we? Why the bloke we work next door to could be one of us and we wouldn't know."

"Well, I tink it all to complicated for the little man. All dem codes and dat I mean. How's a man like mesel to understand all dat?"

Another asked, "Do you understand it all Seamus?"

"Aye he does," the youngest of his companions said. "Tell us again how it works Seamus."

"You all should know it, so you should. But I'll tell you all again. Now you all know who the main man is right?" He did not wait for a response, "Well, just like in any army, beneath the chief are commanders. There' a commander for each of our provinces, they are known as V's."

"Why?" one asked.

"What the fik does it matter why? As long as *you know* what they are called. Now the V's, it's their job to pick their own colonels. Let me tell you this, when one of the colonels is sworn in only two more are there."

"Why?

"Why? Why? Why? Is that all the fiken hell you can fiken say?" The man who asked the question knew Hickey was mad and shut up.

"Right you thick bastard, I'll tell you why. This way if they were ever captured by the Brits and tortured the most they could give away was two names. And the oath they take is sacred. They must swear that they will have nothing to do with the Brit monarchy and be faith full to our darlin' Irish Republic. If they ever told any body the Brotherhood's secrets, they know what they will get. They have to be able to take orders without asking why and be ready to fight at any time."

"Have they got a letter they go by?"

"Yes. We call them the A's. Like I said they're not supposed to know more than a couple more colonels. No chance of anybody betraying loads of them that way." No signatures ever appeared on documents, the validation coming from a seal. In the event of betrayal by an 'A' of a 'V', no documentary evidence could be produced against his superior.

"Then we have the captains who are picked by the colonels," continued Hickey.

"You're one of them aren't you, Seamus?" a man asked. Hickey was furious and sprang to his feet. Pointing down at the frightened man he screamed.

"What the fik have I just told you? You fiken stupid bastard! If you don't keep your fiken mouth shut, I'll shut it for you. *For good.*" The petrified man never spoke again. Hickey allowed himself to slither down the wall until he was re-seated on the stone floor of the cell.

"Now where was I? Oh aye, captains. They are known as 'B's. They only ever meet their colonels and never get to meet their province commander. It's them that picks the sergeants and it's them that picks you lot."

"I never took no oath."

"Privates don't have to," Hickey said, "But you must have done sumten good to get in."

"Aye, I did. I shot a fiken Brit soldier. The bastard didn't die though. Anyways that's why I come to England."

"What's our letter then, us privates?"

"D."

"Is that how you spell private then Michael?" one of the internees asked another.

"How the hell would I know? I suppose so. After tomorrow it might not make no difference."

All these arrangements, meant to reduce the risk of treachery' worked well. Although rare, there had been a few attempts to get the conviction of an immediate superior by a subordinate. Because of the system every instance ended in failure. The letters, V, A, B, C, D, had a constant meaning in conversation among the Brotherhood, but not so in correspondence. The same letters of the alphabet were utilised, but one that meant colonel one week, could mean a private the following, and vice versa. This way if an official letter fell into the wrong hands it would appear unintelligible, or lead to great confusion. Again the same letters written slightly differently altered their significance; a seeming innocent wrong spacing could denote weapons. Reversing the broad down stroke of the letter 'V' could mean a pike, while similarly misplacing the broad stoke of the letter 'A' could mean guns. When vice-commanders or colonels undertook an important mission they were encouraged to use aliases. This was a favourite precaution used by Stephens himself. He was known to have used dozens of different names. Adoption of the identity of a brother or anyone who bore a slight resemblance to themselves was common. Basically anybody who could provide an alibi was impersonated. The problem was, that time and time again, the wrong man, simply the owner of the name, was arrested, tried and sentenced. Anyone who suffered such an injustice dare do no more than protest his innocence. Forbidden, by oath, to say one word they usually stayed silent. Everyone knew that a single word, which might reveal a secret of the organisation, would have resulted in his or her death. Hickey graduated from the Young Irelanders into the Fenian Brotherhood and became a 'B' in every context.

The dock of Durham City Assize court was totally inadequate, as defendants numbered the same as the jury. Hasty extension work had to be undertaken and even after this was finished it would be a tight squeeze. Here Hickey and his eleven indicted associates would face a charge of attempted murder. The courthouse was on the scale of a cathedral or grand opera house. Two giant chandeliers suspended from its ceiling were capable of holding over one hundred candles apiece. At one end a high backed, red leather seatback seat was elevated almost six feet above the court floor. From here the judge would preside over the proceedings. Below, and directly in front of his walnut bench, sat the head clerk and his dominions. Facing, were two rows of church style pew seats, each cushioned and covered in red velvet, pinned down by thousands of round-headed brass tacks. On the front row sat wigged barristers in their sombre black gowns and stiff Quaker style white neckties. Alongside sat the prosecution barrister fumbling though the case papers. Seated in the row behind the barristers, the solicitors who had engaged and instructed them for their clients, sat silently. Their job was done. To their left, lay the two rows of jury seats, and directly opposite, on the other side of the room, the witness box stood isolated and empty.

Almost ten feet above and behind the witness box was a section for ladies of the public. It contained two short rows of long benches, of a similar design to the jury benches. The dock, which rose to the level of the judge's bench was square in construction, and around the top rail, pointed iron spikes protruded at small intervals. The forbidding structure was menacing and did nothing to improve the defendant's image. It conjured up a picture of a place to hold menacing and dangerous occupants. High above, at the back of the court, was the public gallery. Packed for this morning's session, many had queued for hours. So many wished to watch the Irishmen's trial that ticket had to be given out. The prisoners arrived into the dock, via spiral stairs from a small holding cell in the basement. There, iron rings fixed into the support pillars, secured the defendants until they were summoned. They arrived there through a guarded door, which led into a small narrow courtyard. The surrounding walls, which were over twenty foot high, had pieces of broken bottles fixed into mortar around the top. Each one refracted light differently spectrums of light dancing in the mid morning sun.

"Is that a rainbow up there?" one prisoner asked another.

"I don't think so," he replied.

"What will it matter to you lot?" one of the guards asked gruffly. "One way or another there'll be no pot of gold for you lot today."

"Ah fik you," the second man replied as he shuffled across the yard. The heavy strapped door on the other side of the yard led into the main body of Durham jail. It was from here, that Hickey and his companions began their journey to either freedom or incarnation. At the best, they could each expect no less than transportation to one the British colonies, if found guilty. Stepping out into the sunlight of the enclosure between the two buildings none could be certain of their future. Up the spiral staircase they were brought into the court, emerging like a jack in the box. Their burly guards made no allowance for the manacles and leg irons, which made the climb difficult.

"C'mon you filthy Irish pigs. Get a move on," came from down below as chains could be heard clanking against the iron staircase. In the dock the guards tried to control their prisoners, as they turned to scan the public gallery for friends and loved ones.

"Face the front you lot, face the court," the guards ordered. The detainees ignored them as smiles and waves lifted their spirits. Hickey waved to a solitary man in the public gallery and winked. Sadie and their daughter, Bridie, had not visited Hickey during his remand in custody. And as anticipated were not in court for today's trial.

As he turned around he caught his barrister's eye and received a reassuring smile.

"All rise and pray be silent for Her Majesty Queen Victoria's servant. The worshipful Lord Haverton." From a door behind his seat the judge made his entrance. Wigged and wearing a red cape with the coat of arms of County Durham emblazoned on the breast, his white stockings and breeches gave him an almost a theatrical appearance. As the court officials, solicitors and barristers bowed to the renowned arbiter, the defence was under no allusions as to the enormity of the task ahead. After the judge was seated and acknowledged the advocates with a nod of his head, the court usher spoke.

"The prisoners will remain standing, the rest may be seated." The prosecution formally introduced himself to the judge and outlined the states case.

"And who represents the defendants?" he asked. Twelve barristers rose to their feet from the front bench. The judge counted along the line.

"*Twelve* of you? Why so many? Could one not have done the job? I warn you if this is some form of delaying tactic your clients will be sorry. This case is set down for three days, and three days it will be. Not one minute more. Do you all understand?"

"Yes m'lord," a chorus of defence lawyers answered.

The day dragged as each submitted legal arguments. Solicitors sitting behind the advocates constantly passed notes to their colleague, in reverend silence. Legal argument after legal argument were either accepted or rejected until all were spent. Mid-afternoon, the judge declared that he would leave the swearing in of the jury until the following morning.

"This court will adjourn until ten o'clock in the morning. Guards, take the prisoners back to their cells."

"All rise," called the usher.

The following morning the histrionic grand entrance of the judge was repeated. Then the swearing in of the jury began after which the Queen's Counsel, engaged for the Crown, opened the prosecution.

"My lord, members of the jury. During this case I will prove to you that, beyond reasonable doubt, the felon who shot Police Constable Walkington is in the dock of this court today. I will also prove to you that although only one man pulled the trigger, firing the near fatal shot, all were bent on murder. Who better to give you a true account but the poor victim himself? For my first witness I call Police Constable Walkington to the stand.

After a confident start, guided by the prosecution barrister, and constant references to his note book, the police officer gave all the right answers to the QC's questions.

"Can you tell this court if the man who shot you is in court today?"

"Yes sir, he is."

"Can you point him out to us please?"

"Yes sir, it was him", he replied, pointing to the dock.

"Which one exactly?"

"That one sir. The one with the long black hair... and the scars on his face. Standing next to the guard so he is."

"Do you know his name?"

"Yes sir. I have come to know him as Seamus Hickey."

"And the rest of the defendants, did they try and stop him?"

"No sir,"

"In fact they encouraged him, didn't they?"

"Yes sir."

"Thank you Constable, that will be all. Please stay there, I believe my learned colleagues may have a few questions for you" Hickey's lawyer was quick to his feet.

"Constable Walkington, my name is Steen and I am here today to represent Mr. Hickey. How are you? You have recovered well from your ordeal it appears.

"Yes sir. Thank you, sir."

"Constable Walkington let me ask you, do you know exactly how many men were involved in the fracas? Was there more than the dozen you see here today?"

"Yes sir, we couldn't catch them all. A lot of them ran away after the gun fire."

"Would you say there was ... more than twenty?"

"Possibly sir."

"Perhaps more than fifty then?"

"I'm not sure sir." The constable looked nervously for help from the prosecution council. Hickey's lawyer sensed his uncertainty.

"Perhaps your notes might help you? Would you like to look at them?"

"Thank you sir," He said and reached into the breast pocket of his tunic. Rattled by the question he dropped his notebook out of the dock onto the courtroom floor.

"Here let me help you," Hickey's advocate said as he handed the small jotter back to the nervous policeman. He waited while the officer frantically thumbed the pages.

"I don't seem to have that written down sir," he apologised.

"Right. Let us say then that there could have been as many as fifty men involved. Yes or no?"

"Well there could have been I suppose."

"Constable Walkington, I'll ask you again. Could there have been as many as fifty men involved in the disturbance? Yes or no?"

"Yes, sir."

"Thank you, officer. Now would you please tell the court how long have you been stationed in Bishop Auckland?"

"Three weeks, sir."

"Is that all?"

"Yes sir."

"Earlier you said that you *now know* my client, Mr. Hickey. Did you know him before the unfortunate shooting?"

"No, sir."

"Yet you say that today you can recognise my client as the man who shot you?"

"Yes, sir."

"Could you please tell the court how many shots were fired that day?"

"I don't know sir, there was lots."

"Lots? How many guns did you see? More than one?"

"Yes, sir."

"So you are telling this court that several men were armed? Could it not have been another who shot you?"

"No, sir. It was definitely Hickey."

"Constable Walkington. You would not like an innocent man to be found guilty would you?"

"No, sir."

"Do you realise that for the state to find my client, or any of the others, guilty of attempted murder the courts must be satisfied, beyond reasonable doubt, who pulled the trigger."

"Yes, sir."

"You do? And do you still insist it was my client and my client alone who shot you?"

"I do, sir."

"Tell me, Constable ... were you scared when you were looking down the barrel of the gun?"

"Yes, sir."

"Weren't you in fact petrified?"

"I suppose so."

"Yes or no, constable."

"Yes, sir,"

"So petrified that in fact you don't really know who shot you?"

"No, sir, I can remember every detail."

"Can you now? Then can you tell the court with which hand the gunman held the weapon?"

"With his right sir?"

"Are you positive?"

"Yes, sir."

"Would you tell the court was there anything unusual about the hand that held the gun?"

"No, sir, nothing." The barrister turned towards the dock.

"Mr. Hickey would you hold up your right hand and show it to the court." Rolling back his coat sleeve Hickey slowly raised his hand. A gasp ran round the courtroom as the judge beat his gravel for order. The mutilated hand transfixed the court. All could see the missing first joint of the thumb and the missing first two fingers.

"That will be all Constable. Thank you." Sitting discreetly at the back of the public gallery Patrick Bryan remembered the first time he had seen Hickeys hand. It had been when they had arrived at Bishop Auckland railway station from Liverpool.

"I have no further questions for this witness Milord. Thank you," he said then sat down to a slap on the back from his colleagues.

"Has anyone else any further questions for this witness, if not he may step down."

"I would like to call the second officer to the stand if it pleases your worship," another of the defence barristers requested.

"Carry on Mr. Holmes," the judge replied. "But please be quick. Do we really need more police testimony?"

"Thank you sir, I will take but a minute of the courts time. I simply wish to corroborate a point."

"Well and good, Mr. Holmes." Into the dock came the first officer on the scene after the shooting. He stated that he had arrived within a minute of hearing the first of five or six shots. Under cross-examination he concurred that there possibly could have been up to fifty people involved.

"And what did you see when you arrived?"

"I saw several men with guns and constable Walkington laid on the floor. Hickey was stood nearby."

"You're positive it was Hickey and not my client?"

"It was either Hickey or O'Connell, I'm positive. There seemed to be hundreds around him I had to push them back. They were all just standing there. Not one of them came to his aid as he lay groaning." Reading from notes the barrister looked to the dock.

"Constable, you have just said to this court, and I quote, "It was either Hickey or O'Connell, I'm positive", end quote. Is that correct?"

"Yes, sir."

"That, Constable, is as big a contradiction in terms as I have ever heard in a court of law. I have no more questions for you, thank you." Four inhabitants of the town head, the scene of the shooting, received summonses to appear as prosecution witnesses. Their testimonies wildly contradicted one another's, and that of the police. The prosecution was furious.

"My lord, I think it is obvious that these prosecution witnesses have been intimidated. They have not come to this court today and told the same stories they gave to the police. I ask this court to consider them hostile witnesses and strike their evidence."

"I really don't see the point Mr. Holmes. But I will advise the jury that it may be prudent to ignore their testimony. Now get on with your case will you please."

"Yes sir, may I call for the Crown, Mr. David Smythe, gunsmith."

Despite an initial air of self-importance, the gun expert was unable to handle hundreds of questions from twelve defence counsels. The barrister of one defendant enquired.

"How much of your income do you obtain from work undertaken on behalf of the government? For example do you supply weapons as well as collect fees for work such as this?"

"Yes sir, I do."

"Milord under these circumstances would it not be prudent to disqualify this witness as hostile? He obviously cannot be impartial." The court erupted in laughter. Down came the gravel repeatedly, bringing the court to order, as the hilarity ebbed.

"I warn you, Mr. Firbank, any more frivolous remarks and I will hold you in contempt.

"I am sorry, sir."

"And any more disturbances and I will clear the gallery," he barked.

"Is this the weapon recovered from the scene where PC Walkington was shot?" He handed a revolver to the gunsmith. After examining the pistol he replied.

"Yes sir, there's where I marked it. He pointed to an initial scratched on the butt.

"Could you tell from your examination how many bullets had been fired through it?"

"Bye the amount of powder, I would say, one, no more than two."

"But our second policeman told this court that he heard five or six shots. How could this be?"

"There must have been more than one person firing."

"And more than one gun?"

"I would have thought so."

"You have no proof who the gun belongs to have you? Or who fired it?"

"No, I haven't"

"Nor have you any proof that, in fact it is the actual weapon that fired the shot in question. Have you?"

"No, sir."

"Furthermore, you have not been able to match the bullet to this gun have you?"

"No, sir. I have not."

"Would you tell the court why not?"

"Because the bullet could not be recovered and remains lodged in the constable's body."

"Thank you, Mr. Smythe. That will be all," He turned to the judge. "Sir I suggest that this witness's testimony is irrelevant and had no meaningfulness to this case. The defence do not deny that this gun was found at the scene but cannot be connected to any one individual."

"Does the defence wish to call any more witnesses do you know, Mr. Firbank?"

"Sir, I have been asked to inform you that each of the defendants are prepared to take the oath. They readily admit being involved, with others, in the skirmish, but had no intention of murdering anyone, least of all a police constable. Each will deny firing the weapon that caused the policeman's injury."

"I think that will not be necessary. That will be written into the records and taken into account by the jury."

"Thank you my lord." The judge summing up was clear and precise.

"You the jury must find the defendant or defendants guilty of attempted murder *beyond a reasonable doubt*. You must be certain that both the *actus rea* and *mens rea* both existed. The *mens rea* requires proof that there was a 'guilty mind' or that intention, recklessness, or negligence existed. This was so in The Harlot's Case of 1560 where a police officer had been wounded." He shuffled around his ribboned papers before reading from one.

"*Actus non facet reum nisi mens sit rea*. This translated means the mere doing of an act will not constitute guilt unless there be a guilty intent. Conduct, circumstance and consequences must be in place, with such a result of human conduct as the law seeks to prevent. I will try to impartially explain that 'he who asserts must prove'. That means that the burden of proof is on the prosecution alone, and the burden or onus lay upon the prosecution. Throughout a case the prosecution may try to rebut the presumption that a defendant is innocent until proven guilty. But firstly you, the jury, must be satisfied that the guilty person or persons were in the dock. Furthermore you must be certain that it was the intention of the group to murder the police constable. On this you must be certain 'beyond a reasonable doubt' who fired the shot. Reasonable doubt means, that which would appear reasonable to the man in the street.

"If the prosecution convinces you, the jury, that some, or all, of the defendants intended to murder PC Walkington, you should return a 'true bill'. If you feel that the prosecution has failed to prove malice aforethought, guilt or failed to identify the assailant you should acquit." The jury retired but by nightfall had failed to reach a verdict. Sending the jury to a hotel for the night, the prisoners returned to the squalid conditions of Victorian imprisonment.

The following morning at ten o'clock the judge had to send the jury out once more, to continue their deliberations. By noon, having failed to reappear, the judge sent for the foreman, who explained that they were no nearer then, than the night previous, to reaching a verdict.

"Then this court shall be adjourned until two o'clock in the forenoon. Sergeant at Arms, arrange that food be taken to the jury room. Perhaps they can decide while they eat." The court emptied and those able, retired for lunch while the shackled prisoners received a drink of water. At two o'clock the court had reassembled and the jury filed in. The clerk of the court rose to greet them.

"Gentlemen of the jury have you reached a verdict?" he asked.

"We have," replied the foreman.

"Is it in the matter of all the defendants?"

"It is."

"Please tell this court. Have you brought a 'true bill' against the charges or an 'untrue bill'?"

"Being unable to identify who fired the shot, we bring to the court an 'untrue bill'."

"And so say you all?"

"We do." The judge in acquitting all the defendants ordered that the revolver and ammunition be confiscated and destroyed. The Fenian elements of Witton Park and Bishop Auckland celebrated for a week.

Chapter Twelve 1861 - 1865

In the week following the acquittal of Hickey and his compatriots, Sadie, with her now-familiar blackened eyes, wandered the village, avoiding her partner.

"Tell the next patient to come in nurse will you please." Into Doctor McKechnie's surgery came Sadie with her child Bridie.

"I'm wondering if you can have a listen to the child's chest," she said. "She seems a little wheezy to me."

"Is there a cough?" Bridie stood quietly nodding her head. "Right, let's have a listen." He picked up his ear trumpet. The coldness of the rubber made the child flinch.

"I'm sorry, child. Was that cold?" Bridie nodded her head once more and the kindly doctor smiled at her.

"Well," he said, "There seems to be nothing much wrong. Would you like me to make you up a bottle of linctus?"

"No, thank you sir. I can take care of it at home. I wouldn't have bothered you if it had been for myself. But when it's the wee one its different isn't it?"

"Sadie, I know exactly what you mean. Will you tell me why, in all the years I have been doctor here, never once have I attended you?"

"I don't really know, sir."

"Then will you tell me about the bruising on your face?"

"Sir, I'm a clumsy woman always walking into things, or falling down, so I am," The old practitioner did not believe a word, but had long ago decided that he had been put on earth to heal, not judge. "Anyway, it'll be gone by the morning." She became slightly anxious by the doctor's questions she asked how much she owed.

"Nothing, nothing at all. Let's say all new patients get my services free of charge for the first visit shall we? I'd like to see the child again in about a week."

"Thank you, thank you sir," Sadie whispered. "While I might not always remember your face, I will always remember your kindness." The sincerity in her voice warmed the heart of the old man as he watched her leave. Within two days, all signs of bruising had vanished and her complexion was flawless. When they returned to the surgery a week later to have Bridie checked over, the physician was astonished.

"It's remarkable!" he exclaimed. "The child's chest is totally clear and your face, why I would not believe it! Come closer let me see your skin. Do you know I am damned if I know which side was of your face was cut. Why, there is not a single mark. How did you do that? You must have remarkable healing power or do you know something I don't?" She smiled and made no attempt to enlighten this kind man of medicine with her secret. Sadie, like many other Irish folk, believed the blessing that St. Patrick bestowed upon the Emerald Isle dwelt in its very stones, and she held Irish stones in high esteem for their healing powers. A typical stone, brought from Ireland was never allowed to touch English soil. Much sought after for its curative powers it was carried from country to country, house to-house in a basket. Pale blue in colour, they were about three and one-quarter inches thick, the surface was smooth. Although claimed that the stones were effective for anyone it was said they were most effectual in the hands of the Irish women. Carried to a patient with a sore leg, when the leg was rubbed with the stone, the wound healed. Sadie treasured her Irish stone. Repeatedly she had witnessed the healing powers upon others, and herself, but modern medicine dismissed such claims denying the possibility of such 'miracle' cures.

News in 1861 from Samuel in America was not good. The British press for some time had speculated that a civil war was imminent.

"Got a letter of our Samuel the other day, seems the Americans are going to fight each other," William said to Patrick as they nattered away over a cup of tea. Patrick took his hand a wafted away the pipe smoke that separated them over the kitchen table.

"What about?" Patrick asked.

"Seems as those in the south don't want to be part of the United States any more. Others say it's because of slavery."

"It'll not affect me," Patrick said.

"It might affect us. Samuel has volunteered as a chaplain."

"Do you mean he'll have to go where the fighting is, right to the front line?"

"Yes, he has to go wherever men need God."

"Pleased it's not me," Patrick said. "Why do they want to be fighting among themselves? Is there not enough troubles in the world?" David looked up from his book.

"It's only two hundred years since we had our own civil war. Englishmen fighting Englishmen."

"That definitely had nothin' to do with me," Patrick said. "I wasn't even a twinkle in my daddy's eye and all the Bryans were still on their farm in the home country."

"You still call Ireland the home country Patrick. Why? I mean you were born in Cornwall weren't you?" David asked.

"I was that, but of good Irish parents. And I ask you; if a cat had kittens in a dog's basket they'd still be cats wouldn't they? Well the same goes for me."

"I think I understand what you mean," said David, returning to his book.

"Anyway," said Patrick's smoking companion. "Samuel said they'd been to a place called Bull Run and it was awful. They'd had to make a run for it to escape. The men say they would rather die than be captured. They're frightened stiff of being sent to a Southern States prisoner of war camp. Some of the stories he's heard about them he would not repeat to us."

"When you write back tell him we are all thinking of him."

"Would be nice if I could tell him you were praying for him," William chided his friend.

"Na. I leave all that to you, you're better at it than me." William smiled and gently shook his head.

That Sunday, the Methodist chapel added to their prayers a request for peace on earth, and one for the deliverance of family and friends of Witton Park overseas.

Samuel was keen to have news from home and his family wrote even more regularly than before. At this time he appeared to hunger for news. He wrote how he was so sad to have missed his little brother's wedding. He could not imagine Squeak being of that age. Tamar wrote that he had matured into a handsome, lean young man, who looked so happy at his wedding. David kept him up to date on developments in the village and those affecting England.

"It seems we will support the North," he wrote, "And use our ships to blockade the South. From what I read the South will not survive long without their cotton trade. I pray to God that it will be a short war and you can return to New York. Here at home drunkenness continues to be a problem," he wrote. "Two Irish ironworkers had received a fine for leaving their place of work on St. Patrick's Day. Their action had stopped a mill with coals burnt, iron wasted and others laid off. There has been such a shortage of water, due to the erratic supply from the reservoir that people had to lock their water butts at night. The company owners had benevolently agreed to install a lead pipe from the river to help alleviate the problem."

The following year Samuel wrote proudly that the regiment to which he was attached had fought, with distinction, at a place known as Shiloh and many had received promotion in the field. The letters became compulsive reading for all. The news was almost an adventure story, but for the real loss of lives.

"A bullet went through the hat of my uniform that I must now wear. Fortunately for me it was hanging on my tent as I wrote to you. Then at the second battle at Bull Run, I had my horse shot out from beneath me. Poor animal, but I thank God that I was spared, as there is much

168

for me to do here. My days are long tending to the sick and dying. I care not what colour their uniform is. A dying man either calls out for God or his mother. I am about the closest to either that these poor souls get to see before they meet their maker."

David wrote back praising Bolckow and Vaughan for their support in building another chapel for the Presbyterian denomination. Their mother was now at the helm of the Temperance League. She was waging war with a vengeance against alcohol. But she still secretly liked Patrick Bryan.

"Well the president has done it," Samuel wrote, "He has delivered his emancipation proclamation. He intends to free all slaves. 1863 will go down in the annals of American history. Sadly this has infuriated the South even further and increased their resolve."

During the next two years David's regiment was involved in many skirmishes, but no major battles. That was until Cold Harbour in the June of 1864. He thanked his family and friends for their prayers, for he believed that only so many supplications were the reason for his survival. As he attended the dying on the field of battle musket and cannon balls fell all around him. When lying on his cot-bed at night, he wondered how he was spared when so many fell. In his letters home an increase in anxiety and tension was clearly detectable as the war dragged on for four long years. Squeak and young Will-Patrick wrote continuously, attempting to lift his spirits and longed to be with their brother at such a time. To them it sounded like a huge adventure. From thousands of miles away they could not see the futility of civil war.

"The ironworks is overflowing with work and men are earning fortunes," David wrote. "The battleground of alcohol continues but I fear Mother has her work cut out. The Baptists have moved into larger premises, and the Salvation Army has rented the old chapel. Have you seen them? They dress like soldiers and are forever rattling tambourines. They seem a good, God-fearing lot though and are not afraid to take His word to the people. Even into the public houses! Mother now has allies. Perhaps this two-prong attack, against the evils of alcohol, might make in roads, well that's what Mother hopes anyway. Patrick Bryan is in the doghouse so to speak as far as Mother is concerned. He has found somewhere yet another stray dog. That makes two he has now. This one he has called Paddy. Well you remember I told you about him finding the first one, which he called Hadaway? Well they seem to work well as a pair. Two days ago Mother was busy baking when Hadaway nipped in through the open door and stole a ham shank off the table. While she was trying to catch Hadaway, and rescue what was to be the filling for the pies, Paddy stole in and grabbed an already prepared fruit pie and took off. Was she furious?

Anyway Mother and Mrs. Bryan are still busy working at the Co-operative and the hall is in much demand. This might change soon though, for the Catholics are moving out after having held services in the hall for almost twenty years. They had received a gift of three cottages, near the top of Black Road and in future, intend to conduct their services there. In the meantime, the Church of England still appears to be making no attempt to build a place of worship. Their followers still have to walk to Escomb on Sundays and Holy days. Wedding and christening parties are a sorry lot on rainy days, I tell you. St. Patrick's day this year was frightening. Patrick Bryan, mistaken for a Fenian sympathiser, had been warned of an intended riot. People barricaded themselves in their houses and shop fronts were boarded, but the day passed without incidence."

"Good news eh, Margot? That war in America is over." Patrick said.

"It's good new indeed, I thank God."

"And the North won. Guess that's 'cos David was on their side, eh?"

"And God," added Annie.

"Well I suppose so," said Patrick, unconvinced. "Have you had a letter from him yet?"

"Not yet, but I expect we will soon."

Being aware that the 'American war' was over did not detract from the excitement when David's letter arrived. This was the first time they could be sure that he had survived to the bitter end.

"I enclose a small piece of flag, keep it safe for it really is a piece of history," he wrote. "I picked it up of the ground outside a little courthouse in a place called Appomattox. Inside the building is where the famous Southern General Lee signed surrender in April. What a wondrous place it seemed for at last this bloody war is over. Oh, how if I could have as easily picked up those fallen men and boys and sent them home. What has been gained? I doubt there is not a house in America that does not grieve. And what of the divided families? For during this war brother has slain brother and it has set father against son. Countrymen slew countrymen, and while the war is over will the country ever be as one again I wonder. Last week I attended a lavish victory party. While I did not feel comfortable in attending I was left with no choice as I now hold the position of United States Chaplain and am responsible only to the president. Here I met the North's youngest brigadier general. Have you heard of him in England, as the newspapers here seemed filled with his exploits? An unusual man, having a sharp nose he is not the most handsome, but none the less striking. He wears his blond curly hair shoulder length and on top of his uniform he wears a buckskin jacket. This most unusual garb, for an officer, has hundreds of tassels dangling from it, which sway like corn

170

in the wind at his slightest movement. He was with his brother, and both wore identical pearl handled revolvers, not in enclosed holsters as the army issue. 'Made in London, England' he proudly said to me. Like to try them, Chaplain?' I declined gracefully. Apparently now that the war was over, he was going out west to a state called Montana to fight some troublesome Redskins. That's what they call the native Americans here. As you will probably know by now that President Lincoln has been assassinated. The 14th April 1865 will go down in history as a day in infamy. An actor, of sorts, called Booth was the assassin, isn't there a family of that name in Witton Park? I doubt though they are related. Although I only met Lincoln twice or thrice somehow I was strongly drawn to the man. I will be attending his funeral in my official capacity."

Meanwhile in England, the village was setting standards for others to follow. Completing pioneering work, and utilising a supply from the works, it became possible to pipe gas to the houses. This was to be years before surrounding areas, including the towns enjoyed its glowing light.

"The gas light we now enjoy in our homes makes writing these letters to you so much easier," wrote Tamar. "This modern invention is of great value, especially in our dark winters. Sometimes though the pressure is so low, it would have been folly to throw away the candles. Wildness is still a problem in the village, fighting is almost being turned into a sport. Hundreds turn up to watch. Savages I call them. Just last week there was a bare-knuckle fight, held just outside the village. A puddler challenged a pitman to fight for a sovereign. Someone informed the police (no, it wasn't me!) who arrested both pugilists before a victor was obvious. They also confiscated the purse. Apparently both appeared in court, battered, bruised and bandaged, and received a fine of almost ten shillings each. Good enough for them I say. Besides the two fighters many spectators were also arrested. Those who had side wagers also had to appear in court. I'm told there was so many of them they couldn't all fit into the courtroom. Those accused of this illegal gambling simply had their names read out by the clerk of the court and the magistrate fined each person five shillings. Mrs. Bryan is furious for among them was her husband. Michael has prospered at the works as the company has had a relative good year. He tells me though that there is still some unrest among the workers over a claim they made earlier in the year. He is not so optimistic about the immediate future though. Seems there is a new way to make a new steel that is becoming more popular than the pig iron we make, so our order book is not very full. We'll have to wait and see what happens, won't we. On a lighter note I'm pleased to tell you that although the third outbreak of cholera since our arrival here has occurred, once again the village has escaped. Reports have it that the neighbourhood and indeed the whole country is ravaged."

After the escape from cholera earlier in the year, 1865 held promise for the small community. Although Joseph Vaughan was a little downbeat about forecasts for trading conditions when speaking at the annual dinner, there was nothing to suggest the disaster that would soon follow. In the spring, due to a lack of orders, the plate mill was laid idle and workers laid off. Then, within six months of the annual dinner, the giant thunderous hammers of the ironworks fell silent in July. The ironmasters proposed a ten per cent wage cut and in response the northern ironworkers went on strike refusing to accept the cut. The federation responded by locking out every ironworker, nationwide.

Over two thousand Witton Park men, unaccustomed to enforced idleness and the eerie silence, felt uneasy. The absence of the sound of the steam hammers, which for years had beat with the regularity of a metronome, placed a deathly silence, over the men Each day they appeared at the locked gates of the works. Men and boys accustomed to shouting, to make themselves heard, talked in whispers. The squeak of a young house sparrow suddenly seemed like the screech of an eagle and a drip from a tap sounded like a waterfall to them.

"David, I suppose you know why I have called you into the office today?"

"Not exactly, but I don't suppose it can be good news, is it?" David Morris replied curtly.

"Afraid not. The federation has no intention of backing down. You must tell the workers this. If they do not comply every ironworker in the country will suffer. It is intended to insist upon the surrender of company houses, otherwise any monies due will be withheld."

"That's dirty fighting, Mr. Vaughan, and you know it. It's one thing to fight the workers but to threaten their families? Are you telling me that you would put women and children out on the street?"

"If it comes to it, I will have no choice. Can you not see that my hands are tied in this matter?"

"Mr. Vaughan I want no part of this. Why have you called me in? It's the leaders of the Ironworkers Union you should be talking to, not me. I am only a local man."

"Because less than five per cent of the men on strike are members of your union, while you know all the strikers. Please try and explain to them that there is nothing else I can do. They must understand that there is solidarity between all the iron masters. They will not yield I assure you."

The pressures were now mounting on the strikers. The majority of the men received no financial assistance from any quarter. The furnacemen fared better than most with their long local history of joining and forming mutual help societies, or similar organisations. So too did the Welsh community, but for many from the feast it had become the famine. They now knew unless they capitulated they were at the mercy of their masters. The Morris and Bryan families fared better than most. With the family breadwinners divided between the ironworks and the mines for they had 'a foot in each camp'.

Over two thousand voices called to the train that James Croft and David Morris boarded.

"No surrender. Don't give in. Bring back the bacon lads." So the Witton Park lodge of the union sent James Croft and David to a meeting in the city of Newcastle upon Tyne. The attitude of the employers was one that sought to crush the current dispute, forever deterring another. Heading back to Witton Park from the ill-fated meeting James Croft looked to David.

"They will never accept it you know."

"I can't blame them. I mean we gained nothing for our members. No reduction in the fifty-four hour week, either for men or boys. And still we must accept the ten per cent pay cut? Why did we bother going?"

"It's crazy, " James said. "Even if we accepted they still won't let us go back."

"I know. But why? What has the return of work of the original Staffordshire strikers got to do with anything?"

"They are just rubbing salt into the wounds. It's total humiliation they want. They intend to crush us into the dirt, especially the Staffordshire lads who started it all."

Initially, no one had taken the strike and subsequent lockout too seriously. Many chose to take holidays or return to their birthplaces and visit family. Then, three weeks into the lockout, families without support, began to leave the village. At first only those that felt no loyalty to the community left. These were those that by nature were footloose and rootless. Then as the Bryan and Morris families watched long time workmates and their families leave and felt it was history repeating itself, in reverse. Scenes from twenty years ago were being re-enacted. Handcarts and wagons trundled along the village streets just like before, but this time people were leaving.

"Are you going to listen to the man from America?" Squeak asked his brother Will-Patrick.

"Might as well, see what he has to offer. Are you going?"

"Oh aye, I bet the whole place is there. Why they say he says there's jobs in America, for every ironworker, and they give you a ticket to get there."

"Better than that. They say that bastard bosses like the ones here are not welcome. It's supposed to be the land of the free."

"You've been listening too much to our David you have," Will-Patrick jibed his brother. Large numbers of strikers set their sights on America and agents of companies travelled all over England and Wales. The second meeting of men and employers, held at York, again failed to reach an agreement and consequently thirty of Witton Parks' best puddlers submitted their names for emigration. As the dispute dragged on many others were to follow as hardship began to bite. David and his father looked around the marquee in which the annual horticultural show was to be held.

"Well, that's as much as we can do, we can leave it to the judges now," he said to his father.

"They won't have much to do this year will they? I don't know why they didn't cancel this show. Have you seen the tables? Why there's hardly a class with more than two entries. I think there's only the flower section done any good. Do you know we are down by almost seventy five per cent on last year?"

"David you should understand more than most. These are hard times for a lot of folks. All the vegetables and livestock are better on their own tables than in the marquee."

"That's what I was trying to say, father. Why bother with a show this year?"

"It's good for morale lad and anyway the flowers are nice."

"There'll be no brass-band either," David said despondently. "Half of them that played the instruments have up and gone to America."

"I'm sure Mr. Jones will save the day."

"Why, he'll be struggling as well, half his choir has gone too. Do you think anybody will come to see what little there is left?

"They'll come, son. They've got little else to do, being locked out and all. You and the show committee should be proud lad, getting free entrance for as them that can't afford it. They'll come. All your hard work will be rewarded, you'll see."

Despite obvious shortages, the village pulled together and food was abundant. The giant cauldron of broth was constantly added to as folks brought what they could afford. The garden produce from the show was not sold off but added to the bubbling mass of wild rabbit, duck and pheasant Earthy, simple, country games kept the happy crowds entertained until nightfall and Mr. Jones' men sang 'until they could sing no more'.

"Ladies and Gentlemen. The choir thanks you for your applause and now while we rest a while may I ask if we have any other volunteers to entertain us? C'mon now there must be one among you not afraid to come up here."

"I'll sing for you," a voice said coming from the back of the hall. As the crowds parted to let the person through Annie said, "I thought I knew that voice, oh my God, is he drunk?"

"I doubt he's sober, Ma," said Michael. "He's been in the Queen's Head since noon hasn't he?" Patrick, accompanied by his two dogs pushed his way to the front. "Right lads and lasses tonight I'm going to sing for you, 'I Dreamt I Slept In Marble Halls'. If any of you know it you're welcome to join in the refrain. When you're ready maestro," he beckoned to Mr. Jones who would conduct the quartet of musicians. "I'm ready when you are."

"And I'm off," said Annie to Margot and Tamar. "Goodnight."

"How many people live in the village now, David, do you reckon?"

"I think at the last count there was over five thousand, father. But a lot's left since then, hasn't there?"

"Yes, some have, but five thousand is still a lot of people. Look at the crowds—why I think all of them came. I told you they would."

"I think the free broth helped."

"Probably. That's why it reminds me of the scriptures somewhat. It was the feeding of the five thousand all over again. Praise be to God."

"Amen," said his son.

The conflict between workers and management dragged on through the summer months. Gathered together for an outdoor meeting, members of the Ironworks Union met to hear the latest developments. James Croft rose from his seat next to David on a makeshift platform.

"Men, I bring you grave news. The management has informed me this morning that they intend to restart part of the works using men from their Middlesbrough plant." A huge wail and cries of 'shame' reverberated around the station yard.

"We'll not let them in," shouted a furnace man. "We'll lock them out, like they've done to us."

"Kill the fiken scabs," shouted another as the crowd began to turn ugly. As initial anger deflated, David rose and shouted over the din.

"Lads, do nothing to break the law. Sympathy is with us. We must keep the public on our side. There's nothing better than the capitalist press would like than to brand us lawless thugs. Tomorrow when these 'men', and I use the word 'men' loosely, arrive we must show constraint."

"I'll show them something," a man heckled, from the front rows. "I'll show them this." Punching the air with his clenched fist brought a huge roar of approval from the gathering.

"Aye, let them come, well show them," became the rallying call as they dispersed peacefully. And come they did. The empty houses, deserted by people unable to ride out the storm, were given over to them. Daily up to twenty police escorted scabs, blacklegs and management to the works. Morning and evening scenes were ugly. There was spitting, abusive language, and the occasional throwing of missiles. Heavy-handed treatment came back in return from the police guards. With this small labour force the directors managed to restart production and still continue the lockout. The strike committee, headed by David, recruited more and more volunteers and the soup kitchen passed the two hundred gallon mark.

Cracks began to appear within the ranks. The blast furnace men were the first to attempt to negotiate after production re-began but Joseph, under instruction, could do little but refer them to the Middlesbrough plant for discussions.

"How did you get on?" David asked one of their leaders upon their return.

"Waste of time going. They want nothing less than total surrender. The original ten per cent wage cut is now fifteen."

"*Never!*" David exclaimed.

"Oh, it's right. You know the five shilling allowance that furnacemen receive? Well they want to scrap that as well now."

"Why, the furnacemen have always had that. Ever since the works opened so they have."

"Yes, David we have, but it seem not any more we don't. They make me sick. I knew I should have gone to America. If that agent comes back again I'll be the first to go, you have my word on that." David felt dejected; if key workers like the furnacemen were being humiliated what chance had his lowly members?

"Have you heard the news?" David excitedly asked his father. "The North Staffordshire men have gone back. They've surrendered. Suppose with the state of things they had little choice."

"Where does that leave us then?" his father asked.

"In the same boat I suppose. *Up the creek without a paddle.* We'll be able to go back now but things will never be the same. I don't just mean the less money. The management know they now have the upper hand and boy I bet they don't half crack the whip."

Reluctantly, new pay and working practices were accepted and the Witton Park workforce returned. It was not to last. On discovering the introduction of further, undisclosed conditions the skilled puddlers walked out again. No agreement could be reached with the management and another fifteen hundred men rejoined the stoppage. This infuriated the management. They decided to bring down the full force of the judicial system upon the strikers. Chosen at random, a young puddler named Harry Wilson, the inoffensive son of a respected shoemaker was used as an example to the others.

"What next I wonder?" asked David. "Have these ironmasters no scruples? Fancy picking on a young lad who's never been in trouble in his life."

"He's the sacrificial lamb, there's always one you know," his father replied.

"I know what they are up to. But why a kid? Fancy serving a summons on a young 'un for breach of contract."

"What exactly do they say he's done"?

"Well, he didn't much like the job and left. They are saying that 'he left his place of work without giving the due lawful procedure of two weeks warning'."

"What do you think they will give him? I mean they won't lock him up or anything will they?"

"They will do nothing with him. We have a small surprise in store. They think they are dealing with a lot of impoverished uneducated workers. One thing Hickey taught us all, get a good lawyer. The union is determined not to lose this skirmish. They won't have their lamb cutlets from this village. So they wont. We are going to defend, then spring a surprise attack."

Bishop Auckland court was packed for the hearing. The Ironworkers Union hired a Manchester solicitor who specialised in commercial law. He pleaded with the bench that his client, never having received a contract either verbal or written, was unable to be in breach, or guilty. Dismissed upon legal advice the case set a precedent, and the ruling would come back to haunt Bolckow and Vaughan. Within the month, roles were reversed when the union representing a striker took Bolckow and Vaughan to the same court. For the second hearing involving the union's new smart lawyer, people again packed the court. The union claimed the company had made illegal deductions for education and medical care, when the man's family did not reside in the village. Never had they availed themselves of the services. The court had no option but to find in the striker's favour and he received welcome back money.

Only the foolish and the foolhardy chose to work during the strike as tempers often ran to murder pitch. Michael in his senior position had reluctantly stayed at his post, which placed great strains on the relationship with his brother in law, David. His father had not initially elected to strike until, among the endless streams of demands, came one to which he took personal offence.

"They want us to do what?" David's father asked. Never before had David heard his father raise his voice in anger.

"Calm yourself husband," Margot asked him.

"Calm myself? Did you not hear what your son said, Mrs. Morris? They want us to work seven days a week now. On the Sabbath as well, enough's enough. *David* you can add my name to those that will be on the gates tomorrow."

"When you think about it they're not daft," said David. "They will make a fortune if they get this through."

"What do you mean, son?" his mother asked, trying to defuse the situation.

"Well, they want father and the other firemen and fireboys to start noon Sunday making ready the fires. The furnacemen then would start work at six in the evening, followed by the rollers and puddlers at midnight. Before, every body started at he same time but the puddlers couldn't do anything until the furnacemen give them a charge. And the furnacemen couldn't do anything until the firemen got the blasts up to temperature. This way, staggering the starts they don't have thousands of men standing around, twiddling their thumbs. And of course they are not to pay while they stand about idle."

"Well it sounds sensible to me," his mother said innocently.

"Like I said, mother, they're anything but daft." William's decision to join his son on strike relieved tension in the Morris household but also made them vulnerable.

"Well the fat's in the fire now, William," said his wife. "With both you and our David on strike if they go ahead with evictions you can bet we'll be one of the first."

"Mrs. Morris, what is it you're always telling me?"

"The Lord will provide?"

"Yes, that as well. But are you not forever saying 'we've never starved in a winter yet?'"

"Let's not hope there's a first time. It being so near to Christmas and all." Michael's father-in-law's decision to join the strikers left him isolated within his new family.

"Do you know something Tamar?"

"No, what?" she asked as she put down the knitting, which had kept her busy all evening.

"This strike it reminds me of when Samuel was writing home about the American civil war."

"How?"

"He was always saying about how sad it was to see brother against brother, father against son. How the rifts had torn apart families, communities and even the country. He wondered if a healing would ever come about. I see the same things here and wonder the same."

"Do you mean about David, and now my father being on strike?"

"Sort of. Not that it's like that between us. I wouldn't let it happen. No way," he said firmly.

"Why don't you have a walk up to Carwood House and spend the evening with your friend. Play a little cards or something, but try not to talk about work."

"That will be difficult."

"Just try. Go on get yourself out and let me get this scarf finished or your neck will be cold this winter." Michael bent forward and kissed his wife gently on the head. It was then he noticed her first silver hair. Over a game of backgammon the conversation between two friends drifted to the subject of the strike. It was inevitable.

"Michael, you know I have a lot of sympathy with the strikers don't you? Well I have something to tell you which you must promise not to repeat. You probably know that during the past twenty years there has been a great many changes. While the Bolckow and Vaughan families still own a large proportion of the firm they are now accountable to others. They in turn are under pressure to make as much profit as the can to satisfy the shareholders. Most of the directives that have been aimed at breaking the strikers and the ironworkers union have passed down from these directors. So you see it is no longer a family business and matters are outside my control."

"I understand that."

"Good. Well yesterday I tendered my resignation from the board and company."

"Joseph, why did you do that?"

"I'm just not enjoying the job at the moment. I think it's time I saw the world. Maybe meet a nice woman and marry. Anyway, they have accepted my resignation. On the condition that I make no announcement until this unfortunate strike is over. They wish to be seen as solid in their resistance and united in their defiance to the demands of the strikers."

"I'm sorry to hear that Joseph. It means you will leave the village. I'll miss you."

"And I you, but don't worry I'll keep in touch. Anyway it looks like it won't be for a while. In the meantime that's my last counter off the board. Two games to me I believe."

179

Tensions mounted daily, and the first demonstrations and prosecutions began. A married Welsh couple threw stones at the windows of the Old Row home of a fellow countryman.

"It may help the court to understand that the acrimony between these two families since the strike began. As a puddler, John Parton had worked along side Daniel Daniels for years. Mr. Parton has chosen not to withdraw his labour from the services of my clients Messrs Bolckow and Vaughan. They are keen to see justice for good men like him who refuse to listen to the calls of union agitators. Why should their loyal employees not be allowed to go to work, without the fear of such intimidation?"

The magistrate in binding over the Daniels man and wife to keep the peace chose the moment to say, "It is worth noting that since the start of the strike there has been a gratifying side effect. The caseload of this court has been lightened to an amazing degree, since the population of that village have seen a reduction in their income. Cases of drunkenness and violence are at their lowest for years."

A Cheshire man, Robert McTurk had come to Witton Park early in its development and had lived a relative quiet life in Woodside. He and his son both worked at the ironworks and their continuance to do so during the strike upset many previous friends and colleagues.

"I'm afraid I'll have to be leaving my job, as soon as you can let me."

"Why?" asked Michael, "You've been here donkey's years. Are you having problems with the strikers?"

"I'd rather not say Michael, if you don't mind. You know what I mean?"

"I know exactly what you mean. Well, I'm sorry but I'm fed up of it. You will be the fifth skilled man I've lost this week. What about your lad? What's he say? He's been here since he was twelve years old hasn't he?"

"He feels the same way as I do, but he wants to tell you his self."

"Do you really want to leave?" Michael asked.

"No, we don't. But what else can we do?"

"What if Mr. Vaughan could stop them bothering you? Would you stay?"

"I'm not sure. I mean I'm not sure that you could stop them."

"How old are you Robert?"

"I'm coming up sixty four or five I think."

"Well you know if you move how hard it will be to get another job at your age don't you?"

"Aye, I do."

"Then why don't you let Joseph help you? We were talking about this just the other night."

180

The directors sought the assistance of the law once more. The company this time chose to bring a specimen prosecution against the Welshman Alexander Pritchard on the grounds that he had intimidated Robert McTurk. He told a packed court that he lived in fear of his life and believed that it was only a matter of time before he, his son, or another blackleg would die a violent death. The night Pritchard was arrested and placed in the new village police cells the most serious incident occurred. Earlier in the evening, at another open-air meeting, David had introduced the area union man from Newcastle. An unruly element of the crowd, agitated and unhappy with lack of progress or any hint of returning to work, became restless. At the conclusion of the meeting, sixty or seventy of the strikers broke away from the main body, and intent on mischief, set off towards Main Street. David and his senior union colleague pleaded for calm but the gang was in riotous mood. Probably intent on 'blackleg bashing' or attempting to free Pritchard they marched along Queen Street. Inspector Askew, had been informed of the intended lawful meeting, and, just in case, had drafted in extra police. The police strength numbered eight in total.

Spectators watched from the windows of the Queen's Head Hotel as the senior officer stretched his thin blue line across the bottom of the street, facing the approaching mob. David Morris, his colleague, and two stewards from the rally tried in vain to push back the mob.

"Go back. Go back. We said no violence. Go back!" he screamed. Pulling bricks from the surface of the unmade road, they hurled them at the police. All the while David with his back to the police attempted to push back those strikers in the first row. Slowly he was pushed backwards.

"Right men," shouted the police inspector, as the mob drew closer. "Draw truncheons." With drilled military precision their batons were withdrawn from their belts. Each man then placed his whistle to his lips.

"Forward," called the inspector and to the raucous shrieking of the policemen's whistles they advanced. David was unaware of the advancing rank of police behind him. Still he struggled with his determined colleagues who were hell bent on confrontation with the police. They viewed the law with deep suspicion and saw the police as the ironmasters' agents. He never saw the truncheon that stuck the juncture of his neck and shoulder, rendering him senseless. Under indiscriminate blows the strikers retreated, turning the aim of their missiles upon the windows of the blacklegs' houses.

Four people were charged with riotous behaviour, but one had his charge reduced to drunk and disorderly, and was fined ten shillings. The others appeared at the Quarter Session court and received six months hard labour apiece. The judge, Justice Lush in a ruling that would from that day be used throughout that century and the next, stated:

"A man has the right to work as much as a man has the right to legally withdraw his labour."

The strike rumbled on into a third acrimonious month. Developments were to make this the bitterest month of them all.

"What are they building down the bottoms?" Will-Patrick asked Squeak.

"It's a new railway station, just for passengers. Now people will get off there and coal and all that will be loaded at the old John Street platform. From now on we won't get covered in dust when we get on or off the train."

"Why that'll be grand, won't it?"

"Aye, and guess who's just got a job there?"

"Who?"

"Remember that snotty kid, always had his head painted violet? *Him*".

"What doing?"

"He's up in the signal box, his brother says."

"I'd like to have a look up there sometime. Have you seen how high it is? Why I bet you can see right over the works down to the river."

"Will it be called Witton Park railway station now?"

"I doubt it, I bet they still call it Etherley."

"Aye. I bet. Daft isn't it?"

"Aye."

The completion of the new railway passenger terminal made it a focal point. Erected half a mile back down the tracks from the original it became central to the village. Passengers no longer had to dodge coal and other such cargo trucks. The new station yard was a forty-five degree triangular shaped enclosure. From the station buildings, down to the signal box, just before the tunnel entrance to the works, a wooden fence kept the public off the tracks. On the other two sides ran an impressive eight-foot high stonewall. This extended right up to the ticket office and platform. Along the base, broken only by imposing gates, the same style thick stonewall was befitting of a castle. The two support pillars for the iron gates were almost four feet square and topped with a spherical shaped piece of mortar, which reminded travellers of pyramids.

The surface of the yard was composed of fine, rolled locomotive ash; charcoal grey in colour, it was an ideal all-weather surface. Damped by rain it was as effective as tarmac, and in summer, although a boot could raise a puff of dust, compared to other village surfaces, it was a billiard table. From beneath the ashen surface dotted tufts of coarse grass rose, like the grasses of sand dunes. While these struggled for survival the centre of the yard fared better. Used as a turning circle it was unhindered by daily trampling by foot, hoof and cart wheel. This circular became a small green oasis in the volcanic landscape. The new yard soon became popular as a children's playground. It also became the new place for adults to settle arguments.

"Is that right we can't hold our meetings in the new station yard?" a young striker asked David.

"That's right, we're banned."

"Why?"

"In a nutshell, the owner of the line and station happens to also be a director of Bolckow and Vaughan."

"Aye, why, tell them to stuff their yard." Next to the mouth of the works tunnel, beside the station wall, men gathered as they had done daily for the previous three months.

"Not so many of us out this morning do you think?" David's father asked.

"Aye, there seems to be a few less. But can you blame them. I mean, it's freezing isn't it? When I went across the yard this morning, the coalhouse and nettie roofs were white with frost."

"I saw it, nearly got back into bed myself."

"You should have, father. There's no need for you to be here every day. Anyway here they come. Here come the scabs and blacklegs. Does there seem more of them this morning?"

"Na. I don't think so, just about the same I would say," said William

"Here they come." As the police escorted the strike breakers past the picket, the ritual heckling began. After some months of insults, some of the men seemed impervious to the mocking and jeers. Some even came back with their taunts but in the main the majority kept their heads hung low. As the din of the hecklers subsided, a train was heard screeching to a halt at the new passenger terminal behind them. Over the occasional noise of a steam hammer, that the scab work force operated could be heard many voices.

"Seem a lot of folk getting off that train doesn't there?" asked one of the striking iron men. The sounds of many voices intermingled with shouts of commands could be heard. Looking through the small gate just big enough for pedestrians, David and his father saw up to fifty men approaching from the platform area into the yard.

"What can you see?" anxious men asked.

"There's a load of men assembling in the yard," David said.

"Looks like the bloke with the bald head is in charge, the way he's bossing the others about?" said his father. The sun, struggling to break through and defrost the white ground, shone on the baldhead of the apparent leader, making him highly visible. He now led the group towards the gates, which a railway porter struggled to open. With the portal open and the high double gates swung back the full impact of the strangers numbers could be appreciated.

"Who are they?" a fellow puddler asked David. "Are they more iron workers?"

"I doubt it. I've never seen ironworkers dressed so well. Definitely not going to work anyway. Have you?"

"No, I haven't. So who are they then?

"Your guess is as good as mine," said David.

Chapter Thirteen 1865

The leader, as though compensating for his bare crown, grew his hair from ear-level down to his shoulders, and his face was a mass of whiskers and moustache.

"It seems as though they were expected. I don't think it's a coincidence that Inspector Askew and his men were there to meet them," said David. "Also I'm sure I've seen that man before. I mean him there, the one that's bald on top, with the long hair at the sides. Looks like he's the one in charge, doesn't it?"

"They're big buggers aren't they David?" said the puddler standing next to him. "I'm over six foot and I can't see the top of their heads."

"They are that, and they seem to be bursting out of their clothes. It's like they borrowed them for the day. Ironworkers definitely don't dress like that on their way to work. They don't take their own sledgehammers either. Look at those four near the back they're all carrying them."

"Maybe they're going to knock the works down?" joked the puddler.

"Sometimes, I wish they would," replied David. "What are they here for I wonder?"

"Some of them must be carpenters," said his father. See the tools sticking out of their canvas bags?" William observed. "Now what's the inspector doing? He seems to be giving them directions towards the streets. Perhaps they are not going into the works? Maybe they're frightened to pass us and go under the bridge."

"I doubt it, father. Anyway it's the only way they can go, *if* that's where they're headed. Maybe we've got ourselves all wound up for nothing. Maybe they're going to Jane Pit after all."

"Could be," said the puddler.

"I'm not sure," said William. "I've got a bad feeling about this." A man pushed his way though the strikers to get to David's side. "David do you not recognise that baldy bloke with the whiskers? He was at the Middlesbrough office of Bolckow and Vaughan. I was talking to him after the meeting. Do you not remember? You were talking to Joseph in that long corridor and I was nattering to him. Do you remember now?"

"Oh, yes. Well vaguely. Who is he then?"

"That's Jenkinson, he's the head bailiff for the company. The bloke stood next to him he's the bum bailiff he's been here before. He was the one who put John Williams and his family out on the street."

"What's a bum bailiff?" a fireboy asked William.

"He's the under-bailiff."

"Oh?"

"They're only here for one thing then," said David. " Spread the word." And the word spread like wildfire, and within minutes, the number of David's companions had halved. Heads of households rushed to their homes as Inspector Askew led the bailiff's team into Middle Row. Deserting their picket line they were closely followed by the strikers, until they stopped at the front door of a striking puddler.

"It's John Harrison's house they've stopped at," one of the crowd shouted. "Look they're splitting up. Some of them are going round the back." The flimsy ledge and brace front door almost fell apart under the thunderous pounding of the under bailiff. Then the sound of the creaky sash window above them caused everyone to look up. Out of the opened bedroom window appeared the heads of John Harrison and his wife.

"What the hell is going on? What the hell are you doing braying on that door?" asked the man.

"Are you John Harrison?" the bailiff shouted.

"Aye, I am. And who the hell might you be?"

"My name's Jenkinson and I have papers here," he said as he waived them in the air. "These papers say that you must leave this company house immediately. If you refuse to do so you will be forcefully evicted. It'll be better for all if you go peacefully. I don't want to have to throw you out, but throw you out I will, if needs must." Man and wife ducked back into the bedroom and their three stepdaughters, son and lodger, Michael Deghell, replaced them. Rubbing the sleep from his eyes the lodger called down to his workmates.

"What's going on lads?" Seeing David he shouted to him. "Tell me they can't do this to us. They can't, can they David?"

"Who are you?" the bailiff called up to the window. "Tell the Harrisons to come down, now, or we'll break down this door."

"Will you now? Hang on a minute and I'll tell him that. Stay right there a minute will you?" Into the bedroom he vanished to reappear within seconds. "I couldn't find him, but for my part I would like to tell you to *piss off.* And in case you forget what I said, this should remind you."

The contents of the bedroom chamber pot fell from the sky like golden rain. Jenkinson took the main brunt of the downpour but few of the company men escaped. The urine ran down his head and face to the delight of the ecstatic crowd.

"Inspector," he shrieked. "I want that man arrested immediately." At that the front door opened, just before he could give the command to force entry. As the man wiped away at his baldhead and shoulders, John Harrison ignored his plight

"Now what were you saying?" he asked.

"Don't mess me about anymore. You know why I am here and you must get out of this company house now. Here take this," he said thrusting a dishevelled court order into his hand.

"That's no good to me I can't read or write."

"It doesn't matter, I've had enough. You've fifteen minutes to get your things out of this house." Joining her husband, Harriet Harrison reeled from the news, while her spouse surveyed the scene in utter disbelief. Bewildered by so many strangers and police at her door, she clutched their youngest child protectively to her breast. Her husband tried to explain about the non-payment of rent, but was interrupted by the bailiff.

"I'll not ask you again. You now have ten minutes," he said impatiently. Harriet had no intention of being put out onto the streets. Grabbing her husband by the shoulder of his shirt she dragged him indoors, slamming home the bolt. With rehearsed precision, upon a nod of the head from the bailiff, a man stepped forward and sledge hammered the door open. As five or six enforcers entered, the sound of another sledgehammer on splintering wood was heard from the rear of the house. The unceremonious dumping of furniture, chattels and personal belongings into the street left David and the others speechless but helpless. The police were there to ensure that the law was carried out and stood firm in front of the house.

"How could men that claim to be men of God do this to their fellow people?" asked William. Such was the shock that no one answered the lay preacher. The man's wife cried pitifully, while her child, sensing the mother's distress, screamed, and total pandemonium reigned. The husband and lodger would not go without a fight but were arrested and restrained by the police officers. This infuriated the ironworkers and the inspector feared retaliation. Shouts of insults from the small crowd of onlookers were like water off a ducks back to those that threw the family and their belongings into the street. From upstairs windows, beds and bed irons crashed down into the street, as the air filled with feathers from worn pillows splitting open on landing. Within five minutes the content of a cosy family home was emptied onto the roadway, and a carpenter, front and back, secured windows, and padlocked doors. The number of onlookers reduced dramatically as men rushed home to defend their families and homes. Reassembled outdoors, the eviction crews moved on along the row.

"Where they going now?" a concerned workmate of David asked. He could only shrug his shoulders in reply. Methodically, the evictions were repeated a further nine times, until a trail of devastation lay behind the bailiff and his henchmen. The street now took on a pillaged scene as though it had been raided by Vikings or such. David pleaded with Inspector Askew.

"Is this supposed to be legal? Are you going to stand there and watch this? These people haven't done anything wrong except withdraw their labour."

"Or pay their rents," the inspector interjected.

"I know some of them haven't but is that good enough reason to evict poor folk?"

"The court says it is, and as long as it goes ahead peacefully I can't interfere."

"Peaceful? Why they reckon George Merrel's wife from number eight has a broken arm. Do you call that peaceful?"

"I've told you, David, there's nothing I can do." On the streets, side-by-side, a child's broken-faced china doll lay next to a broken earthenware chamber pot. Bailiff and crew walked over clean linen and clothes that lay in piles, while dogs sniffed at, and cocked their legs against, family heirlooms. The breath of crying babies left vapour trails as, in small homemade cradles, they lay screaming in the near-freezing conditions. Still the mayhem continued unabated.

At the last house in Middle Row the eviction team turned right into the narrow single terrace, which faced the high railway embankment. Men, women and boys were being pushed forward into the constricted street and it made progress difficult.

"They're turning into Railway Row," David said to his father. We must get through. Our house is sure to be first. He knew that the home of a strike leader and a striking fireman would not be missed.

"Let us through," he pleaded to the bunched group of spectators, as it was funnelled into the narrow street. Being pushed and shoved slowly they forced their way to the front. There the cordon was being reinforced by the police officers.

"Let go of me, I live there," David said sternly to two of the bailiff's men that struggled to push him back. He saw the bailiff knock on his parent's door and his heart sank. He called to the police inspector.

"Inspector, please tell these men to let go of me and let us through. You can see that's our house they're at. Won't you help us?" Inspector Askew looked to those who restrained David and his father.

"Let those men through," he ordered, and reluctantly they obeyed. William looked to the inspector.

"Mr. Askew. You and I have known each other for some time. I owe no rent but I am on strike, as you know. As I am a man of peace I accept that what is about to happen is inevitable. Another day, those responsible will answer to a higher authority than your court. None the less I ask you to be given a chance to leave peacefully. You said this is why you are here. Did you not? To keep the peace, that is, well this is all I am asking of you."

Inspector Agnew thought for a moment then shouted to the bailiff.

"Mr. Jenkinson. There'll be no need to knock on that door again. The head of the household is here. You may present your papers to him right here."

"But ..."

"Mr. Jenkinson, I won't ask you again. I told you when you arrived that I was in charge while you were in the village. Now do as I say please." As William was served their eviction papers in the street the front door of their house was opened by Margot. Though unaware of what had happened in Middle Row she soon became aware of their circumstances. Meanwhile the crowd had started to grow again. From both ends of the street they swelled the throng. It now took all the bailiffs men and the police to keep the two factions from breaking through and occupying the whole street. As she looked from her doorstep, left and right, she could see nothing but faces. She looked at the men who come and marvelled. As word had spread villagers came together for the first time. Irish stood beside the Welsh, Orangemen beside Fenians. They had found something that surmounted ethnic beliefs, a simple, common cause. In the minutes Margot stood and watched even more men tried to get into the narrow street, as those that tried to keep them out struggled. As word of what was happening spread, many felt their turn would be next, and converged on the company men. Many came prepared to fight, holding spades and other garden tools. Others armed themselves with bed irons picked from the street.

Margot saw P.C. Anthony on the cordon to the left of their house and walked up to him. He waited for her to say something but she just eyed him up and down for a while.

"Gary Anthony is it? Son of Gwyneth?" Police constable Anthony had been the first Welsh immigrant to join the local police force. The Welsh community had been proud to see a countryman become a local officer. As the policeman pushed with his back against the crowd he managed to reply.

"You know it is Mrs. Morris. Why do you ask?"

"Because I didn't know you. Not the Gary Anthony I knew as a boy. For I never thought I'd live to see the day when a Welsh Congregationalist would do the work of the devil and his disciples." Constable Anthony squirmed and fidgeted with the chinstrap of his black conical helmet, but refused to have eye contact with her. Although she had no intention of benevolence towards the Welsh policeman, he was spared further embarrassment. In her excitable state she, lapsed into her native tongue.

While David and the bailiff argued, the inspector became increasingly concerned. His force was trapped in the middle of a street that measured less than ten yards wide. On one side, was a fifteen feet high stonewall, which retained the railway embankment, and on the other, houses that had been barricaded against entry. The occupants leaned from bedroom windows assessing the situation while at either end of the short street the numbers of striking ironworkers grew by the minute. They had allowed themselves to become snared and the mood of the crowd was deteriorating quickly. Having had to deploy half of the mercenaries and police, front and back of the street, he could count on less than twenty men. He was now surrounded by possibly over two hundred and more were arriving by the minute. Those at the rear could not come to their assistance as they found themselves in a similar predicament.

Having got Jenkinson's attention he said, "Look I think it's getting out of hand. If we are not careful this could break out into a full scale riot."

"But it's your job to protect us," a suddenly frightened Jenkinson whimpered, as he looked and listened to the crowds who bayed for his blood.

"David, a lot of these are your men. Can you not speak to them?"

"Yeah, and a lot of them are not. Anyway, why should I try and save the skin of this bad lot? Send for Joseph Vaughan he is the only one who might restore order, if he stops the evictions"

"And how can I do that? We'll never get through to the end of the street, not alive anyway," said the inspector. "What else can we do?"

"Get that lad from the front of the crowd. Stood on my shoulders he should get over the embankment wall. Tell him to cross the railway lines and run to the works."

"Good idea," said the inspector. The boy ran into Michael as he hurried to the works office. Michael rushed to find Joseph and explained the situation.

"You must go and stop this madness. Not just for Tamar's family but for everyone. Joseph you must go before someone is killed."

"I really haven't got the authority to overrule an instruction from head office you know."

"The bailiffs won't know that. Please, just go and speak to them, *before its too late.*"

"Lets be going then," Joseph said as he strode across his office to pick up his hat. " Lets not waste a minute more." Hurriedly Joseph and Michael left Paradise Cottage offices and rushed towards the exit of the works. Surveying the mayhem and despair in Middle Row, Michael and Joseph fought their way through the hostile crowd, and they did not escape their animosity.

"At last ... here comes Joseph and Michael," David informed the inspector as he watched them emerge. Joseph walked straight up to Jenkinson.

"You know who I am don't you?" he said with authority.

"Yes sir, you're Mr. Vaughan."

"And you are in charge here Jenkinson?"

"Yes, sir."

"Then I order you to desist. Stop what you are doing immediately. Return to Middlesbrough and report to head office in a couple of days. They will have my report by then. In the meantime I suggest that you look to your loins and get out of the village. Its no longer safe for you here, I fear."

"If you say so, Mr. Vaughan. Whatever you say sir," said the grovelling employee, glad to be relieved of this assignment. "Will it be safe for us to leave, sir?"

"That, Jenkinson, is not my affair," Joseph said curtly as he turned his back on the man. Hemmed in to the left and right by bodies, while above them thunderous faces glared from the windows and the high embankment, the police inspector pondered his next move. One wrong move from the mercenaries or his men and the tinderbox situation would have gone up in a flash.

"Excuse me, Mr. Vaughan," said Inspector Askew. "If not for the company men is there nothing you could do to placate he crowd?"

"Perhaps there's one thing," said Joseph. "Jenkinson, hand me the remaining eviction orders."

"Gladly, sir" Joseph took the sheaf of papers from the bailiff and one by one slowly tore them up and threw them to the wind. The crowd cheered wildly but did not disperse. As the jubilation subsided David addressed them.

"Friends, the evictions are over. I thank you for coming to our aid as does my father and mother and of course everyone else who was subjected to this humiliation today thanks you. Now it is time to go home to our families. Send these excuses for men back to where they came from. Their tails are that far between their legs they would never dare show their faces here again. Please let them leave. If you do not, Inspector Askew will have no choice but to read the riot act. That is the last thing he wants to do, I assure you. Let them crawl back to Middlesbrough and carry the message that no matter what the ironmasters throw at us the solidarity of this village will throw it back in their faces."

"Now might be a good time to leave," Michael suggested to Joseph.

"Never a better time I think," he replied.

"Follow them," the Inspector said to his men and bailiffs alike. "Stay close together and keep walking whatever happens."

As the crowd divided to let Joseph and Michel through, the others fell in behind. The small police presence, two abreast, began to move slowly towards the station end of the street, followed by a sheepish, nervous gang of demoralised thugs. They had arrived as bold as brass, now walked sheepishly staring only at the ground. From a bedroom window, the contents of another chamber pot rained down on the departing column and men covered them in spit. Inspired, from other open upstairs sash window, fell more urine and excreta upon the hapless cavalcade. By the shovel full, from high on the embankment, men flung piles of black loco ash that adhered to the drenched, stinking evacuees. All the way to the station yard villagers taunted them and spat on them while dogs snapped at their heels. Inspector Askew slammed shut the gates of the yard and left three officers to guard them. He intended to escort them right onto the train and out of his jurisdiction. With the main gates shut only the pedestrian gate had to be controlled. The sergeant and two pitiable constables remained at the narrow entry point. There they stood against the crowd like Horatio and the two Romans at the bridge of Sublician.

The whole village celebrated, for this had been their only moment of glory in an otherwise miserable period of their lives. The following day, Joseph received an urgent summons to attend head office.

"What do you think they'll do to you?" Michael asked. Joseph laughed.

"What can they do to me? I'm already on my way out, and they can't shoot me as a traitor. *Can they*?"

"I hope not," said Michael, " Anyway, good luck."

During the second week of November, while the strike dragged on, Hickey left for Ireland once again.

"Will you be long away this time?" Bridie asked her father.

"I don't know, and if anyone should ask it's me sick Mammy I've gone to see. Do you understand girl?"

"Yes, Daddy I understand." There was much activity in his homeland and radicals thought the time ripe for an uprising. Hickey was to be part of a special mission. There were many Irish-American civil war veteran officers who felt they could help. Pressure was on for a second insurrection. The American Fenians felt that they could raise an army from those that became increasingly anti-British because of Britain's support of the Confederates. Everyone considered the time right, all, except the leader. With the release of thousands of Irish officers and men from the two warring factions in America, the British realised that they must be on their guard. In a pre-emptive strike they raided the Irish headquarters of the 'Irish People' building, and arrested everyone present. The first blow struck directly at the head and resulted in the capture of most of the Fenian leaders. Other arrests followed and most prominent Brotherhood hierarchics were rounded up, and while escaping capture for almost two months, the hunt continued for Stephens.

"I must say these arrests give me great pleasure," said Lord Wodehouse to a subordinate. He was the minister responsible for Irish affairs and nicknamed 'woodlouse' by them. "Although I am a little peeved that Stephens evaded capture."

"It's only a matter of time, sir. I'm sure."

"I agree, but in the meantime I will have to inform the home secretary that while we may have paralysed the movement, we have not, in fact, killed it off."

"Yes, sir but there is more good news for you to deliver? I learned this but a short time a go. One of our Irish informers, Nagel I believe he is called, has delivered up his leaders."

"*Ha*! So much for loyalty among these traitors," Lord Wodehouse scoffed.

"Exactly, sir, and may I add it cost us a lot less than thirty pieces of silver."

In November, Stephens was finally captured along with three other Fenians and a large quantity of guns and ammunition. He did not go quietly. Two detectives, arrived at the building and were shot, although not fatally. After his arrest he was imprisoned in Richmond Bridewell.

"Extra! Extra! Read all about it! Stephens escapes from the Bridewell," called a street corner paper seller. Stephens had vanished less than two weeks after his capture and an immediate enquiry was launched. Almost everyone knew that despite theatrical props and distractions depicting a breakout, it had been an inside job. Stephens had not broken out, but candidly walked out.

"How long do you think we will have to lay low?" an accomplice asked Hickey.

"Just a couple of more days. They'll tire of watching the ports soon."

"I don't get it. Why do we have to lie low? They are not looking for us, are they?"

"No, they're not. But be sure any Irishman crossing the water at this time will be looked at closely. Just relax. C'mon get your boots on and lets go to the pub." Hickey had contacted two of the jail's employees. One worked in the hospital wing and had keys for the whole place. Both were devout Fenians and, when asked, eagerly assisted in the escape plan. Having made copies of keys, a group of armed Fenians, led by John Devoy simply walked in. While Hickey and others stood guard they helped the released prisoner over the wall to freedom. Before they left they tried to make it look like a breakout but to most it was unconvincing. The police and military guarded railway stations and ports and the homes of known sympathisers were raided, but Stephens' hideout remained undiscovered. For a while he lay low in the house of a fashionable dressmaker, before his flight to the United States. Hickey was back in England by the third week of November. After two weeks' continuous drinking in the Bishop Auckland's taverns he set off for Witton Park once more.

At the end of the first week in December, the strikers, defeated, returned to work. The bitter pill of a ten-per-cent wage cut imposed on tradesmen, and even larger cuts on rollers, shinglers and others requiring some swallowing. In an act of total humiliation the workforce had to agree that strikers whose positions had been filled would not be re-employed, and the scabs could remain in the empty houses. In the first week back at work, men had to be stopped from fighting with each other. Out of work hours, the arguments were often settled, behind the wall in the station yard.

Two days after Hickey arrived back in the village the too familiar sight of Sadie and Bridie, now a beautiful young woman, passed Mr. Jones returning from work. Each woman seemed to be carrying their worldly possessions in two cotton sheets, the corners pulled together and tied in one enormous knot. Mother and daughter had wrapped for the winter weather. Although Bridie's beauty was half hidden behind a scarf wrapped around her face, it was still apparent.

"Hello. My, those bundles look heavy," Mr. Jones said.

"They're fine, sir, thank you," Sadie replied.

"But where are you going at this time of night? And it being so cold."

"I thank you for asking sir, but it is no matter. Sure we're just away to visit friends, so we are. That's all."

"Sadie, forgive me for asking but it being so near to Christmas and all I must ask. You're not off to the workhouse again are you?"

"The workhouse? Why not at all. Why what in heaven made you think that now?" Sadie replied half-heartedly.

"Oh, you're not? I'm pleased to here that. For just in case you don't know, I believe the workhouse closed for the day, hours ago."

"Like I said sir, that's no matter to us. Please excuse us now we must be on our way." As they set off to walk away, Mr. Jones said to them.

194

"You're welcome to stay at my house for the night." He got no reply and was about to give up when he watched the daughter drop her bundle, swoon and fall to the floor. The scarf fell from her face revealing a bruise the size of a man's fist along her jaw line. He ran the few steps to where she had fallen as her mother knelt beside her.

"Don't panic. Don't move. I mean don't go away, I'll fetch someone. The doctor, maybe, or someone ... anyone. Just don't panic. I'll be back in a minute." At that, the alarmed Mr. Jones ran for help, returning after just a few minutes out of breath with Richard Blackman who, without speaking, scooped up Bridie from where she lay. He turned towards Stable Row, his long strides eating up the ground with ease. Behind and struggling to catch up, came Sadie with one of the bundles. Still further behind lagged Mr. Jones as, with great effort, he tried to carry the other bundle. Richard kicked open the front door of his cottage and laid Bridie on the sofa. On entering, Sadie asked for water.

"You stay with your daughter and I'll fetch the doctor. Is there anything you might need before I go? Anyway Mr. Jones, my neighbour should be here any minute. He'll look after you until I get back, if that's all right?" Sadie just nodded her head in gratitude.

Halfway along the street Richard came upon Mr. Jones. Totally exhausted he rested on the bundle of clothes.

"Wait there till I come back," he said, "I won't be a minute." He knocked on the door of Will and Margot and explained what had happened.

"Do you think Will-Patrick could run for the doctor while I take Mr. Jones home?"

"Of course he will, Richard. Won't you son?"

"Of course I will. I'm on my way," Will said, already pulling on his boots. The slight figure of his friend had progressed a little further. He was now perhaps twenty yards or so from where Richard had left him, but was again resting.

"C'mon Mr. Jones. Let's be giving you a hand shall we?" Richard lifted up the bundle with ease and carried it off. Behind him followed the grateful little Welshman. By the time Doctor Beddingfield arrived Bridie had recovered somewhat.

"Well, my girl there's no need to asked what caused that," he said on examining Bridie's face. "Are you hurt anywhere else?" Bridie shook her head from side to side, very slowly.

"The giddiness, caused by the blow should soon pass. In the meantime apply cold compresses to the head and stay in a darkened room. You should not try and move until the morning, *at the earliest*. Is that clear? I'll call in and see you again, then." In the kitchen Richard and Mr. Jones s were discussing sleeping arrangements, when Sadie entered. She informed them that when her daughter had rested for an hour or so they would be leaving, and thanked both men profusely for their kindness.

"There's no need for you to leave. Mr. Jones and I have worked it out. Tonight I'll sleep next door at his and you and Bridie can rest here until she's fit again."

"We couldn't do that sir. Although we will be eternally grateful for your offer, no, we must leave."

"Is it your husband you're worried about? If it is, please don't be worried on my behalf."

"Seamus Hickey is not, never has been, or ever will be my husband, he is but the child's father," Sadie said angrily.

"*Oh*, sorry, I thought he was," said Richard.

"No, I'm the one that should be sorry. I had no right to talk to you so, in your own house. And after you took us in, and all. There's more reason for us to be gone."

"There's no need to apologise," said Mr. Jones. "Look why don't we all sit down and have a nice cup of tea? I made it while the doctor was here. At least it'll give Bridie a chance to recover."

"I'm most obliged to both of you good men and I don't wish to ever throw kindness back in anyone's face. Lets have that tea while I fix my daughter a poultice shall we?" Over tea she opened up to her host and his friend.

"Despite knowing it could be dangerous, still you helped me. Why?"

"Because that's what civilised people do, they help each other," said Richard.

"And a Christian thing to do," added Mr. Jones. She tried to explain that she had supported Hickey throughout the years because of a promise and financial responsibility placed upon her by his grandmother.

"That money recently ran out and that made him mad. He took it out on me more and more but what could I do? Over the years I've put up with a lot from Seamus. I told him though, if ever he was to lay a finger on Bridie, I'd leave him. I guess he never believed me but neither had he ever beat her, before tonight. So you see the reason I cannot stay is not for my sake. I'm not frightened of Seamus Hickey; but I am frightened for you two." Richard smiled at her.

"Never be frightened for me, trouble just seems to follow me around anyway. I cannot make you stay the night it's up to you, but I hope you will. C'mon, Mr. Jones it's time you and me were heading off to bed."

After they had gone Sadie went into the kitchen where their two bundles of possessions lay. She fumbled around until she retrieved the small wicker basket containing the Irish stone. After treating her daughters wound she fell to sleep in front of the glowing coal fire.

Chapter Fourteen 1866 - 1869

"How's the young lass this morning then?" asked Mr. Jones as he greeted Richard over the back yard wall.

"She's still in bed but her mother's just said she's had a canny night."

"Sadie up at this time? Why it's barely five a.m."

"She must have been up a while. She woke me up to tell me breakfast was ready."

"*Breakfast ready!* My oh my, aren't you the lucky one."

"Not just me, yours is cooked as well. I was just coming to fetch you."

"Me? Breakfast? Well I could definitely get used to this. I'll be there in two shakes of a lamb's tail, you tell her." Later that morning Doctor Beddingfield called on Bridie.

"And how are you feeling today young lady? A little better I hope? Mrs. Hickey, would you open the drapes a while please, so that I may see to examine your daughter."

"Doctor, please do not call me by that name. It is not one that belongs to me nor would I wish it to be so. Please call me Sadie."

"Fine. Sadie, can you also light the gas mantle, these winter mornings are so overcast." As the gas pressure built and the incandescent light grew the doctor approached the bedridden patient.

"*I don't believe it...*" the young doctor exclaimed. "The bruising ... *it's gone.*" Back at the surgery, Doctor Beddingfield sought out his senior partner.

"Doctor McKechnie. I have just come from treating a woman who had suffered a terrible beating. Last night her face was covered in bruising of the deepest black-blue I have ever witnessed. This morning there is not a trace, her complexion although pallid is flawless. How can this be?"

"Is your patient Sadie Hickey by any chance?"

"No, it's her daughter, Bridie."

"Same thing," the older doctor sighed, "Afraid I don't know the answer, I wish I did."

"Don't you think it strange Richard? I mean, nearly a weeks' gone bye and Hickey has not been round?" asked Mr. Jones.

"Yeah I do, but if he keeps it that way that'll suit me just fine."

"Me too. Do you think he's gone for good? They say after he emptied the house on Thursday he moved into lodgings in Bishop Auckland. Obvious he didn't want his wife and daughter to have ought. Bet ya he sold the blinking lot for the price of a night's drink."

"Probably," said Richard.

"Maybe he doesn't know they are staying at your house."

"You must be joking," Richard said mockingly. "Why, I bet he knew they were here the first night. His cronies will be keeping him well informed, that's for sure. No, he'll live the life of a bachelor for a while, then if they haven't gone back to him, he'll come looking."

"What'll you do then?"

"I'll just take it as it comes. No good worrying about something that hasn't happened, is there?"

"I do worry though," said Mr. Jones sadly.

"I know you do, so I'll let you worry for the both of us, until that time comes."

"What does Sadie say about it all? Is she happy with being housekeeper for the pair of us in exchange for board and lodgings?"

"She seems to be, but she's not one for talking much. Bridie is the one that tells me they are happy with the set up. I just let her get on with it."

"What about you Richard? What do you think?"

"Well I have never eaten so well and I guess you haven't. And while you make the best Welsh rarebit I ever tasted, some of the food she dishes up is great. What do you think?"

"For the first few days I wasn't sure. It's been a long time since I had someone cooking and ironing for me. Not since I left Wales really. I had got into a sort of way with things, but when I look at all the different meals I come in from work to, it's lovely. And another thing, I know you think my high starched collars are old fashioned but I like them. Now I have a clean one every morning. It's fantastic."

"Well it seems that we are all happy with the set up. Let's hope it stays that way, eh?"

"I say my prayers for that to be so every night."

"Keep them up, Mr. Jones, they seem to be working."

"For now they are, but I fear the worst. I fear it is just a matter of time before *he* turns up."

"That's it Mr. Jones. You keep worrying for the pair of us. In the meantime I must get back to work. See ya tonight."

"You're back early, Richard. Something wrong at work?" said Sadie.

"It seems we'll never get back to work proper. It's but two weeks, isn't it, since we went back and we're laid off again."

"Why? They haven't gone out on strike again have they?"

"No, nowt like that. Just the winter weather getting at the pipes—they're frozen solid. We've stoked all the furnaces and with a bit of luck we should be back in a couple of days. If the weather breaks that is."

"Does that mean you'll be at home all day?"

"Possibly. Why does that bother you? It might give us a bit of time to get to know one another."

"No. I was thinking maybe you'd be better off if we were to make our move now. Bridie is well recovered."

"Is she? That surprises me last night she was telling me she still feels a little groggy now and then."

"I think she is trying to kid the troops."

"What do you mean?"

"I don't think she wants to leave. I mean she wants to stay here, not just in the village but here in your house. She says it's the only place she feels safe."

"That suits me, but you're not so sure are you?" Sadie shook her head gently from side to side. "Is it Hickey? Have you forgiven him already?"

"Never," Sadie replied indignantly.

"Then it's settled. Let's talk about leaving no more. The matter's closed as far as I'm concerned. Will you stay?" Sadie stayed silent for a moment, then she looked up at Richard who towered above her.

"Shall we try it, say, till after Christmas?"

"Fine," he said.

Before enough time to repair the frozen pipes had passed, Hickey received a coded message to return to Ireland, for a mission of utmost importance.

"Seamus we've brought you over to tell you that the leaders think that the time is right for the rising."

"And about time too. Let's get at the British bastards and throw them and their kin into the Irish Sea. This time we'll finish the job."

"I knew I could count on your support," Hickey's superior roared with laughter. "We estimate there are about eight thousand Fenians now in the country and the time is ripe."

"It's long over due. I expected to be fighting the day after we got Stephens out of the Bridewell.

"There was a lot thought he was wrong to hold off, Seamus. It nearly divided the Brotherhood as well. That group that broke away and were hell-bent to fight the Canadian Brits almost split us in two."

"I can understand their frustration. If I'd been there I would have wanted to be doing something. Better fight any Brits as sit around on our arses. What's the point?"

"Well it cost him his job didn't it? Do you think though that Thomas Kelley will be as good a leader?"

"He should be, as Stephens chief of staff he should have learned a thing or two. And he obviously doesn't mind a fight, he hasn't been in charge ten minutes and already he's calling us to arms. Seems like a man of action to me."

"We'll have to see. Remember Seamus, a new brush sweeps clean, abut an old brush sweeps forever."

Colonel Kelly, after almost one year in office, was in danger of being tarred with the same brush as his predecessor. Throughout 1866, enduring bouts of boredom and false hopes of imminent rebellion, Hickey remained in Ireland. Eventually Kelly was hurried into a decision to rise in the February of the following year.

"Are all your men ready, Seamus?"

"They are sir, they just wait your word."

"Good, now here's what we must do." The first attack was to be upon the garrison at Chester Castle, only lightly guarded and the huge cache of arms, carelessly protected. The guns and ammunition were then to be rushed to Holyhead.

"We'll then seize what ever steamers lay at anchor, cross to Dublin and begin the rising."

"A bold plan sir, if I may say so, but it's a goodjun. It is that."

"Thanks, Seamus, and good luck." Arriving at Chester Castle, they were to be disappointed. British intelligence had sniffed out their plot and were prepared. The attackers found the garrison stripped of all arms and on alert. There was nothing more that could be done other than send the men back to their homes. The following day while languishing in Kerry, Hickey received another coded message.

"What does it say?" Hickey asked his subordinate.

"It says we're to be ready on the eleventh of February, 1867.

"When's that?"

"It's the day after tomorrow," someone answered.

"Good," said Hickey. "Just two days. Less time for them snooping informers to give us away. Spread the word for the men to be ready."

The first two weeks of the year saw life begin to return to normal after the strike. Since New Year's Day, Mr. Raine had officially replaced Joseph Vaughan and Michael had been promoted.

"There'll be no talking to you now that you're the under manager mate," his friends ribbed him as they walked to work.

"I'll still be Michael Bryan whatever title they give me, except to you of course," he retorted to young Will Patrick, flipping his flat cap off his head. "To you it will be *Sir*."

"Why is Joseph, I mean, Mr. Vaughan, leaving, Michael? I thought he owned the firm?" young Will asked.

"No, he doesn't exactly own the firm. He has shares in it but not as many as his family used to have. I really don't know why he is leaving. He doesn't tell me everything you know."

"I thought he did. You and him being so close and all."

"He'll tell me if he wants me to know, it's not really any of my business, *or yours*. Is it now?"

"I was just curious, for they say he is only moving to Bishop Auckland and starting a new firm there. You won't be leaving will you Michael?"

"Leaving? I wouldn't have thought so would you? Just having been made Under Manager that would be daft now wouldn't it?"

"I'm pleased to hear that and I'm sure a lot of the other blokes who work here will be an all. Most think you're a good and fair gaffer. It's true I've heard many a man say it, I have."

"Stop it you'll have me blushing. Get yersel clocked in and to your post. The hooter will be blowing any minute. I've gotta go and see Mr. Vaughan about something."

"Come in Michael, come in and pull up a chair," Joseph greeted his friend from behind a massive desk that was strewn with plans. "Just going over the final layout of the new factory. Like to see them?"

"Of course," Michael replied. "Pots and pans eh? Who would have thought of it? Why these machines you are getting will make thousands won't they?"

"Thousands and thousands, but the military contract will take most of the production. That still leaves the home market and, of course, the Empire itself," Joseph's tone then changed from exuberant to melancholy. "Are you sure you won't change your mind and join me, we've been a good team for many a year now, I'm not sure I'll manage without your advice and friendship."

"You're going to Bishop Auckland, three miles away, not to the moon. And since you're still to live in Carwood House, for the time being, things will not be so different."

"I hope not," Joseph interjected.

"I assure you they won't," Michael concluded, "And can we change the subject please. Right. Why did you send for me anyway?"

"Okay, we'll speak no more of it. I'll finish by saying that I want you to know that anytime you change your mind the door is always open."

"I thought you said we'd speak no more of it?"

"Oops, sorry," Joseph replied, unable to hide his childish grin. "Why did I send for you? About the party of course. So how's the guest list progressing?"

202

"I've got the list here," said Michael, drawing from the pocket of his tweed coat a dog-eared piece of foolscap paper. "I still think you should have done it though. Why you wanted me to help is still beyond me. Would you like to go over it now?"

"Because, my good friend, while I know almost everyone in the village, you know them intimately. You know their beliefs and their political persuasions. The strike almost tore our community apart I want this get together to be part of the healing. We'll use it to bring together people that haven't spoken to each other since those awful times. I want my leaving party to be of some good not just an excuse for a free meal."

"Has being so paternal to these folks something to do with you leaving the firm so suddenly?" Michael asked.

"Are you asking *did I jump or was I pushed?*"

Humbled, Michael began, "I'm sorry Joseph I didn't mean to pry. Please don't attempt to answer that question. I'm sorry I asked it."

"Do you really want to know, Michael?"

"No I do not," Michael answered firmly. "Mr. Raine is a good man but I know this, the ironworks and the men who work here will both be the poorer for your leaving. And that's for sure."

"Now it's my turn," Joseph replied. "Let's talk no more of the whys and the wherefores of my leaving shall we? One day perhaps when we are both old and retired we'll sit around a bottle of port and reminisce, eh? Looking at the two of us perhaps I should lay down a couple of bottles right now for that day may not be so far away," Both men laughed loudly. "Lets get to the invitations."

At the top of the list, they both agreed, should be the doctors McKechnie and Beddingfield, who had given their services free during the bitter struggle.

To Richard's delight, Sadie, just before the Christmas deadline, agreed to make her stay permanent. In return she would continue to get board and lodgings for herself and Bridie in Richard's cottage. The first two weeks of the arrangement were somewhat of an upheaval for Richard and his neighbour, Mr. Jones. Having become self-sufficient since his departure from Wales, the little choirmaster initially found things very strange.

"C'mon, Mr. Jones," his office colleague chided him, "You must enjoy being looked after, to some extent."

"To some extent, yes, but it takes some getting used to after almost twenty years."

"And how's Richard taking to it?"

"Like a duck takes to water!"

"I thought you looked after him?"

"No, I only did a bit of cooking. I mean … it's as easy to cook for two as one isn't it?"

"Aye, I suppose so, but who did the washing and ironing?"

"I drew a line at that. I did my own and he did his. That's one thing I've never got to like, but I had to learn quick. Now Richard he is a typical bachelor. Do you know he only used to iron the bits you could see of his shirt? I mean he wouldn't dream of ironing the back!

"So, why did you never get a washer woman?"

"On my wages? I'm a time keeper clerk remember, not a puddler. Anyway my late wife would have been a hard act to follow, nobody could starch my collars like her."

"Your late wife? She died did she?"

"Sort of," Mr. Jones answered evasively. "Anyway, enough chattering, I must collect the time cards." With that he abruptly left the office.

"What the hell is that unholy noise?" Patrick exclaimed. From over the rooftops came an off-key melody accompanied by the rhythmic thud of a distant drum.

"That'll be Margot and the league I guess. She told me they were marching today."

"What bloody league?" Patrick huffed as he tried to settle back to his snoozing in his favourite armchair.

"The village League and Band of Hope, it's a pity Patrick Bryan that you never joined them."

"I'd love to, I think not. Band of bloody sober sides that's what they are."

"Then maybe I should join them."

"Don't even consider it woman, don't even think about it. And when I see that Margot I'm gonna tell her to keep her to keep the noise down, some people need their sleep."

"Some people would not need to sleep in the afternoon if they had not been to the boozer would they now?"

"Oh, whisht woman, put a sock in it will you! You and Margot do my head in about the drink. Can a man not have a little pleasure out of life?" At that he feigned snoring until Annie gave up remonstrating.

Nationally, there was a revival in the Temperance movement. Led by Margot, behind their banner of promised deliverance, the Witton Park League marched round and round the village streets. Campaigning seemed to be in the blood of the Morris family. David also worked endlessly for the trade union cause. Although they had been humiliated at the hands of the ironmasters and despite dejection he still worked enthusiastically recruiting new members.

"The next time more workers will be members of the union," he said to his father. "This is the only way to beat these ironmasters. What we need is one hundred per cent of the work force to be members then we will win."

"Don't think you will ever see that day," his father commented despondently.

"Never say never, Da. It'll not be my fault if we don't for I'm never gonna stop trying to get more men to join us. There's always been strength in numbers and that's how I see our future."

"I hope your right lad, I really do."

"I am right, Da. You wait. You'll see that one day the power of the workforce will prevail. It has to, what hope, has the little man got if not?"

"Are you all set for Xmas day then?" Margot asked Annie as they chatted over a mid morning cup of tea.

"As ready as I'll ever be. What we haven't got now we'll have to do without."

"Same as that," Margot agreed.

"Isn't it your young Will's birthday today as well?"

"Aye. He's officially a man now. I can't believe where those twenty-one years have gone. They've flown over haven't they?"

"They certainly have," Annie's eyes glazed over. "Every time I look at young Will I see our Philip and in a way watching him grow has helped me a little somehow."

"There now, Annie, don't go working yourself up again. Let's just count our blessings shall we?"

"It's not as easy as that, Margot. Never a day goes by that I don't think of him. Never a day goes by that I don't weep inside."

"Annie, I'm not going to say that I can even begin to understand your grief. If something like that happened to one of mine I think I'd go crazy. But you, you've been so strong."

"Don't you believe it my friend, it's all a front. I need to put this bold face on every morning I get out of bed. Anyway, your Will, I suppose he'll be getting married next? Has he picked his self a partner yet or is he still sowing his wild oats?"

"He better not be," an indignant Margot replied. "He knows he better never bring trouble to this door or he'll find out what trouble really is."

"I mean has he settled his self down to one lass yet or is he still going out with half the village?"

"Annie, can you remember that day when he came home from school and shocked us all by telling us that when he grew up he was going to marry Bridie Hickey?"

"Of course I can, but he was just a bairn."

"Umm, you think so, eh? So what if I was to tell you that he told me exactly the same thing again just the other night?"

"*Never!*" Annie exclaimed.

"I tell you it's the truth. That's exactly what he said."

"And what has Bridie said to all of this then?"

"Oh, he said he hasn't told her yet!"

"And what did his father have to say about that?"

"Well, William said he and young Will had a long chat about it all. William, while he is not anti-Roman Catholic, explained that it really was an impossible relationship."

"Why?" asked Annie. "Why in Heaven's name should him being a Methodist and her a Catholic stop them marrying?"

"You know why Annie, c'mon you're a Catholic. Can you imagine our Will changing his religion just so he could marry her?"

"And you know he wouldn't have to do that. If he just agrees to be married in a Catholic church and agrees to the children being brought up Catholic then he can keep his religion."

"We know that, but one seems as bad as t'other from where we stand."

"So what's to come of it all then?"

"Nothing, absolutely nowt. It seems we all jumped the gun."

"How do you mean?"

"William told me that young Will had listened respectfully to him then said, "Da you've got it all wrong with regard to Bridie's creed. Her father, Hickey, is a Papist but it seems Bridie's mother has never embraced Catholicism, nor did Bridie."

"My, my, well that explains a lot. I always thought they were just bad Catholics since I have never, ever, known them go to church. Well, me grandfather said if I lived long enough I'd learn everything and there yer go ... I've learned something this day."

"I thought it was Patrick's grandfather that was supposed to have said that?" asked Margot.

"Oh well, it was one of them, that's for sure." Both women giggled as they finished their cooled tea.

Will was determined to court Bridie but up until now this had been difficult in the extreme. No opportunity had seemed to present itself where he could get to talk to her. Now the news that in the company of her mother she had taken lodgings with their family friends was the best twenty-first birthday present he could have wished for. Time

206

ticked by in the village and life seemed idyllic to young Will as he spent more and more of his free time at Richard's cottage.

"How's your Aunt Annie?" Bridie asked. "I see your Ma still marching around with her banners and band but I've noticed Annie is not with her so often."

"You know she's not my real Aunt, don't you? We call her that out of respect. Anyway it's not because Uncle Patrick is drinking less these days that she doesn't go out so much with Ma, but she hasn't been too well this past month so I'm told. Why, although I live next door to her I've hardly seen her myself."

"It's nothing serious I hope is it?" Bridie asked sympathetically.

"I don't know really, I haven't really asked. Maybe I should. I mean, she's no spring chicken now is she?"

"And you say Patrick is off the drink? Why that takes some believing."

"No, I never said he was off the drink. It's just he doesn't drink as much these days. All the crusading in the world would never convert Uncle Patrick. Why, he told me his self that he wouldn't feel properly dressed without his hip flask."

"He's some man isn't he?"

"He is that.... one of life's characters. Anyway, he is spending more and more time with his grandbairns. I bet he's down the fields with them and his dog right now."

Up until the onset of winter, Patrick was a familiar sight playing ball in the fields that surrounded the village with seven grandchildren and the ever-present Hadaway III, grandson of the original Hadaway.

"Can we go down the river today, Granda?" one child asked.

"Not today pet, maybe another day eh?"

"Aw, you always say that, Granda, please, can we not go today?"

"Not today pet, not today. Look, run get the ball before Hadaway does." The giggling children ran through the lush meadow grass trampling the bright yellow buttercups as they raced after the ball Patrick had thrown to distract the conversation. Often they played for hours but always in the fields, never near the river. The swirling water that claimed his son was still the scene of too much heartache for him. Hadaway III loved these hours as much as the children. The ball held firm between his teeth, he would bark, prance and dance, teasing and defying the children to take it from him. When exhausted from chasing him, they gave up and sat making daisy chains while their Granda puffed on his pipe. Hadaway sat guarding the ball until he realized the game was over. Even then he never gave it up but always ran away and buried it.

"You stupid Irish dog, your as thick as your grandfather was. That's another bloody ball you've cost me," Patrick shouted at him. Hadaway wagged his tail and rolled over onto his back in submission. "Stupid bloody dog." Patrick ruffled the animal's almost-silver, wiry coat.

On the third Saturday in January, William Morris, one of the invited guests at Joseph's leaving party, remarked, "Well it seems the sun does shine on the righteous. We could have not asked the Lord for a better day for Joseph's leaving party and the cricket match."

"Looks like there's more people here than we catered for," Michael commented to his host.

"Well, a few more won't make much difference will it Michael?"

"No, I doubt it. Do you know I swear there's more people here than when the works opened."

"Good," said Joseph firmly. He had cut no corners providing a 'sit down tea' for six hundred guests and friends. This would be taken after a hastily organised cricket match. The teams were to be England versus 'The Rest'. Patrick refused the umpire's job and was determined to play. After much lobbying to keep the peace, the captain of 'The Rest' selected him as eleventh man.

"It's a bit early, even for you isn't it, Patrick?" asked Bill Hall, landlord of the Vulcan Hotel as he downed his second Irish whiskey before nine o'clock.

"I need a stiffener before I go out and face that leather ball. Why man, have you seen how fast some of dem bowlers throw the bloody thing at yer? Right I'll have to be going, there's the band leading the teams to the field. Can't miss being in that. It wouldn't do for the all-important eleventh man not to be in the parade. Now would it?"

"No, not at all," said the barkeep satirically. "Go get 'em Patrick, you can do it."

He left the bar holding his head high as to join his team mates behind the band, heading towards the sports field.

"Where abouts shall we play," asked Doctor Beddingfield as he surveyed the field.

"May I suggest the area with the least cow pats," David said. "Some of those cow droppings are bigger than meat plates. Wouldn't like to see our nice white trousers if we slipped into one of them!"

"Good point," said the doctor as he set of to inspect the meadow. "This seems about the best area, drive one set of stumps in here and I'll pace out the distance for the other end."

Stumps in place, the umpires roughly paced out a boundary line, and the captain of Patrick's team, having lost the toss, sent him out to field there. Opening the batting for England, Joseph and Doctor

Beddingfield batted steady for the first two hours scoring over forty runs.

"We'll never get them out," thought Patrick. "I wish they would let me bowl. I bet I could do better than that." The weakness of the bowling was such that, had the playing surface not resembled a sea in storm, the score could have been in the hundreds. With those balls that were not miles off target, the opening batsmen punished the bowlers. Patrick was finding the whole thing boring, having little to do other than occasionally scare off a curious cow. The hours towards the lunch break dragged on until the umpire lifted the bails signalling lunch.

"And where do you think you are going Patrick?" Annie asked him as he tried to slip through the crowd. He leaned forward and whispered to his wife.

"I need te go to the lavvy, that's where I was going."

"Oh, that's all right then, but make sure you use the one at our house and not the one in the Vulcan," she said firmly.

"The thought never crossed me mind," Patrick lied through his teeth. Looking firstly over his left shoulder then his right, confident he had not been followed he rushed into the bar of the Vulcan.

"Set 'em up Ted," he called as he strolled the short distance from the door to the brass railed wooden bar. "Only got time for a quick 'un. Well, maybe two, eh?" Ted the barman smiled as he poured a liberal glass of whiskey for one of his favourite customers.

After lunch, events took a different turn; the captain of the multi-national team unleashed his newly discovered weapon. Over lunch a modest Richard Blackman had asked that he be given a chance to bowl.

"You've played cricket before, Richard?"

"Often at home. You don't think we just lay around on the beach all day do you? Why, it's probably more popular there than here."

"They're bringing on a new bowler I see," Beddingfield said to David. "It's to be Richard is it, well I never."

"They don't play cricket in the East Indies do they? I mean it's a Dutch colony isn't it?"

"Your guess is as good as mine. Let's see what he's made of. If the next half hour goes the same way as the morning session I think we should declare, don't you? Give the blighters a sporting chance. What?" David agreed wholeheartedly. It took the good doctor longer to walk to the crease than he stayed there as his outside stump and bails flew into the air.

"Well I never," he exclaimed as he walked off shaking his head in disbelief before handing the bat to the third man. Sections of the crowd went wild while Patrick jumped up and down in the air exciting Hadaway to a frenzy.

"Lucky ball," someone shouted from the crowd.

"We'll see," Mr. Jones shouted back. Richard took a long, long walk back before turning and building up his speed to an almost sprint. Nearing the crease he brought his long arm high above his head before releasing the ball at an all mighty speed from above seven feet in the air. The batsman never really saw the ball as it hurtled towards him, but simply flayed at where he hoped it might be. His gesture was more self defence than offensive batting and resulted in his bat cleaning out his own stumps.

"Out," shouted the umpire, his call almost drowned out by the enthusiastic crowd. The batsmen were terrified and concentrated on self-preservation as Richard hurled down ball after ball at breathtaking speed. Bails flew in every direction and on every dismissal, Patrick forgetting his age, jumped up and spun in mid air as Hadaway snapped at his heels. As Richard took his now usual long run up a woman shouted from the crowd.

" C'mon Richard just one more. Just for me."

"Ma. What are you doing shouting for Richard like that? People will hear you," Bridie said to her unusually exuberant mother.

"Who cares," Sadie said dismissively. "C'mon Richard. C'mon." When the last wicket fell, caught by the wicket keeper off a wicked Richard delivery, the loudest cheer came from none other than Sadie.

"Well done, Richard," the captain said to him as they gathered before their turn to bat. "Please tell me you can also wield a bat as well as you can bowl. If you can then maybe, just maybe their ninety-six is gettable?"

"Sorry, I'm absolutely rubbish at batting. Never got the hang of it all. Don't put me in early 'cos you will be really disappointed," said Richard.

"Damn, then me and David Morris will have to open the batting. Wish us luck."

"What about me? When do I get a go," interrupted Patrick. "Up to now all I've done is stand out there near that fence and twiddle me thumbs. Apart from when I nearly stopped that ball. And I would have too had I not slipped in that cow shit. I mean, look at my trousers they're covered in it.

"Soon," said the captain. "We're not outta the woods yet. Most of these English did nothing else at school and college but play cricket."

"I know that. But they don't scare me. They haven't got a Richard. *Have they?*"

"Who knows, they may have. Don't worry you'll get your go ... just stay lucky when it comes to your turn."

"I can't be anything else now can I?" Patrick replied. "You know what they say don't you?"

"What's that?" the puzzled captain asked.

"Well, folks say 'shit for luck'. So you see looking at me trousers I can't fail can I?"

Under pressure from experienced English bowlers, wickets fell steadily, but assisted by the poor wicket and more good luck than management, the score of the internationals grew steadily.

"How many's that we are now?" an anxious Patrick asked William Morris. The batsmen were passing each other as the ball was thrown in from the outfield, straight into the wicket keeper's gloved hands. With a graceful swipe he took off the bails before the batsman could get his bat beyond the crease line and safety.

"Out," shouted the umpire and another bowler took the long walk.

"We would have been seventy two if that silly bugger hadn't run his mate out," replied one of the earlier batsmen from Patrick's team. By three thirty in the afternoon Patrick, fortified by the contents of his hip flask, was anxious to get at them. Victory, although a tall order, was not beyond their grasp. If the final three batsmen could get thirty more runs, they could still snatch a victory.

"How's that?" the bowler shouted to the umpire as his ball had been stopped only from taking out the middle stump by the batsman's leg. The batsman looked to the umpire, as did the crowd, awaiting his decision for what seemed an eternity.

"Out," he shouted, to a mixture of sighs and cheers from the crowd.

"It's up to you now, Richard," David said hopefully. "There's only you and Patrick left. Good luck."

"Thanks," said Richard. "I'll probably need it." After Richard had faced his first few balls David turned to their captain.

"Well, Richard certainly didn't underestimate his lack of batting skills. I fear the worst; he's swinging the bat as though it was a club ..." He paused to watch the next delivery. "... But that'll do!" said David as the crack of the leather ball on the willow bat signalled that this was going to clear the boundary over the head of the fielders.

"I hope the ball isn't lost in the hedge, said Joseph, "...it's the only one we've got."

"I hope he doesn't put one of the church windows out," said the verger standing next to him.

"Six," called the umpire.

"Brilliant. Go on, Richard another couple of them and we'll be in with a shout," yelled a teammate. Richard added another five runs before he was caught out from a descending ball, which he had hit straight up towards the heavens.

"Out," called the umpire and Richard to great applause handed the bat to the eager Patrick.

"How many runs do we need Richard?" Patrick asked as he took the bat.

"Eighteen to win," Richard replied.

"No problem. You just watch this. Patrick Bryan will show these bloody English toffs a thing or two."

"Oh, excuse me," he said to a surprised spectator. "Do you think you could lend me that fine cricket hat? It's for to keep the sun out of my eyes."

"Well I suppose I can't say no, can I?" the startled man stammered. "I'm sure that will be no problem, will it Emily?" His equally surprised wife did not answer but stood with her eyes agog. The man took off his neat white cotton hat, adorned in a purple circular pattern and handed it to Patrick.

"Thank you, kind sir. Now, seeing as you have no hair to protect your head from this heat, may I suggest that you wear this for the time being? Patrick handed over his woollen cap. With the importance of royalty, crowned by his new hat Patrick strutted out to the crease. Adjusting the peak against the setting sun, he surveyed the position of the fielders, remembering that's what his captain had done. The English bowlers, in an effort to avoid as many clumps of the meadows grass as possible, were bowling right up to Patrick, but there were still sufficient tufts to send the cricket ball off in all directions. Each ball that failed to have him out, Patrick considered a triumph, and raised his bat to the crowd who, in turn, were getting into the mood of things and cheering. At the other end, his partner was steadily chipping away at the England side's lead. As his partner hit the ball and they ran the twenty-two yards between the stumps Patrick took the adulation. Each time he had to run he acknowledged the crowd by raising his bat and hat.

The patriotic crowd loved it and encouraged the last two batsmen as the score crept closer. During the next run Patrick wondered why the crowd was laughing until he looked down. Running alongside him was no other than Hadaway. Amidst the laughter a righteously angry Patrick led the dog to Michael, leaving his son in charge of the wayward animal.

"Michael, can you not hang on to that stupid animal?"

"Sorry Da, but you know what he's like he just wants to join in."

"Well, it's not a game. Well, it is I suppose. *But not for dogs.* Now hang onto that stupid Irish mutt."

"Yes, Da," Michael said through his uncontrollable giggles. As the opposition rearranged their fielders, Patrick and his partner stood together midway down the pitch.

"Can you believe it, Patrick? We are only three runs from victory. Now then, you have to face the first ball of the over. If we can manage to get a single then that will give me a chance to protect you from the bowlers then possibly get the runs."

"Protect me? I need no bloody protection. Don't you be worrying about Patrick Bryan. He can look after himself. No sir, I need no bloody *protection.*"

"I didn't mean that Patrick. It's just tactics, that's all. Cos it looks like they are bringing their best bowler back on to finish us off."

"I don't care who they bring on, and I don't need any of them fancy *tactics* either. *What ever they are.*" An indignant Patrick walked back to the crease to face the bowler.

The first ball that Patrick connected with was a loose ball from their bowler. Hit square with the middle of the bat, the crack could be heard in nearby Woodside. The ball travelled higher and higher into the air clearing the nearest fielder by over twenty feet heading for the unmanned boundary. It then fell back to earth like a stone but trickled towards the boundary and four runs. A fielder raced after the ball but everyone knew he would never catch it up.

"Go on, go!" Patrick urged the slowing ball. "For God's sake keep going." Meanwhile an astonished Michael stood looking at the leather leader and empty dog collar in his hand, as Hadaway was halfway across the field.

"Come back!" he shouted in vain as the fleet footed animal ate up the yards in pursuit of the ball. Its speed relegated ensuing fielders to seeming slow motion. With only a couple of yards to roll before the ball crossed the boundary line, and victory for Patrick's team, Hadaway was onto it. Grabbing it in his mouth he stood and looked defiantly at the approaching cricketers. A furious Patrick had thrown down his bat and joined in the chase.

"You put down that ball *right now,*" he shouted, the veins in his neck as thick as his index finger as anger and exertion made him turn red. After a teasing friendly bark, ball in mouth, Hadaway set of to run around the cricket square. He deftly swerved around players and spectators alike who had joined in the chase. At last the dog stood still, only about ten yards away from its master.

"Right, you've had your bloody fun. Now drop that ball. Do you hear me, Hadaway? Drop that bloody ball. *Now!*" Patrick commanded. But Patrick's authoritive tone had no impact whatsoever. To tumultuous laughter from the crowd the dog took flight again.

"One word from me, and that dog does exactly as it likes," Patrick said aloud as he watched the animal vanish into the woodland bordering the field. Half an hour later, despite frantic searching, the buried ball could not be located and the game was abandoned as a draw.

"I'll kill that bloody dog when I get my hands on it," a breathless Patrick said to his son as he was handed back the collar and lead.

"Not if your team mates kill you first," Michael joked.

During the opening days of February, much covert activity was under way in Ireland. Despite great secrecy at grass root level, they were unaware that in Liverpool an informer was relaying their every move to the authorities. The discovery almost came too late for some. On the mainland, the Fenian leaders, learning of their betrayal, sent orders across the water: "Send word out to all units. Cancel the rising for February the eleventh."

The news did not reach Kerry in time where Colonel John O'Connor, Hickey and others seized a coastguard station near Cachiriveen. There they captured a tired police dispatch rider.

"Sir, see what the man has in his bag. It's a copy of orders from our HQ and intended for yourself. How the fiken hell did the Brits get hold of a copy?"

"Let me see that," Colonel O'Connor said relieving Hickey of the proffered papers from the rider's satchel.

"Have you read this?" O'Connor asked Hickey.

"Not fully, sir. Is it trouble?"

"It is that. Had we received this message, we would have known that this rising was cancelled. It's a bit late now to be telling us, especially as it says that military and police reinforcements are being sent here to catch us."

"What do you want the men to do then sir?" Hickey asked.

"It says I'm to return to America with great speed and you are to disperse your men and wait for further instructions." Hickey melted into the background of his native country to await further instructions. He did not have to wait long, undeterred by events, Fenian leaders, both sides of the Irish Sea, agreed upon a second attempt, this was to be less than a month after the Kerry incident.

"It's to be March the fourth," the messenger informed Hickey.

"Good, tell the commander my men will be ready."

"I'll do that thing. Good luck, Hickey." The selected night for the second Irish uprising was bitter and snow, driven by a stiff Atlantic wind, chilled to the bones. The leaders were aware that total victory was impossible, but hoped that such an action would further alienate the British from the American government.

"Is there no way that our Irish cousins over the pond could stage some form of military action that might help the cause?" one of Hickeys men asked him.

"I don't think that would be a good idea. If we attack the Yanks it could cost us a lot of friends. Lose them then where would we get the money and guns? No, it's up to us. The best we can hope for is that after we win this fight the United States recognises us as the Irish Republic."

"I didn't mean against the Yanks. I just heard one of them the Yank Fenian bigwigs is saying we should attack the Brits in Canada."

"Well, they can if they want but I think we've got enough on our plate to worry about right here. Don't you?" In the event, the uprising collapsed too early to have any impact. Throughout the country, clashes occurred between the Fenians, police and military, but the informers caused many failures. Outclassed and out gunned, it was a one-sided affair. The commander of Dublin summoned Hickey.

"Seamus, we've been betrayed again. The Brits know everything we're about. We've got no chance now. It was Massey, aide to Colonel Kelly who betrayed us. Last night he was captured and he's turned informer."

"The treacherous bastard," Hickey spurted out, spitting on the floor in a gesture of disgust.

"So he is and may he rot in hell but in the meantime we've gotta make new plans. We now know that they intend to try and finish us for good this time. They've got the police and the soldiers working together."

"And the bloody weather doesn't help," said Hickey.

"It might just help. You see Massey will have told them of our plan to build barricades and that's when they expect to capture us. While they're waiting for us to do just that you must start slipping your men out of Dublin and into the mountains. Move two and three at a time. The storm will give them a little bit of cover."

"Yes, sir."

In the United States, news of the isolated Kerry rising had caused much interest, but the reaction to the March national rebellion caused a sensation.

"I told you that we were not ready for a national rising," Stephens said to Roberts as they sat in the New York office of the Fenian movement.

"I agreed with you. Remember? It was me who said let's have a go at Canada. Let our Yankee lads have a go. It would have trained them up well and then we could have taken them back with us. Anyway the publicity will have done us no harm."

"Publicity? Go tell that to the widows of the patriots that today lie all over Ireland. They'll take poor comfort from that I'll wager. And where was this 'total commitment' from our cousins over here? The reports that I have are that of the thousands of brave Irish lads who fought only one hundred and fifty were Irish-Americans. And what happened to the Fenian fleet that was suppose to leave from these shores?"

"It never happened," Roberts said sadly. "Only one small vessel, the 'Erin's Hope,' with a manifest of five hundred men at arms and thirty Irish officers set sail. They were not to know that it would all be over by the time they arrived."

"Did they land?"

"The officers did and were promptly arrested."

"Oh my God. What next? And what became of the men?"

"They turned round and sailed home I believe."

"Thank God for small mercies."

The elusive Hickey once more evaded capture and this time made his escape to America. Later in the year, Roberts led a force against the British in Canada and was effectively humiliated, although he remained determined that this was the route to success. The following two years, prior to the general depression of 1870, were relatively tranquil and prosperous times for Witton Park. The village's own gas company installed innovative gas lighting in all the streets, much to the envy of the surrounding districts.

"This Factory Extension Act is bound to put costs up," the manager of the works told the production meeting. Under the new rules we are going to have to provide two hours of teaching and give meal breaks to any bairns that we have employed. It'll soon not be worth employing them."

"Why man, that's ridiculous. How did they get that through Parliament?" said one unsympathetic foreman.

In the fall of 1868, millionaire ironmaster John Vaughan died, although many strikers' families did not lament his passing. In the same year his German partner, Henry W. F. Bolckow entered the Houses of Parliament as honourable member for Middlesbrough. Too late to add his weight against the humble Factory Extension Act that he vehemently opposed—an act that meant so much in the fight against child labour.

By the following spring, Margot had collected nearly one thousand signatures supporting Mr. Joseph Pease M.P.; whose private member's bill 'The Permissive Propitiatory Liquor Bill' was before Parliament.

Monday was traditionally washing day. From the wall of every terraced house, across the street to the house opposite, thin rope lines were strung. Like a street filled with bunting, dozens of parallel rows of laundry fluttered in the breeze hoisted high by tall clothes props. On one such Monday, after almost twenty-five years, the village, whose population was equivalent to the total of the three surrounding parishes, was granted full parish status. Formed wholly from Escomb Parish, it would also include Woodside.

Only one shadow was cast over 1869, in the latter part—after an absence of almost two years—Hickey had been seen in Bishop Auckland.

Chapter Fifteen 1869 - 1871

The warm October night the Irish unexpectedly attacked the Welsh signalled the start of the bloodiest period in the village's turbulent history.

"Were you in Robert Longstaff's public house last night ... when the trouble broke out?" William asked Patrick.

"No, not at all. I think I've only been in once in me life. Why you know it's where all the Welsh drink."

"So what were all the Irish doing in here then?"

"Looking for trouble?"

"Aye, but why have the Irish started fighting the Welsh? Has the village not got enough problems with neighbour fighting neighbour and husbands and wives battling? The last thing we need is a large scale nationality thing coming into it."

"Hey, don't forget your David's union lot, they're always at it. They're no angels now."

"C'mon Patrick, now you know that was different. They only fought with them blacklegs. It's not like it is now with the Fenians fighting the Orangemen and now the Welsh and Irish at each other's throats. Why it's getting to be like the wild west of America around here. What were they battling about anyway?"

"I haven't a clue. But I'm told by the time the pollis arrived they found the windows smashed, jugs and glass bottles broken, and the floor covered with half bricks."

"Oh they reckon it was a battle royal so it was. Gareth Jones was telling our David that they had been warned that something was going to happen, so they were on their guard. He said that when the Irish arrived—bent on trouble—the Welshmen blew out the candles and the battle began. He said three of his mates were laid in pools of blood with plaster from the walls and ceilings stuck to them."

"Bloody hell," said Patrick.

"One of them had been hit over the head with the brass fender from the fireplace and lay knocked-out next to his mate whose arm was gashed to the bone. The other lad had his leg broken, so when the police arrived everybody scarpered but the injured that couldn't, and they were the only ones arrested. They were in front of the magistrate this morning."

"How did they get on?"

"They were ordered to pay damages and costs and the magistrate issued warrants for the Irishmen who took off."

"They'll never find them," Patrick said.

"We know that, Patrick. We know that."

"It's every time somebody mentions home rule for Ireland. Either the Loyalists or the Fenians kick off."

"Aye, you're right there, Patrick. But I fear this 'Irish problem' will not be over for a long time. Not in a hundred years."

Young Will came racing up the street.

"Da! Da!" he shouted with great urgency. "Get everybody inside. All hell has broken loose down the bottoms!"

"Steady lad ... take your time and tell us what's happening," his father implored.

"Can you not hear the ruckus? Listen. There's upwards of eighty men battling in the bottom streets."

"Who's battling? Slow down, lad and tell us what's going on will ya?"

"Well, me and me mate were sat on the station wall. Outside the Railway Tavern there was about twenty to thirty Fenians drinking. Suddenly about fifty Orangemen came round the corner and surrounded them. The Fenians tried to get away but the Orangemen started to chase them. The Fenians were getting hell knocked out of them by the time Inspector Askew and some officers came.

"Right, Patrick. I don't know about you but I'm going in and locking the doors. This could go on all night."

"Good idea, William. I'll see you both tomorrow. Goodnight."

By morning two Fenians, Lawrence Holloway and Peter Cairns lay on the village streets in an insensible state. One of them did not regain consciousness for three days. Seven of the Orangemen who'd been seen taking part in the riot were later arrested.

"I see they're out, eh?" said Patrick.

"Who?" asked William.

"Them seven Orangemen Inspector Askew locked up."

"Are they? Why they haven't been in ten minutes."

"That's 'cos they weren't locked up proper. They was just remanded; till they came in front of 'the beak'."

"So what did they get then?"

"Notten really, they were just bound over to keep the peace."

"*Never*. Is that all when they caused a riot and nearly killed a man? Why it's disgraceful."

"Everybody's saying that. A bloke at work said that Inspector Askew was asked by one of them big London newspapers what he thought about it and he told them he was hopping mad. They've printed a story called 'The Witton Park Fenian Riot'. What do you think about that? Seems even the Prime Minister was asked questions about the carry on. He says he's gonna send another thirty-eight policeman to County

Durham. One of them is coming here and another five are being sent to Bishop Auckland."

"Good," William said firmly. It's about time somebody tried to sort this mess out."

"Oh, and guess what else the paper is suppose to have said?"

"What?"

"Well, do you remember Police Constable Walkington?"

"Should I?"

Yea. He's the one that Hickey got off with shooting."

"Oh, aye. I remember him now. What of him?"

"Well, the same papers says, that suddenly, after all these years the bloody bullet has come out of his back."

"Never in the world," exclaimed William.

Hickey mulled over a beer in one of the seediest of Bishop Auckland's public houses as he read a hastily scribbled note. "The shit is really gonna fly now."

"What is it, Seamus?" asked one of his companions.

"Do you remember Tam and Michael that used to lodge with me in Witton Park?"

"Sure I do. Why I was just having the crack with them last week, so I was. Why's dat den?"

"Seems they kicked off last night up Woodside. Seems there was another two of our lads with them. Anyway when the pollis arrived one of the stupid bastards pulled out a revolver."

"Did he shoot him?"

"No, I wish he had. All four were arrested and when the police searched the other three they were all carrying guns an' all. Of course then they searched their houses what did they find? Only guns, ammunition and a fiken copy of the rules of our Fenian society, that's what. Worse than that, the stupid bastard had a list of all the Witton Park area members."

"Did they not have them hidden?"

"They did dat. But the Brits took up floorboards, shifted tonnes of coal and even emptied the earth privvie."

"Will mine be on that list?" his panicking companion asked.

"Every fiker's name will be on it. *Every fiker's,*" Hickey sighed with resignation. As news of the discovery of the secret Brotherhood's membership list falling into the hands of the authorities spread among the Fenian ranks, hysteria seized many villagers. Numerous Irish families surprised their neighbours and workmates by suddenly and unexpectedly packing their belongings and leaving.

220

"If many more of the lads leave there'll be none of us left, Seamus. What can we do?"

"Look, I just heard today that the list and all the other stuff is to be sent to London. The locals cannot make head nor tail of it. This gives us a little space. I'll pass the word and tell the lads to keep their nerve, sit tight a while, and lets see what happens. Bet you notten comes of it. The Brits couldn't organise a piss up in a brewery. They'll not crack the codes, you'll see."

Hickey went daily from house to house attempting to calm his 'soldiers,' urging them not to desert. Days ran into weeks and the weeks became a month and, as Hickey had predicted, no arrests occurred. His faith in the encrypted system, instigated by Stephens, had proved its worth, as the information contained in the seized paperwork proved unintelligible to the authorities. Calm slowly returned to the village. Three men were eventually charged with no more than a breach of the peace, while their associate was charged with treasonous felony.

"It's happened again!" said Patrick to William.

"What has?"

"Have you not heard what the four Irishmen got who pulled a gun on the pollis up Woodside?"

"Don't tell me. Let me guess. An absolute discharge and a guinea from the parish funds?"

"Well, they might as well have. Everybody thought that Owen McDaniel, him who pulled the gun, would get a lot of time, but he didn't."

"Owen who? I never heard of him."

"Makes no matter, I'll bet ya a shilling to a pinch of salt that it's not his real name. Anyway when it gets to court he gets his charge reduced to the same as the others ... breach of the peace."

"Blinking typical," says William. " What does Inspector Askew think about that then?"

"They reckon he's spitting blood so he is."

"I can't blame him. You mark my words. It'll come to murder soon." That prophetic statement became reality too soon for thirty-year-old James McEnany, a married ironworks labourer and staunch Orangeman. The morning of the day of his murder his wife had pleaded with him.

"James, if you go to your Ma's tonight, please don't come home by Woodside. Every night I know you have to walk home through that viper's nest, I worry till your home."

"I'd rather die than let those Fenian bastards tell me where I can and can't walk. Don't worry yersel' pet, they're nowt but a bunch a cowards unless there's a dozen or more of them together." Although aware of the dangers of walking through Woodside to his home, McEnany never contemplated a diversion. James McEnany had vowed openly that he would rather die than submit to intimidation by Fenians, whom he fervently hated. That night, on his way through the Fenian stronghold area to his King Street home, his principles would cost him dearly. Hickey and his companions were leaving the Durham Ox public house as McEnany descended Woodside hill.

"Ah, look lads there's one of them Orangemen," Hickey called to his drunken compatriots. "Bet he was one of them that beat up Holloway and Cairns. Was it you?" McEnany tried to ignore them and walk past.

"McEnany isn't it? Aye it is," he answered his own question. "Married that whore from Belfast didn't you? Never knew who your father was did you? They reckon he was some soldiers. A proper Orange bastard so he is lads." Hickey's cronies thought that hilarious and laughter filled the street. A brave but foolish McEnany stopped and turned back to the gang of six.

"Hickey," he said firmly though gritted teeth, "I might be a bastard but mine was an accident of birth. You are a fiken self-made man so you are."

Found later with grievous head wounds, he lay at death's door for five days. Who threw the first punch can never be truthfully known; no more than who landed the fatal blow that left a twenty-seven-year-old widow to raise four children, all under five years of age, on her own. At a local inquest the jury returned a verdict of 'wilful murder' and warrants were issued against four of the Fenians. The following day Hickey, Hussey, Connel and Casey were arrested and brought before the magistrate's court.

"After hearing the police evidence this court finds insufficient evidence against the defendant Casey and as such he is free to leave. Hussey, Casey and Hickey you will be remanded in custody to face a charge of murder at the next Durham Assizes. Take them down jailer," he ordered.

"M'Lord, before we go may I make a further request of the court?"

"What is it, Mr. Hardisty?"

"Subsequent investigations, sir, have revealed that two others are implicated in this tragedy. As such we request that you order the immediate arrest of the two Fenians McIntyre and Welch."

"So be it, Mr. Hardisty."

"Thank you, sir."

Before the jury was sworn in, a clever defence submission resulted in the dismissal of charges against Hickey, McIntyre and Welch and they were set free. Hussey and Connel pleaded 'not guilty' to a reduced charge of manslaughter. The jury, deliberated for only twenty-five minutes.

"Foreman of the jury. Have you reached a verdict?" asked the clerk of the court.

"We have, sir."

"And is it the verdict of you all?"

"It is, sir."

"In the matter of Hussey, how find you -- guilty or not guilty?"

"*Guilty.*"

"And in the matter of Connel, how do you find -- guilty or not guilty?"

"*Guilty.*"

"Thank you Mr. Foreman and thanks to all of your panel. You are dismissed. May I add I concur whole heartedly in the case of Connel." He made no mention of Hussey before passing sentence on the pair.

"I am sure that this tragedy is the result of a long-standing disagreement between two wretched factions. We heard in this court how the deceased in fact was a member of one of these factions. It is not impossible that in some way he contributed to his own death but this is no excuse for manslaughter. You all came to our shores supposedly in search of work, but brought with you a consuming animosity towards each other, reflecting radical views on your homeland. This has led to a bitterness that people cannot comprehend, as they are not one of you. Here in England we read daily of the problems that exist and we, the courts, must play our part in stamping this out. You will each be sentenced to five years penal servitude. Take them away, jailer."

By seven in the evening only a couple of people remained on the ironworks site, these included Mr. Jones and Richard Blackman.

"Are you nearly finished Mr. Jones?" asked the weighbridge clerk as he tidied his desk for the end of his shift.

"Two minutes," he replied as he cross-referenced the figures in the heavy, blue and red lined ledger. Nightly, he gathered the names and how many hours employees had worked that day. The office could rely on Mr. Jones to have these facts and figures in the paymaster office first thing the next morning.

"Don't know about you but I'm about ready for my grub," the clerk said rubbing around the area of his stomach.

"Me too. Sadie's making a piecrust with rabbit filling. I love it."

"You lucky person. Mind you I hope the rabbit has a humped back."

"*A humped back*? What the dickens for?" Mr. Jones asked quizzically.

"Why to keep the pie crust up." Both men laughed at the clerk's attempt at humour. Richard was still hard at work removing the shingle from the puddling furnaces. Working a split shift, his evenings consisted of taking out the ash from beneath the fireboxes then banking it onto the smelter's fire. During the night, deprived of oxygen, the damping down process would only allow the fire to smoulder until the morning. With over seventy small furnaces to attend he worked tirelessly along the long uniform row, confronted by the endless heat.

"That's well over half of them done," he said to himself as he opened the door to number forty-five. Once again he began by shovelling the ash from the hearth into the wheelbarrow. Then, using the long iron raddle he poked and agitated the fire embers, making more cinder fall through the grate. This caused the level of the fire to drop. From the laden coke truck, dragged in earlier by horse, he built up the fire with over three hundredweight of fuel. The gaseous coke was then capped by throwing into the smelter the cinder from under the fire grate and from the wheelbarrow. The ash was piled on top of the coke, until it was over six inches thick. Once he'd closed the door, Richard then plugged the ventilation holes with clay. The puddlers would remove these the next morning. Then he moved on to the next.

After he removed the bulk of the cinder from under the fire grate of number forty-six, he bent down to pick up the raddle to thrust and dig into the fire. Suddenly, he heard a bang almost like the crack of a whip followed by the whining ricochet of a bullet that struck the open furnace door and disappeared into the puddling mill. Startled, he turned in the direction of the sound. From the light of the furnace he saw a staggering, drunken Seamus Hickey emerging from the dark.

"What the hell are you doing here?"

"What am I doing here? You'll find out in a minute. You fiken big, cowardly, bastard," Hickey was fumbling with a Colt revolver. "You didn't have the courage to try and take my woman when I was around did you? No. You had tee wait till I was gone. Well, now I'm back and after I've seen to you, I'll sort that whore out as well. Say your prayers you heathen bastard."

"Put the gun down, Hickey! Get yersel home. Yer worse for the drink and if you want to sort this out in the morning, *fine*."

"Not in the morning, not next week or next month *but right now*. So long, yer black bastard ... I'll see you in hell." He raised the pistol and aimed unsteadily. Richard felt his knees weaken and his stomach churn. The revolver misfired and Richard dived for cover behind the coke truck. Hickey fired and missed again but kept up his slurred taunting.

"It's no use hiding, yer long stringa pish. I'll find you and when I do, you're dead meat." Another bullet smashed into the wooden sideboards of the truck as Richard looked frantically for anything with which he could defend himself. Hickey, unsteady on his feet from two weeks of celebration following his latest lucky escape from incarceration, staggered towards the truck where Richard sheltered. In front of number forty-six lay the heavy raddle that Richard had bent to pick up when the first bullet flew. Richard knew he'd be an open target if he tried to get to it. As the threats became more explicit, Richard—trapped—turned his back to the truck between himself and Hickey and pushed with all his might. Slowly it began to move. Turning quickly, Richard placed the palms of his hands onto the wooden boards and planting the soles of his feet firmly on the floor. He summoned all his strength and shoved.

"Damn," Hickey said as he fumbled in his pocket for ammunition for the gun. "Don't you worry, mister, I've plenty of bullets left, and they're all for you." There was one more bang of the gun followed by further threats as the wagon gained momentum. Standing in the middle of the narrow gauge railway lines, Hickey felt no threat from the lumbering fuel truck as it approached, but he could not see that Richard was crouched behind it. As Hickey stepped aside he stumbled just clear of the iron wheels as they rumbled past and down the incline. Before he could raise himself, Richard was on him and grabbed his wrists and squeezed as hard as he could to release the Irishman's grip on the gun. The two of them rolled around on the ground until Hickey was on top. The smell of stale ale was in Richard's face as Hickey laughed maniacally.

Hickey head-butted Richard, and delighted in the noise of a bone cracking. Blood ran freely into the corner of Richard's mouth and off the side of his cheek and before his head was clear, Hickey brought up a knee into Richard's groin. The excruciating pain made him nauseous but still he clung onto Hickey's wrists, trying to wrestle the gun away from his grasp. Another round zipped into the roof of the puddling mill as the two men struggled back to their feet and shuffled a macabre slow dance in front of the open furnace. Locked like fighting crabs, they moved around and around as Richard steered his opponent backwards towards number forty-six.

"Oh no you don't, you bastard," said Hickey, realising what Richard was trying to do. But as he turned sideways, Richard seized the moment and forced the gun hand down towards the hot open door. Hickey screamed as the skin on the back of his hand burnt. The gun fell to the floor and Richard back heeled it away from them. Ignoring the pain in his own burned hand, Richard struck out with clenched fists the size of cannon balls at the body and head of his attacker. Hickey stepped in close, biting and gouging at Richard's eyes with deformed fingers.

"Fight fair you Irish bastard!" Richard called.

"Fick off," came the reply.

Just at that moment, Mr. Jones—sent by Sadie to find out why Richard was so late—appeared at the doorway.

"Hoy! What going on? Pack it in, now," he screamed, rushing in. "Hickey, you get off him, *right now*." He looked down and instinctively picked up the gun. Hickey backed Richard up against the door of number twenty-two and, as the skin burnt and blistered the flesh off Richard's back and his screams filled the air, Mr. Jones pointed the gun, fired a bullet into Hickey's head and killed him instantly. Hickey dropped and blood poured from his head like molten metal into the strewn red ash on the mill floor.

"My God," Mr. Jones said.

Richard sank to his knees, exhausted. He raised his eyes and spoke in a quiet voice.

"Mr. Jones, I do believe I owe you my life. A couple more seconds and I would have been a goner that's for sure."

"Richard I've just killed a man. How will I ever forgive myself? What will become of me? Will they hang me, Richard?" Richard looked compassionately at the little man who had been such a friend to him ever since that day they had met on Liverpool docks.

"Nobody is gonna hang anybody. You get yersel home and I'll sort this mess out. Leave it to me. Go home now and say nowt to nobody. Do you hear? *Nobody*"

"But, Richard ..." Mr. Jones began.

"No buts, Mr. Jones. Just go home." Traumatised, the little man turned and hurried home feeling he carried a weight every bit as heavy as the iron pigs that littered the mill floor.

As Richard's breathing became regular and his senses returned he looked over to number forty-six which was by then a raging inferno. He dragged Hickey's body towards it. Despite the excruciating pain of his back, he managed to get the corpse through the door and into the raging flames. The gun followed the body and the clank of the furnace door followed the gun.

Mr. Jones could not bring himself to follow Richard's advice and walked slowly to Old Row where he knocked on the door of Police Constable Anthony. Mrs. Anthony answered his knock.

"Is your husband in Mrs. Anthony? If he is would you tell him I'd like to speak to him please?"

"Why, Mr. Jones, what is it? You look as though you have seen a ghost! Wait a minute I'll get him for you. Will you wait in the parlour?"

"Thank you," he said as he was led into the small front room where she lit the gaslight. The bottom of the gossamer mantle was holed, but still sufficed, while the escaping blue flame hissed continuously in the background. Leaving his evening meal, P.C. Anthony walked along the passage from the kitchen pulling his braces over his shoulders and tucking the tails of his shirt into his trousers. Mr. Jones blurted out his version of events to the amazed police officer.

"Can you tell me that again please, Mr. Jones? Try and calm yourself and speak more slowly if you can please." Once again, but with greater attention to detail, he unfolded the night's occurrence. The policeman watched the pale colour of Mr. Jones's skin turn to a strange grey-green as he continued recollecting and relating minor details.

"Are you unwell, Mr. Jones?"

"I feel a little feint. May I have a glass of water please?"

"Of course you can, and while I'm in the kitchen I'll get my coat. When you're ready I think we had better go to the mill and try and sort all this out, eh?" The constable fastened the ornate silver buttons of his tunic and threw his cape around his shoulders. Securing the garment around his neck by a chain linked to two lion-head studs, he placed the familiar conical bobbie's helmet on his head. The colour returned to Mr. Jones face.

"You ready, Mr. Jones?" he asked as he picked up his standard issue night lantern.

"As ready as I'll ever be, I suppose."

"Good, then let's go shall we?" Together they walked along Old Row past the Vulcan, and under the bridge into the works. Mr. Jones' brain was in disarray, and he could not believe what was happening to him. He hoped he was in a nightmare rather than reality, and that before he had to witness the dead Hickey once more, he would awake. By the light of the lantern they picked their way through the dark shed towards the puddling furnaces.

"Where is the body?" asked PC Anthony. "Is this where you say this thing happened, Mr. Jones?"

"Yes. Right there. He fell right there," he said, pointing to the spot in front of number forty-six where Hickey had lain. "Here's Richard, he'll tell you what happened." Richard, who had been on his way home had returned on hearing voices.

"Richard ... where's Hickey? Please tell the constable I'm not mad and that I did kill him."

"You never killed anybody, Mr. Jones."

"But I shot Hickey! You saw him fall!"

"Well, you shot him but you never killed him. You certainly put a permanent parting in his hair but you never killed him. Just wounded him that's all. You couldn't hurt a thick Irish head like that, now could you?" The policeman raised his illuminating lantern and followed the parallel trail left by Hickey's boot heels right to the door of number forty-six. He looked long and hard at Richard.

"The policeman that Hickey shot—PC Walkington—was a very good friend of mine, did you know that?" he said quietly.

"I did hear something to that effect, yes constable." PC Anthony held his gaze for a full minute.

"Well, Mr. Jones," he said suddenly. "There is no dead body here. There is no weapon. Hickey was never the kind to press charges so I suspect we will not hear from him again. Personally," he added with a glance at Richard. "It wouldn't much bother me if the drunken idiot had staggered in here and fell into one of them furnaces." Mr. Jones could not quite grasp the situation but he had satisfied his conscience by reporting the incident to the police.

"And by the way Mr. Blackman," added PC Anthony as he walked towards the door. "Thank you again for saving my boy's life. Good night to you both. Safe home."

Chapter Sixteen 1871 – 1880

Once again the threat of cholera raised its ugly head throughout County Durham. In a nearby village, a visitor misdiagnosed the early symptoms of his scarlet fever as cholera causing panic to quickly spread throughout the locality. Not knowing it to be a false alarm the village's dedicated doctors, McKechnie and Beddingfield, prepared themselves for whatever may happen.

"You can't blame the folks for panicking," said Doctor McKechnie to his colleague. "They've heard what the plague can do to communities."

"Yes, we've been lucky haven't we? I wonder why? I mean, apart form that incident with Patrick Bryan we've got off scot-free every time, haven't we? There's been what? Four major outbreaks in the last forty years?"

"Yes, it's four I believe."

"And how many died?"

"Phew ... that's a good one. I know that over fifty-three thousand died in the 1831 epidemic. It must be over one hundred thousand in total. Maybe more."

"Yes, and how many have *we* lost?"

"None."

"Exactly. Have you never wondered why?"

"Often, but I've never worked it out."

"Well, I think as long as folks are terrified of the disease they are vigilant. I mean each time there's a scare they carry out, to the letter, what the health board tells them to do."

While cholera had raged all around since the establishment of Witton Park, three times the community had escaped. The village elders took news of any regional occurrence of the deadly virus seriously. At the slightest hint that cholera, often carried on the soles of feet, was on the march, a well-rehearsed drill swung into action. The health board for the village was commendably vigilant and experienced in its efforts to keep the locality free of the disease. Contingency plans were put into place during outbreaks and scares alike, which abounded throughout the nineteenth century. Notices appeared on every aspect of the plague, from preventive measures, and what to do in the event of an outbreak. Instructions, from the whitewashing of houses to the disposal of bodies, were posted on every street corner. The dead were to be wrapped in cotton, or similar material, which was to be saturated with pitch or tar. The corpse was to be buried as soon as possible, preferably within twenty-four hours while all funeral services for victims of cholera had to be held in the open air, and the body carried by a minimum of persons.

It was indirectly due to the false alarm of 1871 that tragedy and sadness descended on the village. Both doctors were working day and night. While most calls were cholera false alarms, many were to patients with scarletina, an equally infectious disease. The workload left the good doctors at their lowest ebb.

"Are you not well?" the old doctor asked Beddingfield.

"Just tired I hope. I think a good night's sleep might do the trick."

"Then that's just what the doctor ordered young man. Up you go and I'll see you in the morning."

"But what about the night calls? How will you manage?"

"Nursie and I will manage. Now lets have you off to bed." The next morning Beddingfield sent for his senior partner.

"I fear I have contracted scarlet fever."

"Now, now. What do we think of self-diagnosis? Let this old quack have a look at you. Have you a sore throat?"

"Yes, and I think a fever is coming on."

"Um, um. Yes, and your pulse is a little fast. I think we had better confine you to bed and get Nursie to keep an eye on you. I'll look in on you after morning surgery." The young doctor, pulse racing, suffered shivering, vomiting and terrible headaches. Within twenty-four hours of the fever commencing, the distinct red rash of scarlet fever appeared, looking like a scald. The rash first appeared on his neck but quickly spread over his entire body. It was at its height after two days, only his nose and lips unmarked. With scant regard for their own health, Dr. McKechnie and the nurse attended Beddington around the clock.

"Is there nothing else we can do, Doctor?" the concerned nurse asked.

"Nothing medically I'm afraid. He is in the hands of a higher authority than I. Has he had anything to eat today?"

"He still hasn't been able to swallow solids, not since yesterday really. I managed to get a few spoonfuls of milk down him this morning. Just before you arrived I tried him with soup but he couldn't manage. He's now struggling to speak."

"Right, let's have a good look at you, young man. Don't try to talk; your throat is pretty swollen and sore. Speak only if you must," Doctor McKechnie counselled. "It must be painful to do so anyway." The day before, his tongue had been swathed by a thick, white, creamy fur. It had since been replaced with a covering of tiny red spots, giving it the look of a half-ripe strawberry. The fever dissipated distinctively by the third day and the rash began to fade as the skin began to peel.

Diligently, the nurse collected the fine bran-like scales and burnt them. Within seven days from its appearance the rash had gone, while the peeling continued.

"What are his chances now, Doctor?" Nurse asked after the examination.

"Well, a lot better than they were. The signs are encouraging, but we're not out of the woods yet. Not by a long chalk." Hopes were high for a full and speedy recovery during the further period of convalescence, until, unexpectedly, the patient suffered a relapse. Dr. McKechnie noticed that his colleague's face and especially his eyelids had become slightly swollen.

"Nursie, collect me a urine sample for when I get back this evening will you?"

"Certainly, Doctor. There's not something wrong is there?"

"I'm not sure. When I've seen the sample I'll know better." Examination of the urine sample revealed a dark red smoky colour and further tests confirmed inflammation of the kidneys and, despite first class medical attention, the village mourned the death of thirty-four-year-old Doctor Beddingfield who had saved the lives of so many others.

Stobbart's Hotel was the venue for the annual dinner of the Cambrian Druids. On this occasion presentations were to be made to Edward Griffiths, the retiring blast furnace manager, and his wife.

"I'd like to thank all of you who have come here today and made this so special for Mrs. Griffiths and me. I'd like to thank the men from the blast furnaces who got me this lovely watch and my wife this beautiful clock. And we thank all our other friends for this beautiful tea set, and especially for the kind words what you've had written on it." The gold watch and clock had cost equivalent to almost six month's agricultural wages. Inscriptions on the tea set bore thanks from the men, and made direct reference to Mrs. Griffiths' virtue and kindness, during various crises at the works.

The erection of a replacement school, the fourth to be built since 1845, took place that year on the site of the original, small educational institution.

"I see your Tamar is getting a new school to teach in, eh?" asked William of Patrick.

"So she is and a grand affair it's to be. This one will be built out of solid stone and will have two wings where kids of different ages can be taught."

"What, they're gonna split the kids up?"

"So she says. She reckons the kids'll learn better if they're with others of their own age."

"I suppose that makes sense. That's progress I suppose."

"It's gonna stand in the middle of a large yard what they're gonna pave so the kids can play. And round the outside there'll be a small brick wall with railings on the top. To keep them in I suppose. Every one of the classrooms is getting a large coal fire, suppose that'll be for the winter."

"Hope the fire doesn't have the same effect on the kids as it does on me. They always put me to sleep so they do," said William.

"I pity the poor little buggers that do that. They say that Mr. Clarke is a proper taskmaster. Our Tamar reckons just a stare could freeze hell over. Anyway, last night she brought home a composition written by one the lads she teaches, Tom Barton. By it was good mind, they gave him a prize for it, anyway."

"What was it about?"

"It was about how many pubs, hotels and ale houses there are here."

"He's not wrong there. Anybody coming here must think the place is full of them."

"Why, I'd never thought about it before. More the merrier I always thought. Anyway he reckons there's fourteen."

"Yeah and in just six, short, little streets. No wonder Margot is always going on about pubs."

"Then there's another three pubs and two ale houses in Woodside isn't there?"

"Ah-ha, and don't forget the New Inn between the top of Black Road and Phoenix Row."

"How many's that make then?"

"That makes, let me see ... *twenty!*" Each pub had its own type of clientele, usually synonymous with the name of the establishment. Indicative names such as 'The Welsh Harp', 'The Shamrock', 'The Hibernian', 'The Cambrian' and many others attracted compatible, regular patrons.

"I think drinking's gettin outta hand all over the country."

"Oh, shut up William. You're gettin to sound more like your lass every day."

"*Hardlys.* Margot would have them all shut down, I never said that."

"Yeah, if it was up to her and that bloody Quaker, a man would have nowhere to escape. The eminent Quaker, Joseph Pease, had his 'Prohibitory Liquor Bill' read for the third time before parliament, and it became law.

"You'll be happy now the pubs can't stay open all day?" Patrick asked William wife.

"Not really, Patrick. It doesn't go any way near far enough."

"Eh? I would have thought you'd have been over the moon!"

"Not at all. When pubs can open and when they should close is to be left to the local magistrates. If they were of a mind they could still let a landlord stay open all day if they wished."

"And who do you think should decide? The League?

"That's not a bad idea."

"*I don't think so.*" Margaret shook her head from side to side.

"Anyway that won't happen, not if we get our way anyway. We're gonna get up a petition and collect as many names as we can and present it to the magistrates. The opening hours must be limited." The village Band of Hope and Temperance League worked in conjunction with other organisations in the area, raising a petition, to present before the district's magistrates. Over four thousand persons signed the petition that they handed to the court, but were dismayed at what little weight it carried. The new 'prohibitive' hours were reduced to the permitted opening hours of six in the morning, until eleven o'clock at night, during weekdays. Contrary to popular hopes and aspirations, licensed premises could still open on the Sundays, for four-and-one-half hours.

"Are you busy at the mill Michael? I haven't seen much of you these past few weeks," his mother asked.

"Run off our feet, Ma. We can't get enough stuff out. There's a war on in France or somewhere so nee iron is coming from ower the watter. Have you not seen the two more blast furnaces we're building? That'll be six we'll have. Why soon we'll be the biggest in England." The Franco-Prussian war meant pig iron from the continent became unavailable and the British ironmasters capitalised on their good fortune. Once again, the community was in a time of plenty, but they also became the victims of profiteers. After disappointment in their inability to influence the courts, the women's leagues turned their wrath onto unscrupulous merchants who, inexplicably, suddenly demanded exorbitant prices for basic foodstuffs.

"It's daylight robbery, that's what it is. We must refuse to buy from the greedy merchants where we believe the prices to be sky high," Margot urged the women who packed the Cambrian Hall. "Thank God our members have the Co-op to fallback on but what of the unfortunates? We will set prices and let no woman pay a penny more." In support of Margot, Mrs. Smith, a shopkeeper's daughter stood up and spoke.

"How is it that my father can sell butter for nine pence a pound yet others are asking over a third more? I urge you to listen to Mrs. Morris and boycott the profiteers."

A 'food strike' swept the county, women boycotted premises whose goods they deemed unrealistic. Butchers, the tradesmen against whom predominantly the women's action became directed, responded by forming the County Protection Committee. Women paraded outside their shops with banners, and bought meat from the less expensive town vendors, boycotting the rest. General dealers and the suppliers of dairy produce suffered the same treatment and retaliated by cancelling all credit, which they blamed for the high prices. Meanwhile, the Co-op, having never knowingly overcharged, flourished and had to engage extra staff to cope with demand. Women who continued to patronise shops considered 'blacked' were shunned or sometimes worse. Paying the extra two or three pence per pound over the designated price the vigilantes set sometimes incurred physically harassment. Prices were forced down by the actions of the County Durham womenfolk, but butchers, in retaliation, stopped slaughtering cattle; turning the beasts out to graze created a demand that outstripped supply, with the effect that prices, over the next two years, steadily climbed.

In February 1872, local newspapers edged the pages with black on the announcement of the death of Joseph Pease MP. He was instrumental in Bolckow and Vaughan establishing the ironworks at Witton Park and had always been a good friend to the workforce.

"Will you be going to Pease funeral, you being under manager an' all?" Patrick asked Michael.

"No. Somebody will have to steer the ship while so many of our big-wigs are there." A large contingent from the area attended the funeral, including the owners of Jane Pit and Witton Park colliery, the coal magnate Stobbart family. Two years later, with the end of the European war, Stobbart's employees received fourteen days notice of a twenty-per-cent wage cut. Behind a band, with the Jane Pit lodge-banner held high, striking miners marched to an open-air meeting at the top of Black Road. While industrial unrest was common in the iron trade, the coal industry had remained relatively strike free. It was felt that a long industrial action this time was inevitable, but it was averted. Miners, persuaded by their union to take their case to arbitration, returned to work. The result, accepted by rank and file was a compromise reduction of pay by eleven per cent.

"Can you believe that, Da? Can you believe that the pitmen have accepted that wage cut without so much as a decent fight?"

"We didn't do much better again did we?"

"How'd yer mean? At least when they told us we also had to take a twenty-per-cent pay cut at least we got it down to ten."

"I suppose we did a bit better than the miners."

Two years later ironworkers became subject to a further six per cent pay cut, as Belgian exports grabbed the British market. Additionally, a new product, steel, which the works could not produce, dramatically reduced the demand for malleable, puddled iron. The price of pig iron had slumped from its high by seventy five per cent following cessation of hostilities.

"Bye the way, I got a letter from your brother in America yesterday."

"Oh? And how is he?"

"He's fine, David, says to tell you he's asking after you."

"Thanks."

"Do you remember him writing once and telling us about that American general he met? The one with the long hair, like a woman's? Remember? General Custard wasn't it?"

"Custer, Da, not Custard."

"That's it. Custer. Well him, his brother and all his soldiers were wiped out by the Red Indians at a place called 'The Little Big Horn'."

"*Get away.* Why I thought them Indians only had bows and arrows."

"Maybe not, eh?"

"Anyway, he was asking about everybody and me and yer Ma is gonna write back tonight."

"Don't forget to tell him about the new church."

"Oh yeah, I will." Twenty-five years after builder's work began on the ironworks, and eight since the granting of parish status, work began on the erection of St Paul's. It was to be the first Church of England's place of worship in the village. Built in the English style, it consisted of a nave, chancel and south porch and could seat three hundred and thirty. It cost two thousand three hundred pounds, seven hundred pounds being given by Bishop Baring, the balance raised by public subscription. A stained-glass window paid for by the villagers was installed, acknowledging the services of Dr. McKechnie, to whom so many owed their lives. One year after the dedication of St Paul's, many dignitaries and a few of the villagers attended a memorial service for ironmaster Ferdinand Bolckow MP who died at the age of seventy-two. That same year, every seat filled for the funeral of Annie who slipped quietly away in her sleep.

"You'll move in with me and Tamar, won't you Da?"

"That's for sure," said a devastated Patrick. "I always told her that I wanted to go first. God knows what I'll do without her."

"We'll be all right Da, you'll see. You've still got us and Jane and all them grandbairns that need and love you to bring up. They'll keep you busy."

"I hope so, son. I hope so."

"Well back to work on Monday. It's been a long time in coming although it could have been worse I suppose," Michael said to his wife.

"How come?"

"I mean at least the weather's been canny. If the shut-down had come in the winter they would have been long days." In the autumn, trade at the works had begun to fluctuate. An acute lack of orders caused temporary closure for a few months before reopening in November. Gone then was the 'feel good factor' that had prevailed in the times of plenty. It was replaced by an alien feeling of vulnerability. Those who previously had thought their future secure at the works did so no more.

"I think the closure was politically motivated myself," said David to his father.

"How's that?"

"Me and a lotta others think the same. We believe that the shut down was a political protest."

"Against what?"

"Against the government's insistence in introducing compulsory education. They've got no cheap labour now have they?"

"*Perhaps* you're right but they won't tell us will they?"

The following spring, over one thousand people gathered in the station yard to greet two prospective Liberal candidates for the area.

"Well, you certainly look the part Mr. Jones," Richard said as the little Welshman fidgeted with the waistcoat of his best suit.

"Big day today Richard, so it is."

"And have you got your band ready?"

"Tuned to perfection. Are you coming to listen to us and the speeches?"

"I certainly am, Mr. Jones. I wanna hear if these Liberals will do anything for the works if they get into power." In the station yard, entertained by the village brass band conducted by Mr. Jones, the crowd waited patiently. They awaited the arrival of the Honourable John Lambton and Mr. Joseph W. Pease, who was following in his father's political footsteps. Mr. Taliesin Thomas, the man who succeeded Mr. Raine eight years earlier as works manager, stood and made the formal introductions.

"Gentlemen, we welcome you here today. And we plead for your help. No place had suffered more in the current recession than Witton

Park. Despite pledging to abolish income tax this current Conservative government has increased it from two pence in the pound to five pence. Our ironworks needs an investment of capital to modernise and enable it to produce steel. For years now capitalists would not invest because of a lack of confidence in the government. We need a new government and we need it now. So we ask: are the Liberals the government we so desire. Would a Liberal government help us?"

"I promise you, that like my father before me I will be a good friend to the Witton Park ironworks and if I am elected will work tirelessly for you all," said Lambton. "My friend has echoed my sentiments exactly. *When,* and mark I say not *if, when* we form the next government I promise we will put iron and steel production at the top of our agenda." A round of applause rang out from the crowd.

"Also when we form the next government I promise you one more thing. Not only will we sort out the ironmasters but also that old chestnut 'The Irish Problem'." A huge cheer went up from the enthusiastic crowd.

"Heard it all before," David muttered into his workmate's ear. "Their promises are like pie crusts, *meant to be broken.*"

"Don't be so cynical, David."

"Sorry. I guess I can't help it. I didn't used to be, you know. It was politicians and employers who made me like this. I think the whole area is doomed. Both the pits and the works."

To the brass band rendition of '*For he's a jolly good fellow*' the prospective parliamentarians left for their next rally. One month later seven thousand northeastern ironworkers, including the Witton Park workforce, staged a one-day strike against yet further pay cuts. Suddenly houses, then whole streets of houses, emptied.

"Talking to Mr. Jenkins this morning," said Patrick to Michael. His furniture warehouse is chocker with stuff. He says he's going to have to rent extra space to get all the stuff stored that he's bought."

"It's 'cos all the young 'uns are leaving. They're fed up and they're young enough to start again somewhere. It could be the beginning of the end."

"What do you mean, son?"

"Why there could be a ripple effect with so many people leaving. If there are no folks to buy stuff then the merchants will start to leave then the place will really start to go downhill. Let's hope it doesn't come to that though, eh?"

"I'll drink to that, son."

Wild swings in trade continued throughout the summer. A shortage of labour from the migration of many of the workers helped those that stayed. Men, animals and machines worked around the clock to meet deadlines gaining orders from overseas competitors.

"All those folk leaving wasn't such a bad thing after all David. Was it?"

"No, Da it wasn't, well not at least for those that stayed behind. It's still a shame that so many good families had to up sticks and move on though. The good side of it is that all the overtime has allowed most of our members to get rid of the debts they'd run up during the strikes and lay offs. That's definitely one good thing."

In the autumn, an elderly William Morris, still with elasticity in his stride that much younger men lacked, walked to the works with Michael and Richard.

"That was some party last night William, thank you for inviting me."

"Our pleasure young man. As long as you enjoyed it."

"We certainly did, Sadie and Bridie also send their gratitude. Bridie couldn't believe that anyone could have been married fifty-eight years."

"Well, we have. Fifty-eight years to the day yesterday."

"So how old are you now Mr. Morris, if you don't mind me asking?" said Michael.

"Me? Why I've just gone seventy-seven."

"So you married young?"

"Yeah, and believe me I wish I'd done it sooner." All the men laughed as they walked along. William had always been proud that he was the only underground miner to make the transition to iron worker and last more than one day. Everyone knew William. Not because he was a lay preacher, or a village elder but because he was the only person at the plant never to work on a Sunday. An unwritten legacy, a concession handed down from Joseph Vaughan, saved him from the humiliation. He finished the hot lunch that Margot brought daily to the works. She had sat beside him on the grass bank while he ate, then watched him light his pipe. She watched the swirling columns of smoke compete with a passing railway locomotive.

"You know what, Margot?"

"What's that dear?"

"We've been here what, thirty five years or so haven't we?"

"About that, yes."

"And we've been back to Wales, what? Only about a dozen times?"

"Yes about that, why?"

"It's just that each time I look down on this beautiful valley and that shimmering ribbon of water I often think that when my time comes I wouldn't mind being laid to rest here."

"Stop being so morbid. That time's a long time off yet. Why, you're as fit as a man of twenty."

"I don't think so, kind wife, far from it I'm afraid."

"All right maybe not twenty," she said as with a smile she collected the utensils. Not far away Sadie was doing the same thing. Walking into the weighbridge where they lunched she melted the men's hearts with her smile of greeting.

"Are you finished?" When she had gone Mr. Jones turned to his friend.

"Didn't Sadie look happy?

"Very. She certainly didn't look vibrant like that a couple of years ago, did she?"

"She didn't have a lot to smile bout though then, did she?"

"No, definitely not. Absolutely nothing." Rising, William walked back to the base of number five blast furnace and resumed his general tidying duties. High above him, trucks laden with iron ore, fuel and flux rolled across the bridge that connected the top of the conical shaped furnaces with the adjacent embankment. Men appeared ant-like as they hurried about their work, emptying the contents of the small rail trucks into the throat of the furnace. Beneath the throat, numerous small channels and flues allowed the rising steam and gasses to escape from the molten charge in the bosh below. Tubs emptied and returned to the embankment for refilling allowed the workers on the vaulted gallery to relax. Leaning against the safety rail that surrounded the top, standing on the stout gangways between the furnaces, they waited the next charge. Beneath them, in the tapping shed, William had watched with some monotony the two hourly tapping of the pigs, before walking outside.

Margot was standing at her front door watching the clouds roll by when suddenly she was flung backwards into the passage of their terraced home. Simultaneously, as she heard the deafening 'boom', the upstairs windows of the all houses in the street shattered. Along the street doors were blown open. Clean washing that had fluttered in the breeze, was blasted down upon the dirty road. It was not the first time Margot had heard an explosion, but that time it came not from the mine, but the ironworks. Michael, who had been in the upstairs offices of Paradise cottage with Mr. Thomas, the works manager, suddenly found himself blown across the room.

"What the hell's happened?" he said as he removed paperwork from his face. Pushing furniture off his chest he struggled to his feet. In front of a large hole in the office wall where moments earlier there had been a large sash window, stood a dazed office worker.

"It's gone, it's blown up," he exclaimed as he gazed on the carnage below.

"What's gone man? What's blown up?" asked Michael as he struggled to lift a cabinet off his legs.

"Number five furnace. It's blown to bits," the man replied in utter disbelief and shock. Michael crossed the wrecked office and gazed out of the hole in the wall.

"My God!" he cried, as hot slag and pieces of metal rained down like grapeshot on the tiles of the office building. Like a volcano erupting, number five furnace threw sparks and debris into the air. The top of the furnace looked as though it would collapse any moment as Michael struggled to see through the thick dust.

"There! There, look, can't you see that big hole, just above the bosh?"

"Where?"

"Why, there man, look again! Look, it's big enough to drive a horse and cart through."

"Yeah. I see it now. What a mess." Through the thick red dust they could just make out the rupture in the wall of the furnace. The large hole, like that of a shotgun upon a tin can, allowed a view of the inner refractory bricks.

"It could have been worse. Look ... the hole is well above the load line. Hopefully the main load will stay inside. If the bloody thing doesn't collapse."

"*If.*"

"C'mon," said Michael. "Tie a hankie or scarf or something over your nose and mouth and let's get over there and see if we can do anything to help." The wooden tapping shed at the base of the stricken furnace lay flattened, the boards stacked as driftwood on a shore.

"Blinking heck, look at that, the joiners' shed must have took the full blast. It's burning like a lit box of matches."

"Yeah, but there's no slag or hot metal running about anywhere is there? That's a good sign, the plugs must be holding." The ground was covered by hundreds of small fires. Tufts of rye grass disappeared in puffs of smoke. The dust cloud blocked out the daylight and the tiny fires looked like flickering candles or blinking stars on a bright moonlit night. The slowly settling dust revealed men running around the gangways at the top of the blast furnaces. Below, hundreds of men deserted their posts and ran around like headless chickens.

The force of the blast that had not been deflected upwards by the hillside had travelled towards Stable Row where it met the railway embankment. Forced upwards by its tremendous power it demolished the signal box before blowing itself out against Railway Row where Margot tried to come to terms with what may have happened. Jugs and bottles were thrown around the three pubs in close proximity. No plans had ever been laid down for such an emergency. The workers who had not run away were joined by hundreds of anxious villagers, making the job of locating of family and friends both erratic and chaotic.

"Have you seen my husband? Have you seen my son?" people called as they rushed frantically around the works. Richard had been passing number three furnace, heading for the puddling mill, when number five exploded. For the second time in as many years he felt a searing heat engulf his body. Frantically, he tore at his burning clothes. Sheltered behind a huge carthorse that he was shoeing, the work's blacksmith was protected from the blast. When he heard the explosion and looked up from his work he saw Richard, burning. Momentarily he watched as the human fireball rolled over and over trying to extinguish his burning clothes. Grabbing his large iron-hooped wooden bucket, he dipped it into the rain barrel and threw the water. Bucket after bucket of water went onto Richard who writhed in agony, but did not scream. As the water cooled and soothed Richard, steam rose from him as it would from a red-hot horseshoe.

"Somebody. Anybody. Get the doctor quick. There's a man badly burned in here. Quick somebody ... get the doctor," the horrified blacksmith called to anyone passing his shed. The blacksmith saw Doctor Beddingfield's replacement approaching.

"Doctor Stokoe! Over here, he's in here. Look he's over there," he said pointing to the blackened figure laying still on the floor of the smithy. "I couldn't believe my eyes when I first saw him. He was just like a fireball. I put him out with me buckets of water, I didn't know what else to do so I sent for you."

"You did really well, smithy. There is no better treatment for burns than water. You did really well." As the doctor bent over Richard he reached into his medical bag.

"Is he still alive, Doctor?"

"Just. Do you know who he is?"

"I think it's Richard Blackman but I couldn't be sure. Why I bet his own mother couldn't recognise him at the moment."

"Right. If I can find a vein I'm going to give him an injection of morphine, that should kill the pain."

"Yeah. That's strange that. All the time he was burning he never shouted or screamed once."

"No? Well he must be a very brave man. Now will you run and get someone with a stretcher so we can get him to the works infirmary?"

"Certainly, sir." When they arrived, the stretcher-bearers were reluctant to handle Richard, so great were his injuries.

"You've got to pick him up and get him to the infirmary or he will die," he ordered the attendants, who just stood, looking aghast. Through the encircling crowd that had gathered, Michael pushed his way forward as he heard the doctor's plea. He instantly recognised the slab-like white teeth that contrasted against the blackened, charred skin.

"*Richard*, Richard can you hear me?"

"I'm afraid he can't hear you at the moment," Doctor Stokoe aid sympathetically. "Do you know him?"

"Very well. Now leave him and I'll get him onto the stretcher." As he kneeled to lift his friend, Sadie's voice cried out from behind him.

"Oh Richard, my darling! Whatever has happened to you?" she wailed.

"Sadie, can you help me get him onto the stretcher? You take his legs. On the count of three. Here we go, gently now. One, two three ..." As the bearers readied to lift she knelt beside his head. Tears ran down her cheeks and fell onto Richard's blistered lips, as he clung precariously to life.

"Sadie, you go with Richard. I'll be there as soon as I can but I've to go see that my father in law is well."

"Of course, you get going, I wish you luck." To his left he could see a crowd of people. They formed a circle like the daisy rings that once grew in Paradise fields but flourished no more. In the centre of the circle he could see David Morris who had run from his place of work to search for his father. He was staring down at a fatality; the face and body respectfully covered by an infirmary blanket. Protruding from the blanket the laceless boots of the corpse were visible.

"Is it your father?" Michael asked.

"Dunno. Haven't got the nerve up yet to look under the blanket. But they certainly look like his boots. He never wore laces. Said they could get fastened up in machinery. Even after he left the pit he never wore them."

"Do you want me to look?"

"No, I'll do it. Can I see the body please?" The nurse was reluctant.

"I'm afraid there's not much to see of the front of him. The poor soul, whoever he is, must have took the full flow of the molten iron on his face and chest."

"None the less ... can I see him please?" Michael nodded to the nurse who slowly pulled back the blanket. David was unprepared for what he was to see as men in the crowd gasped and women howled. He looked at the body, stripped to the waist and burnt beyond recognition. Several people men and women crossed themselves as others prayed aloud.

"Can you turn him over please?"

"What?" the astonished nurse asked.

"Can you turn him over please?" David repeated.

"Why?"

"For there's something I want to see," he said firmly. Seeming not to comprehend David's macabre request, she just stared back at him.

"Please ... do as he asks," Michael said. "I'm sure he has a good reason."

"If you say so, Mr. Bryan," the company nurse somewhat reluctantly agreed. The crowd fell totally silent as the nurse, as respectfully as possible, rolled the corpse over onto his face. The flesh on the back of the body was unscathed, and clearly visible along the spine, was the row of blue-black dots of 'pitman's medals'. Fighting back tears and gagging on each word, David looked at the nurse and spoke quietly.

"Please, cover up my father. I'll be taking him home now."

Chapter Seventeen 1880 – 1882

At the works infirmary Dr. Stokoe administered emergency treatment while assessing the extent of Richard's injuries.

"Nurse, I want you to try and cut away as much of his clothing as possible. Leave any that you think may be fused to his skin. Do you know if there is any borax here?"

"I think so sir, in the medicine cupboard. The key is hanging on the side."

"You. What's your name?"

"Sadie, sir."

"And what is this person to you, may I ask?"

"He's me man, sir."

"Right, Sadie, I want you to put some water on heat and get it just warm enough for your elbow to stand it."

"About the same as a baby's bottle, sir?"

"Exactly. Now hurry." When the water arrived, he added borax and a mild antiseptic solution then transferred some of it into a jug.

"Stand back nurse — I don't want to wet you as well. This will help the burns and also help us get more material off him." He doused the burned body and clothes of the sedated patient, pouring jug after jug until the bed and floor were awash.

"Right, that should do it, let's get on shall we?" Patiently, and with the utmost gentleness, they separated skin from attire.

"Sadie, can you assist us further?"

"Certainly, sir."

"See the earthenware bath over there? I want you to fill it with warm water so it's about ... well ... like a baby's bottle"

"Yes, sir."

"Use this if you like," he said offering her his thermometer.

"No thank you sir, I'll just use my elbow." Despite the gravity of the situation they managed to smile at each other. From the rows of coloured bottles that lined the shelves, the doctor measured a larger amount of boric and added a quantity of tincture of iodine. Adding it to the bath water he stirred and stirred it around.

"Now, nurse. We've got to be extremely careful with him. We've got to get him into that bathtub. Can you stand back a little Sadie, please?"

"Can I not help, sir?"

"No, not at the moment. The nurse and I will manage this one, thank you."

"You won't hurt him sir, will you?"

"Not if I can help it. Ready nurse?" With infinite care, the nurse and doctor lowered Richard into the water, and momentarily his eyes opened. If the move caused excruciating pain, Richard did not murmur.

"Now ladies. Here's the tricky bit. I want you to try and keep the temperature of the water about the same. You'll have to take out and add more warm water as necessary. Do you think you can do that?"

"Definitely," Sadie said, answering for both of them. As the nurse and Sadie maintained the water temperature while pouring the soothing liquid over his head and shoulders, the doctor watched closely for signs of shock.

"I'm just popping into the next door office. I won't be far away. I need to refer to my textbook just to check what the latest recommendations are for burns of this nature. Since I left Edinburgh medical college opinions seem to change annually."

There were various options open to him: dry dressings, thickly powdered with starch and boric acid in equal parts, would have sufficed in other circumstances. Having received almost fifty per cent burns Richard's injuries were so extensive that this method seemed inadequate. As he read the passage on the danger of loss of body fluids due to blistering he said aloud, "Good old Smithy, you and your buckets of water may just have saved a life."

The cold water had prevented major blistering which in turn could have caused subsequent kidney failure. Because of the hysterical blacksmith's actions, Richard had escaped those complications. The doctor considered the alternative method of treatment. Oily dressings of Carron oil that contained limewater and linseed oil in equal parts had previously proven successful in the treatment of major burns, according to the writer of the journal. In Dr. Stokoe's limited experience, however, he found that even with a little eucalyptus oil added as a mild antiseptic, septic changes often still occurred. Another major problem with oily dressings, he had found, was the difficulty in removing them should surgery be required.

"No. Neither of those is for us. I think we'll stick with the boracic solution," he muttered under his breath. Returning, he instructed the nurse.

"Can you prepare long strips of lint and soak them in a fresh boric-iodine solution, please? Sadie can continue to douche him." Sadie gently ladled water from around Richard's body then, just as gently, let the healing solution trickle down from the top of his head over all the parts of his face, neck and shoulders that could not be submerged.

"Now comes the awful part again. We've got to get him out to dress his wounds. Wait—I think we'd better put a clean linen sheet on top of the rubber blanket. The risk of infection is at its highest at this moment." This second man handling still did not cause a murmur of complaint from the patient as they lifted him back onto the iron railed bed as carefully as possible.

"Right, Sadie. Can you pass the bandages as we need them please?"

"Certainly, sir." Working in unison, the doctor and nurse started at his feet and wrapped his limbs, body, and head in the wrung-out gauze dressings until he looked as though embalmed. Only slits for his closed eyes remained. Through these small apertures, Dr Stokoe opened one eyelid then the other and shone a small light into the pupils.

"How is he, doctor?" Sadie asked anxiously. Inwardly, despite numerous hopeful medical signs, the doctor had his doubts as to his patient's chances of survival. Although sedated, Richard should still have reacted to some of the extremely painful processes he had been forced to endure.

"I'm not sure. On one hand the clinical signs are good, on the other his reflexes belie this. He is either a very brave man, or so close to death that pain does not register on his nervous system."

"I assure you sir, he is one of the bravest men on Gods' earth."

"I hope you're right Sadie for the next twenty-four hours will be critical and prove one way or the other." With the bandaging finished, the doctor instructed his nurse.

"I want you to put another rubber blanket on top of him, but a much lighter one if you can find it. If not, dispense with it and just add extra thick woollen blankets. It's imperative that he is kept warm. Nurse, I must go now and see who else needs my help. If you are required elsewhere make sure someone is left with him at all times."

"I'll be here," Sadie reassured him.

"Good. Let me know immediately if there is any change." With that he left the room.

Through the glass in the surgery door, Sadie could see several peering faces. She felt like a goldfish in a bowl until she saw the concerned face of Michael.

"Nurse, Richard's friends are in the hall. They must be desperate for news. Is it all right if I pop out for moment?"

"Of course, my dear, take your time. I'm not going anywhere as yet." Among the crowd, Mr. Jones stood next to Michael.

"What's wrong with Mr. Jones?" she asked.

"Oh he's just upset that's all. He'll be all right in a minute. How's Richard?" Unaccustomed to seeing men cry, Sadie was surprised at Mr. Jones's reaction, yet somehow his tearful face held a wondrous, loving beauty. She turned to him.

"Come now, Mr. Jones, Richard will be fine. He's fit and strong and that alone will see him through. Remember when his back got burned before? Did it bother him? Why not at all. Any other man would have cried for a week, but not Richard, now did he?"

"No, I guess not, but did the doctor say he was going to be all right?"

"Well, not exactly. What he said was that some of the signs are good but the next twenty-four hours arc critical."

"You mean that if he is still alive in twenty four hours then he'll be all right?"

"That's how it sounded to me," Sadie tried to reassure the distraught little man.

"Well, in that case, if I could wish my life away I would and wish it was tomorrow night."

"So do we all, Mr. Jones," Michael interjected.

"Oh, I nearly forgot. Did you find your father in law? How is he?"

"I'll tell you all about it tomorrow shall I? C'mon, Mr. Jones. There's nothing more we can do here right now. We'll see you tomorrow, Sadie. You'll be staying all night are you?"

"As long as it takes. Tell me, Michael, have you seen anything of my Bridie?"

"Yeah, she's outside shall I tell her you want her?"

"Yes, please." While the little Welshman headed home to pray Michael set off to comfort his hysterical wife. Sadie leaned to her daughter and spoke in a whisper.

"Please bring me some food, for I may be here a while, and bring also the Irish stone. Good girl ... be quick now."

Sadie had been so preoccupied that she heard no sounds through the thin walls of the medical centre. Next door, William's family gathered around his corpse, Tamar crying hysterically and her mother whimpering uncontrollably. Squeak and Will-Patrick stood together with their eyes fixed to the floor. William lay before them beneath a clean cotton sheet. What they could not see were the horrific injuries he had sustained that sickened even the young doctor. As they looked at the ironed linen that covered their father, they gazed at the creases that formed squares like the grid on a map. Each four-sided area conjured up memories of what lay hidden beneath the sheet. Looking at the square that covered the head, Margot thought of the grey hair that had never receded and the unkempt walrus moustache that she constantly told him to trim. As she lowered her gaze she could make out the broad shoulders of the man so used to hard work. Farther down she looked on where his legs lay. Legs which so often she had teased him about.

"How come you've got such ample shoulders but legs like a sparrow?" she would mock.

Tamar, standing next to her mother, looked at the shrouded figure and also thought of happier times when she was a child and her father had entertained and puzzled her for many hours with his double jointed fingers and elbows. Squeak remembered the hole in the side of his father's leg. For years he fooled his children into believing that it was where the French had shot him while he was in the war. As they grew up they had discovered an abscess caused it. Will-Patrick, who had thought his father immortal, was dumbfounded. To him, his father had always been old. Since childhood he had believed his father would never die, just remain old forever. But there he lay, and young Will could not comprehend why.

The entrance of Patrick brought each of them back to the stark reality of their surroundings. He looked across the room as though looking for an explanation, but no one had one to offer.

"I came as soon as I heard. I'm really, really sorry." He was underground when he got the news and along with all the other men dropped his tools and surfaced. Black as the coal that he had been hewing, with laceless boots and the bottom of his trouser legs tied with string to prevent rodents from climbing up, he looked like a scarecrow as he stood next to David at the bottom of the bed.

"I really don't know what to say either. I mean, William and I were such good mates. I'm gutted so I am." For the first time that anyone had seen, outside his late wife, tears ran down Patrick's cheeks, washed away the coal dust and dropped onto the well scrubbed floorboards like ink blots.

"Are you really sure you want to see this? I urge you not to," said David. "That's not the Da you knew beneath that cover. He's gone from us and is in a better place now. Please, take my advice and keep the picture of him that you each have in your heart. That's what you should do. Remember him as he was and not the poor soul that lies beneath that sheet." No one spoke for a long time.

"David," said Margot. "Can you take the family home? I'd like to stay with your father a little while longer. "Go on, run along, I'll be home shortly."

Obediently and sorrowfully her family and Patrick left her alone with her husband. The emptiness that she felt gnawed at her very being.

"Tamar," said David. "I'm off to see the undertaker. Did you telegraph Samuel?"

"As soon as you asked me."

"Good, right I'll go and catch this train into town. I'll be back as soon as I can. Keep an eye on Mother will you?"

"Of course I will. See you later."

248

The following morning, the undertaker arrived from Bishop Auckland and removed William in a closed coffin to the parlour of his home. Behind closed curtains, Margot continued her mourning and sat in silent vigil beside the simple casket.

"You all right, Mother? You've been in here so long and it's so cold. Squeak and I have brought you a drink and something to eat, won't you try, please?" Tamar asked. It had been over twenty-four hours since Margot had eaten anything.

"Thanks pet, but I'm not hungry, but I will have a cup of tea though."

"Here you are then, Mother."

"Thank you, Son," she said taking the cup and saucer from Squeak. "How are you?"

"I'm fine Mother, but we're all worried about you. I wish you'd try and eat something. Look, Tamar has made your favourite sandwiches."

"Not just now, Son. Maybe later eh?" Squeak and Tamar moved closer to their seated mother and stood either side. They joined her gaze at the sealed pine coffin, raised up on trestles. On the top of the coffin Margot had placed one of the two family bibles. The other lay open on her lap, at the gospel according to John, chapter fourteen. Around the temporary mausoleum lavender water had been scattered. It helped, but could not alleviate the pungent smell of burnt flesh and death. The atmosphere was too much for Squeak and, bidding farewell, he hurriedly left the claustrophobic, darkened room. Tamar soon followed him into the kitchen, where her twin sons occupied one of the kitchen chairs.

"And what have you two been up to?"

"Nothing, Mammy."

"Then, how come you both have jam all over your faces and there's breadcrumbs everywhere?"

"We were hungry." Tamar smiled at them with a look that let the twins know how special they were to her.

"I know. You really have been good children for your Mammy."

"Can we go home now," one asked.

"Not yet pet, but we won't be long. As soon as Uncle David comes back we'll go and make your father's tea, shall we?"

"Can we see Granda Morris now?

"No, I'm afraid not," she answered, her voice drowned in sorrow.

"Why not, Mammy? Has he gone to heaven?"

"That's right pet. Granda Morris has gone to heaven," she turned to see who had entered the room. "Hello Jane, oh ... and Bridie too. Nice to see you both, how are you?"

"We're both well thanks, Tamar. Your David asked us if we could pop in and see if there was anything we can do."

"Oh, thanks. It seems I've never stopped making tea. In the last three hours there must have been fifty people here paying their last respects. Will you hold the fort while I take the twins for Michael to look after? He should just be about coming home right now. And ask Mother if she would like another cup of tea and try and tempt her to have something to eat. There's a cake in the larder, try her with that. She hasn't had a bite to eat since yesterday. Right I'm off, tell David I won't be long."

On the seventh day of mourning Samuel arrived with his new wife. It was not the ideal circumstance to be introduced to her new family, but she coped well considering.

"Please accept my condolences. I know what it is to lose a close family member. Only last fall we lost both Mamma and Papa all in the space of one month. It was the saddest time I've ever known in my life. Even my fervent belief in the resurrection and afterlife was tested. I'm sure despite my faith that at the graveside, as the casket was lowered, I felt not one jot better than the worst atheist." David thanked his sister in law for her kind thoughts.

"Yes, I understand everything you've said, and the burial is the part that I also dread. That's when everyone knows it's not a nightmare and reality sinks in. When we walk away from that hole in the ground and leave father's earthly remains I think that's when it will hit a lot of people hard. Especially Mother. I've arranged that the internment side of things will be a private, family affair."

"Where will he be buried?"

"At Escomb."

"Oh, and where's that?"

"Just over a mile away."

"But did I not see a magnificent new church as we arrived in the village?"

"Yes, you did, but it hasn't got a graveyard, so we'll have to go to Escomb."

"How strange," his sister in law concluded. As the cortege left for the Methodist chapel at the end of the street, near to the works entrance, Sadie respectfully watched. Not until the last mourner had gone in did she hurry back to the infirmary to Richard who had by that time regained consciousness. The service, led by Samuel, was conducted with the reverence and dignity that befitted William's standing in the church and community.

"My father dedicated his life to the work of God and the benefit of his fellow man. It is therefore fitting that so many of you have come to pay your respects. I understand that several of you wish to say a few words in his honour so I stand aside and thank you all for coming.

Before I go, my mother has asked that I read a verse from a hymn of which she is particularly fond."

"Adieu, go thou before us
To join the angel throng,
A secret sense comes o'er me
I tarry here not long,
Adieu, there comes a morrow to every day of pain,
On earth, we part in sorrow
To meet in love again."

His passing was lamented by so many that members of the congregation took over three hours to deliver their individual affirmations.

"Have they decided what caused the blast Michael?"

"Well Da, the engineers say it was a freak build up of steam. They seem happy enough with that explanation for they've started work on its repair already."

"Bloody hell, that was quick. Why, the dust has hardly had time to settle. Do you know I think everyone in the village has a story to tell about that day. Even in town people are talking about it and what they don't know they make up."

"I believe that, but it also said that the explosion could be heard six miles away at Shildon."

"Yeah, I heard that."

"Well, I hope that when they are talking they mention Mr. Morris. What was is that one of the speakers at his funeral said? Wasn't it something like 'A man is not dead as long as his name is spoken'?"

"Yeah, it was something like that."

Outside the village the disaster soon became remembered only for the stories of miraculous escapes. As yarns grew into incredulous comic book inventions, Richard lay in the hospital and considered his plight.

"Right Richard," said the doctor. "Here we go again." And, once again, Richard's bandages were removed and he was lowered in to the saline solution for his daily treatment. Dr Stokoe thought he detected a definite improvement in his condition.

"Sadie, I've heard about your seeming ability to heal yourself quickly but tell me—are you working your secret formula on my patient?"

"I don't know what you mean, sir."

"I think you do. Dr. McKechnie has told me of incidents in the past where you seemed to have had miraculous recoveries. I wish I had that power, could you not share them with me? I promise I wouldn't tell anyone else."

"I really don't know what you mean, sir," she said, pushing the little wicker basket farther under the hospital bed with the back of her heel.

"I mean, Sadie, that something incredible is happening to Richard. His burns were so severe but for his physical strength he would have been dead. Having survived I would have expected him not to have reached this stage of recovery in months, not weeks."

"It must be that stuff you put in the water, sir."

"Hmm. It's good, but not that good." Richard sought Sadie's hand as doctor and nurse peeled away dead skin using sterilised tweezers. Not once during these daily painful handling did Richard complain before being re-wrapped, mummy fashion. The following day, when unbound, his healing skin would reappear as that of a freshly dug onion, and be similarly peeled away.

"Now that you are much better, Richard, I am thinking of moving you to Darlington hospital. What do you think?"

"Why, doctor?"

"They can look after you better there. They have better facilities."

"Doctor, you're just after telling Sadie how well I am doing. What more could they do in Darlington than is being done here?"

"That's true, I suppose."

"No, sir, I don't think they could do more than you good folks have done right here. Just send me home, that's what I'd really like."

"Well, I tell you what. We'll give it a couple of more days and then see."

"If the nurse popped in, me and her could give him the baths, and do the bandaging and things, sir," said Sadie.

"I'm sure you could, my dear, like I said—we'll look at it again, say at the weekend."

The chair next to Richard's bed had never been empty. Since his admission a rota system operated between Sadie, her daughter and Mr. Jones, augmented after William's funeral by Michael and his family.

"Would you like me to do a couple of nights for you mother? You must be about on your last legs."

"No thanks, pet. The nights are the best time for me and Richard ... and the stone," she answered softly. By the weekend, the doctor was able to reduce the dosage and frequency of the morphine, and the skin continued to heal at a healthy rate.

"Well, Richard. Amazingly, I think we can safely say you are now through the critical stage. You will still feel pretty groggy for a while I'm afraid but I think I can let you go home now. The risk of infection is receding with every passing day so I think we can also reduce the bandaging. This will lessen the workload once we get you home. You'll take good care of him won't you, Sadie?"

"Of course I will, sir."

"That's settled then. I'll arrange his transfer and as requested have the nurse call in each day."

The same day, Samuel and his wife called to say their goodbyes. The new Mrs. Morris had never met Richard prior to the accident. Their arrival coincided with the disfigured man being prepared for his treatment. Although shocked at the sight of him she conducted herself with great diplomacy. Sadie could sense she was uncomfortable around Richard and invited her outside.

"Yes, you go on out, I'll just sit and have a few more minutes with Richard, then I'll join you."

"How is your family taking it about your father?" asked Richard. "They talk so little to me about it."

"Perhaps they think, as I do, that you have enough on your own plate."

"Samuel," said Richard. "You lot have almost been like family to me. Remember you were among the first friends I ever met when I came here."

"I know that, Richard. Like I said since we feel the same about you, none of us wish to burden you. For my part I feel robbed. Not because he is dead, but by the suddenness of his departure. When you nurse someone in his final days or months you get a chance to prepare yourself somewhat. When it comes like a bolt from the blue the shock is awesome. Not having the chance to tell them things you always meant to say, or to even say goodbye. That's an awful feeling. Mother has taken it very bad, but worst than that she's bottling it up. That's not good."

"No, that's not good at all, let's hope she comes to terms with it soon." Outside, Samuel's wife talked to Sadie.

"What was Richard like before the accident?"

"He was a strong as a bull, yet tender as a lamb and quite the most handsome of men."

"Where did he come from originally? Samuel is always telling me that almost everybody came from somewhere to here."

"He was from the East Indies."

"But ... I mean, I thought people from the East Indies were ... coloured?"

"Richard is Dutch. Well, his folks and grandfolks were I suppose. No, he wasn't black if that's what you mean, just a beautiful bronze," Sadie replied.

"I'm sorry, Sadie. I didn't mean to offend but I hope you can understand I couldn't tell what colour he was under all those awful burns."

"Does it matter what colour a man's skin is anyway?"

"It does in America, but that should change slowly now the war with the South is won."

"The sooner the better, I say."

"Anyway, I'm off to Scotland tomorrow. Getting to meet some of my ancestral relations that I've never met. Really excited about meeting my grandpa who's nearly ninety years of age."

"Does he wear a kilt?"

"I don't suppose so, I don't think many do."

"No, and not many people from the East Indies are black."

"Point taken."

Over the next month, endless days of bathing and peeling away of skin continued. As layer upon layer of burnt skin, like black paint beneath a blowlamp, was peel away pink skin begin to reappear. The healing process varied form one part of his body to another, mottled from white-yellow to dawn-tinted red.

"How are you today, Richard?" asked Patrick. "I've brought two of the grandbairns to see you."

"Good, come on in my old friend, pull a chair up."

"So how's it going then?"

"Well, it's going well, so the doctor says. He says he can't get over how well I'm doing.

"That's good, but from where I'm sitting it looks as though there's a long way to go yet. Why you remind me of a patchwork quilt me granny once had!" Both men laughed.

"As long as I don't end up white with an Irish accent, I don't care." Both men laughed again. Outside, as they left, one of the children looked up to Patrick.

"Granda, Richard won't turn white, will he?"

"If he did, then it wouldn't be the real Richard anymore, would it? No, Richard's not going to turn white, no more than I'm going to turn emerald green," he reassured the concerned children.

Over the following eight weeks, Richard was entrusted into the loving care of Sadie. Each day the nurse would call and assist with the change of the dressings while Doctor Stokoe monitored progress. Richard knew that, in Sadie's capable hands, he was getting the best modern medical care, plus the most mystical and ancient.

After the demise of the Fenian Brotherhood in Ireland, the 'Land League' formed its own branch in the Witton Park. Originally created following the ill fated uprising of fifteen years earlier, the legal organisation dedicated itself to the destruction of the power of English landlords in Ireland by peaceful means. Their composed protests suffered a serious setback when Lord Cavendish, the Liberal party chief secretary and a colleague were knifed to death in Phoenix Park, Dublin. The savage, murderous act lost the Land League much support in England and prominent, sympathetic people distanced themselves from the organisation. In Witton Park, Father Kyte chaired the association's meeting and passed a resolution imploring the British government "not to punish the many for the actions of a few."

"I'm getting worried about Mother," David said to his sister. "Have you not noticed how strangely she acts at times? Since father went and she hears the sound of men's boots on their way home from the works she still puts on clean apron."

"Old habits die hard, brother."

"Perhaps ... but ... what about the last few days? Did you know she turned up at the works, each day, with a plate of dinner?"

"Who for?"

"Why, father of course. She knows I've never eaten at work."

"What did you do?"

"I took the food off her and made sure it went to a good home. The young 'uns who got it thought it was Christmas. I tried talking to her but she seemed distant and didn't understand. Just to make things worse she kept mumbling on in Welsh."

"We had better keep a close eye on her, don't you agree?"

"I sure do, but what about the food?"

"Look, for now let her carry on, if it makes her happy. We'll just have to play it by ear."

"What if she gets worse?"

"We'll have to cross that bridge if we have to come to it, brother."

Margot lapsed more and more into speaking only Welsh. It was a source of great frustration to those who tried to help. This effective shunning of lifetime friends led to whispers regarding her sanity. It came to a head when Will told his mother of his plans to marry.

"Ma," he said proudly. "Bridie and I are going to get married as soon as possible. Well, aren't you pleased for us?" The announcement did not even cause her to stop fidgeting with her shawl, as she rocked incessantly in William's favourite chair. Later that day, Jane moved her mother in with her family, but Margot continued to wander back to the house that held so many happy memories. After their simple civil wedding ceremony, Will and Bridie took up tenancy of the old family home and were able to walk Margot back to Jane's care whenever she wandered in.

Strangers in such a tight knit community stood out like a sore thumb. The respectably dressed man who arrived from the train on an otherwise mundane Tuesday morning drew a few stares from curious railway station staff.

"Excuse me sir," he enquired of Mr. Parr, the new railway master. "Can you tell me how to get to Stable Row?" Satchel in hand, he exited the station yard and turned right. Standing in front of house number nine, he checked the number against a piece of paper produced from his bag and knocked at the door. As it opened, the sight of the disfigured Richard took his breath away.

"Can I help you?"

"I'm looking for a woman called Sadie, known as Hickey, and her daughter Bridie. Do they live here?"

"Why do you want to know?" Richard asked defensively.

"I have some news for her."

"Is it bad news?"

"No."

"Then you had better come in and wait. She shouldn't be long. She's just popped round to her daughter's to borrow some milk."

"So her daughter doesn't live here?"

"She did till a couple of weeks ago. She now lives in the next street over, since she got married. I'd make you a cuppa tea but, like I said, Sadie's away getting some milk."

"It doesn't matter, thank you. I had one at Darlington railway station, while I waited for the connection to here." In the parlour they sat in silence, occasionally glancing at each other. The visitor was immaculate in a black three-piece suit, starched white shirt with winged collars and an old fashioned bow tie. A little too short in the leg, the front crease of the trousers ran straight down to his instep, exposing black socks in black shoes, shined to a lacquered finish. Only the absence of a black stovepipe hat with bow and tails at the back prevented him from being mistaken for an undertaker. Richard concluded that if he were not an undertaker, he must belong to one of the other two professions of men in black: doctors and solicitors.

"You a solicitor?"

"No, I'm only a solicitor's clerk."

"So what does a solicitor's clerk want with Sadie and Bridie then?"

"I'm sure that you will understand that the matter is confidential. May I ask what relationship, if any, you have with Sadie?"

"She's my soul mate."

"Oh," the clerk responded, unable to comprehend. "And what, may I ask, happened to you?"

"Me? Oh, you mean this?" he said, holding out his mutilated hands. "It was an accident at the ironworks."

"I believe I read about that in the newspaper. Wasn't a man killed?"

"Yes, I suppose I was lucky not to have joined him."

"Did you know him?"

"Very well. William Morris was his name." The visitor noticed dust from the station yard on the surface of his shoes. He produced a piece of cloth from his satchel and cleaned them. As he waited he fidgeted with his necktie, crossing and uncrossing his legs continuously. He checked and rechecked the cuticles of his fingernails and reached down often to touch his black leather satchel.

"Do you think she will be much longer?"

"I doubt it, but who can tell? When two women get nattering, time means nowt. Hang on, that sounds like our back gate, this must be her." Sadie entered by the front door and as she came along the passage she could see Richard standing in the parlour.

"What you doing in there?"

"You'd better come in, you have a visitor."

"What?" With impeccable manners the visitor rose from his chair, and waited for a formal introduction. The stranger's unexpected presence set alarm bells ringing in her head. Sadie refused his outstretched hand and chose the seat farthest away from him.

"Who are you and what do you want?" she said sharply.

"My name is McMasters. I am junior partner in a Durham City law firm. We act for a London barrister who was originally instructed to find one Seamus Hickey and his family." The mention of Hickey's name sent simultaneous cold shivers through both Sadie and Richard.

"I don't think I can help you," she interrupted. "I haven't seen Hickey in years and never wish to again."

"Some around here think him dead," Richard interjected.

"Our enquiries have drawn a blank as to what has become of him," said the clerk. "We have studied the police report appertaining the last sighting of him and have concluded that he must have gone off somewhere. Alternatively he might have died. Either way, this does not affect the business I have with you and your daughter."

"And what do you want of them?" asked Richard.

"That I cannot reveal right at this moment. I come to find you and ask that mother and daughter come to our chambers, in Durham City at their mutual convenience."

"Will you not tell us why? Just the mention of that man's name around here, especially in this house, makes us extremely nervous. Anyway how did you find us? "

"That was easy. The home office has tracked Hickey for years. Up until his sudden disappearance that is. Bye the way, their checks in America have revealed nothing and they are of the opinion that something must have happened to him."

"The home office cannot be interested in Sadie and Bridie though?"

"No, not at all."

"Thank God," said Sadie. "Now Mr. Clerk whoever you are, let me tell you again I have not seen Hickey in years. Furthermore I wish to have nothing to do with anything that might involve him, past or present so I'll bid you goodbye." Begging Sadie to be re-seated, the solicitor's clerk capitulated and revealed that Hickey was not his main object of interest, simply a means to an end.

"I'll tell you this. Come to our offices next Tuesday at ten in the morning and I promise you that you will hear something to your advantage."

"And it has nothing to do with Hickey?"

"Not really, not at all. Will you come?" Sadie fell silent.

"We'll talk about it and let you know. Is that all right?"

"It is your prerogative, but remember ... I said that you will hear something to your advantage. My advise that you to deliberate carefully and hopefully I'll see you Tuesday."

"Mother didn't come home today."

"What do you mean? She went back to he old house?"

"No, she didn't come home from the works? I gave her an empty plate, and knife and fork, which seems to keep her happy and off she went as usual. When she wasn't back by two o'clock I went looking for her."

"I took the plate and that off her as usual," said David to his sister. "That was about noon."

"Yes, well, when I found her she was just sat where her and father used to sit, babbling on to herself in Welsh. Sitting there like a dog that refuses to leave its master's grave so she was. I felt so sorry for her as I brought her away. I cried."

"She'll speak nothing else but Welsh these days."

"Don't I know it? And after all this time." Margot's condition deteriorated fast. Each day, she delivered an empty dinner plate to the works. Day after day she would sit at the tunnel entrance, until led home to her daughters, by family or friends. Her steadfast refusal to speak in anything other than Welsh fuelled rumours of her committal to the lunatic asylum. On a typical day, after delivering her dinner plate to the works, Margot headed for Stable Row. She headed for the cottage where, thirty-seven years earlier, she and William had lived upon arriving in the village. Oblivious to her surroundings she headed for the little row of houses, nestled among the active railway sidings.

John Croft sat high up in his new signal box, replaced after the explosion.

"Mrs. Morris. What are you doing? Don't cross there. There's trains coming," he bellowed. Indifferent to the danger she crossed the busy tracks as trains and trucks rattled by. The driver of a passing locomotive blew the whistle of his little shunting engine.

"Get off the bloody tracks you stupid bloody woman. You'll get yourself killed!" The fireman dropped his shovel with which he had been fuelling the boiler.

"It's Mrs. Morris, I'll get her," he shouted to the driver as he jumped from the moving engine. But even as he raced down the track, Margot stood in the middle of the rails and stared blankly at the laden, freewheeling flatcar coming towards her.

"Move, Mrs. Morris, move!" he screamed frantically. As the engine whistle screeched, Margot was impaled on the coupling hook and dragged down the steep incline before dropping beneath the wheels of the bogey.

For the second time in a year, the Cambrian Society covered the cost of a Morris family funeral, and the whole Welsh community mourned for the society's founder member, and tireless worker.

Chapter Eighteen 1882 – 1884

"Do you fancy a look to Darlington tomorrow, to see the trains?" Squeak asked his younger brother.

"To see trains? Are you kidding me?"

"C'mon Will, you must know I always wanted to be a train driver?"

"And a stage coach driver and a cowboy, c'mon why do you really want to go?"

"Well, Samuel and his wife are arriving there from Edinburgh before spending a week or so here. Then they'll be setting off back to America."

"So what?"

"I want to have a word with Samuel, in private like."

"You're not thinking of going back with them? Are you?"

"We'll see." The brothers waited at Darlington railway station for the arrival of the train from the Scottish capital.

"You weren't born the last time I was here," Squeak reminisced.

"Can you remember all that way back?"

"I surely can. There was mother and father, David, Samuel and Tamar, the Bryan family, Richard and Mr. Jones. We all stood about here, it hasn't changed much at all." The train entered the station and moved at a crawl alongside the long platform. Finally it came to a shuddering halt.

"What a surprise!" Samuel said on seeing his brothers. "Fancy meeting you here. Are you off somewhere?"

"Not really, I came to see you."

"To see me? Couldn't it wait until we got back to the village?"

"Not really. See, I wanted to have a word with you in private."

"Oh? Well, if you've come all this way it must be important. Look we have over one hour to wait for the connecting train. Shall we go and sit in the waiting room and talk?"

"Who's coming with me to the cemetery in Escomb?" Samuel asked his family the next morning.

"Husband, I'll walk there with you, if you wish."

"And I'll come an' all," Tamar said. The other three brothers declined.

"You go, Samuel. Who knows when the next time will be that you get to visit their graves. We can go anytime. I'll probably wait until father's headstone's in place."

"Not places for me. Can't understand why folks want to go there," observed Patrick whose view on cemeteries was set in stone like the names inscribed on the headstones. "I mean, if we are to believe what we are told, there's nowt there. Not as we knew anyway. They're supposed to have gone to heaven ... or somewhere ... aren't they? I might not be a church going Christian but I know where my wife and son are, and it's not in Escomb graveyard.

"Of course you're right Patrick, these are just places of remembrance that's all, but that's why people go," Samuel concurred.

"I don't need no graveyard to remind me of Annie and Philip, thank you. Every minute of every day they are in my head and in my heart so they are. Every night I talk to them, through my prayers. No, I know where they are."

"We all know where they are Da. And they're probably with William and Margot right now. But it's different for Samuel him going away and all."

"I suppose so," Patrick reluctantly agreed with Tamar.

"I tell you, lads ... now is the time to ask for the reinstatement of our wage cut plus a significant rise. This upturn in the fortunes of pig and puddled iron is making the iron-barons even richer!" David told a packed union meeting. A great cheer went up from inside the Cambrian Hall as men endorsed their union's stand. But the union demands met with total refusal, so the men went out on strike.

"Well, brother, at least we'll get to spend a bit more time together before you have to leave," David said.

"Do you think you can win, this time?"

"Well, the company has full order books and needs to get those orders out. That should help us."

"I hope so, brother. I'll pray for a speedy good outcome for the men."

"You won't need to pray very hard. This note I just received says that today's arbitration board has handed down a temporary settlement in our favour. We'll be back at work in the morning. When the full board convenes in a few days time it should go well for us. The board will be chaired by our new liberal member of parliament."

Back in the meeting hall, David once more addressed his union members.

"I have here the findings of the full arbitration board. Before I tell you their findings I ask you ... can you remember the honourable J. W. Pease? Well, he chaired the meeting. You remember him don't you? The fancy gentleman who promised full support for us? He would be the one that would stand behind us he said. You remember don't you?"

"Hurrah!" a few men cheered.

"Take my word lads: J.W. Pease is neither honourable nor a gentleman. He stood behind us all right ... and stabbed us in the back.

He has refused to endorse our claim." Pandemonium erupted. At the works, disgusted puddlers downed tools and walked out again, the resulting shortage of iron closed the mills. A week of bitter arguments among the various factions ensued.

"The only democratic way to settle this is to have a ballot," David told his members. "We'll vote whether we should go back or stay out." Against this backdrop of continuing turmoil the ballot was held. Only the puddlers voted to continue strike action and, by a majority of sixty five per cent, the workforce returned.

The night before Samuel and his wife were due to leave they held a farewell party.

"Listen folks," Squeak started. "Now is as good a time as any to say this I guess. Although mainly for our David and Tamar's ears, you might as well all know. Tomorrow our oldest brother leaves us again for America. Shortly after them, me, Will, and our wives will be setting off there as well."

"What?" Tamar gasped.

"Did you know about this Samuel?" she asked.

"Yes."

"And you didn't say anything?"

"I was sworn to secrecy and, anyway, they simply sought advice. No decision was made then. This is the first I have heard that they have made their minds up." As the stunned party tried to recover, Patrick broke the silence.

" Good luck to you all I say. Wish I was younger; I might have had a crack at that mesel. Don't shake your head Michael, the ways things are going round here, you might need Samuel's help yersel, so you might."

Richard and Sadie, too, were planning a trip.

"Do you realise this will be the first time I've really been out of the house since the accident?"

"Are you sure you're up to it Richard?" Sadie asked.

"Of course I am, why we're only going to Durham City, not to the moon."

"But I worry."

"Why? The doctor said I was fit enough didn't he? I'll be fine stop being such a worrit. C'mon or we'll miss the train."

"Ma, why are all the people staring at Richard? It's making me embarrassed for him, that it is."

"Maybe they've never seen such a fine figure of a man."

Richard looked at the caring young woman and smiled.

"Bridie, don't concern yourself, it's just human nature. It doesn't bother me don't let it bother you. But thanks for being so considerate anyway." Bridie and her mother smiled at the great man's fortitude. In Durham City they walked through narrow cobbled streets looking for Old Elvet.

"My, oh my," said Richard. "Look at the size of that church." Overlooking the river, upon which punts abounded, the magnificent building dominated the city and the skyline.

"That's a cathedral," Bridie corrected Richard.

"Is that so now? And what exactly would you say a cathedral is?"

"It's a massive church I suppose."

"Isn't that what I said?" he laughed. Arriving at the given number in Old Elvet they entered the old building.

"Could do with a coat of paint I think."

"Could do with some fresh air I think," said Sadie. " Phew, it smells like a tin of snuff."

"A tin of snuff? Never heard that one before," said Richard.

"All right, mister perfect, it stinks of stale baccy smoke."

"Don't get serious, Sadie. I was only kidding."

"Sorry, can't help it. I'm as nervous as hell."

"You'll be all right," he reassured her. That's why I came wasn't it? To look after you?" She smiled lovingly.

In the small waiting room, Richard stood while the ladies sat on the only two chairs. Horsehair escaped from under the worn covering and the unsteady legs creaked at the slightest movement. A half glazed door allowed them to see into the adjoining office. Solemn men in black sat at rows of desks, as though at school. As they silently scribbled away, their grave faces were as solemn as pallbearers. On creaky hinges the heavy door swung open and a boy of about fifteen or sixteen years addressed them.

"Sadie and Bridie Hickey?"

"It is," Sadie reluctantly agreed.

"And may I enquire as to who you are, sir?"

"He's with me," Sadie said firmly.

"Very well, will you follow me please?" He led them through the main office to an oak panelled door.

"Bridie, look at all the books. Why they're wall to wall and floor to ceiling. I bet there's more books here than what's even in David's library." Richard mused. The office junior tapped reverently on the door.

"Come in." Seated behind a desk that seemed to fill the room was an elderly, distinguished man. His portly figure filled the leather chair and he looked relaxed as he puffed away on a huge cigar. The surface of the desk was strewn with paper in seemingly chaotic order on top of which numerous leather books lay open. Deeds and letters were piled so high that only the top of the feathered quill, which stood in the inkwell, was visible. As they entered his office he tried to clear a small area in front of him. Standing behind him and slightly to his right was the clerk who had come to their home.

"This is Sadie and Bridie Hickey, sir. You are expecting them. The gentleman is a friend of theirs."

"Thank you Trimble, I think you had better bring another chair in for our guests, then that will be all."

"Yes, sir." Extending a well-rehearsed smile from over the desk he greeted them.

"Good morning ladies, my name is Booth I am a senior partner in this company, and you are, Mr. ...?" he asked looking directly at Richard.

"Blackman."

"Good. Mr. Blackman, why don't you pull up that chair and we can all be seated?" He turned to the women. "Now your papers are here somewhere, I went over them just this morning. Here we go." He opened the ribboned bundle.

"First and foremost, we must get the legalities out of the road." Like a vicar waiting for his congregation to settle down, the lawyer paused before commencing. "You are Sadie, known as Hickey are you not?"

"Yes sir, but I'd prefer not to be." The barrister managed a small smile.

"And you, my dear, must be Bridie, also known as Hickey, are you not?"

"I was, but my name is Morris now," she answered proudly. The old man untied the ribbon that constrained the folded sheaf of papers and carefully laid it down.

"This document is a certified copy of the last will and testament of Lord Edward Septimus Lowery."

"Who's he?"

"Ssh," Bridie's mother urged her.

"Lord Lowery left the bulk of his estate to his wife, having no heir by that union." His eyes scrolled down the parchment until resting upon the relevant paragraph. "But Lord Lowery acknowledges an illegitimate child, Seamus Hickey ..." Both Bridie and Richard drew breath and Sadie reddened. "However, as an Irish peer, Lord Lowery has been kept appraised of Hickey's terrorist activities, and had no choice but to disown and disinherit him. He was also aware of yourself and your child, Madam. The paragraph that really is of concern to you both states, and I quote: 'Should she survive, the sum of five thousand guineas shall be given to Sadie Hickey and a similar sum shall go to Bridie Hickey, my grandchild, should she survive to the age of twenty-one years. Congratulations ladies, it seems that you are both wealthy women. I hope you use it wisely and if our firm can ever offer investment or legal advice I hope you do not hesitate to contact us."

On the return journey to Witton Park the two women were so dumbfounded, that they could not recall changing trains at Bishop Auckland. It would take hours for the magnitude of their good fortune to dawn on Sadie and Bridie. On their arrival friends crammed in the little cottage to hear of the day's events.

"When he mentioned Seamus I thought it was to be more trouble, did you not Bridie?"

"I did, Ma."

"And what was he on about?" asked an eager Mr. Jones.

"Us, and good fortune at last!" Sadie and Bridie revealed all to their stunned friends.

"Five thousand guineas? Why even a puddler would have to work twenty years or more to get that sort of money," said David.

The following morning, after a sleepless night, Sadie left her room, wrote Richard a note and set off with the intention of walking to Bishop Auckland. When he got up, Richard was surprised not to see her in the kitchen or pantry. Assuming she was across the yard in the privy or still in her room, and not noticing the note on the table, he went into the pantry to wash under the tap. Opening the back door he shouted across the back yard.

"Sadie. You in the netty? Hurry up woman, I'm dying to go," Towel in hand he crossed the small yard and knocked on the rough wooden door. "Sadie, I said are you in there? If you are hurry up please or I'm going to have an accident." There was no reply so he lifted the cast iron snack and pushed open the door.

"Where the hell can she be I wonder?" he muttered as he seized the opportunity and entered the empty privvy. Back in the cottage he nervously opened the lacquered door into the inner sanctum of Sadie's private quarters. Her bed was folded away and, as it did each day, had transformed back into a settee, changing the bedroom back to a parlour. Puzzled, he wandered back into the kitchen where he finally saw, blending into the white tablecloth, the piece of paper. It was written in a semi-literate childish hand, and Richard digested the contents with incredibility. Sadie referred to the events of the previous day and how she wished Richard to share in her good fortune. She wrote of things she had never told a soul. How as a girl without a dowry she had never married, then as a piece of property lost in a game of chance, she found herself given away to Hickey. She wrote that her fear of rejection had forced her to leave the house and what she described as 'the cowardly note'. But right at the end she added a line that made his heart leap: *Richard, will you have me for your wife?*

Richard had long dreamed of this day. Throughout the time that Sadie had lived under the same roof he had never made advances toward her and had masked his inner feelings. His hope was that some day she may get over her bad experience with men and come around. At times he doubted that this might ever happen as time past slowly, it seemed that the best he could hope for was that they would be the best of mates, like him and Mr. Jones. He never pushed her. What he did not know was that Sadie had slowly fallen in love with the kind gentle giant. She, in turn, became frustrated by Richard's seeming indifference towards her. But she was determined that one day he would know her feelings. This was the day.

Right at that moment the front door opened. He stuffed the note into his trouser pocket and sat at the table. Sadie walked in and stopped at the entrance to the kitchen, looking first at the table then, seeing the note gone, at Richard.

"Well?" she asked with a strange confidence. Richard stood up and took the couple of short strides that separated them and looked down at her.

"Sadie, are you sure you want to do this? Yesterday hasn't gone to your head has it? You are still a beautiful woman in the prime of your life. Why you could get any man you wanted, and that's without your money."

"I'm as sure as sure."

"Sadie, I ask you again. Are you sure? Think about it. With your money you could travel the world with any man as your husband. One whose appearance would not embarrass you."

"Richard Blackman," she said. "It is you, and you alone, that I wish to marry, and I'll be having your answer now, if you'd be so kind."

"Of course I will marry you," Richard said as he stooped to kiss Sadie full on the lips. News of the impending wedding caused quite a stir in the community and grand preparations hastened. For Sadie it was dream come true. She had hardly allowed herself to even think that one day she might marry Richard; now to marry him with a full wedding service was blissful.

"Jane, I'd like you to personally make the dresses. Spare no expense, you've no idea what this means to me!"

"What colour dress would you like? White?"

"No, ivory please, with matching bridesmaid's dresses. That's one each for you and Tamar and our Bridie plus five for the Morris and Bryan bairns.

"Sadie, words fail me. Never have I been so honoured," said Mr. Jones. "It will make me so proud to be the one that gives you away. Thank you."

"If you'd asked anyone else I'd have been pretty miffed mind you," Michael said in thanking Richard for asking him to be the best man. After the wedding ceremony in St. Paul's church, the guests enjoyed a lavish party in the function room of the Vulcan Hotel.

"So you're leaving tomorrow then are you, Squeak?" one of the guests asked.

"Yeah, we're off tomorrow. I'm pleased all our family and friends are here enjoying themselves it'll keep their minds off it. Especially our Tamar."

"She's taking it badly then is she?"

"Why you know what lasses are like. In fairness though it's not long since we lost father and mother and now her two brothers leaving ..."

"I can understand that mind," said the fellow guest.

"See you all in the morning," Richard shouted as they prepared to leave by pony and trap to spend their wedding night in Bishop Auckland. A little boy, no more than three years of age, looked on from the edge of the pavement, his feet in the gutter. In his mouth was the remains of a clay pipe. Pulling fresh air though the empty bowl he sat and mimicked his grandmother.

The year eighteen eighty-three saw the iron industry once again in the doldrums, and periods of layoffs were frequent. The intervals of enforced idleness were enjoyed by some, hated by others and utilised for the good by a few. At every opportunity Mr. Jones fine-tuned the male voice choir which, after almost forty years loving development, was progressing to a national musical icon. Midweek, during strikes and layoffs the choir practiced daily in the chapel.

"Do you know what, Mr. Jones? I do believe more of my congregation attend these rehearsals than come on a Sunday to hear the word of God."

"Both are sweet music to my ears, minister," Mr. Jones diplomatically replied. David, as he always had done, watched the revolving head of the choirmaster in fascination. Although it had never actually fallen off or rotated a full three hundred and sixty degrees, it had forever held him spellbound. As though disjointed from his body, the neck, in the stovepipe collar, moved the head like a ventriloquist's dummy as sweat trickled down his face. Oblivious to his surroundings, only aware of the music, Mr. Jones moved his hands like a ballerina's as he conducted. Unexpectedly he dropped the baton and bent to retrieve it. The disciplined choir continued for a few bars but came to a faltering halt as first their leader dropped to his knees, then rolled sideways, baton in hand. His eyes remained closed, forever.

"What shall we do?"

"Go get Richard," David said. "And run tell Doctor Stokoe as well."

"But he's dead, what can the doctor do now?"

"Cos he'll know what to do—now go. Hurry!" As David knelt down and replaced Mr. Jones spectacles, he crossed the choirmaster's limp arms upon his chest before saying a small prayer. Richard was the first to arrive.

"I'm sorry Richard, there was nothing we could do. He just sort of keeled over and died. I've sent for the doctor, I just didn't know what else to do."

"It's all right. I can't think of any other way he would have preferred to go. Here he was with his beloved choir, baton in hand. No, I think that is how he would have wanted it." With that he bent down and scooped his friend into his arms and made to leave the chapel.

"When the doctor arrives tell him I've taken him home."

Mr. Jones death devastated Richard. He had lost both a great friend and brother figure. He intended that his companion should have a quiet Methodist funeral, but the occasion was effectively taken out of Richard's hands. The Methodist circuit minister, upon hearing the news, arrived to take the service, and the Welsh community organised an occasion befitting a statesman. Forty musicians played requiems and funeral marches as they accompanied the hearse over its two-mile journey to the graveyard. In the church graveyard over two thousand people attended the internment of the area's undisputed maestro of music.

"I bet he didn't know hc had so many friends and admirers."

"Well, Richard, he obviously had, didn't he?" said Sadie.

"I'm not looking forward to this."

"Someone's got to do it and you're as near as he had to next of kin."

"I know, but going though a dead man's things, ugh ... it's not proper. I'll feel like a vulture."

"Don't be daft, Richard. Can you think of anyone else who he would have wanted to do it?"

"Sadie, if that's suppose to make me feel better I'm sorry it doesn't. Anyway will you help me?"

"Of course I will."

"I think we'll get the worst over first?"

"How do you mean?"

"I mean let's do his bedroom first. That's probably the most private part of the cottage. I mean it's not like the kitchen or sitting room is it? Do you know, I think I've only ever been in here twice when he was poorly." With the moral support of his new bride Richard first checked the contents of the bureau. A small brass key protruded from a central keyhole at the top of the sloping front.

"This is where he probably kept the manuscripts he held so precious."

"It's not locked," Sadie said.

"What do you mean?"

"The key, it's not even turned."

"Cos there'll be nowt to steal will there? Open it up and let's see what's in there." Beneath manuscripts and the like, folded neatly and tied around by a purple thin ribbon, lay a very official looking document.

"What's this?" Sadie asked, handing the document to her husband.

"Why, it looks like a will, but he never mentioned anything to me about such a thing."

"Maybe he intended to but never got round to it, before he was cut down so sudden."

"Maybe, let me read it." It turned out that Mr. Jones, despite his frugal lifestyle, had made some shrewd investments and had left a tidy sum.

"What's an executor?"

"Somebody who hangs somebody isn't it? Why?"

"Cos he's written down what he wants doing with his things and he wants me to be his executor."

"Well, it can't mean that then can it? You'll have to ask somebody who knows about these things." Mr. Jones wished that any personal possessions not desired by his friends should go to those unfortunates in the workhouse. To parish relief he donated one hundred pounds and a similar amount to the Mechanics Institute library. The village brass band was to receive one hundred pounds, and a trust worth two hundred pounds was to be set up for the village choir. A further fifty pounds was to be set aside for in the event they ever won through to a Welsh eisteddfod. The residue was to become equally divided between the Welsh Independent chapel and Richard. He wrote of Richard that he had been no less than a brother to him and that he could not have been prouder or loved him more if he had been his own flesh and blood.

"Blimey, that still leaves nearly two thousand pounds. Do you hear that Sadie, the wily old Welshman left nearly three thousand pounds and one of them is to me!"

"Really? Does that mean that now you are a man of independent means you'll want a divorce?" Richard smiled sadly.

"All the money in the world cannot replace my old friend. I would gladly give it all away to have him back for just a moment to say goodbye."

"I know that, I was only joking."

"I know that too," Richard said as he hugged the love of his life.

The ironworkers were becoming more unsettled by uncertainty and when, in January eighteen eighty-four, a sale of parts of the works took place there was much concern.

"Do you think it's going to close David?" many of his union members asked.

"They say not. They strenuously deny that they have any intention of closing the works."

"I've heard that all the machinery is going to the Middlesbrough plant and that's where the work will go."

"I've asked them time and time again about that but I tell you they deny such a thing."

"What's your brother in law say?"

"Michael knows about as much as us."

"Aye, that's maybe what he says. I mean would he tell us if he knew?"

"I'm sure he would," his tone tinged with a hint of uncertainty.

"Have you seen yesterday's paper, David?"

"No, why?"

"There's a letter in there from Thomas Taylor Williams, do you remember him?"

"Didn't he use to work in the rolling mill?"

"Yes, that's him, and his father before him."

"What's the letter about then?"

"Oh, it's saying how well he's done since he went to America. After he left here, during the strike of seventy-one, he got a job managing three large American ironworks. Seems he made a fortune but lost it again when he had a go at farming. He wants his friends in England to know that he is building a new mill, in conjunction with his wife's brother, who also worked here as a puddler. The plant's to be known as the Minneapolis St. Paul's Iron and Steel works."

"Where about's is that?"

"Minnesota, it says."

"No wiser," says one of the interested men.

"Says there's three hundred good jobs gannin beggin' and wants to hear from the likes of us."

Michael was on leave the day of the sale and was relaxing when Tamar rushed in to tell him they had an unexpected visitor.

"Why Mr. Raine, how good to see you. Have you come for the auction of machinery?"

"That's one reason, also I've come to see you."

"I'm over the moon to see you. How have you been?" Michael said excitedly. "How long has it been?"

"It's been twelve years since I left but coming back today, it only seems like yesterday. Nothing seems to have changed."

"Afraid you couldn't be more wrong my friend, these are times of the utmost uncertainty."

"I'd heard that, and that's the other part of the reason I'm here."

"Are you still at that Newcastle mill?"

"Yes, I am. Since we reopened it we have gone from strength to strength. I wanted to write to you some time ago but the terms and conditions on which I left here stopped me."

"What do you mean?"

"Since the day I left I've always wanted you as my right hand man. You are the best I've ever known. I'm here today to finally ask if you'll come and work with me."

"I don't know, Mr. Raine. Don't get me wrong, I'm grateful and flattered by the offer but I feel I've still got a job to do here."

"That's another quality I admire in you. Loyalty is sadly lacking in a lot of people these days. Will you promise that if this place does close you'll reconsider my offer?"

"I certainly will, sir. Oh, you'd better know though, I once made such a promise to Joseph Vaughan." As they sat and reminisced over a cup of tea, Tamar re-entered the room with a beaming smile upon her face.

"Guess who's here now?"

"Who? Two visitors in one day? I don't believe it ..." Totally surprised, Michael looked in amazement as Joseph Vaughan strode into the house.

"Speak of the devil and he will appear."

"Strange, I remember a long time ago your wife's mother saying exactly the same about me."

"I'm sure she didn't mean it."

"No, I don't suppose so, after all it was the first time we'd met. Anyway I must be off or I'll miss the start of the sale. You'll consider my offer won't you?"

"Definitely Mr. Raine. Thanks for calling." Although it had only been some weeks since they had seen each other, Michael and Joseph greeted one another like long lost brothers.

"I knew Mr. Raine was here. I was talking to him earlier as he viewed the items that are going under the hammer. He told me he was coming to see you to make you an offer of employment. I think I have first call on your services if I am correct. I seem to remember a certain promise made."

"I never promised you anything, you scoundrel."

"Oh yes, you did."

"I never did, but why do you remind me?"

"As you probably know my business now keeps me abroad more and more of the year. Our empire is expanding thanks to good old Queen Victoria. Do you realise in three years time she will have reigned over us for fifty years?"

"She hasn't done a great deal for us here, I'm afraid."

"Now, now Michael."

"Let me come straight to the point. I need you old friend. I don't suppose I spent more than three months here in all of this year. I've lost a lot of interest in the manufacturing side but the sales side I am really enjoying. Although I'm picking up business as I swan around the Empire it's really just one giant holiday. C'mon, give it ago, just think about it, we'd make a great team."

"Let me sleep on it will you?"

"Of course, but remember one thing ... with my offer you could stay in the village." Michael walked his friend to the front door, promising again an early answer.

"Well, what do you make of that? Two offers in one day. Can you believe it?"

"Don't forget about that man in America who is looking for good men as well."

"I hadn't forgotten about that, but do you really want to go to America?"

"No, I'd prefer not to leave here, given the choice."

"Me neither."

In February, the company formally announced that on May the nineteenth of eighteen eighty-four, thirty eight years after Miss Vaughan tapped the first 'litter of pigs', the plant would close forever. After writing to Mr. Raine, Richard was the first person who Michael told of his intention to work for Joseph.

"It was what Joseph said that day about if I went to work for him that swung it. I'm fifty-eight years of age and have no fancy for emigration to America. At my age even Newcastle seemed too far. Then there's me Da, he over eighty now and doesn't want to go anywhere. Our lass is the same she doesn't want to move either. What about you?"

"Me? I'm officially retired. Sadie and I are going round the world. First we are going to see Ireland then we'll sail for the East Indies. Then we're coming back and when we are ready for some more sun we're off again. Probably go and visit Bridie and Will in America one day as well."

"So you're not going for good then?"

"Not likely. Did you think you could get rid of us that easy?"

On the day Richard and Sadie were to leave, Michael, his father and two of Michael's children decided to accompany them as far as Darlington.

"Are you sure you want to come all the way to Darlington to see us off?"

"All the way? Why, I bet it's no more than ten miles by train."

"All the same."

"All the same nowt. Anyway, it's a day out for the bairns, they love going on the train." As they stood on the village's railway station platform—on the threshold of their journey—the party looked over at the ironworks, unused and silent in Paradise. From where they waited, they could hear the melodic song of a male blackbird. Sitting high on top of one of the blast furnaces, it watched over its mate building a nest amongst the abandoned mills. At Darlington railway station, as they awaited the Edinburgh to London train, Patrick kept the children amused, as the two families said their goodbyes. They watched and counted the comings and goings of small shunting engines that sent up intermittent clouds of black smoke and white steam.

"All aboard!" The guard checked the compartment door through which the friends were saying their ultimate farewells. From somewhere along the platform a whistle blew, then after the hissing sound of released steam, the couplings between the coaches tightened and the train began to move. In a final act of parting, Richard thrust a large manila envelope into Michael's hand.

"What's this?" he shouted after the parting carriage.

"It's a present from me and Sadie. So long, see you in about three months." As the family waved to the fast disappearing train, Michael opened the envelope and stared at its contents in disbelief. In his hands were the deeds to Carwood House. As the tail end of the guard's van vanished out of sight, one of the boys looked up to his grandfather.

"Granda, how old were you when you first came here?"

"To be sure I don't know son, for it was dark when we landed."

ISBN 141202640-7